THE PET THIEF

KASSTEN ALONSO

TUSCALOOSA

FC2 is an imprint of The University of Alabama Press

Book Design: Illinois State University's English Department's Publications
Unit; Director: Tara Reeser; Assistant Director: Steve Halle; Production
Assistant: August Cassens
Cover Design: Lou Robinson
Typefaces: Bell MT and Garamond

⊗

The paper on which this book is printed meets the minimum requirements
of American National Standard for Information Sciences—Permanence
of Paper for Printed Library Materials, ANSI Z39.48–1984

Library of Congress Cataloging-in-Publication Data
Alonso, Kassten, 1968-
 The pet thief / Kassten Alonso.
    pages cm
  ISBN 978-1-57366-171-3 (pbk. : alk. paper) — ISBN 978-1-57366-839-2
(ebook)
  1. Human experimentation in medicine—Fiction. I. Title.
  PS3601.L59P48 2013
  813'.6—dc23

                              2012040236

For Kaspar, for Benjy, for all the
innocent souls, real and imaginary

"In the Realms of the Unreal, innocence lives in the constant shadow of danger."

—Henry Darger, *The Story of the Vivian Girls, in What Is Known as the Realms of the Unreal, of the Glandeco-Angelinian War Storm, Caused by the Child Slave Rebellion*

"When you notice a cat in profound meditation,
  The reason, I tell you, is always the same:
His mind is engaged in a rapt contemplation
  Of the thought, of the thought, of the thought of his name:
    His ineffable effable
    Effanineffable
Deep and inscrutable singular Name."

—T. S. Eliot, *Old Possum's Book of Practical Cats*

THE PET THIEF

Tsokka tsokka tsokka.

Running comes. Tsokka tsokka tsokka tsokka. Black boots run. Huh huh red lips puff Huh huh Little fists swing Torn red stockings tic toc tic toc tic tocking. Long brown coat flaflaflap. Allee puddles Black boots splash. Pale throat, black collar Yellow tail wags Red mouth hollers Tsokka tsokka tsokka tsokka tsokka tsokka tsokka.

Allee splits. Corner bricks. Black boots cht cht cht Hand slaps bricks Brown coat spins Red stockings kick Gravel allee Black boots slip, run run run. Yellow tail fish flash sunlight.

Bee bee bee cars redgreenwhite.

Little brown coat black boots byebye.

Komp Komp Komp. Black shoes come. Komp komp komp. Black cap blue shirt Komp komp komp komp. Allee splits. Stone allee. Gravel allee. Clotheslines. Green shutters.

Cheeks blow huh, huh, huh. Merde.

Blue shirt bows. Black trouser knees sparkly hands grab. Ouaa. Ouaaaaa. Sparkly cheeks nose pour onions salami brie.

Alors. Blue shirt tummy puffs big, little, big, little. Spits sour. Black cap turns. Black shoes come. My finger Doberman puppy tooths gnaw. Kick kick, little brown paws. Gravel allee.

Spinny top Blue shirt hides, babump babump babump. Scratches, big black shoes. Dirty black trouser turnups.

Alors. black shoes says. Which way she go. A droit. A gauche. The blonde. Hep. Im talkin to you. My tootsies Dusty shoe touches. Hollers come my head my fist hits. Foot kicks.

Cest quoi ce connn Door swings, flashes, Jinglelee Brown shoes come Green sweater Wrinkly hands Bon jour, officer. Mister says. May I help you.

I ask your grandson he saw my suspect, but he does not respond. huffing black cap says. Babump babump babump. Chin drips. Brown eyes my eyes. Hurt. Brown eyes get big.

Why does he yell. Im the one got kicked.

Grey trousers crouch. Grappa. Tobacco. Pink tummy spotted wrinkly hand pats. Yellow fingernails. Shiver. Shshsh. Its okay, my boy. Okay. Okay. My, this little puppy sure is happy, isnt he. What fun, to chew soft pink fingers, yes. Its okay, my boy.

Come on, kid, shes gettin away. says huffing blue shirt.

Mister says, Im afraid he couldnt tell you anything if he wanted to. He cant speak.

Well you can damn well point cant you.

Officer. Take a moment. Le regarder. Comprenez.

Hm. You got one of those, then. says trouser hips hands. Maybe you seen the girl, eh, Granpapa. Blonde, brown leather coat.

No, Officer, Im sorKomp komp komp komp komp komp. Running blue shirt black trousers black shoes get little. Little black cap turns sidetoside. Red neck hand rubs. Shoulders shrug. Merde alors. Little black cap Hand throws. Little redwhitegreen cars zoum zoum.

Little blue shirt arm shakes, hollers, What good are you.

Mister rises. Lets go inside now. O dear. The puppys into something over there. Here, dont eat that. Eeesh.

Flap flap torn yellow awning. Shivery window. Greywhite stones Green shutter taps. Tic, tic, tic. Sun shines. Greywhite stones Shadows climb. Drainpipe. Little pink wings flutter.

Red tip cigarette. Smoke, my eyes. Mister says, There Henry is, my boy. The rainwater head again, as you surmised.

Pink w w w wings. Little black Henry eye blink blinks. Little black beak clics. Gettin thoisty up here.

Brown sweater shoulder. Pretty Boyd rainbow wings tha tha tha. Feathers puff. O boy. says Pretty Boyd. Hes a gonah this time.

Now Pretty Boyd. says Mister. Mister coughs. Smoke. Dizzy. Wrinkly mouth Wrinkly hand hides. Goodness, me.

Cough cough. Goodness me. says sky.

Rooftop. Sun. Yellow hair. Moon. Pointy chin has yellow hair moon. Red glasses bingbing. Goodness me.

Stones come slow. Fingers, tootsies, climb. Yellow awning my hand grabs. Streetlamp.

Stones my fingers tootsies climb. Clicky green shutter my hand shuts. Boiled cabbage. Burnt toast. Splintery planter box. Windowsill. Rainwater head comes. Blinky metal eyes clink clink.

Metal mouth says, *Me from away bird get.*

Henry wings flare, yellow feathers show. Cars zoum zoum. Shooooo Redorange crest feathers plume. My ears hurt. Tootsies slip.

Careful up there. Mister says.

Rooftop moon. Yellow hair shines. Red glasses bing bing. Sunlight. Careful down there.

My fingers hurt. My arms legs shake, burn. Drainpipe my hand grabs. Tootsies push, hurt

Old cloaks, suits or coats Coat rack squeaks, rolls, Old satten, old taffety, or velvet

Black beak shimmers, clic clic. Grey Henry claw shaky finger pokes. My hand grey Henry claws grab Stones my fingers Pinkyellow wings flap flap My shoulder Henry perches, claws pinch.

Rainwater head says, *Everytime me poops bird pink.*

Haw haw. says Henry. See you round, Bucket head.

Careful on the way down. Mister says.

Haw haw. says Henry.

Stones slow rise. Pink Henry wings flap, my eyes. My ear beak tickles. Shiver. Sweets. says Henry flaflap.

Mister, Pretty Boyd, get big. Green shutter my elbow bumps. Streetlamp. Torn yellow awning. My foots Cobblestones clapclap. Henry wings flap, claws pinch.

Ach, luck run out sometime.

Now Pretty Boyd.

Sweets. says Henry.

That clinches it. says rooftop. Goodness me, yes. Yellow hair flutters. Red glasses bingbing sunlight.

Wrinkly Mister hand says, Come here, Henry Tudor. Wrinkly finger curling grey Henry claws take.

My fingertips dusty white. My tootsies.

Mister says, I dont know whats more silly, a cockatoo afraid of heights, or a cockatoo afraid of heights who repeatedly gets himself stuck in high places.

Sweets. Henry says. Wings flaflap.

Brown sweater. Tobacco. Grappa. Wrinkly hand comes. My mouth chokes. Hollers.

Mister says, Im sorry, sorry. Just wanted to say, some young man is an extremely proficient climber. Anyone else would have broken their crown scaling a façade like that. And how many times. Mais jamais ce jeune homme parfait. How he does it is a wonder that may only find explanation in the besprung watchworks of science, nay, beyond. The inexplicable, the divine. Old Henry owes him yet another debt of thanks. Dont you, Henry.

Thanks. hollers Henry. Desoive sweets, now.

Desoive sand in craw.

Now Pretty Boyd. We none of us can help our basic nature. Of course you may have a treat, Henry. says Mister. Theres a dried apricot for you back at the shop.

Whoa whoa whoa. says Pretty Boyd. Rainbow wings flare. Dry apricots, this plotz.

Okay, Pretty Boyd, okay, treats for you too. says cawing Mister, shoulders hunched. My ears my hands hide. Owie.

Rooftop. Sun. Dust spins. Green shutter tic tic.

Peanut butter biscuit my fingers show. Doberman pup whines. No. My lap panting pup lies. Furry head my hand cradles. Pink tummy cries. Pink tummy my hand rubs slow, Sososo. Brown eye, my eye. Moonpie, brown eye shows. Blink blink. Dry nose.

Cui cui cui. Cage birds hop.

Jinglee. says bell. Rain. Wind blows.

Wood stool creaks. Ahem. Bon soir, miss. Horrible wet out tonight, yes. The door, allow me.

Jingleelee. says bell. Shop door shuts. Pink hurty tummy my hand rubs. Little hidey top spins t ta, t ta, t ta, t ta. My fingers little tongue licks. Tongue pink, rough. Thirsty.

Clic. Clac. Clic. Clac. Clic. Fish tanks, cages, black boots stalk. Cheep cheep. Clic clac clic. Clic clac clic. Clic clac boots come.

Ach, O boy. says Pretty Boyd. Cat drags self in. Ha ha.

Pink tummy whines. Green bird bottle my hand takes. Metal spout shines. Soft black muzzle metal spout rubs.

Clic clac clic. Wet black boots. Long brown coat. Red stockings, wet. Black collar, white throat. Metal tag clinkclink. Metal spout, water drop. Water drops, red glasses. Eyes hurt my eyes. Blink blink.

That mutt looks sick as hell. torn red stockings says.

Cold, my neck. Wet yellow hair red lips chew. Fweet fweet Tell us a secret. Yellow hair Skinny finger pulls. Black crosses have fingers.

Tooths show. Im bustin you out tonight, chickpea.

Red lips say, Hsst. I know you hear me.

Bright smell, shop. Wood shavings. Feed. Fweet fweet fweet birds. Bloop, bloop, fish tanks. Puppies Yip yip.

O boy. says Pretty Boyd. Rainbow wings flare.

Pink tummy cries. Pink tongue licks metal drop. Red glasses drip. Eyes hurt my eyes. My eyes water. Groan.

Brown shoes come. Mister shoes dry. Black boots wet.

Were you looking for something special, miss. says Mister. We shut soon.

Red mouth yawns. Are you a witting or witless accomplice.

Pardon.

Very clever. Long brown coat turns, boot heels clic, clic, clic. Yellow tail shivers. Cheep cheep cheep.

Tell him all that rocking is making that mutt seasick.

Swish swish. says yellow tail. Clic clac clic clac clic. say black boots. Water drops, floorboards. Jinglelee. says bell. Water drops, floorboards.

Doberman pup, green bottle fall. Pup yelps. Floorboards my tummy lies. Water drops big, my eye. Hollers come. Pretty Boyd wings flapflap Cage birds Cui cui cui Mister jumps Holy Moses what a racket Tranquille my boy Calm down Take it easy now Whats wrong.

My shoulder Hand pats. My shoulder shakes, my shoulder burns, my back Floorboards hits bam bam bam fire jumps Floorboards my hollering foots kick My head my fists hit hit hit. Fireflies spin. Hollering.

Im sorry, my boy. I forgot. Im sorry. Dont hurt yourself.

My eyes nose mouth wet. Burning. My eyes blink blink blink. My throat hurts. Mister hands show. Tranquille my boy. Mister says. I mean, theres a wonderful good boy surrounded by friends. We should like him to know he is safe.

Fire gets little. My eyes my sleeve wipes. Floorboards my tummy lies. Water drops sparkle. Sparkle my fingertips pet. Sparkly tails water drops make. My throat hurts. Byebye.

Whats got under his skin this time. says Mister.

O boy. says Pretty Boyd.

Purple closet curtain sways. Tippy toe closet window, rain. Grey fog, window makes. My cot creaks. Whistle. Cheep cheep. Fuzzy green blanky twitches, pulls. My tummy little blanky legs kick kick. Growl.

My foots rub, rub, rub. My chin my hand sits.

Raggedy Ann, my hand, pages turn.

O boy. says Pretty Boyd.

Glow glow glow Purple closet curtain shows. Little tooths gnaw my elbow. Little tongue wet little wet nose. Green blanky kick kick kick. Cot creaks. Clic clic clic, sleepy beaks. Siamese cries. Cracked ceiling sighs, snores, Uhhh hhh. Uhhh Hhh. Uhhh h h h.

Page my fingers turn. Raggedy Andy. Raggedy Ann. Hookie The Goblin. Cookieland.

Breaking.

O boy. says Pretty Boyd. Trouble, trouble, trouble, us.

Jingleelee. Purple closet curtain flaps. Rain gets big. Clac clic clac. Birds whistle, squawk, Who Who Door broke O my Shop shut Who Begone You Barmy Cutpurse You.

Clic clac clic clac clic. Bang.

Green blanky yelps. Cot rattles. Raggedy Ann falls floorboards. Floorboards cold my hands, my foots. Bangbang Raww fweet fweet. Doberman pup green blanky shows. Pup my hand puts crate.

Thief Thief. Pretty Boyd hollers. Wake up old lush. Ach wots use Help Mac Grimalkin robbin coop.

Rusty dusty, purple curtain my fingers taste. Neck tickles. Grey sweater top spins badum badum badum.

Purple curtain peeks my eye.

Shop. Darkness. Fish tanks glow glow glow. Budgies spin, bump wings, bump ceiling, fall, flutter no no no Tippy toe kitty paws swat. Crate puppies say Yap yap yap. Doberman pup says, Oua oua, rattles crate. Cockatiel drape Brown coatsleeve pulls. Opens metal gate Cockatiels sputter dart Brown coatsleeve chases bang bang bang. Shaking blue tail, bang bang bang. Long brown coat spins. Blurry hands.

Hands have wings.

In you go Brown coatsleeves throw, Big cage, wings beat tho tho tho Birds cry My ears hands hide My tooths bite Ach Stop er, Mac My knees clac clac Swinging cages somersault My back my head hits. Cough. Darkness.

Shadows dart, flicker. Your insides are either made of cotton or sawdust.

Ring ring. Ring. Ring ring.

Where are we going. asked Raggedy Andy. To the Deep Woods in search of adventure. replied Raggedy Ann, as they scampered down the stairs.

Ring ring. Ring.

Falling bubbles, goldfish tank. Broke door kitties sit, tilted heads, rain. Mouillé, mouillé.

Bell shines broke door. Ring ring. Bell hides.

Bell shows. Ring ring. Rolling floorboards. My elbows hands push, my botty sits. Head hurts. Bell hides.

Ring ring. Ring ring.

Broke door comes, rain. Kitties turn, cry, Mouillé.

Water drops floorboards. Owie. Hard water bits hurt. Red dot, my finger. Red dot drips. Shiver.

Ringringring. says darkness rain.

Cobblestones glitter. Mouillé, mouillé. Shop pups yap yap yap. My shoulder flittering finch passes tha tha tha tha, streetlamp, rooftops, black sky, smoke.

Byebye.

My eyes rain pokes. Blink, blink.

Broke shop door shuts. Handle my hands pull. Broke door rattles. Hole, sharp glass. Door shows Pretty Boyd rainbow wings flaflaflaflap. Push, Mac, push.

Handle my hands pull. Hollering. Not pull, push.

Ring ring, ring ring.

Glittery stones, gravel allee. Flashing cage flapping wings Little brown coatsleeve swings. Tsokka tsokka tsokka.

Ach, come back, Mac.   Mac, come back.

Cold wet stones. Bits, butts, apple core, bones. Rain. Streetlamp. Raindrops float, dart, yellow light. Streetlamp hollers Zreeeeeee. Allee goes byebye. My eyes hurt. Bang Metal ash can falls, cough cough rolls. Fireflies. My back hits, top spins d da d da d da d da, lamp hollers Zreeeeeee.

Tippy top windowsill. Red tip cigarette. Hollering.

Sahd dap dwon trehe, I tlel you.

Breaking. My hair my hands Glass bits hit. Hollering. Cobblestones hard wet. My foots slip, push, slip.

Window. Little bottle waves. Red tip cigarette hollers, Telnilg you for the lsat tmie.

Long hair Window shows. Little bottle little hand takes, caws. Esay, Leo. Lokos lkie hes trppiin on smoe good siht.

Wlel, he sholud be mroe qeiut aubot it.

My head hollers spin. My head my fist hits. Fireflies.

Ring, ring, ring. says bell. Ringringringringring.

Rain. Glittery stones. Allee, fireflies byebye, darkness. My hands foots run. Stone steps come. Downhill tree branches wave, clatter. Black boots skip, tic toc, tic toc, toctoctoc. Brown coat shoulder. Bingbing eyes. Little long brown coat goes byebye, White picket fence. Gate cage bangs. Birds cry.

Dont be shy. says darkness rain.

Ring, ring, ring.

Stone steps. Tippy toe tree branches shake. Shadows wave. White pickets, broke gate. Weedy court. Ivy rattles. Peely door. Darkness. Bell Ring ring. Miaou darkness doorway come. Miaou. Ivy rattles. Darkness hums. Wet grey sweater top goes da dum da dum da dum.

Dry. Stairwell flickers, yellow light. Popping rain Doorway shows. Miaou. Miaou. My wet pantleg blue Korat rubs. Eyes bingbing. Pointy ear my fingers scratch.

Faim. Faim. says blue Korat.

Salty dust have shelves, staircase. Bootprints shine wet, dusty steps. Cracked ceiling shadows clic clac clic. Clic clac clic. Stairwell, feathers float. Birds holler Who What How Where Why.

Stairwell says, En haut. Viens ici, chickpea. Dont be shy.

Ring, ring, ring, ring, ring, ring.

Wet bootprints flicker Yellow light. My hands, foots climb. Cats follow, scamper prip prip prip My arms, legs, Coats rub. Flickery tails. Wet steps say Hee. Hee. Hee.

Cats byebye. Doorway. Candlelight. Torn brown sofa. Pale throat, black collar. Tag shines. Wet yellow hair. Red stockings cats rub, miaou. Blue eyes bingbing my eyes.

Floorboards bell hits, bounces, jingleelee.

My grey sweater Fists grab. Black crosses have fists. Red scratches. White tape. Hollers come. Stand up. says fists. You should like to become a horseman like your father.

My arms fly. My arms flap, swoop, dive. Hollering. Blue eyes stare, hurt my eyes. Keep howling. red mouth says. Step right up Hear the forlorn kvetching of the wild man of Burundi Watch him take flight. Listen chickpea, no one can hear you and even if they did they wouldnt bloody care.

Pale throat, black collar, smell. Legs, sweat, crouch, dirt, hot, jump, salt, ash, flowers, owie, bangbangbang.

My grey sweater fists push My heels ch ch ch, my arms spin. Hands clap Hollering red mouth caws Hahaha Black boots stomp dam dam dam dam Book hand throws Kicking shadows Cage birds cry, hop Wings thrash My ears hurt My hands hide Arrooooooo.

My arm cold hand takes, squeezes. Ear tape hand cups. See. red mouth says. Nada.

Candlelight flickers. Cages. Birds rabbits snakes. Aquariums. Rats hamsters. Lizards. Wet cage Wet birds flap wings, shake heads, say,

Why.

Where.

Help.

Ha ha, help. dry birds say.

Thop.   Thop.   Thop. Wet ceiling boards drip. Shiver.

Détendez, tu es libre. shrugging brown coat says. Youre a million kilometres away.

Brown coat flaps Cats scatter Waterdrops my cheeks eyes forehead. Broke chair Coat flops. Black sweater, long red stockings, skinny, wet. Cold, my neck. Black sweater sleeves hands push. Yellow tail white tape fingers pull. Hair shakes. Wet yellow hair Red towel hands rub.

Red towel says, Doctor Dolittle and his Allee Cat Allies thought they were going to do their usual dance number on another one of our kind. Doctor Dolittle, all smiles and charming old world bows, wot friendly white hair yodeling off his conniverous old head. His warm sweater vests and worn loafers. All those safe kindly earth tones. All those ravished grappa bottles in the allee. Hes just another sawdust Caesar. Just another collector and conspiracist on the take, is Doctor Dolittle. Betting you were just another sucker.

Wet red towel flies. Shadows flap. My arms wet towel hits, burns. Damp hair Pale hand lifts. Blue eyes. Red stockings says, But tomorrow Dolittle will stir headache powder into a little hair of the dog and when his vision singles, he will see who the real sucker is.

Torn red stockings turn, ceiling shadows stalk. White tape fingers take little box. Box opens Wood stick fingers pinch. Red tip. Box stick scratches Flash snaps Pssshou.

My eyes my hands hide. O boy.

Ha ha ha cawing red mouth says, That old parrot taught you more than Dolittle ever did, huh. O boy.

O boy. my mouth my hand hides.

Red mouth caws. Haha. Lets run with that. Oboy. You got yourself a street name, kid.

Fiery stick lights wick. Wick. Wick. Little stick hand shakes My nose Smoke comes. Torn red stockings come. Little fires flicker. Eyes bingbing. Wax. Skin. Sweat. Damp chin.

Black sweater leans. Black collar. Metal tag white tape fingers pinch. Freda. fingers says. Tag shines. Freda. red mouth says. Say it. Blue eyes watch my eyes. My eyes hide.

Youre all wet. yellow hair says.

And your toes must be ice cubes. torn red stockings says.

Rolled black sweater sleeves says, Yet you crouch there like a darling little caveman with those big worried shoe button eyes.

I know, I know. says red mouth. Youre out of sorts cos whatevers happening here to you right now is all wrong cos its never happened to you before Contiguity Disorder the same thing must happen samely lest the laced get loost and the least get lost But you must also know some part of you chose to come Lust list liced last Au revoir to the past I didnt stuff you in the cage with these birds O no I rang a bell and you followed so some aspect of you knows whats happening here was supposed to happen. Aujourdhui, cest le jour.

Cage birds spin, rankle, cry.

How.

What.

Who. Who. cage birds say.

Red mouth says, A little bird told me its about whoness and whatness, Oboy. Whoman in another way.

Brown sofa red stockings sit. Black boot hands pull. Boot tumbles klonk klonk floorboards. Black boot hands pull. Klonk. Bruised bare foots walk. Shadows. Hands lift window. Squeak. My ears hurt. Windowsill carton pale hand takes. Hole tape fingers tear. Carton hand tips. Red mouth drinks, pale throat moves. Lips tongue licks Mmm, thisll put an end to your whimpering. Half and half. Just like you and me.

Carton cold hand pushes, my hand. Fingers black crosses red scratches says, Take this. Go on, damn you. Its organic. Fingers grab my wrist. Take it. My wrist burns, my arm, my throat. Hollers come, burn. My hand carton hits Take it Carton falls, milk splashes O for christs sake Cats come, my wet pantlegs coats rub Miaou cats red stockings push Outta the way Carton hand takes, green bowl. Milk carton pours gug gug gug gug. Pale hand pushes Drink green bowl slides, comes. My hand green bowl bumps. Floorboards jumps. Milk spins, milk cold, milk thick, milk sweet. Miaou. Miaou. Cats come.

Black sweater says, Ah, the bigness of your eyes. The pretty of your face. I knew it the instant I saw you in that forlorn allee outside Dolittles. Almost forgot animal control was hot on my little tail. Then you climbed up and rescued the pink cockatoo here. That was the clincher. Youre just like me. We are broken telephones. We are bent as thieves. We were born from the lions sneeze. Now, we are all designed by mathematics, but unlike the math of god, the math of man is irremediably flawed. What do the anthro do when experiments go poopoo. Back to the drawing board. Thanks for playing, do come again. Only we are the lovely living breathing parting gifts wot remain. I perseverate. And you have such a long long ways to go. You dont even have shoes and you have to have shoes if youre going to fit in

My grey sweater Fists grab, pull

Stand up Andy you have to walk on your hind legs and shake hands How do you do and smile on demand and no matter how much we despise them we still look like them, so we have to make use of that abuse if only so we can do what we need to do, otherwise the anthros lock us up until we get too old and uncute and uncuddly and they send us without regret to that great big shop for pets where the light is too bright and the sound is too loud. And its so cold. I will have the last laugh at so called mankind. You are going to help me laugh. Do you know how.

Cats crouch. Milk purring red tongues flick.

Ha. yellow hair black collar red mouth says. You dont even know what you are. Yet.

W hen Raggedy Andy was first brought to the Dollhouse he was very quiet.

Birds fweet fweet fweet. Book pale hand turns, shows me dollies. Black crosses Pale fingers. My eyes my fingers hide. Top spinnedy spins inside.

WhyyyyMeee. caged pink Henry cries.

Raggedy Andy did not speak all day, but he smiled pleasantly to all the other dolls. There was Raggedy Ann, the French doll, Henny, the little Dutch doll, Uncle Clem, and a few others.

Broke window ivy leaves scratch. Broke window snores. Bird cages. Tail high, comes greeneyed Korat. Ceiling shadows pitapat. My back hard cold wallpaper hurts. Torn wallpaper flutters.

Some of the dolls were without arms and legs.

One had a cracked head. She was a nice doll, though, and the others all liked her very much.

All of them had cried the night she fell off the toy box and cracked her china head.

Raggedy Andy did not speak all day.

But there was really nothing strange about this fact, after all.

None of the other dolls spoke all day either.

Torn wallpaper flutters. My fingertips fluttering tickles. My hand shines, candlelight. Hair shines, my hand. My hand. Hair shines, little hairs shine, my hand, my hand shines, little hairs shine. My hand. Blink, blink, blink, blink little hairs flickery candlelight. Bam. My tummy jumps.

Skinny black pantlegs stand, groaning armchair. Book flies, pale hand, book brown sofa bounces, tumbles.

Hand pulls black sweater sleeves. Skinny arms hide. Red lips says, Wots with all the distractions. I brought along your sleepytime books cos I thought theyd make you feel apples n spice, send you on your dreamy way to lala land. But you havent slept since I rescued you. Still all big eyed, cowering there behind the sofa, tripping on that ripped wallpaper. Whatre you nervous about. You cant think and you cant dwell so whatre you nervous about. You mustve forgotten Dolittle by now.

Korat sits, torn brown sofa. Green eyes my eyes. Ouille. Korat says, blink blink.

Fluttery torn wallpaper My fingertips touch. Torn wallpaper tickles.

Black boots clic clac clic. Yellow hair shines. You know, youre driving me mad playing with that wallpaper. Cest tout que tu fais. Then again, wot had I expected. Sparkling conversation. Rapier wit. Ha. Jesus. Here, you want that bleeding scrap. Shadows Pale hand black crosses makes, wallpaper hand tears, Take it eat it choke on it for all I care. Hand throws. My cheek Curling, fluttery shadows scratch. Hollers come. Hiding eyes, hand hand fingers thumb. Wood floorboards Foots scrape, Brown sofa foots kick. Hollering.

Korat jumps, hides. Head peeks, blink blink big green eyes. Broke window sighs. Window Ivy leaves scratch. Water ceiling boards drip. Plip. Plip. Plip. Shiver. Wood floorboards shines drippy water. Floorboards cold, hard. Hurts my hip. My back cold, hard wallpaper hurts. Cage bird Wings flip flip flap.

Yellow hair shines, candlelight. Brown coat Pale hand takes. Red stocking hat. Creaky big cage Hand lifts. Cage says, Its that time again, got to make my rounds. Another week or two, once youve stopped obsessing about the decor, youll come go with me. But for now, youre still for the birds. Wheres my hook stick. O, and heres a little something to even the keel.

Red pebble taped fingers put my hand.

Clic clac clic. Doorway, dark hall, candle sputters, byebye, smoke. Hollers come.

Dont be such a fraidy cat. clic clac stairwell says.

Red pebble my tongue tastes. Sweet. Candy.

Raggedy Ann and Raggedy Andy lay in their little doll beds, smiling up through the dark at the top of the playhouse. It was very still and quiet in the playhouse, but the Raggedys were not even a teeny weeny speck lonesome, for they were thinking so many nice kindly thoughts. And, you know, when one thinks only lovely, kindly thoughts there is no time to become lonesome.

The playhouse was an old piano box and was all fixed up nice and cozy. There was an old rug upon the floor, two doll beds, three little chairs, a table with pretty little play teacups and saucers and plates on it.

Book black cross fingers shut. Book Lap sits. Black sweater arm waves. This is our abandoned ship, our grounded wreck, our dead star. red mouth says. Its the perfect hide out for me. For us, chickpea. The Favelle, this whole areas been left for dead. Haussmanns going to tear down these sad sack buildings, bring in new blood, new bees n honey, make it trendy, toney. Gentrified, sunny. Loft art living space. Bring on the middle class, the hipsters, bohemians, artistes, guppies, the upper crust. The private speculators and property developers. The washed. All of them running the allez cats and criminals and norway rats and poor widdle scuts like us into the dust. Reduce our natural habitat, our range. Making us, then, deranged.

My lap Korat sits. Tongue licks paw, purrs ron ron ron.

Until then, in the meantime, its all ours. Et personne ne sait que nous sommes ici. Well, no one knows beyond the others. Swan. Our king. Youll meet anon. He found me this corner of the map, this old piano box, he gave it to me, A dollhouse for a doll, he said. The others, the Vivians, are in this district. Youll meet them too. Swan keeps us all Cling Clang rattle tattle ding dang, jumping Korat claws my lap, Hollers, cats slink redgreyblack, ears back, eyes big. Door, hallway hollers Merde, Questce que cest que ça, Tais tois, Booige.

Cages, twittering wings, shadows scatter ceiling Goddammit Bedtime book falls Skinny black pantlegs jump My arms flap flap flap Bouncy brown sofa Black boots chakk chakk chakk Hook stick Pale hands grab. Darkness, hall, yellow hair hollers Cant you read my sign.

Read this sign, granny.

Bitch fuck you we can to here, is free country.

Darkness.

Clic clac clic, doorway darkness clic clac clic, Three triangles, the cat, my sign over the door you brats, what, have you come to get high with the cookie people, well my my my theyre all dead you bloody stupid Aurolac shits you goddamn paint sniffing toadstool twits, dead dead dead, we ate them all up every crumb You in search of freedom Then get the fuck back into the womb before I snatch those wormy mops right off your tops and tuck into your cookie crumble brains.

Holler, crash, bang bang bang. Korat skips, flanks flash, byebye. Wood floorboards comes, hands, foots. Doorway comes. Darkness. Hallway cats crouch, curling tails. Hook stick Black sweater arms wave hit little dirty coats, little curly heads, plastic bag drops, dusty splintered floorboards Silver splatters You bitch Red tom turns, runs prip prip prip Black sweater arms hook stick push Arrêtes, Arrêtes, emmerdeuse, My head My hand hits wanggg stars holler Fuck yourselves right out the window trolls Youre lucky Swan int here otherwise hed march you up to the roof to see if you could fly Little legs little foots trip over pans, pots, cans, window, trip trap trolls byebye.

Redbluegreen window Black sweater arms shut bang.

Fuck you, bitch.

Black sweater black pants turn, yellow hair flashes. Collar tag blinks. Hook stick hand puts hallway floorboards, black jeans kneel. Grey rope hands take. Pots pans lift, clang clongety bang.

Our foolproof security system. cawing black sweater says.

Pots pans Pale hands stack clnkclnk cardboard box. Grey rope pulls tight. Redbluegreen window shines. Hook stick Pale hand takes. Black boots come, clic clac clic. Cats come, prip prip prip, Korat, green eyes my eyes, soft blue coat rubs my arm, my thigh. My hands foots turn, follow Korat, cats, flickery doorway comes prip prip prip Torn brown sofa jumps hands foots Brown sofa squeaks Caged birds sing fweet fweet. Clic clac clic clac clic. My tummy, warm purring Korat curls. My eyes Fingers hide. Black boots come. Hook stick falls bow w wwood floorboards. Clic clac clic. Armchair groans. Skinny black pantlegs cross, worn black knee, black boot bounces.

Shiny mirror has pale hand, blue eyes blink. Red lips white tooths caw. My god, the burnt out little nose pickers are right I am getting fucking old. I could pass for thirty.

Blue eyes get little. Blue eyes get big. Cheeks turn sidetoside, shiny glass. Tooths shine.

Have you ever seen your own face, Oboy. Its a pretty sight, though your whiskers could use a little dig in the grave. Glass pale hand turns. Candlelight flashes. My eyes hide.

The magic of Imagination may at times be very lovely, when one imagines beautiful melodies, lovely thoughts, or kindly deeds. But, when the magic of Imagination is forced upon one who is not strong enough to escape, the experience is likely not to be a pleasing or beautiful adventure.

Raggedy Andy looked thoughtfully at Raggedy Ann and said, You speak like a very wise person, Raggedy Ann.

Book white tape fingers shut. Raggedy Ann my hand takes. Book my fingers open. Pages my fingers turn. Pages dry. Pages smell dusty. Bright red Raggedy Ann yarn hair my fingers pet. White sailor cap Raggedy Andy wears. My eyes Colours hurt. Broke window sighs.

Raggedy Anns been a wonderful addition to the collection, chickpea. You appear to be enjoying her more yourself. Least, youre sleeping. Like you, I wonder why cant the world be more like Raggedy Ann.

Tumbled floor books Pale hands pick.

Red lips say, Here are some other treasures from the canon wot inform our mission. My guide to bird identification. Always good to know what youre rescuing. The index medicus, cos we get hurt out there. My map of the city showing all the best rooftop pathways in red ink. Its how we round round get around. We can cross entire districts without touching the ground. Heres Fox in Sox, to practice talk.

Books brown sofa catches. Red tom Tortoiseshell jump. My foot books touch.

And the most important piece of my library. Construction of Biologically Functional Bacterial Plasmids in Vitro, by Stanley Cohen and Herbert Boyer.

Wrinkly yellow papers white taped hands rattle.

This describes how to isolate and amplify genes and insert them into other cells with precision. Recombinant dna technique. Our bible, the book of genesis, you see.

It explains how you and I came to be. says wrinkly yellow papers. Yellow papers turn.

My eyes hide. Candles flicker. Birds fweet fweet fweet.

Caged Henry coos, Sweet, sweet.

Maybe nows the good time I should give you the highlights. red lips says. Black collar tag Pale fingers black crosses poke. Clink clink. Pale candlelight Tag shines. Pale throat shines. Freda. My eyes Blue eyes watch.

Pale throat says, One day when the real for sure folks had gone away from home and Raggedy Ann and Raggedy Andy had been left out in the little playhouse in the orchard, Raggedy Ann said to Raggedy Andy, Raggedy Andy, do you know what.

Tell me, Raggedy Ann.

Raggedy Andy, you and I were constructed in a cell free environment. A test tube. In vitro. Its true. We are factories, not breeds, not specics, not dollies nor even earthlings.

Our original a to z was to make the anthro stronger and healthier. Vaccinate against bigger, badder, wolfier diseases. Protect it from untimely, inconvenient dying, or even just the sniffles.

Andy, did you know you and I were pure. Raggedy Ann said. Purified and homogenized, anyway. And we wouldve gone on forever, our bits begot from immortalized cell lines, spun free of birth and death, simply enzymes, proteins, bare naked segments of genes. Anonymous, sure. Patented and trademarked, okay. But nonetheless authentic, without fear or desire, without need or neurosis or pain. Simply free. Free not to be a you and a me. Eternally.

What Im saying, Raggedy Andy, is we never were supposed to live.

Now dont cry. The real sob story begins with an experimental allergy fix for Feldee one, the cat glycoprotein wot triggers rashes and wheezing and red eyes and sneezing. Some pharmaceutical companies tried to nix the protein the old fashioned, barnyard way, testing untold thousands of kitties, searching for that one in every 50000 wot lacked the allergen. Those lucky few were then greenlighted to fuck their brains out. Tee hee. Pardon my french, Andy. This method was, quote, natural, but took too much time, and supply couldnt keep up with demand.

Other companies tried genetic engineering to knock out the protein. Not only didnt gene therapy save on time any better than artificial selection, it didnt save on bees n honey either. Who but some rich ponce is going to pay four grand for a feline. No one knew feldee ones purpose in cat metabolism in the first place, so removing it couldve had unforseen side effects, like o, say, death.

Raggedy Ann said, And whether you use selective breeding or gene therapy, any dandling between allergenfree cats and regular cats would indubidously restore the sneezy gene, undoing all that well wrought husbandry.

My nose sneezes Atchoum.

Gezundheit, Andy. So along comes Doctor Frankenstein. He cooked up a less drastic solution, so they say. By fusing the fiddledeedee protein with an anthro antibody, he created a flashy designer molecule wot trumped the allergy. Gamma feline domesticus, a so called alternative to genetic modification and a safe way to retrain the immune system of anthro allergy sufferers. Just go to hospital and get pricked.

Doctor Frankenstein opined, But vhy shtop at allergy proteins. Did not hybrid cells behafe like embryonic shtem cells. Like cow und rabbit, could not cat eggs be used as cost effectiff shortcut to making cloned embryos vhich could yield human shtem cells. After all, clones are crucial for research into illnesses like Parkinsons und motor neurone disease. No longer over somevuns dead body vould my fellow Wissenschaftler have to harvest the cells. No longer like a magpie vould he have to vait for those all too fewly precious human eggs in vhich to grow the shtems. Just scrape off some skin or blood cells, then fuse those patient cells viss plentiful, accezzible animal eggs shtrippt of their nuclei. Upon fusion, the eggs vill direct the patient cells to grow as embryos. The cells created vould be identical to the patients und contain the gremlins wot caused the diseases, vhich could be shtudied to unravel the puzzle of the diseases und test new drugs.

Raggedy Ann snapped her cotton soft fingers. Et voilà, our daffydown dilly Daddy Frankenstein, who started out wanting to do good, began wanting to do god.

Know what a chimera is, Andy. Raggedy Ann said. In biology a chimeras a plant or animal wots got more than one set of genes. Animal chimeras, mosaics, they dont blend so nice as plants. Since each gang of cells fights for expression, the resulting animal is a ragtag of mismatched parts.

What Frankendaddy really wanted was something wot looked anthro and was not protected by god or law or decency, but by patent alone. What he wanted was a proprietary hybrid. A ready supply of organs for transplantation into o so deserving anthros.

The prize winning discovery of restriction endonucleases made gene splicing possible. What the forest sprites call recombinant dna. Raggedy Ann laughed. O, Andy, through recombination, Daddy Frankenstein could choose a piece of dna, cut that piece of dna with a restriction enzyme, then glue that insert to other restricted dna with ligase. The recombined dna is then loaded into a vector and driven into the host cell.

Have you ever heard of vector control, Raggedy Andy. Not rats or mosquitoes, but self replicating dna molecules. In gene therapy, vectors are typically made from plasmids, harvested from the cytoplasm of bacteria. But a virus can be a vector, and so can dna, reengineered and used as molecular carriers, vehicles for delivering genetic material. Beep beep.

Were we conceived in the backseat of a virus. Raggedy Ann said. Couple a crazy bacteriophages drunk on lambda juice on a hot Saturday night in a petri dish. Or maybe we were contrived via Saturday Night Special. Biolistics, with its lovely gene gun shooting high velocity nanoparticles of gold beads coated with dna into the host cells nucleus.

Bang bang youre born, huh, Raggedy Andy.

Or perchance we came to be via proprietary transfection reagents like lipofectamine, aka the cats pajamas. Ah, lipofectamine transfection, with its zesty lipid and dna blend, given a dash of electricity and baked to perfection inside the cell by phagocytosis or membrane conflation. Its alive. Alive.

With all these toys at his disposal, Frankendaddy began pairing feline genes with their orthologs in anthro genes and worked his way out from there, fusing the most unlikely genetic traits last.

Spoilers of embryonic research said the creation of embryos from animal and anthro cells, or anthro animal chimeras and hybrids, was like, wicked, and shouldnt be allowed. The regulatory body for embryo research, and for cleaning up the mess, the Center for Animal Care and Industry, or CACI, were nervous nellies, calling townhall meetings to discuss and debate and avoid making a decision.

Our jolly Daddy Frankenstein was not only a mad scientist, but a master politician, always saying the right things, such as Hybrids can help us defelop cures und treatments for a host of anthro afflictions, but vee are in no vay interested in the creation of dog faced boys or mule arsed girls.

Of course, Daddy had secretly decided the more similar to anthro the animal, the better research tool it would make for testing new drugs or growing spare parts to transplant into the worthy anthro. To give himself room to work, he had to appease regulators and silence the watchdogs at the same time. Knowing all too well that anthro disease is genetic by design, Papa Franks used recombination to develop antibiotics, hormones, and other biologics to increase resistance and not just treat but prevent genetic diseases, reduce the sideaffects and cost of medicines and improve treatment for preexisting conditions.

Its all very dog and pony, Raggedy Andy, but of course Daddy Frankenstein wasnt mix and matching dna segments just to defeat disorder and disease. Make yourself a hero, win a nobel prize, and whos going to criticize you. Whos going to tell you youre wrong. Whos going to fick mit dich. Raggedy Ann said. The CACI set forth voluntary ethical guidelines like the infamous Assisted Human Reproduction Act for the pick and choose of criminals like Daddy Frankenstein, then with a little grease from lobbyists, concluded that creation of such embryos was perfectly legal anna neagle. Why not.

Black boot Raggedy Ann kicks. Boot bounces, spinning. So, we arent considered Gods creatures and weve got no rights, regardless of the huffing and puffing of watchdog groups. To Daddy Frankenstein you and I have only ever lived on paper, dead end calculations to be crumpled up and thrown away.

Cotton soft hands clap. My ears hurt. Raggedy Andy. Remember when you were nothing more than a twined strand of genes, a dna fragment from a cat spliced together with dna from an anthro, sticky ends attached by ligase, pooled feline microsomes and pooled anthro microsomes centrifugated from fragmented endoplasmic reticulae and integrated into a cellular chromosome, evolving into a microscopic leech, or were you a peach, clinging to some blat of yeast or morsel of moldy cheese or truffle or mushroom, from which you gained stability and nourishment, a base from which you could receive instructions for transcription and translation of new characteristics encoded by the inserted genes, mass producing proteins, dividing into cells upon cells, replicating your way from hybridized culture to fertilized egg to fullblown fetus, gestation in this way the only answer to how you got here. What mother would have you. Literally.

I am an omphaloskeptic. Raggedy Ann said. Black sweater, white shirt, fingers lift. Cotton tummy glows. Tummy finger pokes. I have a navel, but I dont adam n eve I was born.

Think of it, Andy. To say we were never born is right on the money, honey, and for Daddy Frankenstein and his rabblous team of hucksters and hustlers and vultures and venture capitalists, this excuse has got sex appeal, it letsm off easy. What harm if our adhesion molecules fail and we burst like shredded wheat into so many unraveled threads of dna, or if we should be poisoned by e coli O157H7 or some other rogue gut flora hidden in a castoff sandwich and, at best, we contract bloody shits or inflamed bowels or kidney failure, or at worst, our cells get confused whos boss and begin accepting signals from the verotoxins promoters and terminators, gobbledeegooking protein expression until we eventually collapse into a steaming, bubbling blood pudding, or if we get picked up discreetly and carted off forever and a day by the CACI, or if we simply get rubbed out by the street or prim and proper gentrification or just mournfully fade away under greasy pizza boxes piled high in a banged up dumpster. No soul. No harm. No bloody foul.

Raggedy Ann shook her head. Because how can we die a tragic death if we were never born. How do we exist when we are a chemicular novelty. How can we hurt when we are naught but a mixed infection, a therapeutic protein. A dead end vaccine.

Of course, even without the worst case scenarios, Daddy Frankenstein overlooked a few variables in his rush to be the smartest and the richest. Some of us, ha, most of us, developed fault ridden genomes or replication origins or expression factors. Or maybe transfection was unstable, treacherously transient, physiology reverting or degrading. Raggedy Ann coughed. Black crosses, cotton soft fist. What Im saying is, even after you recombine and transfect and replicate and fuse and fertilize, you still got to get the monster to walk, dont you Andy. You still got to give it a chance to live normal. But no, our proteins got miscopied or misunderstood until they lost key functions, telephones without buttons, no dial tone, halfbreeds and halfwits, feral and astray, defective, detritus, expendable. Even the idea of growing us for organs to be harvested was quashed cos, well, like eating cloned meat. Who wants a liver or kidney or heart from a genetically modified retard. That shit might be catching, you know.

Raggedy Ann sighed. The long and short of it is, Frankendaddy implanted a modified anthro cell into a scraped out feline egg, and here we are. Cat people. Fucked.

While I share our story with you Andy, Papa Frankensteins out there brewing up newer and better gmos, for the benefit of future generations of anthros. Bottom line, whether mill raised or backyard bred or pound seized, we have to stop him by saving the animals. And you have to help me, Andy. Help me rescue the cats and birds and bats and rabbits and pigs and noahs whole goddamn ark, one by bloody one, though we know theyre marching two by two. Its not the best way, in fact, we are on a loser that will kill us eventually.

But the butterfly effect is all we have. Raggedy Ann said.

Raggedy Ann and Raggedy Andy turned over and over as they fell. Part of the time Raggedy Ann was on top and part of the time Raggedy Andy was on top. But all the time they were sailing through the air, each Raggedy held the others hand.

It was quite dark, but that did not worry them for both Raggedy Ann and Raggedy Andy have bright little shoe button eyes. One can see very well with shoe button eyes if one is a rag doll stuffed with nice, clean, white cotton. And, of course, being made of cloth and stuffed with nice, clean, soft, white cotton, the Raggedys were not hurt even a teeny weeny bit when they finally lit with soft blumps upon the bottom.

The bottom of what, was just what Raggedy Ann wished to know. Where are we, Raggedy Andy. she laughed.

I guess we are at the bottom. Raggedy Andy replied, as he stood up and helped Raggedy Ann to her feet.

Dear me, yes, I know that, Raggedy Andy. laughed Raggedy Ann. But where is the bottom and where are we now.

Raggedy Andy scratched his yarn covered rag head and looked all about him.

Scritch scritch scratch.

Scuffly rats torn wallpaper hides. Cage birds whistle coo Rise and shine Yoo hoo hoo Wake up sleepy head FweefweefweeFweet.

Pink Henry cockatoo cries, Ssssweets.

Ear hurts. Stinky pillow my arms knees hug. My legs, head, warm kitties curl. Purring. My back, cold wallpaper scratches. Scritch scratch rats stained ceiling hides. Broke window Black Ivy leaves Sunlight. My eyes hurt. My side.

Little red candy white tape fingers show.

An apple a day. crouching black pants says.

Wood floorboards little red candy sits.

Ears flat, dirty cat sniffs. Hssst. Dirty cat goes, legs stiff.

Little red candy my tooths bite.

Sweets. caged Henry cries.

Crouching black pants. Black boots. Blue pullover Red mouth Red glasses bingbing. My eyes fingers hide.

Purple glasses white tape fingers show.

Irlens of your very own.

Stinky pillow purple glasses shine. My hands take. Purple glasses my tongue licks. My nose sniffs. My eyes purple glasses hide. Metal wings my ears hold. Glasses pinch my nose. Sunlight soft. Purple. Hahaha.

The Irlens, they use prisms to tame colour frequencies. Scotopic sensitivity, too much glare on our shoe button eyes. Contrast so highstrung it vibrates. We are wired to respond to contrast, so we are always in response mode. Sudden movement further causes sensory confusion, agitation. Its bloody debilitating, the severe aptitude of our senses.

Blue pullover turns. Blue pullover sleeve lifts. Earphones. says pale wrist. For noise isolation, reduction. See. Ears earphones hide. So you dont get so surprised. Yellow tail shakes Red mouth hollers, Lalalalalalala Boots klonk klonk. My ears my hands hide.

Stinky pillow Earphones bounce. My hands take. Sniff sniff. Lick. My ears earphones hide.

Boots stomp Hands clap. Lalalalalalala.

Wood floorboards tumbling white slippers come.

Ballet shoes, for your hind paws, since you refuse to wear hard soles. says clic clac clic black boots.

My foots white shoes hide. Haha.

Yellow hair grey cap hides. Guess it doesnt really matter which foot they go on. Black pants crouch. My heel white tape fingers pinch. Here, the drawstrings make them snug. Like gloves. See. String white tape fingers pull. White ballet shoes pinch. Haha. You like it tight, eh. Thats good. More on that later. Now, lets go shopping.

Black boots clic clac clic, hallway, byebye.

Corner. Torn newspaper. Holes, floorboards. Floor hole my pee sprays. Steam. Ring ring.

A fuera. hallway says. Es la dia ventecuatro. Venga ahora.

Ring ring. Doorway comes. Chattery cage birds say,

Wait.

Help.

Sweets.

Hallway. Dust floats. Light shines little downstairs entrée door. Downstairs cats chirp, tails flick, prip prip prip.

This is your skills development home, chickpea. Theres no going back to Dolittles, no going back to the simple life of the vegetable or tea cozy or whatever you thought you were. Your old so called life ended twenty four days ago. Twenty four days means you are acclimatized to your new environment. Twenty four days. Just like any other stray.

Stairs. Dust. Big breath blows. Earphones soft. Bubbles go. Downstairs bubbles spin, bubbles fall, get little. Pop. Pop. Pop.

Tiny bubbles. Hahaha. My hands clap.

Not just any bubbles. upstairs says. Supermiracle bubbles. This, the supermiracle bubble wand. And Im Freda.

Bubbles my hands ballet shoes chase. Stairs go Hee hee hee. Clic clac downstairs comes. Entrée door gets big. Doorlatch hand pulls.

Creak. entrée door says. Sunlight soft, purple glasses. Dust.

Orange supermiracle bubble wand Bottle hides. Wand shows, drips, red lips pucker, blow. Bubbles green. Blue. Purple. Bubbles say, Ha. Hee. Hey. Viens dehors jouer. My finger, bubble perches, shivers, pops. Breath blows. Bubbles come, bubbles go. Bubbles bobble Bubbles roll Bubbles twinkle, twinkle, pop. Bubbles my hands catch, bubbles spin, float.

Clic clac clic says, When my tormentors, the collectors, began to be turned away from shelters and faced competition for the freetogoodhomers, the random source animals, they stumbled upon the labs, Frankenstein and the big CACI giveaway of science rejects. Perfect for folks with a big heart and a bigger penchant for torture. They only had to restrain us n retrain us and theyd collect big from the taxpayer.

The collectors put me and the others through the hells of remodeling, cure and habilitation, in order to teach us how to speak when spoken to, how to groom ourselves, how to sit still. They went with the program, for a while. The touchy feely therapies, the ihp, the diet restrictions and of course the neurocorrectors. But results were hard won. The collectors began to rely more and more on their bread and butter tactics. Reward and punishment. Negative reinforcement. Fear. They used water to overpower and control us. Whether we or they didnt like something, water was often the answer. The collectors would haul us up, check us for fight, plunge us under again. They would use the tub, use hoses, hot water bottles, squirt guns, soaking rags stuffed over nose and mouth. You have to learn, they would say. Bad kitty. Splash.

Why would anyone think they could reprogram us, when our programming is in our dna. We are not behavioral or developmental. You and I are spooky actions at a distance, chickpea. We exist in two diametrically opposed conditions at the same time. Anthro, not anthro, feline, not feline. The many worlds hypothesis. We exist in the decoherence of the quantum suicide machine. In the cat state, not dead and not alive, but the superposition of dead and alive. Alive and dead. The idea of superposition means as long as we dont know an objects status, its in all possible states at once. So there we are, spinning in opposite directions. Schrödinger, naturally. Entanglement, necessarily. Quantum immortality, not likely, for how can an electrical current circling in opposite directions simultaneously be anything but numbered, daywise. Dead and alive and two and a half times more sensitive than the anthro. Thought experiments. Probability waves. Collapse of same.

Supermiracle bubbles bob tippy toe. Greenblue bubbles sparkle spin float. My hands clap, mouth says Hahahaha. Hands ballet shoes chase. Bubbles tumble, dart, shine. Hep. Ha. Ho. Maintenant volons. My arms flap, hair flutters. Chasing.

Clic clac Grey cap Yellow tail says, New applications in quantum computing and cryptography, in techniques for ultrasensitive measurement, atomic clocks or interferometers wot measure microscopic distances. Surveyors to the gods is what science would have our purpose be.

Marrons, marrons. hollers white apron. Chauds les marrons, chauds

Yet here we are. Market rue claire. Without a god in sight. Not hide nor hair.

Buy a rabbit, a rabbit

Ripe Speregas

Oranges, oranges. Qui veut mes belles oranges

Sausages hiss. Lamb steams. Rainbow paper Hand gives hand. Gyro Hand gives hand. Gyro Mouth chews.

Green melon block White tape fingers take. Red mouth chews. First pass, we take samples. Espy what we want more of. So if all else fails, least we had a snack.

Boots clic clac. Stroller hands push. Little booties kick, fuss. Bundle carrots. Tomatoes. Purple flowers rustling green paper wraps.

There you are, madame.

O. Ces orchidées sont si belles.

White bowl. Burnt peanuts, red. White tape fingers takes. Burnt peanuts, my hand takes. My tooths crunches mmmnnnn.

Crunching red mouth says, They would have us forecast disaster like seacats on a ship. Short of that, theyd settle for optimizing credit default swaps on sovereign debt, developing fraudproof digital signatures, or simulating complex biological systems for use in drug design.

Oublies, oublies. Elles sont bonnes mes oublies

Orange wand plastic bottle says, As a simulacrum, I have tested a lot of their drugs. You have too.

Clipclop clipclop snorting hot Just a horse Oboy

Apples, red yellow green. Box tips, falls. Apples roll. Sacré merde. Green onions red radish purple beets. White leeks. Pickles has glass jar. Strawberries Strawberries, scarlet strawberries pears, rhubarb.

Rather than open the kimono and expose us for all to see, They would have us encrypted, broken into secrets, beyond scope of the media, the masses Buy any Dutch biskits Theyd have us break into secrets, detect eavesdroppers, target whole villages for liquidation.

Buy a fork or a fire shovel

Candy oranges, chocolate bits, tray has. Black cross fingers take. Pastry, scones, cookie bits. My fingers take.

Samples for paying customers, eh. says fat hairy arms crossed big tummy. So scat.   Damn gypsies.

Innit rich. Aint we a pair. Superpositioned on land, at sea, in midair. Its measurement wot causes an object to be limited to a single possibility. To be defined, ergo incomplete. To be. To be or not to be means one is lost or free.

Round and sound, cherries O. Ripe cherries O

Mommy can I have a Fanta Please Mommy Please

White lion mane comes. Its Rozlyn. says red mouth. What one might call a cat lady. Black trunk Wrinkly spotty hand holds. Wheels has black trunk, rolls, dirty curly goblin shoes bump. Tied purple cloth has handle. Dirty goblin shoes grunt, whistle, toe toe rubs, walks. Black paint have eyelids. Wrinkly forehead, cheeks. My arms flap.

Little Nanny Etticoat, In a white petticoat, And a red nose. The longer she stands The shorter she grows. A candelstickell do the tricke

When she saw Raggedy Ann and Raggedy Andy the funny little woman stopped and nodded in a friendly manner.

Buy a candelsticke. she asked as she took one from her basket.

How much are they, I want to know. Raggedy Ann said. She did not need a candlestick, but she always believed in being polite.

They are foive cents. the little woman answered as she took more of the candlesticks from her basket. And, if ye wish a candle in the candlestick, that will cost one cent.

Raggedy Ann winked one eye at Raggedy Andy and said to the little woman, If we should take two candlesticks with two candles in them, how much would that cost.

The funny little woman thought for a long time, then she took a pencil and figured for a long time on a piece of paper. Ha. she said. If ye take two candlesticks wit candles in em, it will cost ye exactly nothing.

Then here it is. Raggedy Ann said as she held out her empty hand. We shall take two.

The funny little woman handed Raggedy Ann the two candlesticks with candles in them, asked, Wan any noice small pinted matches. Raggedy Ann shook her head. Then thanking Raggedy Ann very kindly, she put the rest of the candlesticks back into her basket.

Rozlyn.

Ah. Heya Freda kitty cat. cawing brown tooths says. Thought it was you. Aint seen you in a while.

Grey cap tape hand takes. Yellow hair leans. Wrinkly hand pets. Hand is spotted, dark, strokes yellow tail. How yuh doin kiddo. says brown tooths. Red mouth purrs, ron ron

ron ron. Metal tag clinks, black collar, pale neck. Gettin too skinny, dearie. Got some noice sahdines fo yuh next toime I sees ye.

Black eyes, my eyes. My eyes hide. My arms flap flap.

Sardines would be great, maman. says red mouth. Maybe we will see you at the library. My elbow Candles tap, black boots my shoes follow. Toes turned, dirty curly goblin shoes whistle, walk byebye.

A candelstickell do the tricke

Yellow tail says, How dispiriting it mustve been for Frankendaddy, that all we, his creations, could do was sit and bluster like irritated vegetables. A kings ransom down the test tube. And what pray tell to do with us now. So the powers that be devised IAM, the perfused organ program, manufacturing cells, tissues, and subcellular fractions from our nontransplantable organs in service to a global network of pharmaceutical, academic and biological organizations. Advanced Research and Development Activity of the National Biopharmaceutical Security Council. Department of Defense Multidisciplinary University Research Initiative Program. Institute for Biological Standards and Control.

Knives, sitthers and razors to grind

How many of these noshing bastards are sewn together with bits of our thread. They dont even know how scourges like you and me have propped up their paltry crop of organs.

Bicicletta ringring. Red mouth says, This was your walk through, Oboy. Next time youre going live. Here. For you.

Wand, bottle, my hands take. Tic toc tic toc. Bottle my nose smells. Bottle my tongue tastes. Wand my tongue pokes. Soapy. Wand my hand puts bottle stir stir stir. Orange supermiracle bubble wand My mouth blows Drops jump. Wand my hand puts bottle, stirs, rakka rakka. Wand hole shows, wet shiny. My breath goes. Bubble comes, pops byebye.

Hot baked wardens hot

Crab, crab, any crab

Soapy water my mouth drinks. Spits. Bottle my hand tips. Wand soapy water pours, plouf. Cobbles shine, wet.

O boy. my mouth says.

Look. That mans wearing ballet shoes. Funny. Crazy, is more like it. He looks like one of them, doesnt he. Cant tell. Well, look.

Pointy shoes walk, bare heels soft pale pink. Black shoes. Brown. Grey shoes. White. Dirty shoes stink hmph hmph hmph. Red pantlegs drag. Blue jeans rolled turnups. Look, cippolini. Big shoes. Little shoes. Dog poop. Blast. Clic clic clic, dog paws trot Hot spiced gingerbread, smoking hot Shoes bounce walk Boots buckles Skirts show pale ankles Shoes slip stumble tummy falls Ow, hands knees cobbles hit. Are you alright. White cane taps. Flip flops dance Red tootsies walk slap slap slap Spare some change for a bite of bread Black shoes shine. Purple corduroy stuffed boots. Yellow laces flicker Japan your shoes, your honour Shoe sock metal stalks make legs walk. Hole sole shoe shows dirty white sock. Pedals sneakers bicicletta zoum zoum.

Tsokka tsokka tsokka. Blue pullover black pants run come tsokka tsokka tsokka My shoulder hand hits Vas vas Plastic bottle falls, rolls, bump bump Bell goes ring ring ring Black boots run Hands flash, elbows swing, coats turn, stumble, gasp. Black boots my ballet shoes chase, Les Arrêter Hands come, my grey sweater pulls, Knee shoulder ballet shoes climb Ballet shoe pushes, jumps Hep Coat stumbles falls

Emil Stones Elbows cheek hit Oof Watch out My ballet shoes run. Boulevard comes. Arms legs swing Big eyes blink Bell Ring ring Downstairs black pants blue pullover runs, tummy arm hugs, cawing black boots tic toc tic toc. Ring ring ring.

Lamps glow stone stairwell. Steam. Ring ring. Wood boardwalk comes. Canal. Wet stones rat dogs lick. Ring ring.

Puddle boots plouf. Yellow tail twitches. Pale throat. Black collar. Metal tag flashes. Black boots walk tictoctictoc.

Corner comes. Dooryard. Paper. Plastic wrappers. Cup. My eye orange wand hides. They never chase us far. For what. Does some bruised turnip trump a knife thrust to the heroism.

Black pants blue pullover crouches. Pullover tummy big. Pullover tummy Hands go. Hands show. I scored an heirloom tomato. Little soft. Deux croissants. Little hard. We can have sandwiches. Preserves. More sandwiches. Dried cherries. Grapes. Ugh. Grapes go in the canal. Plish. Chocolate bar. I dropped one in my haste, damn it. But I did get a great sausage. Was the sausage man wot chased me. And look. Still warm. Quick, have a bite. Non. Mm. Now look. Honey bee pollen. Good for allergies, I read. Okay, not the best haul, but with your help, we can do better.

Blue eyes my eyes. My eyes Purple glasses hide. Me, wand hides.

I know what youre feeling. But your good Doctor Dolittle was no different than my collectors. Lots of sweet in the coffee. Loving when anyone was looking, genteel to a fault. Reputable. Credible. But dont you adam n eve it. A honey tongue, a heart of gall. When they couldnt twist me into a pretzel, or drown me into submission, the collectors decided to try one last thing and bury me under the foundation of their new big house. For good luck. I escaped then, and ever since.

What Im saying is, I wouldnt be trying to teach you how to be like them if this were our world. But I have to teach you how to be like them. Cos even the anthro has to pretend to be anthro. Its the difference between life and death.

Loneliness. Im not the first to say this. But how else to describe it. Cold and grey. A crow perched on a wire. Silhouette. Objective correlative. The outside reflects the inside. Arent we loneliest on grey cold days. Arent we less lonely on sunny bright days, warm fuzzy days, pretty pollen days. Loneliness is the skin wrinkling across the back of a hand. Crows feet etching round weakening eyes. Loneliness is that aspect of death wot makes us sad, as opposed to fearful.

I remember cowering in the crawlspace of the collectors big new house, shivering, hissing and spitting, doing my damnedest to ignore the collectors disingenuous commands. I can still hear them, their breath, see in that square of light the flexation of their thin lips from smile to grimace, the fingers snapping, the palms patting then slapping the ground, the falsehood, most gentle and sweet, harmless and innocent coaxing wots but a pale disguise for oblivion.

Here, kitty kitty. Here, kitty kitty.

In that moment, I knew loneliness. In that moment, I woke up.

Red mouth says, Do these introspective interludes amuse you, Oboy. Do you think me funny. Tragic. Wretched. Tedious. We cant all waste away in a cozy little pet shop, you know.

Id heard a rumour that the collectors had had enough of me. They had a black body bag, unzipped and glimmering plastic in the sun. They were going to put me in the bag, drop me in the drink. And that just made me so god damn sad. What could be worse than realizing you are unloved and in the way and doomed to deadness. So god damn sad. I didnt want to be put to sleep. I had only just awakened. I had to get out.

Black cross fingers says, I clawed through the mesh over the vent where I cowered. I scratched and pulled my way through that cement hole, the mesh scraping across my back, the pain was inconsequential. I ran. I escaped. I was free.

I know where I came from but I dont know how long Ive been here. On the boulevard. I met Swan. King o the cats. Wet and cold, he took me in. He told me I was real. He showed me loneliness is loveliness, too. I looked into his eyes and knew he was true. He was lonely, just like me. Just like you.

Like sticking my finger in a light socket, the realization that escaping my collectors didnt mean life was now happily ever after. It was nouvelle hell, the street. So beastly lonely and ridiculous, sleeping in store fronts wrapped like codfish in dirty newspaper, trying to stay dry if not warm spending dayafterday in the arcades, malls, subways. Trying not to starve or get cracked. Or pimped out. Or tracked. Others of us appeared, escapees clueless n trembling. We knew it when we saw each other, like you in the allee outside Dolittles. Some would run, too feral, trusting no one. The rest started running together, telling each other where to sleep and where to eat though more often sprinting en masse through the markets, snatching food and scattering, or pantomiming warnings when CACI vans were on the prowl.

Rawwww. says hyacinth macaw, flared wings. Budgie chuckles, Funny man, funny man. Ceiling shadows flicker. Black sweater torn red stockings long brown coat. Yellow hair red hat hides. Red sunglasses, blue eyes.

Collar tag fingers pinch. Im Freda. fingers says. Freda.

We taught each other who was who. We taught each other what we knew. We helped each other get by. It was the only way to survive. Comprends, Oboy. We found the missing pieces in each other. We put our pieces together. We had no one else. Until Swan.

Window ivy rattles. Cage birds whistle, chuckle. Terrarium mice snuggle. Cats curl, lick. My head, black stocking hat, warm. My foots ballet shoes hide. Grey sweater black coat. Purple glasses. Flickery candlelight.

Red mouth says, I remember the northbound subway train left Goblin station and there Swan was in his mismatched three piece suit, worn black fedora atop his long silky hair, striding across the rails to the southbound side, daddy longlegs stepping up to the platform, gold chains, gold rings, gold toothed flamenco smile and heat and smell of gitanes gathering us round, Youre safe now, Papas here, but lets keep one thing clear, my dears, the straightest edge you will ever find in this sinuous world, and thats No snitching, cause bitches wot snitches get found in ditches, nest ce pas. Swans long arm snakes round your shoulders, his finger to his lips. Never talk to cozzers. Never use real names, always aim to be faceless. You may say Im king of the cats. You may say Im Going Places.

Hook stick pale hand takes. Black plastic sacks my hand holds. Brown coat bows, red mouth blows. Candleflame shivers, goes. Smoke, darkness. Cage birds snore, coo. My ears earphones hide. Cat eyes bingbing. Miaou. Miaou.

Long brown coat turns. It wasnt till Swan that I found purpose beyond survivals despair. That I found I could have purpose.

Every day, right now, animals of all kinds are getting sold to the biomedical research industry and its lovely spokesmodel, Doktor Frankenstein. Every year hundreds of thousands of animals are trashed by research and testing laboratories, universities, medical and veterinary schools, pharmaceutical companies, the military. We just cant wait for milky thin legislation to pass the mustard and save these animals. Not when dear Daddy Frankenstein and his cadre of lawyers and liars and hobnobbing lobbyists simply bury such profit margin annoyances under an avalanche of taxpayer bees n honey. Yes, everyone, from the snot nose flipping burgers, to the prune drawing a pension whilst withering in her half pension, to your own Doctor Dolittle paying tithes on every little shop pet he sells, everyone works for Frankenstein.

Except us. We work for Swan. Alors.

Hallway. Black boots clic clac clic. Following cats prip prip tails flicker. Hallway says, Swan got fed up anon with panning n mugging n nicking newspapers n tchotchkes to sell for centimes. It made him scream, Time is money, honey, even when you have neither, so lets build us a moat. But he didnt want to just float. Not Swan. Swan craves real scores to finance his machinations on behalf of our kind. Hes got the mind does Swan to waylay this fucked up heartless world wot thinks it can play with dna like toys on christmas day.

Hallway comes. Downstairs black boots cht cht cht, splintery handrail hook stick scrapes. Ballet shoes Chirping cats crisscross. Entrée door creaks. Ivy rattles, shakes water. Cold dark. Red hat Ivy leaves scratch. Water drops shine. Cats prip prip prip, turn, rub, mew, moonlight.

We set up camps in parks and under bridges, thinking we had upped our living standards from newsprint bedding and storefront headboards. But when Swan saw this he scoffed. Ay carajo. Are you trolls awaiting billygoats. You know what befalls trolls in the end, my dears. Trip trap, trip trap. He showed us the anthros were rats abandoning the Favelle, what with Haussmann tearing everything down. He told us the coppers wont come, no surprise raids, because cases cant be built when Haussmanns mandate rolls over any evidence cordons. So, here we all found places to make our own stability. If only a while.

Entrée doorlatch pale hand pulls. Door shuts Bang. Paint flakes flutter, fall. Water drops my purple glasses. Black boots cats swarm. Meouing cats white picket fence scatters.

The Dollhouse is mine. says long brown coat, torn red stockings. Brown coat arm lifts. See that symbol over the door. Three triangles. Cats head. Shows Im here. So anyone, feline or anthro, knows not to enter uninvited. Sure, those batty Aurolac kids break in every other full moon, huffing and puffing, but I cant get too mad at them. The new Aurolac, they dont know. The older ones forget their own names with each sniff of silver paint. So, I tug a few dirty ears n kick a few dusty rears n they stay away again.

Ballet shoes shwip shwip shwip. Hook stick clic, clic, clic, picket fence taps, dusty bricks taps, clic, clic, clic. Clic clac boots says, Swan showed us the streets a hypertension between freedom and needom. We recalibrate the balance of these factors with cookies and crackers, potato chips, all in their original packages, of course. Yogurt n cheese, tossed when theyre past date but still good as you please. Pizza, still warm in the box. We mine dumpsters of restaurants, cafés, soup kitchens, the docks. Sneak onto University and find all kinds of brilliant remains thrown out by coddled collegians.

Court, allee, square, broke fountain, rubble, Buy my singing glasses big hole, tumbled wood beams, creaky footbridge. Canal water gurgles. Dizzy me. Horse buggy goes clip clop clip clop, voices grumble, cigarettes fingers pinch, red sparks mouths suck, smoke. Darkness, yellow lit windows, shadows swing.

Çaaaa vaaaaa.

Torn grey coat, stubbly cheek, shiny wood. Shiny wood string bow saws Frayyydaaa. Red hat says, Khatskelev and his violin. Hook stick brown coatsleeve swings, black boots tippy toe, leg kicks, spins. Movsha. Quest qui ce passe.

Allo, Freda kitty. sawing string bow says. Dented can dirty tootsies tap. Cough. Cough. Stubbly cheek says, Ten francs, anything you want. Bartok, Mendelssohn, Brahms. Cough cough.

The philharmonic should pounce on you with many tens of francs. says twirling brown coat. Adieu.　　　Adieu, kitty.

Black boots my ballet shoes follow. Streetlamp sputters. Puddles shine, gutters. Windows dark. Yellow dumpster hook stick bangs. Tail whips, jumps Jesus, You see the size of that rat Wow　　　　　Anyhow, we always start here, at the boulangerie. They throw marvelous stuff out every evening. Insane. We want to be first in line, but that fat ole king rat beat us to it. O well. Hold open the sack.

Dumpster garbage Hook pushes, pulls. Red glasses says, Whatre those, bagels. Plastic sack hook lifts, swings, hisses, Hold the bag open, Oboy. Bagels hook drops. My hands sack pulls.

Croissants. cawing red mouth says. Chocolate, almond, plain. Strawberry tart. O la la, Saint Honoré. Olive quick bread. Blueberry anglaise. And of course, les baguettes. We will go by Movshas corner, put a tasty tip in his violin case.

Black boots my ballet shoes follow, gravel allee climb, archway pass. Stone helmet stone beard has archway. Stone mouth whispers, *Me with play, want you. Attends, attends.* Stone eyes follow. Drainpipe hook stick bangs High window hollers Hep ballet shoes run, black haversack bumps scampering cats, lamp flickers, Metal rail torn red stockings jump, stone balustrade black boots run choc choc choc. Puddle blinks, shines.

Grey dumpster sighs. Metal lid pale hand lifts. Bricks lid bangs. My ears earphones hide. Garbage hook stick stirs. Red mouth says, Sole inserts. Toothpaste. Sundries, which we can certainly use, but Movshas wheezy rattle reminds me, if we find antibiotics and antihistamines, we keep them. We get pretty banged up in our line of work. These chemists, though, they never throw any drugs out. But we always hope.

Black plastic sack hand carries, bumps legs. Allee, square, bright lamps, black horse, black helmet, black sword, Dieu et mon droit, trees rustle, leaves fall, spin. Owl calls.

No no no dammit. Red dumpster Fist hits. Black boot kicks. Allee hollers Bangbangbang.

Tippy Toe window hollers, Stai zitto, diavolo.

Bloody locked. kicking boot says. This is where we get our cream, our milk, our cheese. Dammit. I shouldve never let Fouroclock join me on my rounds. Idiot mustve gossipped. Never share our sources, Oboy. We do, and dumpsters get locked. Fuck. Gonna have to come back with a hammer or a skeleton key. Lets go, allons y.

Black boots tic toc tic toc. Ballet shoes shwip shwip shwip. Green dumpster.

Brown dumpster.

Blue.

Black boots tic toc tic toc. Ballet shoes shwip shwip shwip. Black plastic sacks get heavy. Allee stones rise, stone steps fall. Canal, mist hides. Stone steps black boots scuffle, torn red stockings sits. Put those down. Black plastic sacks pale hands pull. Sacks drop, touch my ballet shoes. My arms flap. My black coat pale hand pulls.

Sit.

My botty, cold hard steps. Long brown coat says, We take more than we will eat, so we can barter. But we always eat first. Sacks brown coatsleeves dig. Lets see. You want a. Bagel with cream cheese. Only a day past date. A dented can of fanta. Not brie n chablis, but itll do.

Bagel dirty fingers black crosses show.

Miaou. say shadows.

My mouth my hand hides. O boy. my mouth says.

Bagel shakes. Come on. Take it.

Yellow bagel smells. Black spot. Throat chokes. Streetlamp moth bumps, wings purr. Black crosses, hands, fingernails dirty. O boy. my choking mouth says.

Raggedy Ann says, Hundreds of thousands of animals, cats, are burnt and irradiated, blinded and mutilated, deafened and bludgeoned, whipped, chained, restrained, strangled, starved and bled to death. The Lethal Dose 50. The Draize Eye and Skin Irritancy Test. Animals are force fed any number of cleaning agents, pesticides, drugs, lipstick, for gods sake. They are induced into heart attacks, convulsions, shock, paralysis, suffocation, bleeding from mouths, noses, eyes, ears and, joy, assholes. Theyre used for practicing vivisection, testing transplants and other surgical maneuvers. Painful, invasive testing on just one animal can go on for years and years. All this, in the name of product safety and toxicology studies. In the name of new and improved. And yet, none of this is anything like what they did to me and you.

Cotton soft fingers rub black shoebutton eyes. Says Raggedy Ann, Im telling you, Andy, we must eat if we are to have the strength to rescue all those poor dear creatures. Besides raiding the market, one way we eat is by scavenging. What, you think we can conjure popcorn clouds n ice cream mud puddles n candy covered cookie bushes n ice cold soda water springs.

My knee bagel taps, choke. Raggedy Ann says, Shit. If we follow your lead, then we shall have nothing to eat but wind sandwiches. Know how you make a wind sandwich. First you cut two thin slices of air, then you spread a lump of soft wind on each slice, then you stick the slices together. The haute couture crowd will simply die for Oboys haute cuisine.

My arms flap flap flap. Hot sour my mouth tastes. Eyes water. Hollers come.

Christ, shut up, what, did your puppy die, are you attending a wake. hollers Raggedy Ann. Fcuk it, dnot eat it, die for all I crae you dumcfubk. Bagel flies. Stone steps bagel bounces, spins, byebye. Shadows chase, pounce.

Raggedy Ann hands clap. Stone steps holler clap clap clap. Earphones my hands grab. My ears hide.

Non, pas sandwich à vent. Youd have us waltz down to some salvation army or mission or youth outreach wot serves up two hour Sunday brunch, or buffit tables filled with hot tacos n barbeque, like a goshdarn picnic. We get a little sermon all apples n spice, pledge allegiance to the flag or hitler or god or gold. Yeah, n maybe they take dna samples from the wrappers n plastic silverware we leave behind. Confirming suspicions. Dotting tees crossing eyes. Those vans wot deliver snacks n hot cocoa, o so yummy, warming our daffydown dilly lil cotton stuffed tummies, have surveillance cameras snapping pics of us point blank as we slurp their tainted cocoa. Are you bloody daft.

Torn red stockings rises. Hips cotton soft hands. Red sunglasses. Red lips. Red eyes bingbing my eyes. Darkness.

Okay, fine, you misbecoming mournful little walleyed goat. Plan B it is. Longs we fill your gut so you can work. Thats the important thing. Our purpose.

Long brown coat turns, black boots cloc cloc cloc cloc upstairs. Get the sacks n lets go. Black boots my ballet shoes follow

Get the sacks Oboy

Black plastic sacks my hands grab, steps ballet shoes climb shwip shwip shwip, run, my thighs sacks bump. Gravel allee, corner, boulevard, metal barrels fires burn, big hole, yellow lobster, crumbly leaning bricks.

Bricks corner red hat peeks. Orange dumpster. Black door. Red hat hand pulls. Yellow hair shakes, shines. Red glasses hands take, blue eyes. Blue eyes, my eyes. Black plastic sacks my hands hold.

Wait here. pale throat black collar says. Hector cant see you. He might get jealous n stop feeding me. I mean us.

Brown coat turns. Black door. Miaou. Miaou. Red mouth black cross fingers steeple. Goddamn it. Miaaaooouu.

Black door swings, dirty white apron shows. Brown arms. Black moustache, big shiny tooths. Black moustache hisses, Hola, pussycat. Havent seen you in a while. Tienes hambre. Lasagna, garlic bread. Tengolos, para ti.

O Hector. long brown coat says, shoulders turn. Id die without you.

Espera aqui, I get a box.

Could you give me a bit extra. Im reeeeally hungry. And its getting so cold out.

Esperate, pussycat. Luigi en la casa. White apron byebye. Doorway, lightbulb, water sprays, holler, clink clink.

Brown coat turns, shows thumbs, tooths. Lasagna. red mouth says. Theyve got the best Italian in town.

Black plastic sacks heavy. My arms hurt. Brown arms black door shows white plastic sack. Here. says black moustache. Luigi gimme a funny look, so I make like is the garbaje. You take to go.

White plastic sack pale hands take. Gracias, amor. Brown cheek red tongue licks. You taste so good, Hector baby. red mouth says. Spicy mozzarella.

White apron brown hand holds, wipes brown hand. Yellow hair brown hand pets. Black moustache, lips, pale cheek. Hector, mucho macho. Gotta go. Luigi, recuerdas. Big white tooths shine. Black moustache says, Stay out a trouble, pussycat. Come by my crib again sometimes.

Black door shuts. Wotsa goin on out there, Hector.

Nada, jefe. Basura.

Black boots torn red stockings skip clic clac. My tummy white sack smell hurts. You like the fresh saucy stuff, eh, Oboy. swinging white sack says. What about your principles.

Black boots my ballet shoes follow, grumbly tummy.

Broke drainpipe black waters dripdripdrip. Shiver. Black waters glitter, wet uphill stones. Freda ballet shoes my ballet shoes follow, shwip shwip shwip, wet uphill stones. Windows glow, moon glows, darkness.

Dim hallway black ballet shoes bounce tippy toe, tippy toe. Look. A new trap, complete with freshly welded and oiled CACI cage. Regulation gauge. Yesterdays news covers the bottom wire, and the trigger tray, bien sure. So clever.

Metal cage shines. Blue bowl has cage. Black raincoat crouches, black collar tag winks. Freda. Red glasses shine.

Where do all these powdery old ladies come from, Oboy. Sprouting like mushrooms behind yellowed lace curtains, conniving with tremors to trap us to sell us to labs to bolster their meager widows pensions. Fick.

Rear door handle white tape fingers lifts. Rear doorway black raincoat sleeve goes, blue bowl hand takes. Trapdoor shuts Snat. Cage rattles. Earphones hide my ears.

Fish heads blue bowl shows. Red stains have silvery heads. Sharp Freda tooths glow. As if needing to put food in your mouth is any excuse. Lifes tough all around, whether youre feline or fraulein. And when youre both, like I am. Es wird sogar noch schlimmer.

Bowl tape hand lifts. Crooked nose sniffs. Red mouth says, These little metallic heads with their gloopy staring eyes. Herring. Ach, shprinkled mit paprika. Probably the dead hubbies favourite dish, huh. Probably why hes dead.

Blue bowl falls Wet leaves Thump. Silvery fish heads jump. Tilted allee Black ballet shoes shwip shwip shwip.

Shwip shwip shwip greenyellowblue crumbly allee say.

White ballet shoes follow. My hands cold, hurt. My nose purple glasses pinch. Allee windowsills white clotheslines cross. Stripe meridien hangs. You like that shirt up there. You always wanted to become a fisherman like your father, eh. Stripe meridien passes, waves. Dark eaves, black wings Brrrrr flutter.

Black raincoat stands, hips, hands. Metal cage red shrub hides. Shaky yellow tail says, And this one. Every time, the same wretched potato mash and watered milk, with telltale ambrosia of doddery hunters flowersick perfume.

Black Freda pants crouches. And look who gets herself caught in here everytime. Boutin, you dunce. How many times. And for this shit. Dont meou me. Youre hungry, youre always hungry. Its an old excuse.

Trapdoor white tape hand lifts. Okay, come out of there. Dirty yellow cat comes. Kitty runs prip prip prip. Usually we escort trapped cats to the Dollhouse. But dirty boutin knows her way there, if nothing else.

White bowl Hand lifts. **Bang**. Cage jumps, trapdoor shut. My arms flap, spin. Bowl Freda hand shows. Food dirty thumb pokes. Shivers, me. My cold hands coat pockets hide. Bubble wand. Catsup packet. Cream cups.

Cold potatoes. dirty tape thumb says. Bowlful of cheap unpeeled insults, no proper last repast. Can you believe Boutin goes for it. Dumb cat.

Cobblestones white bowl skips Bowl spins Yee, yee, yee. Dirty thumb red tongue licks, red mouth spits. Least we foiled madames budget for the week. She herselfll be lapping up mash and sour milk. Here, biddy, biddy. Ha.

Crinkle crankle allee. Black ballet shoes shwip shwip shwip. My ballet shoes follow. Yellow lamp. Shadows seesaw come, go.

Crumbly pink corner. Black raincoat leans. Dripdripdrip. Yellow tail glows. Black collar, pale throat. Tag shines. Bricks fire escape zigzags high. Shadows, bricks. White moon sighs. Dripdripdrip.

Stones toe taps. Red glasses tilt. Hes up there. The Leperm.

Black pants kneel. White ankles show. Ballet shoe strings white tape fingers pull. Black raincoat rises. Black pantlegs kick, kick, kick. White smoke puffs. Eyes flick flick Red mouth hisses Ha Crumbly pink cob Hands slap Ballet shoes run fa fa fa Elbows knees Grrrr Black pantleg lifts Ballet shoes ch ch ch ch climb bricks Metal ladder White tape hand grabs squeeee Skinny legs swing, twist Bricks Shadows sway, kicks. Skinny legs twist, twist, cough.

Ow. hanging Freda says. White smoke mouth huff huff huffs.

Shadows bricks ballet shoe kicks Arm swings Rung hand grabs. Hanging Freda grunts, legs pedal, black raincoat sleeve lifts, rung hand grabs, rung hand grabs, skinny knee bends, ballet shoe kicks, black raincoat climbs. Fire escape balcony. Church bell chimes.

Skinny Freda leg steps, balcony railing ballet shoe stands. Skinny Freda leg steps. Black ballet shoe stands. Balance is key Black raincoat sleeves seesaw Railing ballet shoes walk With balance comes stealth Ballet shoes hop, balcony grate ballet shoes pittapat. Yellow tail shakes, red glasses shine.

Ring ring, ring ring. says bell. Ring ring.

Moon. Shiny cobblestones. My ballet shoes Dark damp leaves hide. Crouch. Ballet shoe strings my fingers pull. Tight. My back Crumbly pink flat leans, damp cob grit my hands. Leaves my toe taps My legs kick, kick My mouth smokes

Ringring ring

        Ha Allee stones run Bricks spin, come sh sh sh My ballet shoes climb Fire escape balcony falls sh sh sh Grate my fingers grab hurts Shadows my shoes push Bar hand grabs Bar hand grabs Balcony ballet shoe pushes Railing hands pull Legs jump, swing

                    Grate ballet shoes

                        Bam Bam.

Quietly, Jumbo. upstairs balcony says.

White smoke my huffing mouth makes. Handrailings cold, metal steps My ballet shoes climb. Balcony comes. Black pants crouches. Window Freda fingernails taps.

Sill. Red curlicoat rex cat sits, dirty window. Blinky green eyes Green plant hides. Hi honey. says Freda hands. Remember me. Green eyes blink. Dirty window red paw rubs.

Youu. says red curlicoat rex.

Black raincoat sleeve hand pushes. Metal bracelet, wrist. Metal bracelet white tape fingers pull, bracelet ravels. Watch what jimmy can do. Metal shakes straight, wang wang. Window sash. Bracelet Jimmy Freda hand pushes. Lips red tongue pokes. Black collar, tag glitters, pale Freda throat. Jimmy pushes, pulls, squeak, squeak, squeak.

Got it. yellow tail says. Jimmy slides. Windowsill Jimmy taps, Jimmy curls, wraps skinny wrist. Metal bracelet black raincoat sleeve hides. Sash Freda fingers push Reeeeee. Warm darkness comes, tobacco.

White tape hands show. Windowsill, stretching red curly back arches, sash rubs. Miaou. Red head bobs, fingers pink nose sniffs. White whiskers flick. Miaou.

Its that bloody dankish herring. No, Im sorry curlicue, we dont have it. That was for someone else. For you, something much better. Curly back Freda hand rubs, fuzzy chin tape fingers scratch. Red curlicoat rex purrs. Black raincoat sleeves purrs, hugs.

Loveable sweet baby. Oboy, say hi.

Red glasses Freda eyes, green eyes, my eyes. My hand shows. My hand purring red head bumps. Fuzzy ear my fingers scratch. Black raincoat hug.

Ramon. hollers darkness.

Light comes, my eyes hurt. Red sofa, black rug. Black hair hangs. Blue bathrobe. Ramon. hollers blue bathrobe. Blue bathrobe Big arm pushes, hairy chest, green pajama pants come. Black eyes hurt my eyes. My eyes hide. Qué chingaos.

Yellow tail hollers, Qué diablos, qué carajo, qué hostias haces.

Hairy arms come Window black ballet shoe kicks Window falls, hits hairy arms hits cheek Ah Green plant tumbles Rex tape hands put black raincoat sling Zzzt raincoat zipper Black raincoat spins Come on Metal stairs Black ballet shoes kick kick kick, climb Window blue bathrobe arms Hairy arms lift Squeeee Oboy Grate spins My shoes Railing hits Rusty metal ladder jumps My hands grab, rungs fall tungtungtung My top spins Dum ditty dum ditty dum

Metal steps green pajama pants climb pangpangpang Handrails hands grab Malditos ladrones, detengaos

Rooftop. Brick chimneys puff. Stove pipes steam. Black wires bob, metal poles gleam. White moon dark sky, winky little lights. Downstairs little black Freda shoes climbs, little black tummy bounces, rasp rasp rasp.

Ayúdame. little dark hair little blue bathrobe hollers.

Lights windows show, crumbly pinkwhiteorange allee. Windows Black shadows lift. Squeee. Shutters bang.

Whats going on.

Whos out there.

I ring police.

Metal ladder rungs Freda hand hand hand climbs, raincoat, tummy sways. Moonlight, damp throat shines, tag winks, black collar. Rooftop Freda ballet shoes jump, tummy black raincoat sleeve hugs, runs

Shshsh my Lovely just a little jump ahead

Chimney stacks stove pipes raincoat black, runs. My ballet shoes follow tsa tsa tsa. Darkness little lights,

       Geronimo

               black pants jump, yellow tail flashes, moonlight. Byebye.

Darkness little lights blink.   Breaking.   Fuck.

Rooftop end comes. Little Freda stands little roof, big tummy arm hugs, ballet shoe kicks, moonlight. God damned ancient terra cotta tiles This is the biggest absurdity about Frankensteins experiment, how bleeding big we are and slow and clumsy and always breaking things just trying to function. Dont just stand there with your big useless mouth and bigger eyes, jump, fool.

Hep ladder top Hairy chest Green pajama pants hop Te tengo, bastardo Gitano rooftop comes arms fists knees wink pwa pwa pwa.

My breath comes, my ears white smoke blows. My hair flutters. Downstairs allee passes. Freda, tiles come, get big, tiles cold break My hands ballet shoes pap pap pap stumble, tumble, my knees back Tiles hurt, roll, spin. My botty sits. Purple glasses fingers push. Earphones my hands push.

High roof green pajama pants hairy chest huffs. Black eyes watch my eyes. Allee black eyes blink. Black eyes watch my eyes. Hairy chest big little, big little.

Madre.

Quest ce qui ce passe. hollers window.

Hairy chest bent elbows hands mouth hollers, They steal Yvonne gato. They on your roof. Ring policia.

Ring yo mama, coulero. red Freda mouth hollers. Pale skin glistens. Hot salt dirt flowers, glistens skin. Black collar tag shines, moonlight. Freda eyes, my eyes. Black raincoat turns, black tummy arm hugs Arm shakes Ring ring ring Ballet shoes run, jump roof, run jump, run jump Ring ring ring Freda shoes my shoes follow, downhill rooftops run, allees jump, tiles break, ballet shoes hop, skip Viens Oboy Metal roof bang bang black pants botty sits, ring ring, ring ring, metal roof falling botty slides shhht Raingutter Bang Yellow tail waves byebye.

Moonlight. Thump.

My botty metal roof hits Lights, gutter bangs, Tummy tickles, falls My foots Downstairs balcony hits, my hands, railing. Little wet stones has allee. Cawing Freda stands.

Hows that for intuition. red glasses says. Didnt even know this balcony was here.

Miaou. says black raincoat tummy. Fussing. Black raincoat zipper Tape fingers pull zzzt. Ça va bien, curlicue. Green eyes peek, blink.

Woww. curly coat rex says. White whiskers twitch.

Fuzzy forehead crooked nose rubs. Rex purrs. Good sweet kitty. red Freda lips says. Oboy and I are going to take you somewhere safe where you never have to worry about anthros killing you with syrupy kindness ever again. Back you go.

Black raincoat zipper Fingers pull zzzt. Balcony railing Freda hands, ballet shoes climb, stand. Railing squeaks, shakes. Black pants black raincoat jumps. Drainpipe Bong Falling hands grab, yellow crumbly cob falling ballet shoes scrape shhhht. Wet stones Black ballet shoes hits. Allee little Freda stands. Tummy arm hugs. Red glasses shine bing bing. My eyes hide.

Ring ring ring ring ring ring ring.

My foots Railing comes. Railing wiggles, squeaks. Balcony door lights. Orange curtain peeks. Qui est là. My hands tummy Drainpipe hits Bong My ballet shoes crumbly yellow cob hits, yellow grit crumbles Shhht Rising pipe burns my hands. Stones jump, hit ballet shoes. My ankles sparks hurt My knees, my palms slap. Earphones fall.

Oww. my mouth says. My fingers dirty. Earphones my hands take. Hide my ears.

Darkness. Rain comes. My eyes, blue Freda eyes. Okay, Oboy. Lets get our curly little friend back to the Dollhouse. Nightschools out.

Stolen Cat Reward Offered. says Freda. Early Tuesday morning a moonlit rooftop chase failed to rescue a rare ginger and white Laperm stolen from a flat in Bercy.

Torn brown sofa. My lap black Patty Cake curls, licks. Catsup packet my fingers rub. Ceiling goes dripdripdrip. Shiver. Pots pans quiver, water spills. Wood floorboards wet. Picture my fingers pet. Raggedy Ann Raggedy Andy hold cotton soft hands, run.

At one ay em, the neutered male, Rufus Hi Rufus was snatched from the fire escape window of his third storey flat by an experienced duo of, well, cat burglars. O, thats clever. The cats owner, Yvonne Gutierrez, and Ms Gutierrezs fiancé, Ramon Playaduro, chased the thieves to the roof. The pursuit stalled, however, when the thieves leapt 5 metres to the rooftop of a neighbouring block of flats.

Five metres. says Freda. Was that all.

It was impossible. Señor Playaduro said, dumbstruck. They are crazy, taking that jump. They should have die. Rufus too. Which of course would have been berry berry terrible. But for Yvonne, not knowing a thing, this is worse I think.

O Rufus. Did you and Ramon have issues. Hm.

Candlelight flickers, shadows. Torn armchair red curlicoat rex meous, snuggling blue Korat, Dirty Boutin. Dirty Boutin grumbles Faim, faim, faim.

Caged Henry caws. Cage wings thapthapthapthap.

Citywide, the theft of pets is on the rise. Last year, witnesses alleged an unidentified female had stolen pets from districts all over the city. Authorities believe Rufus may have been taken by the same suspect, whom they have dubbed the pet thief. While Tuesday mornings daring theft and escape closely matched the pet thiefs em o, this time she had an accomplice. Thats you, chickpea.

Newspaper flaps. Black Patty Cake twitches, my lap. Despite offering a 4000 franc reward for the safe return of her prized cat, Mizz Gutierrez admitted that the whereabouts of the frizzy feline remain a mystery.

Skinny black pantlegs cross. Thats cos we arent after dinero. says Freda. No mystery there. And good thing for Yvonne, tambien, cos whats to stop us from stealing him again, and demand another ransom. Cha ching. But no worries, Rufus. We wont send you back there.

Orange ears black cross fingers scratch. Pale hand Dirty Boutin licks. Window ivy rattles. Kitchen cat eyes bingbing candlelight. My nose Hot wax smell tickles.

Mizz Gutierrez says she remains optimistic that 10 month old Rufus will be returned. We have been phoning vets up and down the mainland on the chance that somebody has dumped him off. If thats the case we hope they would be able to identify him because he has been microchipped.

Microchipped. Who int. says Freda. Rufus, whose pedigree name translates to Red Rabbit haha Red Rabbit how bloody anthro is described as medium sized and of slim build. Anyone with any information is asked to contact Yvonne Gutierrez at 096 142 8424 or Ramon Playaduro at 014 586 6121.

Im earning quite the rep. says Freda. Newspaper flickery fingers tear. My ears hurt. Torn paper dirty black fingertips pinch. I should show this article to Swan. Hed be pleased.

Ceiling water dripdripdrips. Shiver me. Catsup packet my fingers squeeze. My arm purring blue Korat cheek rubs. Golden conure hollers, I cant take it no mo. Raggedy Ann crinkles, page turns. Burnt cookies Raggedy Andy throws.

Freda says, I cant wait for you to meet him, Oboy. Swans divine. Il est tout l à mien. Freda and the Swan. He has other aliases, Gypsy Dan, the Magician, the Bandolier, and of course, Street. But to me he is Swan, my one n only flame. He promised we would leave this ding dong bell one day. Just the two of us. In the meantime, he makes the street bearable. He makes our lot in life credible. Swan is merry like a dream. I keep fearing Im going to wake, and realize he had never been.

I remember I first saw him slinking toward me down rue Bataille, his Vivians prowling the pavement about him, eyes shifting, murderous, but Swans brilliant gaze straight on me, his gold flecked smile, the surety of his footedness, made the hair stand up on my arms. I thought he was going to walk right through me, but he took me in his embrace and said he saw me coming for miles, he saw the ache inside me, the pain, the way I burned from my two selves stitched impossibly together. He saw me coming. He saw me. Follow me to the rooftops, bo peep, he said. I adam n eved him. Swan. I saw his pain, too. I was meant for him, and he for me.

You will meet him anon. He already knows about you.

Red coat, blue jeans botty, shiny black boots crung crung climbs metal fire escape stairs. My ballet shoes follow. Ivy rattles, leaves red, wet, fire escape hides, windows, bricks, parapet. Purple glasses, cheeks, hands Ivy water sprinkles. My stripe meridien. Stripe meridien my hand pets. Oboy, viens, red glasses, black boots run, crung crung crung, byebye. Red ivy sprays, fluttery grey sky.

My nose Ivy tickles. Ankles, earphones, sleeves Ivy scratches. Metal ladder, rooftop comes Metal boxes Spinny fans hum. Egg shells. Pee smell. Pigeons snore. Peely brown Bulkhead door.

That leads to the stairwell. says shiny yellow hair. If anyone comes, theyll come from there.

Bulkhead skylight Blue tarp hides. Tarp Wood boards trap. Clic clac clic black boots walk.

Ballet shoes follow scrit, scrit, scrit.

Red ivy parapet Black boot stamps. Blue knee bent, red coatsleeves wide. Freda says, This beautys the perfect reconnaissance point. Personne ne peuvent nous voir. But we can see all, down Rue St Antoine, up Turenne, straight down Saint Paul. All the way to the Canal. Stags cavorting in le Bois.

Bongg, bongg, bongg. church bell rings, hurts my teeth.

Boot, boot, ankles trembles, parapet Freda walks, red leaves crunch, coatsleeves wide, white tape wrists twist twist twist. Rooftop pigeons flock. Canal, little sandbags, dock. Mist. Little shadows walk. Little boats glide. My big eyes purple glasses hide. Earphones my hands pull, ears damp. Lappy water. Sleepy me.

If this wasnt the perfect place for scouting pets, we would squat here. A pity Haussmann will tear her down, tear it all down. Anon.

Trees, spinny yellow leaves, broke pavement. Metal rooftops slant, rusty rain gutters pant bloop bloop bloop drippy water. Shiver. Little rooftops, metal hats, metal boxes shine. Brick chimneys huff. White smoke tall metal stove pipes puff. Canal horn blows.

Tall Freda walks, Freda sways. Red glasses flash. All these flats. says Freda. All the animals imprisoned in these flats. You can hear them. Freda eyes shut. What do we have. Parakeet. From that scream, maybe Alexandrine, maybe rose ringed. Macaw, the old blue and gold standard. Two mice running on an irritatingly squeaky wheel. A hungry Siamese, very close. Yellow Freda hair tilts. There. That window two floors up The broken red shutter. She hears the mice. They piss her off too. Crooked Freda nose wrinkles. And, jesus. Dog dog yappy dogdogdog. Whats with this town and dogs. Picayune. All we need do is keep our eyes and ears tuned. Once we pick this neighbourhood clean, we reconnoiter another scene, for a while. Then we return here to rescue all the replacement animals. But never dogs. Bloody vile.

Street hollers. Street hums. Trees, pavement, swinging arms legs come, heads blackgreybrown. Magpies fly. Tree branches wave, La la, la la, la. Pissoir. Paving stones. Twirly pink umbrella Colly Molly Puffe Courtyard, allee, wet blackswhitesgreys swaying clotheslines hang. Bricks, stones, broke red shutter. Ashy brown elbow, metal railing. Sill dark paw pats, brown elbow dark Siamese cheek rubs, cries. White cigarette Brown fingers hold. Smoke fffffeathers. Fingers flick. Cigarette tumbles, wet pavement, little red spark.

Siamese sits. Okay Francie you lil croona, be back in a hour. Bring you that tuna.

Slam. Clump, clump, clump.

Windowsill. Siamese sits. Siamese cries. Tummy hurts. Blue eyes, my eyes.

How best to liberate Francie. Freda says, black boots turn, parapet. Note the mannerisms of the façade. We can climb the rustication, at the quoin, the corner. There. Inch along the string course, balcony to balcony, et voilà. Window wide open. Or do you prefer the banded columns on either side of that door. The way the bressummer juts above, makes it a snap to simply heave ourselves up to the sill. Get a workout, the fingers will. Youll want tape, my dear. On the bright side, since the jailer is gone, we just walk out the front door, easy as pie.

Little streetcar dingdingding, my tooths bell rings. Earphones my hands put, ears hide. Purple glasses finger pokes. Stripe meridien hand pets. Thump thump streetcar passes. Yellow car says beebee. Door opens, shuts. Downstairs green raincoat skips. Yellow car door opens, green raincoat hides. Yellow car says Bee bee, goes byebye. Tree branches bob, black starling. Starling calls Brrr, b bee b bee b bee.

Freda hollers, arm out, There he is. Swan. The Vivians too. Lets not fuss wih Francie just yet. Swans running down some dirty little rat.

Fog comes. Rooftops Fog crosses, hides crates, chimneys clotheslines, hanging wash fog ruffles, wires, trees, fog flutters, spins, parapet little grey arms little green legs jump, run metal rooftops, bang bang bang, sheets grey sleeves flap, grey jacket spins, green pantlegs run run run, fog seesaws, voices holler, caw, arms legs chase, bang bang bang, jump parapets, balconies, drainpipe swing Theyre closing in Green pantlegs stumbles, hands knees tumbles, O god, fumbles, Gonna getcha mouse, bang bang bang.

Fire escape. Black boots, red coat, yellow hair, byebye.

Come on. bobbing red ivy leaves cry.

Raggedy Ann knew just which way the strange man had run, for she had watched him, so after jumping from the window and catching hold of his hand, Raggedy Ann and Raggedy Andy raced through the yard, scooted across the field, and climbed through a hole in the fence.

Balcony grate My fists hold, arms hang, legs sway. Rooftops dark ghosts leap, fly whoosh, whoosh, hahaw, bang bang bang.

Come on, Oboy. hollers allee.

Fog scatters, allee stones jump, hit my hands, ballet shoes. Ankles hurt. Tsokka tsokka tsokka. My hands ballet shoes follow.

Corner comes. Bricks ivy climbs. Climbing black boots fog hides. Ivy shakes, rattles. Wet ivy my hands ballet shoes climb, follow thumping, rattly wet leaves. Pigeon wings shooshooshooshoo. My ballet shoes, hands Rooftop hits. Rooftop pigeons bob, scuttle. Green pants black stocking hat Fog shows. Grey jacket arms comes, tic toc tic toc.

Shit. hollers black twisty mouth, grey sleeves wave fog, sneakers stomp stomp stomp. White fog twisty mouth makes, huh, huh, huh. Grey chest goes big little, big little. Black twisty mouth hollers, Clear out, Freda.

Hey. Freda says, hands, hips. I know you. Hookie, right. Hookie the goblin.

Fuck out the way, bitch. Now. pale lips holler. Pimple throat bobs. Black eyes roll. Black stocking hat turns, huh, huh, huh, huh.

Freda says, But theres nowhere to go. Except down.

Fog twirls, seesaws, running, jumping ghosts, brown pants, white coat, black fedora, arms legs follow, run, jump, get big, bang bang bang, fog curls, hollers Miaou, miaou, haha,

Miaou, We see you, little mouse.

Black eyes big, skin shines. Twisty mouth says, Warning you, bitch. Two a you better clear out or

Whats the rush, Hookie. Swan only wants a word.

Grey jacket, green pantlegs turn, run. Hands hands parapet, hats shoulders Peekaboo voyons vous petite souris Sharp tooths show, parapet legs jump, stalk.

Grey jacket turns. Shit.

Crouching legs Fog shows, bent knees hands hold. Eyes.

Wheres the fire, jeremiah. crouching fogs say.

Black stocking hat, grey jacket, green pants, spin. Chakk chakk, chakk chakk, boots sneakers coats arms sunglasses legs mouths meous meous follow tall black fedora, dark glasses, gold tooths, gold necklaces.

Dark glasses Long fingers take. Green eyes. Green eyes, my eyes. My eyes hide.

Swan, this is Oboy. red Freda mouth says.

Tall green eyes come. My eyes hot perfume waters. Fog drifts. Nose sniffs. Gold tooths say, Johnnie Jump Up made a bet, he could pass for Violet. What spoiled the little rascals game. The scent he used was not the same.

Long furry coat comes. Toothpick Mouth chews. Street say your new boy look like a fuckin reetard, Freda.

Pining for a kindred spirit, are you, Dainty. says Freda.

We dint need yo help ketchin this fool. Vraiment, Street.

Black fedora, green eyes turn. Redblackbrown sleeves Grey jacket sleeves push Fuck you bitch Sleeves push, pull, grey jacket fusses.

Freda, how you been, girlfren. stripe coat silver sunglasses says. Cigarette Yellow tooths bite. Red tip glows.

You know how it is, Mignonette. Freda says. Sometimes Peter. Maybe Mary.

You lookin all neat and pretty. says black bowler hat.

She aint seen Swan in a whiles. says spotted coat green sunglasses. Got new threads. Got the boots spankin polished.

Bet she wash that pretty blonde hair at the liberry.

Bet she vagazzled.

Fuck you, Pussy Willow.

Aaahhh, hahaha.

Grey jacket hollers, Get your fuckin paws off me, you twisted freaks arms grab, push I aint done nothin. Voices caw, bump, slap, Say he aint done nothin That what he says I is fo sho innocent Why you runnin then Hookie whachoo missin yo flight Did he call us freaks Miaou.

Grey jacket Long furry coat brown hands grab, pull. Grey jacket sleeves swing. Furry coatsleeves shake, brown hand slaps, toothpick wiggles, brown finger hiss,

Chill bitch.

Long furry coat shoulder Long hand pats. Gold tooths say, Now, now, Dainty. Snap Dragon is so very bold. He plays his tricks on young and old. He hides behind the old stone wall, and shoots his pop gun at us all.

Nuh o, now you done it. rooster hair says.

Street the tax man. says stripe coat.

Long white pantlegs big boots stalk Grey jacket green pants. Black fedora long finger pokes. Damp forehead shows. Excuse me a moment. the king said to the pirates and Raggedy Ann and, dancing round and round, the king lunged and gave the goblin doll six hard thumps, one after the other, so fast it sounded like a drum. Before the goblin doll could get to his feet, the king had given him three more hard thumps which sent him rolling head over heels again. And all the guards and the men of the court who liked to see fights yelled with the king.

Black stocking hat lies rumpled wet, rain puddle. Torn yellow hair glows. Sitting green pantlegs stiff, wet. Sneaker sole hangs flap flap. Cawing. Hoo, you seen how hard Swan hit im. Fog comes, grey sleeve wipes. Red shows. Drippy lips, tooths, nose. Shivery me.

White coat black fedora spins, long hands clap. Twisted freaks, he called us. I like that.

My cars hurt. My arms flap, spin fog.

Hummm, Oboy. Freda says. My arm hand squeezes.

My mouth says hum.

Long jaw long hand rubs. Gold tooths glow. Say, let me tell you all a little story about our blond judas here.

Tell us, Swan.

Ouai, we like stories.

Mullein grew up rough and tumble. He was Irish, very humble. Still he was a jolly fellow, With his funny head all yellow. And his crooked teeth. And his spine. And the stain spreading on his dungarees. O, Mullein.

Yellow hair drippy red nose say, Aw Stweet, I tole you, I doe dnow how dey foud oud aboud de sbokes.

Grey jacket arms Fog hands hands hands grab, Hop là grey jacket green pants lift, stand. Red drip, drip, drip shines.

Shiver me. My mouth says hum.

Grey jacket shoulders Long hands fingers gold rings brush brush, pet yellow hair. Shush. Shhh. Now look. Ive mussed you all up, Mullein. And your hairs so fetching. Almost as pretty as my girl Fredas here. But I feel bad. I, I hope youll let me make things right.

Hand Gold rings White coat hides. Hairbrush hand gold rings shows. Yellow hair Hairbrush brushes.

Hairbrush says Rasp, rasp. There we go. Better already.

Stweet, Ib tellid yuh, id wudda me. Pwease.

Hairbrush says Well, if not you, Mullein, then who.

Hidey wood stick hands hands hands pass. Wood stick Dusty brown fists takes, squeezes, lifts. Fog snickers.

Ah. A leaf. gold rings say, fingers pluck. Leaf flutters, falls, perches red drops, worn sneaker.

Hairbrush says, Hold still, little one. Almost done.

Yellow hair, eyes wet, blink, red mouth cries. Stweet.

My mouth says hum.

Shiny yellow hair Hairbrush pets, rasp, rasp. Yellow hair Pale lips kiss. Your hair is lovely, dear. says gold tooths. So very lovely. But you know, Sweet William, sad to tell, you rang the Canterburys Bell. Just for that, your father said, William, come out to the shed.

From the back the stick struck the goblin doll so hard upon the top of his head that it smashed him right down to the floor where his shoe button eyes hit with two clicks.

My mouth says hum. Darkness hurts my head.

Wake up. Wake up, Raggedy Andy. Raggedy Ann said.

Merqurius. Mircurios. Mercury. The Ram, the psychopomp, herald of the dead.

White coat turns. Cane white coatsleeve lifts, stripe coat cane pokes. Fouroclock. Cover the door.

Bien sûr, Swan.

Être et durer.

Être et durer, Swan.

White coat, Freda turn Steps boots tromp tromp. Cane goes tap tap tap. Black fedora says, We witnessed it, bo peep. Caught sight of it departing his beady little eyes, disappear through the hole behind his skull. The instant Daintys bat tapped that little rat it, shoo.

Long hand flies.

I saw it, too.

No matter how many times we have seen it, we will never fully consummate the experience. We tried. We inhaled at the moment of impact, our face centimetres away, trying to capture. It. In the comic strips, they put x x for the eyes when a fellow gets the top hat, and that was exactly right. Poof. Double x. As though he were eager to die,

Gone pecan, Swan,

just awaiting Daintys signal.

Well, Hookie had it coming.

Who.

Steps Boots tromp tromp. Dust puffs. Cat eyes shine.

Oeufs. hollers Siamese.

Me too, meilleur, mieux. holler cats.

Gold rings hand holds cane. Steps cane tap taps, climbs. Long hand Freda hand holds.

Entrée door window shines, pale light. Entrée door Stripe coat blocks. Black glove black glove holds. Eyes glow, my eyes hurt. Hsst. stripe coat says. Degages. Scram.

Oboy. Freda says. Never mind about Fouroclock.

Stripe coat Sharp tooths says, Ouai. Never you mind, boy.

Black boots, brown boots, my hands ballet shoes follow, dusty steps, climb. Blackorangegrey hallway cats come miaou, miaou, push, hungry, eyes bingbingbing, cats round boots, miaou, miaou. Darkness. Fweeta fweeta fweet. Cats Brown boots follows, follows Freda boots, caws.

A thriving enterprise, bo peep.

Brown boots my hands, ballet shoes, follow.

What we have read about you in the papers. C'est vrai.

O, Swan. You read the latest. The scarlet macaw.

Miaou, miaou, white pantlegs cats rub. Long gold rings fingers snap. Cats sit, ears twitch, tails flick, eyes blinkblinkblink. My back torn wallpaper pushes.

Gold tooths say, Apparently the two of you made your escape by rapelling down a bloomer filled clothesline.

Claro. And we took a few of those with us, too, ha ha. says Freda. Black cross fingers snap. Fire comes, hissy match. Candle, candle, candle, fire lights. Red Freda glasses Fire dances. Freda hand shake shake, smoke.

Cage Gold ring fingers stroke. Hello, precious. Scarlet macaw screams, thrashes wings. Cage bars Beak bites. Shadows flicker, cracked ceiling. Water drips. Shivery me. Plic plic plic pots pans. Shiver. Window Rain taps. Wings flapflapflap.

Broke window Ivy leaves scritch scratch. My back torn wallpaper holds. Purring Maine coon comes, my lap paws knead.

Long white coatsleeves open. Freda goes. Freda Long white coatsleeves hug. Red Freda lips opens. Black fedora drops. Noses, cheeks, lips, rub wet, soft.

Swan. I missed you. sighing Freda says. Im so glad youre back, safe and sound.

Brown coatsleeves Long hands rub slow. Black fedora says, We always land on our feet. Bo peep.

Freda purrs. Brown Freda coat presses white coat, gold chains. Gold tooths shine. Wet mouths push. Black fedora Freda hand takes. Long red hair shows. Yellow Freda hair Black fedora hides. Mouths push. My hand Rough Maine Coon tongue licks.

Green eyes, my eyes.

From where did you flush this suspicious big eyed creature. gold tooths say. Freda White coatsleeves hug. Red hair shines. Red tongue licks.

I rescued him from a nasty, death dealing little man. A CACI collector posing as a pet shop owner.

Freda eyes, my eyes. My back wallpaper hurts. Freda says, I had to rescue him, Swan. Hes one of us.

Torn brown sofa White pants sit. Gold chains shine. Korat comes, white pants lap Korat hops. Korat ears Black thumbnail scratches. My brown sofa White pants botty touches botty touches botty touches. My brown sofa. Closet. Metal hangers. Hangers my fingers push, g rrrring, g rrrring.

Whats he on about.

He thinks the sofa belongs to him. Oboy, hum. Oboy.

Korat chinny chin chin gold ringed finger scratches. One of us. Yes, I see. That fainting interlude on the rooftop.

My mouth says Hum. Gold tooths flash, candlelight.

Hes no cozzer. gold tooths say. No badge wearing serf, undercover in the underworld. Broken sofa as your turf. Mooncalf. Are you.

My mouth says Hum.

Freda says, He is balance like youve never seen. So true and natural. I show him a movement once and hes got it.

A pure specimen. He is beautiful, we can see. Very so. Untested, yes. We shall sometime put him through his paces.

My mouth says Hum.

Freda says, Hes going to help me. Us. I, Ive taken him out on a few runs. Cats. The scarlet macaw. Oboy was great.

Korat gold rings hands push White pants rise. Thump thump blue paws. Hand hand dusts. We can always use another for the cause. Just remember, bo peep, any headaches, you provide the aspirin.

Yes, Swan. Black fedora pale Freda hand takes, yellow Freda hair shows. Fedora Hand hangs, wallpaper. Yellow hair shines, candlelight. My eyes Red glasses flash.

Maine coon ribs my hand rubs. White coat white pants come, gold chains shine, purple shirt. White pants crouch, gold chains sway. My ballet shoes, my hands, stripe meridien, green eyes watch. Meridien my hand rubs.

Beautiful sweater. gold tooths say. On the border of the wood, all alone the Ghost Flower stood. Like a moonbeam dressed in stripes, such a very pretty sight.

Long hand comes. My knee Black fingernails scratch. Gold rings sing, hurt my eyes. Hairbrush white coat hides. My head torn wallpaper hits thumpthumpthump. Hollering. Maine coon jumps, my lap claws hurt.

Fabulous. gold tooths say. White pants stand, turn, wood floorboards boots tic toc, turn, brown sofa arm white coat hits, purple shirt sleeves flare, turn, tic toc, tic toc. Long red hair hangs, flickers, candlelight. Brown boots tic toc, shadows spin. Blackbluewhite cats follow pripprip, pripprip. Wood floorboards Brown boots stomp. Gold tooths hiss. Cats scatter, ears tails low. Gold rings hand Freda hand takes, Freda spins, holds hand, Freda falls, Freda purple sleeve catches. Birds fweet fweet fweet. Red hair hangs, touching mouths hide.

O, Swan. says Freda, breath big. My lover.

Lovely bird. hanging red hair says. Purple shirt rises, Freda purple sleeve spins, yellow hair flashes, candlelight. Cage bars Long gold rings fingers pet. Gold rings Beaks peck. Gold tooths say, Lovely menagerie of birds. So difficult to trace. For the papers the gendarmes talk a good game, but surely they have more pressing tea parties than sour old dames missing pretty polly. Else youdve been nabbed by now. No offense. Youve done a laudable job rescuing these animals, bo peep. Cats, mice, o, and the snakes. But these birds in particular. Cheep cheep. We admire your commitment and your effort. Its time to push our plan ahead.

Swan.

We have others would better care for these birds. No questions asked. We would strike a bargain, of course, something to reflect street value.

But, Swan. I can care for them. I am.

You only have so much room here, my dear. And so few resources. The feeding and watering alone. Time. And if the prefects men decide its time to bring you in. What happens to these birds then.

Freda says, But the cops dont come. They dont know I. How would they.

Continue caring for the cats and rodents and reptiles. And mooncalves. Let us be concerned with the birds. Fouroclock comes up, collects some of these beauties.

Which.

The most gorgeous. Scarlet macaw. Or perhaps youve something of greater value hidden around here.

No, Swan.

We thought you questioned us as a way to broach the subject.

No, Swan.

Youd tell us if you did have something of greater value.

Yes, Swan.

You know our disgust for secrets.

Yes, Swan.

Mullein knew our disgust, going in.

Yes.

And he knew, going out.

Yes. Yes, Swan.

Ceiling shadows flutter. Floorboards mattress white pants sits, tangled blankets elbows rest. Hanging red hair Dirty pillows curl. Floorboards Boot heels toc toc.

Our feet. gold tooths say. Ache, from the chase.

Freda kneels. Brown boot Pale hands take, pull. Red glasses turn, bing bing my eyes. One moment, lover. Freda says. Freda comes. My hand Pale hand takes. My hand pulls, holler. Gold tooths shine. Long white pantlegs cross, pale foot bounces.

Johnny jump up made a bet.

Stripe meridien sleeve Freda hand grabs, Freda hand pulls. Hallway. Redbluegreen window comes. Wait down here, Oboy. Freda says, my arm Freda hand pulls. Theres milk in the bowl. A treat.

Red candy Hand shows. My fingers take. Hallway Freda goes, flickery doorway, byebye. Redbluegreen window. Hallway cats meou. Prip prip prip Eyes bingbing. Milk bowl cats crouch, lap lap lap.

Never you mind, boy. downstairs says. Hsst.

Milk bowl, redbluegreen window. Come eat. Korat says.

Non, big. Siamese says, drippy chin. Drink all.

Flicker doorway says, Swan, you goddamn gorgeous rogue. I tell Oboy it was you who found me, who saved me from crashing and burning on the genetic scrap heap.

Such language, bo peep.

You are from the same accident of science as us all,

Doorway throws torn red stockings, hall.

only you were the first to clue in to the whole idea of, not just survival, but revenge, of standing up to the system from the outside

A sudden blow

You rounded up us all, took us under your wing,

The great wings beating still

and we accept you as our king, Swan, King of the cats

Stammering girl, am I cob or tom

I know theres that little bitch downstairs, the other Vivians, females, though I will scratch out their surly eyes, leave those malkins battered and bruised

Rage, lamoureuse

I know there are others you keep like birds in a cage, but Im your muse, your ay number one female, Im your queen

Freda and the Swan

Yes, my Swan, regal and towering and lithe in disguise, with your beating wings you part my thighs

Déjà vu le jour quun oiseau la fist Femme en lieu dune pucelle

Your fist gripping my lapel, tumble me pell mell down the stairwell, you, leopard, me, gazelle, rasp the hollow of my neck with your beard, Whisper things in my ear, things wot make my skin shiver,

Le cruel Amour veinqueur De ma desir sa sujette, Ma si bien escrit au coeur Vostre nom sa sagette

yes, your thighs across my thighs, your chest across my helpless breast, hold me down, fuck me, Swan, Im so weak and wet,

My beak inside your scarlet mouth

The burn the pain the glorious domain you own wot is me. Work your cock inside, Swan, fuck me, o, fuck me, dont ever stop, baby, Someday,

Laid in that white rush despoiling your springtime of its rose

when you want to settle down, when our mission draws to a close, when you no longer want to be king of the cats, when all the mewling big eyed brats can fend for themselves, I want you and me to run away,

Yea, being so caught up

So far away, to the country, to the sea

So mastered by the brute blood of the air, Je suis celuy qui deserte Le tonnerre audacieux, ma chere. A duck and a drake, And a halfpenny cake, With a penny to pay the old baker. A hop and a scotch is another notch, Slitherum, slatherum, take her.

Floorboards my fingernails scratch. Darkness. Redgreenblue window. Downstairs, cawing. Flicker doorway hollers. Cawing, crashing, crying, Freda.

Survival of the fittest. More like hyperpropagation of the most alike. While youandeye were engineered as simulacra, as jolly pastiches, for us to survive on our own, Oboy, we have to do more than respire as homage to limage dhomme. Swan says we have to act like them too.

Black Freda boots Dirty ballet shoes follow. Streetlamps, pavers, black Shadows walk. Maids in your smocks, Look well to your locks, Your fire and your light and God give you good night White corsets, shop window. Wood gate. My shoulder rough stones brush. Dark doorway, hand shows. Ein Paar Groschen, bitte. Black boots walk tsokk tsokk.

Freda says, Like all of us who sprang from the test tube with this demeaning demeanor, you went from polished and sparkling intellectual property to defect riddled reality to gum stuck on the loafer of bureaucracy to a quantified docketted microchipped christlike Nothing in need of a good home as they say, as they say. Humble Doctor Dolittle filled out all the requisite paperwork in triplicado, passed some perfunctory knee taps and, just to make sure he wasnt obviously a sadist or, worse, a biotech operative after trade secrets, a psychiatric exam. Then Dolittle toddled off to the pound to select you. Hmm. How to decide. Theyre all so cute, we dont know whether to cuddle or cudgel the little darlings, eh wot. Awful. Lets see. I believe the one drooling No the one picking imaginary nits No the one with the big brown eyes gnawing its paw is the one for me. Sold. Just like that, Dolittle became your collector. Jailer. Spy. You became his supplement. Vitamin. Mineral. Retirement. Until the day you die. Five years. Ten. Then ole Doc Doody doos it all over again.

Clinkclink tag black collar pale Freda throat. Square. Fountain. Grate, steam Black boots kick, kick mist, stones.

Atget. hollers doorway, smoky guinguette.

Lamplight, yellow Freda hair shines. Crumbly stone walls Fingernails scrape, rattly ivy pulls, yellow lit windows show. Stones, leaning red dress. Black boots pass.

Un moment, lovah. red dress says. Wha she got I aint.

Dirty white ballet shoes prip prip prip.

Red glasses Skinny finger pushes. Freda says, Those of us like me who struck that self revelatory spark could finally see to escape the pet shop, the kitty mill, the foster farm. We struck out on our own, wild and free, potential media embarrassments autonomous and unpredictable.

But we dont want exposure any more than the CACI does. Can you imagine soapboxing for our rights. Right. Drawing attention to ourselves makes us vulnerable. Easy to mop up. So Swan tells us to study the anthro, learn to act like the anthro. We survive by fitting in with the fittest. But pursuit of the sincerest form of flattery demands a ridiculously precarious balance. When we try too hard to act like them, when we get so focused on behaving just right, on walking and chewing gum at the same time, we lose all appropriate emotion and intonation and evocation We give ourselves away We give ourselves to parody, stiff and grotesque as Frankensteins burlesque. Then we get plucked off the boulevard and dishevelled by the CACI.

Pavement arms shoes ears legs mouths shadows streetlight, waving trees Buy a candlestick Café tables, chairs, chests, bottys. Ill be out of town a few days. A funeral. Glowing cigarettes fingers pinch. Smoke. Je lui ai dit que cétait lui. Son fini. Good for you. Glasses, hands Moon shines. Pavement, stained red carpet, bright lights.

Marquee. says Freda.

Red glasses shine. Brown coatsleeve lifts. Film. Lew see nay ma. Its the best and quickest way to learn everything there is to know about them, about what makes them tick, to observe without being observed, without the messiness of direct contact, the impossibility of living those stories ourselves. Drama, comedy, pathos, peccadillos, mores, manners, love, hate, the whole interpersonal schmeer is here, on the silver screen. Film taught me what I know about anthros and how to behave in their world, all in these convenient warm dark dry cozy little two hour lessons. Quick studies, crash courses, slices o life. Of all the hoary drugs and reprogramming the collectors laid on me, popcorn cinema therapy was one thing they never bloody tried.

Corner comes, Black boots go. Allee. Boxes. Ashcans.

Buy my matches, maids, my nice small pointed matches

Gutter puddles shine. Fried fish. Rotten vegetables. Dog barks. Red doors. Red paint peels, splinters, black ink scratches, doors. Freda head turns, skinny bracelet Jimmy have pale hands. Doors jimmy goes. We have to be. Afficionados not just of anthro. Behavior. But of linguistics because. So much. So much is verbal with them. So. Almost got it. So much information, eh, comes out of their mouths. Heartfelt confessions. Mundane trivia. Baseless opinions. Baldfaced lies. They think in words, damn it. O, there we go.

Red door Freda fingernails pull. Doorway, darkness. Door black boot holds. Pale wrist Jimmy wraps, brown coatsleeve hides. Black collar Tag trembles. My back hand pushes. Go on. Freda says.

Red door shuts. Darkness, mold, dust. Smoke, must, heavy curtain. Heavy curtain Freda arm pulls. Chairs, caps, shoulders, hands, knees, eyes. Darkness flickery light purrs,

Tippy Toe hole. Light shines, big voices, big noises. My hands earphones. Butter, coughing, rustle, burnt, slurping, sweet.

Seat Freda hand pushes flat. Freda sits, chair squeaks. Collar tag twinkles. Seat Pale Freda hand pushes flat. Black coatsleeve Freda hand pulls. Freda hand my black coat elbow knocks.

Assieds. pulling Freda says.

My botty sits. Seat squeaks. Chair back Freda boots stomp. Chair back Dirty ballet shoes tap.

Love stories are the best for learning. says Freda. This one looks particularly instructionary.

Bright shiny ears eyes mouths noses hair. Holes cheeks show, powdery skin. Voices big. My ears hurt. Wet mouths open shut, Oua oua oua. Moist big eyes blinkblink. My purple glasses Supermiracle bubble wand presses. Pocket catsup packet My fingers rub.

Freda says, See whats happening here, Oboy. The anthro male has asked the anthro female on a date. A date is where two anthros go and do things together and try not to say something daft. Observe the levels of communication. Internalizing the levels is crucial, if youre ever going to pass for one of them. Theres the factual level. Will you go out with me. The emotional level. Cos I like you. Then theres the interpersonal level, the intent behind the question. And I want to get to know you better.

Shh. darkness says.

Last is the nonverbal level, something we are more familiar with in ourselves, but in this context parallels spoken language so is tied to the verbal, and thus can be woefully lost on you and me   Hair flips noses mouths moving staring eyes flashing lights yellow tooths hairy mole puffy cheek wrinkles eyebrow shiny skin bitten lip pimple chin Voices little voices big Voices voices Eyelids itch Hand lap bubble wand tap tap tap Eyes stare hurt my eyes My eye my eye my hands hide

See the way he smiles at her, and runs his hand through his hair, he varies looking in her eyes and looking off into the night. I know, Oboy, youre filled with fright, but eye contact is paramount. So is physical proximity, in love situations. Youre going to have to get used to it   Shiny   rings dangle Ears Flashing moon chandelier thumping noises Thats the beat Music Oboy stomping feet Its a disco, ils dansent Arms legs pirouette red lips hanging cigarette smoky darkness gold barette shines Long red hair shines

See how he moves closer to her, the way his voice is quiet and soft. Observing him, she in turn responds favorably, cos shes tantalized, she enjoys the sensation of his attraction to her, see it in her eyes, so she smiles and twists her shoulders sidetoside and bites her lip and finally says

Shhh. Quiet.

His smile is big, hes elated, you can tell cos hes showing all his teeth Anthros show their teeth when theyre really happy, chickpea, their mouths make that infernal racket you think is crows cawing

Tais toi

its called laughter, risa, rire, Gelächter, gargalhada, I laugh, too, but its the pastiche I dont bloody mean it.

Big bright arms hug, lips lips push, coat shirt skirt slip Before you despise me You must know Ive fallen in love with you My purple glasses Bubble wand taps, legs pants hands shoes. Seat squeaks. Catsup packet fingers squish. Breath gets big, Groaning Hands pulls clothes Mouths touch Eyes close Sleepings so sad Chest arm pushes Bed squeaks Bare back Bare legs Bare arms squeeze. Neck mouth bites. Big lips big eyes big nose turns, cries, I dont want to be in love with you

My neck hair tightens.

This is the intercourse level, Oboy. The physical. My cheek hot Freda lips. Something else you should learn about. For your own good. red Freda mouth says.

Would you please be quiet, please.

Red carpet Light flashes. My eyes Flashlight flashes, red Freda glasses. Votre billet. says flashlight.

Freda yawns. Think I lost it in that pit of a loo.

And your friend.

No, I didnt lose him.

Flashlight flashes. You both better come with me.

To the boxcars, eh, Himmler.

Pardon.

Now you know nookies always the best part of the movie. Let us watch this scene. He needs to learn.

Mamzelle. If you and your friend dont come with me Im going to ring the police.

Okay, okay. Madre de dios. Can a lone muchacha an her tonto catch a break. Eets heez first time joo know.

Mamzelle.

First time at the bloody seenayma, with a real live cheeky cheeky cheek. He was even going to get un poco suerrrte,

Mamzelle

just like el romeo in the fleek. But thass outta the queshion now, eh. Preek.

Shut up.

Mamzelle. says flashlight.

Freda rises. Seat flips up, squeaks. Freda turns, purring flickery tippy toe light shines.

Freda hollers, Raggedy Ann and Raggedy Andy were two rag dolls. They were stuffed with nice clean white cotton

Groans, hollers, cups darkness throws. My shoulder crumpled bag hits. My eye Supermiracle bubble wand hides.

Mamzelle. waving flashlight says.

And their faces were painted on them. hollers Freda. My shoulder pale Freda hand slaps. Skinny legs bump my botty. Hollers come. Bubble wand my pocket hides. Floor is sticky, my hands, my ballet shoes, run.

Both Raggedy Ann and Raggedy Andy wore very cheery smiles and were friendly, happy little creatures. Freda hollers.

Mamzelle. The police.

But they focking hated getting focking hassled by focking candycoated baboons like focking joo. Flashlight pops, hits floor, tinkling Vassily the police Arms legs run thump thump thumping dirty carpet, door opens, yawning light, popcorn pommes frites fly Bright hole light purrs Red vest Freda hands hit shove Hep Freda runs Allons y chickpea Darkness spins Curtain comes, my cheeks curtain brushes, red doors Black boot kicks Bang damp darkness, run Blue puddles My hands ballet shoes plouf Pale fish moonlight tsokk tsokk tsokk darkness

Think anyone noticed us. cawing Freda says.

Hands ballet shoes, shp shp shp. Black Freda boots tsokk tsokk tsokk. Allee, rue, allee, run, moon shines, bright windows, cat cries, darkness. Fweeet.

Blue lights flash.

Hollering comes, pin pon pin pon pin pon.

Shit. Brown coatsleeves flap, Freda head turns, yellow tail twitches. White cars red stripes come.

The CACI. Run, Oboy, run.

White cars flashing lights pin pon pin pon White cars get big pin pon pin pon pin My earphones my hands press My shoulder Hand hits, pulls my coat Forget your ears vamanos White cars holler, squeal Car doors flap, stones black boots clac clac pin pon pin pon pin Black gloves hold buzzing sticks, holler, Alto, Arrêtez, Stop where you are Boots come chakk chakk chakk, splash water.

Freda turns, brown coattails flap Black boots tsokk tsokk tsokk Rooftops holler pin pon pin pon Freda My hands ballet shoes follow, stones cold, wet, plif plouf. Red Freda glasses flash, boots swing Freda runs. Arms legs buzzing sticks come Pin pon pin pon Squealing white car blocks allee, Freda jumps White car bonnet Black Freda boots run bang bang bang Red stripe doors flap Fweeet fweeet Freda jumps, black Freda boots tsokk tsokk tsokk, byebye.

Door red stripes Slam black helmet black gloves Flashlight flashes My eyes hurt Stehenbleiben My head ducks pin pon pin My stocking hat Swinging flashlight brushes Spak Bricks flashlight hits Buzzing stick rises

    my ballet   Helmet
         shoes   Shoulder
          climb   Bent knee

ballet shoes climb crumbly bricks tsa tsa tsa Fire escape ladder My hands grab Cold rough ladder falls Stones jump, hit ballet shoes Bang Flashlight falls bounces, bumping light rolls, Black arms black legs fall Oof Black helmet Buzzing stick bounce Boots come chakk chakk chakk My hands, ballet shoes, run, corner comes.

Courtyard, flickery light. Wood fence brown Freda coat jumps, byebye. Courtyard, fence come Ballet shoes sha sha splintered wood Fencetop Hands push, slivers bite, big red car roars, huffing white Wet stones jump, hurt My botty.

Freda hollers, The bus, get up Brown coatsleeves wave, boots run tsokk tsokk tsokk. Big red car gasps, steam puffs, windows windows windows have eyes, darkness hollers pin pon pin pon Whistles fweet fweet My ears hurt Platform Freda jumps black bars hands grabs Vites vites, Oboy.

Hands, ballet shoes run. Dirty black rubber platform comes. Mud, seeds, chewing gum. Red stocking hat Freda hand pulls Red stocking hat brown coat pocket hides. Yellow Freda hair. Greasy hair pale fingers brush, red glasses show. My hands, ballet shoes follow. Yellow lights. Grey seats coats scarves hats sit. Green coat coughs. Windows fog.

Big black wheel Brown arms, brown hands twist. Black glasses shine. Red lips. My eyes hide. Window, darkness, flashlights bob, whistles blow, running boots.

Freda.

Dez.

Where to.

Anywhere.

Pedals Sneakers push, white knob brown hand grabs, pulls metal stick. Scree. Growling, shaking. Window rattles. Streetlamps shake. My legs crouch, my fingers grip torn plastic seat. My tooths chatter. Hollers come.

Shut up, Oboy. Freda says. I dont like it either but I dont have a pet carrier to stuff you into. Just hum. Here.

Red candy. Sweet. Grey seat Freda sits, huh huh huh. Pale damp skin, shiny. Metal tag flutters.

My mouth says hum.

Freda.

Little papers brown hand gives Freda hand. Freda eyes big, red glasses. Metal tag trembles black collar. Freda chest goes big little, big little, huh huh huh. My hand, Freda hand. My ballet shoe, Freda boot. Groaning. Streetlamps, doorways, windows pass.

I saw that. Grey puffy hair, tongue licks chapped loose lips. Yellow tooths click. I saw that, driver. You just gave these allee cats those transfers. They didnt pay. No, sir, they did not. Vermin. Stole my canary I know you did.

Black glasses turn. Old woman. I know you dont want me to put yo crazy arse off my bus for seein things n causin a disturbance. Not when you got to get to yo rabbit hutch all the way in Passy to soak them tire ole feet a yoze.

Old grey lips sputter. Grey hair flutters. Crooked greasy nose Crooked finger scratches. Dirty yellow sack Pink coatsleeves hug. Old grey lips smack. Hmph. Youre all allee cats.

See ay see eye. Freda says. Fingers, red glasses shirt rubs. Eager to erase their mistakes.

They did not pay.

Thats you and me, Oboy. Freda says. Red glasses black cross Fingers put, cover blue eyes. My eyes Freda eyes watch. My eyes hide.

Growling stops. Sighing. Steam coughs. Earphones my hands hold. Red wood handle Brown hand pulls. Squealing door folds open. Steam huffs puffs. My head says bum bum bum, hurts. Freda head turns. Red glasses shine. Freda rises.

Thanks, Dez.

You and yo boy take care. Them sirensll shorten yo lifespan.

Allee cats.

Miaou. says Freda. Brown coatsleeves swing, Freda jumps. Boots chok chok pavement. Freda turns. Metal tag flickers. Come on, Oboy.

Dirty rubber steps come. Pavement comes. Roses red roses. hollers red roses. Steps red roses climb. Door folds shut. Big red bus gasps, hollers, steam puffs. Big red bus gets little, byebye.

Black stocking hat My fingers tug, touch purple glasses, wiggle earphones. Supermiracle bubble wand My pocket hides. Catsup packet. Tall bricks leans.

Grey stone lions sit, watch me. You. lions say.

Chickpea. Come on.

Black Freda boots k k k k stone steps. Arms legs sit, legs walk. Red tips cigarettes. Look my music came in. Its the latest. Thats great. Lets go back to your place and check it out. Lions watch.

Pin pon pin pon pin. sirens say.

Oboy. Vamos.

Freda boots my ballet shoes follow, stone steps. Freda says, Flashing lights mean run, Oboy. Sirens mean run. And if you hear anyone sprechen zee deutch while holding a buzzing stick. You run.

Big wood door opens. Freda goes byebye. Arms legs come, go. Buckles have black shoes, pink hearts. Lets find Amelie. To the winebar. Small pink moonboots dot dot dot. Come along, Mavie Shoes say drip drip drip. Shiver. Shoes say toop tee toop tee toop. Metal walker Hands hold push bang bang bang, shuffling shoes.

Oboy.

Warm. Dim. Arms legs swing bump me. Hollers. Shut up. says Freda. My arm Freda hand squeezes. Calmate. Lets go. My eye Supermiracle bubble wand hides. Freda boots Ballet shoes follow. Folded paper Freda hand takes.

Dewey decimal system. says Freda. Paper Finger taps. This little brochure lets the anthros manage all the printed knowledge in their world. Sometimes what we do is slow them down. For instance, we can move books on mythology to the medicine section. Or we can mix books on ghosts and witches and ESP with books on religion. We can switch books on genealogy with books on gynecology. Why would we do this, youd ask if you could. Because we must confuse and constern the anthro, we must slow its thirst for knowledge, retard or even divert development of even more screwed up ideas than us. Its a small thing. But we are small things, and every little bit helps. Come on.

Freda boots clic clac clic. Shoes clomp clomp. Red stockings Paper sacks smack smack smack. Long skinny shoes. Dirty shoes. Swollen fat ankles have red Shoes. Pink pants. Black pants, white polka dots. Bare foots, dirty heels Excuse me, You cant be in here without shoes Aw come on Big doorway, yellow walls. My eye Supermiracle bubble wand hides.

This is the little anthro kiddies room. Freda says. Picture books. Chapter books. The real world.

Little arms little legs bluewhitered shoes run. Hey, its mine, I saw it first. Blue shoes tumble, fall. Owie. Crying.

Kiddies. says Freda. Cute enough to eat, arent they. Ugh. Book Pale hand black cross fingers takes.

Heres one of my favourites. says Freda. Book opens. Colours, eyes, dog, fox.

Look, sir. Look, sir. Mister knox, sir. Lets do tricks with bricks and blocks, sir. Lets do tricks with chicks and clocks, sir.

My arms flap flap flap. Page crouching Freda hand turns.

Ah, and heres a new trick, mister knox. Socks on chicks and chicks on fox. Fox on clocks on bricks and blocks. Bricks and blocks on knox on box.

O boy. my mouth says. Ha. Bubble wand my tongue pokes.

Pale Freda fingers turn pages. How about this. When beetles fight these battles in a bottle with their paddles and the bottles on a poodle and the poodles eating noodles. They call this a muddle puddle tweetle poodle beetle noodle bottle paddle battle.

Carpet greenblue vines rolls, my botty, my back. Carpet ballet shoes thump thump. My hands clap clap clap. Supermiracle bubble wand flies. Lights shine, my eyes.

Back rolls, hands knees crawl. Supermiracle bubble wand greenblue vines carpet. O boy. my mouth says, wand fingers pinch. O boy.

Freda says, I taught myself to enunciate using this book. You can never have too many copies.

Freda eyes flicker. Book black haversack hides. Now where are the Raggedy Ann and Andys. Your favourite. My hands, ballet shoes follow Freda, greenblue vines. Books Freda hands take. Freda says, Raggedy Ann in the magic book.

Book black haversack hides.

Raggedy Anns secret. Freda says. Will be our secret. Raggedy Ann and Andy and the nice fat policeman.

Books black haversack hides.

Raggedy Andys pillow fight. You and I should have a pillow fight sometime, chickpea. Of course, youd probably die of fright.

Book sack hides.

Freda says, Periodicals next. Librarys closing anon.

Carpet greenblue vines Black Freda boots clump clump. Arms legs coats come, go. I read that book. It was only okay. Shiny shoes, black pants. Dirty shoes, brown pants. Ankles. Shoes thump thump. Wheres the elevator in this place. These stairs are killin me. Red shoes. Blue pants. Pants swish swish swish. Black Freda boots clic clac clic grey steps, grey leaves.

Upstairs. Freda says.

Black Freda boots my hands ballet shoes follow. Grey stone steps cold. Black Freda boots go, carpet pink roses. Yellow tail goes. There. Freda says. My shoes follow. Carpet pink roses.

Newspaper Freda hand slaps, wood table. Todays news. says Freda. Wood chair Freda sits, black haversack drops, pink roses carpet. Pages black cross fingers turn. O, yeah. Freda says. Lookit, our latest capers here. Pet thieves nab gold crown conure.

Pages black cross fingers turn. Ah, the classifieds. Little black ants Fingernail traces. Freda says, Theres no way we can stop demand. So we try to dent supply. Labs place orders for a specific type of animal to class b dealers, who in turn call on bunchers to do the dirty work. Pale fists shake. Bunchers. The sunzabitches are the real pet thieves.

Shh.

Bunchers usually work the pounds first. Then they look for animals on the street. Then at residences. Homes and backyards, Oboy. Pale hand waves. Or here in the city, flats. Or the bunchers answer the classifieds. Rattly newspaper hands shake.

To beat the bunchers and the brokers, we have to be first in line for random source animals. We have to steal the dearies from homes before daylight comes and the animals are given away. Or we have to answer the bloody ads. Free to a good home. No questions asked.

Shh.

Lets see here. Em gee ar says no pets. Purebred Ragdoll, gorgeous, lovebug personality. Free to good home. Seal bicolour. Approved only. 014 016 5949.

My eye Supermiracle bubble wand hides.

Gold crown conure needs new home. Approx 6 years old quite sweet never bit anyone, needs single bird home. Wannabes dont waste my time bird rescue people need not contact approved homes only. 014 26 Ironic, the ad for this birds still here, even though we stole the little dear back on page 5. Freda says, Heres one.

Due to a separation with mi esposo I need to find new home for quaker parrot he left behind. My husband could handle him but Im scared. I can get in cage to give him food and water but thats it. Cage included he is about 2 years old.

Paper Pale fingers flick. Lost job, failed marriage, need to get rid of the family pet fast. Thats what we look for. Cos thats what the bunchers look for. The free and the easy. Rozlyn. Hey.

White lion mane turns. Black paint eyes blink. Thin lips pull, brown tooths show. Heya kitty cat. brown tooths says. Dint reconize ye at foist. Black eyes, my eyes. My eyes hide. Dirty whistly goblin shoes come. Smell tastes dirty. Poo. Musty clothes sweaty skin. My eyes water. Tummy hurts.

Wrinkly hand shows. Hand is spotted, dark. Freda leans. Yellow hair wrinkly hand pets, strokes yellow tail. How yeh doin kiddo. says brown tooths. Freda purrs, ron ron ron ron. Metal tag clinks, black collar, pale neck.

Whos ye friend. says white lion mane. Ees a looka aint e. Well, ees lookin at everythin cept me. Brown tooths caw. Mouth coughs. Big white lion mane shakes. Scare ye dearie. Dont care so much for my joy do veev, eh.

My coat Wrinkly spotted hand touches. My tummy hurts. My eyes hide.

Hes afraid of his own shadow. says Freda. But hes one of us. And we are hungry, Rozlyn. Can you help.

Well, dearie. Eres a nice baguette. Fresh. Foind me later Oil have some milk fo ye.

Black paint eyes blink, watch my eyes. Long black lashes hang loose. Black eyelid paint thick, gritty. Brown tooths Orange tongue licks. Lips pale, split, dried blood. Hairy lip. Hairs curl, trembly chin. Mouth has scabs. Wrinkly skin. Cold, damp, my eyes.

How bout a kiss dearie. says split lips.

Rozlyn, you old letch. cawing Freda says. Oboy just fell off the turnip truck, you know.

Toinips are me favorite veggie. Brown tooths go clic clic. Orange tongue pushes brown tooths. Coldness goes updown my back. My tooths clic clac. My lips curl.

Red wrinkly lips says, The othah night I was standin outside Killys guinguette and this man, I dint know im, nevah seen him before, he runs across the street, grabs a loose pole.

Shh.

Ow anyone knew that pole was loose, is beyond me. Anyhow, he comes n swings the pole at me. Foive toimes. I duck each toime. He coulda kilt me. I report it to the police and what do they say.

They couldnt help you.

Cozzahs. And the prefects a woman, can you believe it. Well, gotta go.

See you later. says Freda.

Arivoir.

Curly goblin shoes sh sh sh sh. Trunk hand drags. White lion mane gets little. White lion mane goes byebye.

Newspaper Freda hands roll. Paper black haversack hides. Carpet pink roses.

Freda rises. Black haversack hand takes. Did that security geek see me nick the paper. Freda says. Finger diggin for nose gold says negatory. Lets go. I lost my old bird guide climbing the other night. And theres a parrot I want, the one we keep hearing at that brownstone in Belleville. I think it might be a Senegal.

Purple glasses my fingers tap. Freda, my hands, ballet shoes follow. Shoe sole paper sticks. Long skirt moves, shines, bright light. Checked pants. Stains have pants. White cane red tip Dark shoes bright laces follow. Cane goes tap tap tap.

Cawing.

Whatre you laughing at. Freda says. Havent you ever seen a service animal before.

Pink roses carpet, grey stairs, pink roses carpet. Youve got to walk on your hind legs, Oboy. The whole point of today was to start learning how to behave like them. Not that they all behave like them. But positively, youre not exactly stealthy or unnoticed padding along on all fours. Or maybe its the dirty ballet slippers. Its important that we instill confidence in Swan, that we show him youre fully capable of running with us. Here we go. Book Skinny pale Freda finger pulls. Pretty birds. Red glasses Fingers lift. Pages flutter. Yeah, yeah, this is great. Eyes glasses hide. Book Hands clap shut. Book haversack hides.

Viens. Freda says. Freda turns, black boots chachachacha pink roses carpet. Clickety clic clac, clickety clic, grey steps. Ballet shoes follow. Big wood doors come.

Wait. says Freda. We check out the community board before we go. They post new random source stuff today. Freda coughs. Okay, hmmm. No, no, nothing new, no. O, fuck.

White paper Freda hand snatches, crumples, stone floor crumpled paper bounces byebye. Freda eyes, my eyes. Lets go.

Door opens, darkness.

D im wet allee. Long furry coat. Red tip cigarette, crooked white tooths. Brown finger tap taps cardboard box.

White plastic bottle caps.

Oily brown hands, dusty dry knuckles. Bottle cap fingers pluck.

Red pea shivers.

Skinny white chick win again. says long furry coat. Rainbow paper Freda hand takes. Cardboard box rainbow paper taps.

Thats it for me. says Freda.

You aint gonna gimme a chance to catch even.

Rainbow paper Freda hand waves. Your games too easy. Freda says. Id hate to be the one who put you in the poor house.

Brown fingers say snap snap snap. Who here can show me fotty. I only gonna play fo fotty now, fotty francs, cuz when my roll go down, the stakes go up n the payday get dat much bigger. Allez, allez, somebody, all you got to do is keep yo eye on the bride n the dowrys yours, come now, pipples, step on up, only fotty francs, now I know somebody here got to be tall enough fo those awwwwds.

Hands coats hide, hats fingers scratch, scuff scuff shuffling shoes. Aw, venez, venez, somebody got to.

My coatsleeve Freda fingers pinch, pull. Stand right here. Freda says. My ear breath tickles. Stand close to the box.

Box dirty, wet. Box my black coat brushes. Tape. Cardboard box my finger rubs.

Cabeches Cockels Hartti chaks Makrill

Freda turns. Green coatsleeve Freda arm hugs, pulls. Green coat comes. Red ear Freda mouth brushes. You saw how easy that was, didnt you, handsome. You were reaching for your pocket, but then you backed off. Dont be shy.

You sire. scratchy voice says. You feelin it, aint you.

Freda tooths shows, head nods. Hes got you all figured out.

Aw, non, non, non.

Venez, sire, step up to my altar.

Rainbow paper Freda hand shows. Look at this loot, handsome. Riggers a hack. If I can take her, you surely can.

Rainbow paper Pale hairy hand short fat fingers shows. Rainbow paper drops, cardboard box.

Quarante.

Heroes like you make le monde spin round, pardner. says red tip cigarette. Red pea White plastic bottle cap hides.

Men like you deserve a wedding night to knock yo socks off. Brown fingers bottle caps cardboard box.

Ch, ch, ch. say white plastic bottle caps. Arms legs stand, walk, swing, dim dark allee.

Thass yo lady, bro, you bess keep yo eye on her, peekaboo, now you sees her, now you dont, inside outside here come d bride, she wearin her pride but she done hide cuz she shy, clyde, did her stride make you all crosseyed o weak in yo knees.

Pale balcony moons peek. Railings Red sleeves roost.

Its a trick. balcony moon hollers. Dont fall for it.

She n her friends work this corner all the time. says window moon.

Long furry coatsleeve waves. Now all you crows up there shut yo beaks. Im juss a single mom tryin to make a livin, daccord.

Dont move, Oboy. My ear Freda breath tickles. Stay in front of the box.

Cigarette glows, crooked white tooths, white smoke, my eyes sting, my mouth coughs. Caps oily brown hands switch ch, ch, ch. say white plastic bottle caps. T t, t t, t t, hidey red pea says. Bottle caps glow, dim grey light.

So where that lil woman be, pardner.

Thin white lips Short fat finger presses.

You saw it. Its that one. Pale ear red Freda mouth hisses.

Shushah blondie. You had yo fun.

Short fat finger taps cap. Celui ci.

Sure now. You sure. Okay. White cap Long brown fingers lift. Cigarette flashing white tooths wiggles. Nicely done, sire. You jus won yoself fotty. But befo you go pocketin that dough, why dont you occur to yo mind the spoils of doublin down.

White cap Brown fingers lift. Red pea shines. You got you another peek, sire. Alls you got to do is keep yo eye on d bride n d honeymoon in d bank.

Dont pass it up, honey. Freda says, ear mouth brushes. Its a steal, I won 40. You can win 120 just playing it safe. Even more if you put in your whole bankroll. You cant lose. Ill make sure of it. And after, Ill let you buy me a drink.

Cardboard box edge My finger rubs.

Achetez mes lavettes, mes bonnes lavettes de laines

Red tip cigarette says, Gimme a bet. Ill match you bill for bill.

Rainbow papers Short fat fingers drop, cover rainbow papers, cardboard box. Cinq cent francs. says green coat.

O my. says wiggly black eyebrows.

Cover him. says Freda. Rainbow papers Brown fingers drop, cover rainbow papers, cardboard box.

He covered.

Red pea Long brown finger taps. Cap Brown fingers put, pea hides. Caps move sh, sh, sh, sh.

T t, t t, whispers hidey red pea.

Round and round she go, where lil bride stop dont nobody know, her beau got his woe blowin to an fro gawkin high an low, Didja you seen her, bro It fotty below n she lost in the snow yea even so I wanna drink pernod, is my lil bride lyin low did she stub her toe on her way to the altar.

Shes a fake. hollers high balcony moon.

Dark hat turns, tilts. Thought I tole you to shut yo beak. Dont make me climb up there. Brown fist shakes.

Youre lucky we aint rung the prefects men.

You jus jealous old man you done loss yo mojo wit yo teef settin in a broke glass a dirty pickle juice.

Freda leans, says, Quick, handsome, look. Cap Freda fingers lift. Red pea shines. Cap Freda fingers puts.

Long furry coat turns. Alors. Which it gonna be, sire.

Go ahead and take im. says Freda. Lady luck, handsome.

White plastic bottle cap Short fat finger taps. Celui ci.

You sure.

Ouai.

Long brown fingers lift cap. Aw.

Pas, attente. Mais vous. Cest quoi ce bordel. Green coat turns.

Freda hands show. You saw it just like I did. Freda says.

Gotta sting, pardner. Rainbow paper Brown fingers take. Rainbow paper long furry coat hides.

Elle ma montré où il était. Je. Je suis volé.

Now, nobody robbed you, sire. See. Cap brown fingers lift. Red pea shivers. They she is.

Voleurs de merde.

Mm hm. Dassa ladies fo you.

Wet stones Dark shoe stomps, turns, coats pants move sidetoside five hundred forty francs he lost, dark shoes clomp clomp gravel allee, gets little, bye bye. Long Cigarette cawing mouth wiggles.

Black eyes, my eyes. Learnin somethin, shithead.

My eyes hide.

Who next maintenant. Allez, that was jus some bad luck back there. Tourist should always go home happy.

Police are on the lookout for a pair of cat burglars who creep into downtown flats between 2 and 5 am. Miraculously, the duo penetrates locked windows and balcony doors often located several stories above street level, then make their getaway via fire escapes and rooftops.

More incredible than their skill at breaking and entering is the fact these thieves arent after the usual money, electronics or jewels. Rather, they covet family pets. Cats, rabbits, rodents, reptiles, but especially, exotic birds.

Police have noted one glaring exception to the hit list, which only amplifies the aura of mystery. In a city known for its canine lovers, these pet thieves dont like dogs.

Its not that we dont like dogs, its that we are allergic to slavering shit breath. says Freda.

Stained ceiling holes drip drip drip. Shiver. Flickery upsidedown candles Puddle shows. Newspaper Skinny black cross fingers hold. Wet black boots crossed, wet pantlegs, wood floorboards. Wet yellow hair hangs, drips. Newspaper Dark spots plif plif. Shivery me. Ginger tabby purrs, my lap paws kneads, my pants damp, thin soft ear my fingers rub.

Freda says, A female burglar christened the pet thief, suspected in 30 breakins targeting birds and other pets last year, has returned to the district, according to Gobelins Police Inspector Antonini Finocchio. Finocchio said several Gobelins flats were recently broken into in a manner similar to those during last years spree. The breakins occurred in the area from Rue de la Sante to Avenue des Gobelins and from Boulevard Arago to Boulevard August Blank.

We are certain this is the same gal from last year, Detective Finocchio said. And now she has a partner.

Here that, Oboy. Freda says. He called me a gal.

My fingers Ginger tabby tongue licks. My neck trickle tickles, my back. Purring fuzzy tabby chin my fingers scratch.

I cried as if somebody had died when he was taken, said 26 year old Mimi Sissen, lamenting the theft of her likewise 26 year old red macaw, Zoltan. Zoltan was torn from his rooftop aviary on 3 November.

Despite disguising themselves in long coats, stocking caps and sunglasses, victims describe the woman and her male accomplice as either Caucasian or Hispanic, in their late teens or early 20s, up to one point eight metres tall and of slender build. The woman is believed to have blonde hair. Believed to have. Is that like alleged. Are they implying I bleach.

Citywide, the number of pets stolen in the past 12 months has shot up to more than 100. In addition to a multitude of cats, during one four month stretch reported thefts ranged from moluccan cockatoos to california kingsnakes, and a plethora of rabbits, guinea pigs, mice and ferrets in between.

Freda caws, newspaper Hands shake. Parakeet whistles, head bobs. Cuddly guinea pigs has cardboard box. Purring ginger tabby stretches, my wet pantleg claws scratch, hurts.

The pet thieves even broke into a pub and stole a duck. Edvar Kriek, owner of Hurdlemakers, said, The duck is one of a pair and though she didnt have a name, she was well loved by both myself and my customers. Im very upset about the loss and the duck left behind is very confused.

Wet yellow Freda hair shakes. Blue eyes watch my eyes. Freda says, Was there a second duck. Well, we will have to make an encore appearance to Hurdlemakers, wont we. Cant have daisy feeling alone and blue, right, donald.

Green plastic pool. White pekin duck floats. Candlelit feathers glow. Ceiling drops plic plic green plastic pool. Qua

qua. duck says, flaflaflaflap, hurts my ears. Brown water Yellow bill scoops, white feather head shakes sidetoside. Wood floorboards papers books shiny drops speckle. White pekin duck Red burmese watches, pink nose leather damp, eyes blinkblink.

Inspector Finocchio said his team is burning the midnight oil to catch the thieves, but leads are few and positive descriptions scant. Finocchio believes there are more victims than have come forward, and so would like to remind citizens to do their part. Report any suspicious activity or information on the case to the investigations department at 014 952 5354. Callers may use the anonymous tip line at 014 482 7400.

Newspaper Freda fingers tear shhht. Ginger tabby ears flatten, paw pink tongue licks. Newspaper falls, Freda rises. Floorboards creak Freda clac clics Cats prip prip prip rub black Freda boots. Ceiling holes drip, drip, drip. Shiver. Torn newspaper scraps Freda watches. Heres a good spot. Freda says. Torn wallpaper, newspaper scrap pale fingers pin. Cage birds whistle. Bearded dragons Aquarium shows, staring black eyes. Freda comes clicclacclic. Black pants crouches.

Lets see what Belleville has to say. Freda says. Newspaper pale hands shake, open pages. Cat eyes shine, window, sofa, candlelight, darkness. Here it is. Freda says. Reward offered for cockatoo pinched from pet store. Belleville Police say a two person team is burgling this southwest district and has struck again over the past weekend.

The culprits, whom authorities believe to be the notorious pet thieves, broke into Señor Zorros Pet Boutique on Rue LaCross Sunday morning and snatched a 10 year old umbrella cockatoo named Kipling. Witnesses report seeing a man and woman in long coats fleeing down the allee, cage in hand. They clambered up an office buildings fire escape and disappeared over the rooftop.

Jeri Luna, manager of Señor Zorros, is still trying to make sense of the crime. I thought it would be puppies, you know, the purebreds, wot got stolen, or other merchandise, aquariums and such. Who in the world would actually just steal a bird. And why, whats the purpose for it Luna said.

It appears the thieves knew exactly what they wanted when they robbed Señor Zorros. However, no one can say who took Kipling or why.

Belleville Station Commander Hermann Kurt says Their motivation, whether its for cash, from selling the stolen pets, or the thrill, only the perpetrators can tell us that for sure.

Brown sofa arm sits Freda, boot heels thunkthunk wood floorboards. Freda says, O sure, those are the only reasons. Cheap bees n honey or cheaper thrills. Couldnt be cos theres something really fucked with this world theyve made and that animals should have no part of it.

Ginger tabby rises, stretches, claws scratch. Tabby hops, wood floorboards tabby walks. Clothes pile quivers. Devon rex jumps Ginger tabby tail Paw swats Devon rex spins jumps byebye Crouching Ginger tabby hisses, eyes black.

Luna is asking for the publics help and is offering a huge reward for Kipling, who is worth 24000 francs. The amount of the reward is only being disclosed to the person who finds the cockatoo Twenty four grand. Freda says, watches cage. Who knew you were worth so much.

Shadows Umbrella cockatoo wings flare, crest flares, black eyes blinkblink candlelight.

Swan will know. says Freda. Newspaper rattles.

Rawww, three cheers for pizza. says hyacinth macaw.

Newspaper pale hands flap. Freda says, Police believe the pet thieves are linked to as many as 150 burglaries in and around the downtown area over the past two years. They primarily strike between 11 pm and 6 am, stealing only pets. The thieves have no qualms about hitting homes when residents are present, even entering bedrooms when people are asleep. On the rare occasion theyve been confronted, they simply scamper up building walls or down drainpipes and disappear, their acrobatic escapes too much for the average pursuer.

Commander Kurt believes the pet thieves broke into at least nine Belleville flats between 11 and 29 November, stealing cats from four victims, one of whom, a woman in her 70s, was pushed to the floor when she grabbed the females coat O come on, I didnt knock her down, she fell when I pulled my arm away. says Freda. Bloody yellow journalism.

If you know the suspects, their whereabouts or have any other information on the crimes, ring Belleville Police at blahbiddyblahblah. Freda says. Paper Fingers tear shhht.

Freda rises, walks clic clac clic wood floorboards creakcreak Paper Freda fingers pin, torn scraps. Black pantleg calf chinchilla persian rubs, tail raised. Black pantleg shows long white hairs.

Brown coat hips hands hold. Freda says, Weve got the booboisie running scared, Oboy. Look, we are front page of almost every district rag. Passy Pet Shop Hit by Theft. Daring Thieves Swipe Cockatoo. Angora Stolen, Kids Bereft. Reuilly Police Havent A Clue. Bird Thieves Terrorize Flats in Bercy. Thieves Turn Pet Store Arsy Versy. Salty Cat Nicked from Stevedore. Rooty Hill Burglars Strike Twice More.

Freda hands clap clap clap, hurt my ears. Birds cheep cheep, flap, ruffle feathers. Cage bunnies huddle, noses twitch. Floorboard cats sprawl, mattress, brown sofa, watch aquarium mice.

Qua qua qua. says white pekin duck.

Thats right, Donald. Freda says, twinkly black collar tag. No mercy, from Belleville to Bercy.

Creamm. seal point Siamese says, my knee paw taps.

Freda says, You know, we should start conducting large scale assaults on breeding facilities. We should hit the zoo. Can you imagine that. Lions and tigers and bears, Oboy.

Ginger tabby Freda hands grabs, swings tabby high, ceiling. Furry legs stiff, eyes blinkblink.

Dowwn. tabby cries.

Freda turns, arms raised, tabby eyes black. What if we freed every bloody cat, bird, rabbit, mouse, tadpole and daddy longlegs in town. In the world. What if we were all free to start over again. To be who we are, who we always shouldve been. What kind of world would this be then.

Ginger tabby head Freda lips mwah, cat Freda hands put wood floorboards. White hairs black pants Ginger tabby sniffs. Broke window Ivy leaves rattle. Freda shoulders shake, wet brown coat falls Notice none of the papers said how cold and wet our mission is Coat arm flings, mattress coat hits. Tortoiseshell jumps, back arched, eyes black. Red towel Freda hand takes, rubs wet yellow hair. Red towel says, Thats the thing about the papers. They never tell the whole story.

Red towel falls. Blue Freda eyes, my eyes.

Black sleeves Pale Freda hands push, arms pale, candlelight. Belt black cross fingers pull. Buckle flashes.

Im going to take off my pants now. says Freda. Theres something I want to show you. Something you need to see.

Belt tongue, buckle, Freda hands hold. Candles flicker. My foots, cold. Red mouth says, We are intellectual chattel. Fabricated to cure anthro ills, to replace worn out anthro parts. But with insanity the skys the limit, so might we be crosspurposed to noiselessly infiltrate enemy installations or, like cats to sailors in marine lore, alert itchy palmed market makers to the next financial bubble. If only.

Buckle Freda hand pulls. Tongue hisses sssss belt swings. Shadows swing. Belt falls wood floorboards Ta ting.

Raww. hollers Capri Macaw. Red tongues lick paws.

Freda says, Doktor Frankenstein thought our tails were an abomination I cannot unveil my maztahpeez to zee vorld viz diz grosz appendage So he tried to nix our tails through a cocktail of genetically encoded checkpoint mechanisms and deletion constructs, dna damaging mixers like oxidation, hyperthermia, starvation, suppressor proteins.

Shiny black pants snap Freda fingers pull. Pkk. My toes curl. Freda says, Heavy metals, olives for this martini, could directly induce gene expression through the actions of metal responsive transcription factors and Hic signal transduction pathways. Cadmium, mercury, arsenic. Down the hatch. Make mine copper, iron and lead. And keepm coming.

Zipper thumbfinger pinches. Zzzzzt.

Using mineral and amino depletion to underexpress metallothioneins, the good doctor induced heavy metal stress, catalyzing cell cycle arrest, and with a splash of unbalanced translocation, a dash of unequal crossing over and a spritz of breaking without rejoining, he was sure he could ultimately shake and stir us into tailless perfection.

Black pants Freda thumbs push, hips sway sidetoside Like the lapping of the tide Freda bows, yellow hair hangs, blue eyes hide. Freda shoulders rises, yellow hair flips, clink clink tag. Skinny thighs. Blackyellowgreen bruises. Shimmer is black underwear.

The deletion voodoo was more blindfolded bingo game than exact science. Imprecise excision only contributed to serious genetic snafus and loss of function mutations. Lejeune syndrome. Monosomy five p. Sick sick. Menkesnwilson. Fragile x. Cri du chat, crying cat syndrome. The CACI discretely ensured none of these mistakes suffered long.

Broke window whistles. Miaou. says Big Orange David, shiny green eyes. Tummy hurts. Miaou.

Smaller deletions, instead of murdering us, gave our kind such bricabrac as malocclusions, cleft palates, harelips and high anxiety. Right. Medium sized deletions led to seizures, gastrointestinal malfunctions, immune system dysfunctions, hypoplasia of the cerebellar vermis, aberrant antibodies in the blood.

Freda foots step, black pants foot kicks Black pants slide shhht. Devon rex hops Paw swat swats Devon rex byebye. My eyes Freda eyes watch. Shiny yellow hairs Freda thighs. Bruises, shins. Scrapes, knees. Thumbs black underpants hide.

Freda sighs. Then theres you n me, the crème de la crème, with our upper respiratory infections, our synesthesia, our oversized and overwired frontal lobes and amygdalae, our chronically inflamed lame brains. We are always ready to blow from the struggle to integrate disparate cognitive functions and assemble coherence in a world made up of complete and mindboggling randomnity.

Black underpants thumbs pull, rub thighs, knees.

Black underpants fall.

Oops. Freda says. Foot kicks, black underpants fly, byebye. Skinny bruises Freda thighs. Yellow fur. Peepee hides. Freda says, Youre the one with a peepee here, Oboy.

Moist fur. Fur soft.

Itll be soft to other parts of you besides your eyes. Freda says. And more than moist. Freda comes, foots pf, pf, pf. Dusty floorboards footprints glow.

Freda turns, pale botty. Grey tshirt hand lifts. Candlelight flickers. White stripes has Freda hips, has botty. Botty finger touches. See this scar. Freda says. No matter how hard Papa Frankenstein studied and analyzed and reduced and oxidized and postulated and hypothesized and tilted his great bald head side to side, he could not deprogram my tail. So, snip snip the old fashioned way. The stupid irony. The ironic stupidity. He mutilates our main source of expression then wonders why we cant communicate. Vhy do you not sprecht. I have only cut out your tongue.

Botty hand slaps.

I remember my birth. He pulled me yowling from the oven with my very own tail and teeth and claws and whiskers and, cue heavy sigh, hopes and dreams. I was fresh and piping hot but I was all bloody wrong and I remember him shaking his big fat fucking head and his thick tongue clucking Nein nein dies wird nicht machen as he snipped off my parts. Lip finger lifts. Tooths show. See here. He ground down my beautiful teeth. Cheek fingers pinch. Electrolysis to burn out the whiskers. The memory of that burning stench still sickens me. But I try to take comfort in the knowledge his obsession with eliminating our tails sunk the whole hybrid program.

Skinny arms fold. Just look at you, next big thing. No functional speech, just mimicked exclamations and yowling. Rolling eyes and flapping arms yiyiyi. You dont even know you have a body unless it gets touched by something else.

My wrist Freda hand grabs. Hot Freda hand pulls. Freda turns, Freda botty my hand touches. Botty hot. Hollers come, my hand pulls. Hollering.

See what I mean. Freda says. Chut chut. Settle. Blue eyes yellow hair hide. Soft moist fur. Soft pale thighs. My hand shakes. Mouth whines. Puffy red Freda lips. Freda hand lifts yellow hair. Blue eyes. Cui cui cui cui. My chest Freda nonees bump. Soft dark fur my hand brushes.

Oboy, I want to take your pants off now. says Freda. My ear red lips tickle. My pants pale hands pull. Darkness flutters.

I want to show you youre just like me. Freda says. Freda smell, hot sweet, sunflower, rooftop, onion sweat. My pants black cross fingers pull. Hollers come Freda hands my nails scratch. My arm Freda hand squeezes Arm hurts Cage birds fweepfweepfweep Wings flaflap Ceiling shadows jump Red yellow green Heads tilt sidetoside. Little black eyes, my eyes.

Hum. says lovebird.

My mouth says Hum. My arms flap. Pants button pulls, zipper zzzzt. My mouth says Hum. My pants Black cross fingers pull, candlelight. My legs. Black blue purple bruises.

Oy, ye been wearin these alan whickers far too long. We need to make a clothesline run.

My underpants Freda hands pull Freda kneels. My peepee yellow hair brushes. My legs jump My ankles Underpants, black pants trap Stumble My arms flap, wave, stripe meridien Freda hand grab. Calmate. My mouth says Hum. Darkness curls, parakeets chatter, my eyes blinkblink. My mouth says Hum. My ankle Freda hands grab. Freda hair my hand pulls.

Ouch, fuck, easy. yellow hair says. Abyssinian runs, flicky tail. My wrist Freda hand squeezes, my hand opens. My mouth says Hum. My ankle pale hands lift, my dirty foot kicks. Jesus. My ankle Freda hands lift, my dirty foot shows.

Freda rises. Yellow hair hand pushes. Whew. Blue eyes flicker, candlelight. My eyes hide. Cage birds hop, twitchy ack ack ack, black shadows flutter, ceiling cracks. Miaou.

My arm Freda hand pulls. Broke mirror comes. Turn around. Freda says. Stripe meridien lifts. My botty Freda finger touches. Check it out. No, the mirror, chickpea. No, stop. Just. The mirror. Smoky red candle Freda hand holds My botty fingertip touches. Shiny mirror botty tightens. Groan.

See there. Youre an amputee, like me.

Stripe meridien Freda hand lets go. Freda stands. In mirror, blackgreenyellow bruises have skinny legs, arms. Collar tag Freda fingers fumble. Im looking like a leopard, arent I. Freda says. Its a hard fork n knife, scaling flats when youre 45 kilos too heavy.

Smoky red candle sits. My hand Freda hand lifts. Youre looking thrashed yourself, chickpea.

My hand pulls. Burning.

Nailsre splitting. Ive got formaldehyde I nicked from the taxidermist. We will harden them.

My wrist Freda hand takes Freda spins Pulls my arms hugging. Hollers. Yes, I know it burns, skin to skin contact burns me too, but hold me We are brother and sister, you and I, arent we, Oboy. Cats of Frankenstein.

Hollers come, arms burn, Fah Better get used to it Freda hands pushes, Freda spins Tummy arms cross, grey tshirt hands lift. Grey tshirt falls, floorboards. Bruises, arms. Freda spins, yellow hair flashes, torn wallpaper shadows jump, My peepee Freda hand touches Floorboards jumps Skindiddy, skiniddyskinskinadidididdy. my mouth hollers, peepee tickles, gets big. Candlelight, pale shiny Freda comes

Boum Boum

My ears hurts. Wood floorboards shakes. Ceiling dust sprinkles. Hollering Freda jumps. Cage birds hoot, haw, flap wings. Scrambling cats Sofa hides. Freda runs hallway, pale bruised botty flashes byebye.

Doorway comes. Hallway cats hunch, ears twitch, eyes blink blink blink my eyes. Dust falls.

Freda, redbluegreen window come. Window Pale hand bangs. Graffitti wall jumps, hits my shoulder. The dance hall. Freda says. Theyre pulling her down. Goodbye red lady.

Long yellow arm Redbluegreen window shows. Rusty lobster claw has yellow arm. Bricks Claw scratches. Bricks fall. Crows wheel, squawk caw caw. My tooths big boum boum hurts, my eyes. My eyes thumbfingers hide. Dust, smoke, float.

My neck Freda breath touches. My shoulders twitch.

The sky is falling, chickpea. Haussmanns only two blocks away now. We dont have much time left.

Flashing light Yellow lobster has, smoky black pipe. Dance hall window hole Yellow lobster claw scrapes. Hoses spray water. Little yellow hats little orange vests. Bricks boum. Black dirt falls, dust twirls, floats. Window hole, bricks byebye. Broke floors, doorways show. Yellow lobster claw drips. Shiver. Heart spinnedyspins sidetoside. My chest hurts. Air hot, chokes my throat.

Take it easy, Oboy. Freda says little. Hum, baby, hum. My shoulder Hot hand touches. My shoulder Fire burns, hollers come. My hand flashes, fire my hand hits. Freda hollers little, light gets little, bricks crash little   black dust   darkness

Thats the time I fooled you Raggedy Andy cried as he ran with the saw through the woods. When he came to where the magic wooden sword was tied to the stump, Raggedy Andy cut the strings. And just as Mr Doodle ran up to catch him, Raggedy Andy jumped on the magic sword and cried, Magic sword, carry me after the paper Dragon to the Magicians castle. And the magic wooden sword flew over the ground so fast Mr Doodle was left far behind.

Light comes. Dust Ceiling cracks sprinkle. My foots kick, elbows hit, stand Hey, watch it you idiot. Freda says, nonees shake.

Broke roof Whining yellow lobster claw pinches. Smoke sputters, black pipe. Lobster whines, roof sags, breaks, crashes, black dusts rise. Little orange vests little yellow helmets, black dusts firehose sprays, yellow lobster. My eyes thumbfingerholes hide.

My mouth says hum.

Progress. Freda says. Lots of noise and banging and smoke and rubble piled to the sky. Meanwhile, the Favelle is eradicated. Loss, retreat, regression, recession. Reversal. Who knows this better than Frankensteins monster stitched together with different body parts. Brought to life. Overjoyed and overwhelmed by life. Sent packing by those who fear and misunderstand him, those whom he would gladly embrace, but who judge him based on nothing but their neurotypically narrow world views of what life is supposed to be based on the light refracted through their weak little excuses for eyes. Banishing him to the northernmost extremity of the globe. North, to le bois. Thats where we are headed, you and I. Or maybe south, to florida, where the pickings are ripe and the weathers fine and my joints wont ache from the rain. Though we would have to convince Swan.

Dusty wood boards Yellow lobster claw clutches. Black smoke lobster botty farts. Yellow helmet orange vest runs, pushes wheelbarrow bricks.

Progress is inevitable as death. Freda says. Red candy Freda hand shows. My fingers take. Our little white picket fence will be unpicketed, our quaint little ivy covered shop shattered, our peely, moldy appartement collapsed. Sweepm up and throwm away. But who cares. Certainly not us. Because theres more than one kind of progress. And not even that big bad lobster can stop our kind.

Metal postcard tree my fingers spin. Ee aa. Ee aa. Tree wobbles. Postcards flash redyellowgreen. Flower smells dizzy my eyes. Pantlegs walk sidebyside. I forgot they had the bird market here on Sundays. O sure. Lets get those lilies then come back and take a look. Finger spins metal tree. Ee aa, ee aa, ee.

Il est tres jolie, eh.

Yes, I can see. Lovable little guy.

Freda says, Look. One of the parrots wot caught my eye. Ces petites vieillards are buying him. See. Gramps in dark blue sailor coat. Wrinkly wench in green polka dot trench coddling the potted carnations. Bloody grey hairs, like your Doctor Dolittle.

New laid eggs, twenty centimes. Chicks and hens

Buy a fine singing bird

Redyellowpink flowers smell big. My mouth says hum. Purple glasses my fingers poke. Earphones. Crouching ballet shoes. Postcards my fingers spin, redblack, whitegreen. Aa ee, aa ee, aa. Cage birds hop, twitter. Rattles. Sawdust. Bird seed. Cheep cheep cheep. Ee aa ee. Ee aa ee.

Book Freda hands open. Lets see. Pages flutter. Legs swing toandfro. Pointy Freda knees long brown coat hides. Black Freda boots, black haversack shiny buckles. Black pants. Long brown coat shows vest. Pink fringe lapels pink fringe waist. Studded belt.

Buy a linnet or a goldfinch

Pages Freda fingers turn. Blue eyes squint. Page finger taps. Here we go. In addition to their brilliant colouration, the fig parrots fascinating and vivacious nature make it among the most attractive of psittacines. They are gregarious, active and playful birds, which become tame easily. A fig parrot, Oboy.

Wings thapthapthapthap. Easy. Easy, feisty good boy. Hand puts parrot wood wire cage. Cage hand takes.

Merci.

Merci beau coup.

It should be borne in mind that fig parrots are very active birds, which enjoy bathing. Fig parrots housed in outdoor aviaries have the charming habit of bathing by sliding down large, wet leaves that Id love to see they are also very curious. During the breeding season, however, they can become very distressed, which can result in them abandoning or even killing their chicks. This does not necessarily take place at the time of the disturbance, but often occurs some days later. Yeah, Im not too keen on motherhood either.

Ringring pass biciclettas. Moped buzzes zzzzmmm

Lilly white mussels Oysters Buy any shrimps

Canal seagulls hang, swoop, shriek wah wah hahaha wah wah wah haha.

Book shuts. Book black haversack hides. I want that fig. Freda says. I want all these birds even that bloody rooster strutting around this ever so genteel Sunday socalled bird market, just a black market full of the stolen and abused, birds nicked far from here. Thus doomed. But with the prefecture next door. Approving. We have to tail someone.

Freda boots jump clompclomp. Metal tree My hand spins.

Come on, enough with the postcards. My arm Hand squeezes. Eeee aa. My back Knee bumps. Oboy. Aa eee. Allons y. Clic clac clic. Stripe meridien my fingers scratch. My ballet shoes spin, follow Freda, shwip shwip. Sawdust. A candelstickell do the tricke. White lion mane, travel trunk wobble Nice small pinted matches Blackgrey sneakers pass, loose wet laces flap flap. Wrinkled grey pants. Green pants frayed turnups. Big shoes walk clip clop dirty little heels peek, peek, peek. Black haversack Freda hand swings.

Bird houses hang. Shadows sway. Door holes black.

Freda says, Theyre tied up, they wont fall on you.

Clac clic clac. Dirty sneakers shuffle, cane passes tap tap tap. Flower dress comes. Excusez moi. Legs waddle. Wheezing. Move it, showstopper. says Freda. Flower dress. Wheezing. Pardon. Freda jumps sidetoside. Bloody hell. Freda bumps, Flower dress arms Freda hands grab. Spinning, table, bump bump, bird seed bags jump. Youre taking up the whole bloody aisle. says Freda.

How incredibly rude. Unhand me.

Rude is the sight of you chewing your cud.

I never.

O yes you have, bossie. Far too many times.

Gasp. Clic clac clic. My coat Potted flowers brush. Flower smells dizzy. Come on, my cowardly lion. Freda says. Nows not the time to drowse among the poppies. Our old baa baas are going astray.

Shadow arm shadow hand holds. Walking. Shadow birdcage, shadow wings flaflaflaflap. Shadow flowers. Sunlight. Dark blue coat, polkadot green. My eyes blink blink.

Do we take the metro, sweetheart. Wood wire cage Hand lifts. Cage finger taps. Green wings flapflapflap. Why dont we walk. Its become such a lovely afternoon. Isnt it wonderf hooosh sunlight hollers. Hurt.

Quiet, chickpea. Its only contrast. My glasses my hands hide. Arms legs swing toandfro. Le metro.

Bird seed sack Freda hand shows.

I used the venus of willendorf as a diversion. Didnt even see me lift it, did you. Bird seed sack black haversack hides clac clic clac. We are going to need more than this, of course. All the refugees we have back at the dollhouse. When we rescue lil figgy, we want to take her feed, too. Remember that wont you.

Fountain sprays. Quai. Cars zoum zoum. Leaves swirl greenyellowredorange, spin, blow. Tall trees groan. Freda passes, leaves black boots kick. Pigeons flapflapflap. Cars zoum zoum.

Buy my drops, twenty a half franc, peppermint drops

Tiddy diddy doll

Yellow Freda tail swings sidetoside. My shoulder Freda hand hits Come on Freda runs tsokka tsokka tsokka haversack bounces cars squeal, holler bee bee bee pavement Freda turns, arm waves Come on, Oboy leaves poof, spin, float. Cobblestones.

Cars sit. Arms legs walk. Burbling.

My hands, ballet shoes run. Freda, pavement come. Freda caws. I love it. Like any dutiful anthro you awaited the light.

Black Freda boots jump. Canal parapet Boots walk. Greygreen water gargles. Dizzy me. Streetlamps. Arms wide, haversack swings, tall walking Freda says, I was only a kitten for one autumn, but I so loved to dive into piles of dry leaves. To feel the crackle against my body. To find bits of leaves later in my coat. Secrets. Glourious. The air smells different. Like the underground has opened up somewhere, some gaping hole we cant see but its letting all the cold damp earthy stuff into the air. That smell is death, Oboy. Innit glourious. Dost

I repeateth myself. Autumn is the best time, its high time, but its no time to relax. Autumn has quickly had its way with the trees. Ravished. Roughed up raw. Left naked and bruised without a farthing for cab fare home. And winters right on autumns heels, ready to fuck with our plan. Anthros wont be leaving their windows open. The rain will be cold and unremitting. Petsll less willingly be rescued. Winter is hard.

Bridge comes. Pavement rough. Freda jumps boots clompclomp. Shadows dart. Arms legs walk. Wheres our happy couple. Freda says. Black strap hand pulls. Prams Hands push, sneakers jog. Puddle Black shoe splashes aw goddamn Clogs make horsey clop clip clop. Bird seed sack Dark blue arm cradles Wood wire cage Fingers holds. Grey hair Pink hat shows. Dark blue arm green polka dot arm hugs. Polka dot arm hugs pink carnations.

Dizzy me canal water makes.

My forearm Freda hand takes.

My forearm pulls. Hollers. Okay okay, kayase, tonto. Just trying to make us fit in with the throng. You, mostly. Hells bells, at least walk on your hind legs. Its supposed to be romantic along here, not jungle book. Watch how the old folks do it. Watch bloody everything. Romantic. Autumn. Scenic walk. Pleasure cruise. All the components are here. If only Swan, instead of you. Sigh.

Big boat comes. Water plumes. Bridge. Boat hides. Little anchored boats water slaps. Boats rock. Upsidedown boats, bank. Dizzy me. Sour throat. Fishing poles dark coats hold. Water. Downstairs cats crouch, fish heads eat. Miaou. Miaou.

Seagulls turn, wheel, wah wah hahaha, wings slash. Dark hand shows metal cage. Cage has clicking crabs. Cuatro franc, cuatro franc. gold belt buckle, red shirt, white tooths say. Dark hand lifts cage, turns. Cuatro franc.

Straw hat coughs, says, Lets have a look, young man.

Cinco por quince. says red shirt.

Crosswalk. Boulevard. Arms legs coats walk, burble, bump. Burn me. Hollers. My hands my pockets hide.

Hush. Freda says. Freda boots clic clac clic, puddle boot skips, steps kerb. My ballet shoes follow. Cars zoum zoum. My mouths says hum. Clic clac clic clac, lights shine, red awning. Metal tables. Flickery glowing jars. Wicker chairs, sitting botties. Legs cross fingers wiggle hands turn. White coats hold metal trays. Movsha plays violin. Hand throws clink clink violin case.

Ping ping. says violin.

Tuaca make a good sidecar, señor.

Uh, lets go with a manhattan.

Ill do a lemon drop.

Tables have plates saucers. Glasses hands hold. Then I go to the spa for five days. He owes you that much. Red, yellow, black waters have glasses. Shiny bubbles have glasses. I jibe well with Pisces always have. Black straws, little umbrellas. Black water Cups have Je ne le crois pas My eyes burnt smells stings.

Its coffee. Freda says. Clic clac clic. Black haversack swings. Its café society. Polite, selfindulgent, all cozy in scarves and cocked hats, chattering about this and that, which is to say nothing at all, aglow with ephemera, whimsy, badinage, the trivialities wot comprise and compromise their existence, striving to fill space and time to the brim and ignore the detritus and silence closing in. The anthro at its pinnacle of normalcy is nothing you need to assimilate.

Freda boot kicks, pigeons thap thap thap, hop, clic clac clic. Mopeds cars zoum zoum. Violin Bow saws. Fahree fahrou. Tray White coatsleeve holds. Pastries has tray. The special is the seafood bisque. Pastry Freda hand grabs. Clic clac clic clac. Pastry Hand puts violin case.

Ping ping. says violin. Gold tooths shine.

Glass pot White coatsleeve tips, black pours. Would you like to see our dessert tray.

Tweedle deedle dee. says violin.

Feather hat. Pomeranian. Saucer little pink tongue flick flicks. Freda says, Mm, tarte aux sardines. Pie Freda hand takes huh Pomeranian squeaks oua oua oua Feather hat hollers Long brown hair jumps, wicker chair falls thump Arms wave garçon garçon White coat comes quescequicepasse Feather hat Voleurs Ma tarte Freda hollers Bloody rat dog runs tsokka tsokka tsokka, sardine pie cawing Freda chews, metal tag black collar clink clink clink. My hands ballet shoes run, follow bouncy haversack.

Buy any clover water

Songs, three metres a centime

Fingers Tongue licks, licks lips. Maybe we should move to rome. says Freda. They know how to treat cats. With an easygoing honour and respect peacefully coexisting, egyptiana, a link to the past rather than an antidote for the future, romans have no interest in conducting worthless misguided selfserving experiments. We can hang out in one of the ancestral centers, behind the pantheon, or the palazzo spada. In the ruins of the piazza vittorio frolicking in the park at the center of the square. Or ride on the back of vittorio emanueles horse Lets just get out of here, chickpea, Lets go somewhere else, things are so fucked up here, anthros are so fucked up. Good hors doeuvres, though.

Allee. Broke sticks. Broke stones. Torn bricks. Biciclettas ringring. Wet newspaper, cups, cans Black boots, ballet shoes pass. Twisted spoon. Pigeons roost, flapflapflap.

Brown shoes. Broke pavement. Orange leaves. Parrot cage. Dark blue coat. Green polka dot. Pink carnations. Noses rub. Lips touch. Tooths show. Cage hand holds. Seed sack. Arm hugs. Blue coat green polka dots hugs. Pink hat blue shoulder rests.

My hand Freda hand grabs.

My hand pulls, hot, hollers, my hands pockets hide. Freda says, Christ. Can you walk any slower. We are not losing these old farts comprends moi. We are going to get that bird. We are going to rescue it from their cozy comfy snuzzling evil. Their well worn, broken in malignity, so gentle n kind.

Its been a beautiful day, ezra. Yes, maddy, dear, it certainly has. Im ready for an early supper. What shall we have. Tomato sandwiches and pommes frites. A bottle of that pinot gris. What about you, Jack. What would you like. We arent naming him Jack, are we. I was thinking Berthold. Well he certainly looks dramatic.

Green feathers plume. Blue coat, polka dot, caw.

Crutch, boot, crutch, sandy stones boots walks. Pavement, corner. Green grass. Red balls Hands juggle, un, deux, trois, quatre. Black coat black hair brown skin. Curled arms legs hands sleep, stone bench. Sweat. Smoke. Pee. Mouth open. Yellow tooth. Snoring.

Windows. Wires clotheslines tremble O look my favourite colour Freda runs Wood planks boot stomps Huh Boots climb bricks chokchokchok Red sweater hand grabs

Clothesline jumps thwip thwip clothes shake, falling boots clomp clomp cobblestones.

Oua oua. Oua oua. Broke stone wall. Dirty orange chow barks Oua oua. Oua oua. Fucking dogs. hollers Freda. Red sweater swings, rocks hand takes, rocks fly pak pak pak hit stones dog yie yie jumps byebye.

Whats wrong with Charlie.

He doesnt like my sweater hanging on the line. Spooks him.

Freda turns, Freda chest red sweater covers.

Its dreadfully pretty. Freda says, red glasses shine. Just like you Freda Oboy said brightly. Ha. If only.

Red sweater Black haversack hides.

Stone steps. Dark blue coat green polkadot coat stand.

Home. Im glad you suggested we walk. Beautiful. All for us.

Wood wire cage swings. Steps shoes climb. Metal tinkles. Door opens. Byebye.

Maybe instead of roma we should run away and join the circus. says Freda. We could move from town to town, wowing audiences with our daring feats of derring do. Maybe we should rescue jewels instead of poor hapless pets, huh. Move to Vienna. You William Powell, me Kay Francis. Liberate zee jewels, ha ha. Wouldnt that be rich. Ding dong bell, theres nothing we could do with jewels. Who would trust buying them off a couple allee cats. No, we will stick to what we do best. Our meeshon. Our raisin detour. Our cousin celery. Rescuing the less fortunate than ourselves.

Freda head tips. Up there, on the north side. See. The light that just went on in that oriel window. See. I guess you do see. I see youve already figured how to get up there, in the span of an eyeblink. Pilaster, moulding, sill, corbel, quoin. Window. Systemizing. If I did a samba you could do it easy, just from watching me. Ive been watching you. The way you move. Silky smooth. A physical savant. Almost as good as Swan. You see relationships, connections, with little effort, judging instantly how far to jump, always landing on your feet. You dont have a thought in your crust o bread, but your body is filled with measurement, analysis, reflection. Your eyes gauge distances, for cartwheels on parapets, for backflips off flagpoles, running on tip toe across wires and cables.

Do they know what theyve made. Arent you as valuable as the hybrid the technocrats had dreamt about. Moreso. No they just want to destroy us for being different, for being an accident, an embarrassment. Like Tobermory.

But the horror is forgotten when I see you move. When you climb and prowl, your tongue between your teeth, the tendons standing out on the backs of your hands, the tops of your feet. The way the muscles in your arms and legs pulse and tighten, and you **aaaah** jump. A mixture of gravity and waggery, the way you run on the edges of things, on brims and brinks, on crooks and corners, on fringes and hems. On donners and blitzens. We are the grinch who stole Berthold, Oboy. And I suddenly realize cooperation has become counteroperational. Two working separately can accomplish twice as much as working together. What Im saying is, dont take it from me. Time you hunted on your own, chickpea. Tomorrow you fly solo. Man the reconnaissance point. See what you can see.

R usty drain hole has rooftop corner. Orange leaf. Brown shoe. Sky blue.

Black tar roof, blue tarp poofs, pointy metal hats shine sun. Rusty fan Metal box hides. Green ivy, parapet. My wrists ankles Ivy scratches. Brick chimneys. Black smoke. Seagulls dive, float, wee wee, ha ha ha ha. Hum. Little narrowboats white plumes. Little cars whiteredblue holler Bee bee bee. Tootoo. Streetcar Dingding, dingding. Burnt smell, dirty smoke smell. Hum. Pavement trees lean, branches whisper wave, little wings flutter browngrey. Tweet tweet. Fruit white apron stacks. Yellow lemon, lime green, orange tangerine.

Parapet moves. My fingers Ivy scratches, ballet shoes. Prip prip prip Corner comes. Mouth hums. Tall metal stovepipes. Tin rooftops shine bright sun. Church steeple green. Fluttery wings. Dormer windows flash, purple glasses brush my lashes. Blinkblink. Allee gutters shine. Sooty broom sooty shoulder bounces Chimney Sweepe Wicker basket skirts brush. Pink tongue mongrel trots clic clic clic clic.

Parapet moves, hands, ballet shoes. Hum. Corner comes. Little allee, little turret. Turret windowsill pigeons roost, snore, coo. Window. Burmese. Window. Monk parakeet. Window. Pekinese. Oua oua puffy paws paddle dirty window.

Hello.

Little courtyard. White hair black dress brown broom. Biciclettas zoum zoum. Stones brown broom sweeps. Shh. Shh. Shh. Shh. Little streetlamps flic flicker little wood carts picture frames chairs. Cool, my forehead, hands, hair.

Us to hello say, come.

Blue tarp flaps snapsnap. Neck hair tingles.

Parapet. Sun. Wings thathatha pigeon lands. Head tilts, blinkblink. Purple glasses Fingers touch, earphones fingers tap paw paw my ears. My eye orange supermiracle bubble wand hides.

My mouth says hum.

Parapet comes. Pigeon struts, flutters, Howdy chum. Parapet warms my hand.

Bricks. Stone heads, shoulders, pigeons roost. White poo streaks grey stone hair. Stone eyes stare. Stone arms, stone hands hold columns. Pigeons coo, scuttle, streaked stone foots hop.

There are you, know we, though you hides wand orange, thee. Unafraid be. Down come.

Orange supermiracle bubble wand Coat pocket hides. Parapet my tummy lies. Mouth hums. Parapet hands grip. Ballet shoes pantlegs coat slide, fall Warbling wings flaflaflaflap my pants, hanging coatsleeves, hair Hum Stone shoulders my ballet shoes tap. Parapet my hands let go. Knees bend Pantlegs my hands brush, hands grab stone hair. Ballet shoes slip, fall Stone neck Arms hug My legs hang Hum White bird poo black specks cracked stone cheek. Stone robe Knots folds my tootsies scratch, fingers hold. Hum. Stone foots jump my spinning ballet shoes Uff ledge hits, arms wave. My botty sits. Big cracked stone tootsies my cold hands take.

Welcome. Before, gargoils see to came ever nobody.

See me.

Everything see we. Toes your of tips, on moon of side dark see, can we. Going are you where, and from came you where, see we. Knowledge this, here up lonely so is it. Lonely so.

Coat pocket, bubble wand, catsup packet, seashell. Catsup packet comes. My mouth says Hum.

Gargoils say, *Matter not does loneliness, then.*

Catsup packet fingers squeeze. Stone heads, shoulders, ledge Pigeons coo chortle roost, beaks duck dart peck. Little turret orange pigeon lands flaflaflap. Little court. Street. Little heads blackyellowred little whiteblackblue shoulders little browngreyblack legs walk tic toc tic toc Heres that Indian restaurant. Is it buffet style. I need to get to the bank. Ich geh gern mit sprühgebräunten Mädchen aus. Giselle wouldnt fuck me cos I was wearing an Armani exchange shirt plus Im too fat n hairy. A alguien le tengo que caer bien allá arriba. Ha ha.

My bent knees black coatsleeves hug. Ledge ballet shoes scrape. Catsup packet Fingers rub. Rough edges scratch. Street, turret, window Fweet fweet fweet says parakeet. Hand lifts earphones, hot ears, cool. Fweet fweet.

Animals loved, steal you, wants she. Animals unloved take, well, would you. Be animals leave, well, would you.

Fweet fweet fweet. Monk parakeet. Hides. Flappy green wings, hides. Ears earphones hide. Catsup packet Fingers squish. Hum.

Fog comes.

Miaou.

Fog slides, canal hides, rooftops rides. Comes.

Miaou. Miaou.

Yeow. Ha ha ha.

Fog blooms. Ghosts come. Shadows flutter, jump, run. Miaou. miaou.   Ha ha ha.   We see you little mouse.

Cracked stone tootsies my hands hold.

Run.

Ballet shoes, botty, rise. Stone robe my hands ballet shoes climb. Rooftop. Pigeons hop. My hands shoes run. Ivy parapet. My black coat ivy scratches, my arms hang. Downstairs window ledge jumps tup tup. Ballet shoes turn. My botty window bumps. Allee. Ashcans. Shingle rooftop. Brick chimney puffs. Fog curls, huffs. Breath goes. Shingles come, hit, Scrat scrat scrat my hands, ballet shoes, climb. Jump peak. Shingles my botty slides shhht hurts Valley hits my shoes Wee wee hahaha Shingles my hands climb scrit scrat Tootsies kick kick Fog says, Miaou. Where goest thou.

Boat hollers awoogah. My ballet shoes jump, arms flap Top spins bahdum bahdum bahdum Fog flutters, rooftop comes hits hands, shoes, bahdum bahdum Somersault Run Duck ropes, wires Chat chat chat chat shingles Shoes boots come Bang bang steel rooftop.

Bricks Hands My ballet shoes Whaaa my elbows, arms, chest Parapet hits, hurt, ballet shoes climb Chimney comes Pigeons thapthapthap Fog hides Rooftop slides Cawing shadows run sidebyside He movin He movin Arms legs flash, puddles splash, rooftops shadows jump Drainpipe Hands grab shhwiii fall Metal rooftop comes bang bang Hands run Bangbang comes Boo gotcha my spinning coatsleeve fog grabs Stomp stumble Aw fuck Rooster hair trips tumbles, metal rooftop elbows knees bang bam bang, fog puffs, rocks, byebye.

My throat Arm chokes purple sunglasses twist Streetlamps flic flic flic You done fo sucka Hollers come, choking arm my claws scratch, shoes kick Fog pokes, pushes me fog has pants, boots, gloves, coats Eyes watch my eyes Hes a fast lil jackrabbit aint he Bien sûr Not bad not bad atall Ay ay ay he do holla though Tais toi crybaby Here you be Street jest like blondie said it was.

Fog flutters Rings fingers white coat spins, gets big, hands clap clap. Black fedora. Green eyes. Gold tooths says, If it int the new little cookie kitten with the red cinnamon eyes. How is Blackeyed Susan.

Fog says, Just broke her wrist, Street. Nothin terrible. We gonna get her fixed up.

Muthafucka spun me off the damn roof. I mo killim.

Hidey seagulls Wee wee wee, haha, haha.

Brown fingers snap, my coat collar brown hands grab, shakes me, hurts Shit head, you dont know what the fuck you doin up in here Red tip cigarette crooked white tooths Yo hula hoop dance could a got my girl Suzie kilt.

Composure, Dainty. No one is dead. Yet.

Brown hands push, brown finger pokes, my chest hurts. Autre temps, shit head. Give you somthin to yell about.

Gold rings, long fingers. Hairbrush long pale hand holds. Green eyes. This brush can be pleasurable. Or it can be a menace. Regard the handle. Filed to a point. Cant slice baguette or cheese, but can excise eye, puncture jugular, impale hand or foot. If you please.

Yo Swan. Member that time you jam it up under the chin a that fulanowhatshisname.

Le Basc.

Hoo wee, Street hoistit that fool right off his feet.

Oom oom mmm. Sounded like a dang seal, with his mouth all stabbed shut like that.

Sho was funny, Swan.

Ouai. Quite a sight, Maidenhair.

Être et durer, Swan.

Être et durer.

My stocking cap flies byebye. My hair hairbrush brushes. My legs kick, shoes kick, arms hold my arms, hurts. My chin Glove pinches, hurts. My chest big little, big, little, top spins bahdum bahdum hollers come. Hurt.

Hairbrush pulls, rasp, rasp Rooftop my ballet shoes kick scuff, Rasp rasp rasp Hollers hot fire my ears, wet eyes, my tummy hard knee hits Oof My knees roof hits Head shakes sidetoside, Huhh huhh Fog hollers awoogah Hairbrush pulls rasp rasp Hair burns Top flutters bahdumbahdumbahdum Hairbrush says, Crimson Rambler one day said he didnt like the old homestead. Thought hed travel, so he went, over the wall on mischief bent.

Streetlamps flic flic flicker. Shadows spin wee wee ha ha ha. Wee wee wee. Ha ha ha. Darkness.

When the men came riding up they were very angry.

What are you doing here beside my ice cream mud puddle. the large man who galloped up first asked in a loud angry tone.

This is a magical ice cream mud puddle. Raggedy Andy said. And we were eating ice cream cones because we thought the ice cream was free.

Oho, you did, did you. Well let me tell you, I am King Growch the Great, and everything in this deep deep woods belongs to me. You shall pay for each ice cream cone you have eaten. Hand me five cents for each cone and hurry up.

All we have is one penny. Raggedy Andy said. He had hardly said it when he knew that he had spoken too soon

Cold wet cheek
      White pants
            Flashing gold tooths say, He ariseth.

My cheek pavement scrapes My hands, knees push, leg crouch. Cough cough. Magpies cry. Court. Trees. My throat Earphones pinch. Purple glasses, black stocking hat lie sidebyside. White pants rise. White coat, red vest, spin, brown boots chak chak. Red hair Black fedora hides. Dark neck Gold chains clink clink, gold rings fingers.

Bo Peep boasted you could run, mooncalf. We saw for ourselves, and are duly impressed. You even neutralized one of our best. But you dont know the heavens yet.

White coat turns, walks. Purple glasses my hands take. Black stocking hat my hands take. Spigot long fingers twist. Water comes, bwoop bwoop splashes. White coat says, Hands, because of the tasks they perform, are middlemen. Hands cater to lower body needs, but also at times must be wuzho.

Washing hands becomes an important ritual. Hands are washed, using separate soap and towels, anytime they may become ritually unclean. Making the bed, putting on shoes, even adjusting ones belt.

Gurgly water White soap Dark hands rub wish wish Dark cheeks dark hands wash Gurgly water Dark hands catch splash splash water. White coat turns. Gold tooths show. Dark wet forehead Dark chin glow, drip drip water. Shivers me.

One may even wash his face and hands whenever he feels his luck leaving him. gold tooths say. Or when he decides to test his luck on an unknown.

Red tip chest pocket. Long fingers pinch, red pulls. Shake. This mouchoir reminds us how brutal life is. How quickly our blood can be snatched from our breast.

Red hanky pats chin, cheeks, forehead.

We remind ourselves we are not Julius Caesar. Keep your enemies close and your Romans even closer. Close enough to strangle.

Red hanky chest pocket hides. Red tip peeks.

Like we counsel all strays we bring in from the cold, dont talk to cozzers, and dont keep secrets from us. Secrets get kitties snuffed. Ha. Saying we hold court over who lives and dies is like saying you decide what befalls the lint in your pocket. What is no jive is our whiskers can pick up within as little as five nanometres thats two thousandths the width of a hair the most incipient dissension or deception, intrigues furtive as field mice tiptoeing in darkness. Intery, mintery, many have tried. Cutery corn, the lot of them cried.

Black fedora long white coatsleeve tumbles. Black fedora long fingers catch. White coat bows. Red hair shines. My neck Long white coatsleeve hugs. My mouth says Hum.

Once we pick up the vibe, we must elucidate which way the fur lies. So, the embrace.

My cheek beard scratches sidetoside. My eyes darkness pushes. My mouth says Hum. Scratchy beard says, We just cleave to whom concerns us, our face pressed to throat, and take some quick shallow breaths through mouth and nose. Those whiffs are always in the money. If we dont like what we smell, kitty cat gets the top hat. Foe, friend. Recruit. Nimporte quoi.

My ear Lips touch. My throat Nose touches. Black fedora fans. Sniff. Sniff sniff. Black fedora fans. Cool.

My mouth says hum.

Long arm goes byebye. Hollers sigh. White coat white pants spin, Gold tooths flash, magpies cry. Red hair Black fedora hides Black brim Long finger traces. Hands clap clap. No mice hiding in your field. Not much of anything. Perfecto.

Dark hand white coat hides. Dark hand shows. Little brown bottle. Lid fingers twist. Lid fingers show, wave. Crouching, hissing grass, shadows jump, thighs, sweat, dirt, fog, bangbangbang, flowers, ashes, blood. Freda. Gold tooths say, Pretenders can fake a tat, can make finger puppets, can name names. But they cannot fake scent. Bottle mouth Palm presses, tips. Shake shake. Dark cheeks, jaw Palm slaps. Little lid gold ringed fingers twist. Bottle white coat hides.

My coat Long fingers grab, pull. My chest, white coat red vest bumps. My cheek rough beard scrapes. My cheek rough beard scrapes. Hollers. My cheeks my hands rub. Dust. Apples. Flowers. Fog. Ha ha ha. Freda. Hollering.

Calmate. Scent says no one can touch you. Scent says you live in our world. Your scent joins our scent. Comprends.

My mouth says hum. My cheek my shoulder rubs.

Boum boum.

My earphones my hands hold. Whine.

Ah, the herald of progress. gold tooths say. Haussmann, le grand croquemort. Even the cemeterys slotted for burial. We admire the irony. At the same time, we must solidify our cash position before the Favelle is completely annihilated. Escape to that île de soleil so far away. Être et durer. Ha. Être et durer. We just need one major score. With so many kitties working on our behalf, yourself now. Ha. Être et durer.

White coat white pants jump, fire escape hands boots climb. Rooftop fog hides. Brown boots cha cha cha cha metal ladder. Gold tooths green eyes holler, You belong to us now. Brown boots byebye.

Miaou. Miaou. fog says. Ha ha. Catch you later, Oboy.

Dirty stone columns. Splintered grey shutters open flat. Windows dark. Street, corner, windows hide fweet fweet fweet Door opens shuts ringring arms legs swing ringring, bright window moves, my eyes hot food smell waters ringring.

Courtyard. Allee. Red candy paper Little black shorthair pounces. Ashcan lies Torn plastic sack Big grey cat hunches Sardine tin tongue licks. Black shorthair trots prip prip prip. My ballet shoes prip prip prip. Black shorthair pounces Big red mouth opens wide, hhhiiihhh, grey paw swats, shorthair tumbles, hops, back arched, legs stiff, see saw.

Crouching big grey cat Ballet shoes pass. Green eyes burn my eyes. Miiine. says big grey.

Me you. my mouth says. Me you. Black shorthair turns, blue eyes my eyes. Little tummy Hungry hurts. My tummy hungry hurts. Blue eyes blink. Shorthair sits. My hand coat pocket hides. My hand shows. Cream cup.

Me you. my mouth says.

Knees, stones. Black shorthair comes prip prip prip, tail raised. Purring. Little cup Fingers hold, purring red tongue laps. Little back, bones Hand rubs. Scabs. Cream cup falls. Cup Black paw bats. Blue eyes, my eyes.

Coat pocket. Cream cup my hand takes, lid hand tears, holds cup, little red tongue jabs. Little white drops fingers, whiskers. Red tongue flic flic flics. Purring.

Shorthair sits, lips tongue licks, whiskers, nose. My fingers red tongue licks, white drops.

Allee stones, my dirty white shoes. Little black paws flicker, follow. Shoes run thapthapthap. Black shorthair comes. Broke wood cart My ballet shoes hide. Black short hair comes Cobblestones shoes slide Peekaboo Shorthair jumps. My shoe Black paw bats.

My legs crouch. Little black shorthair my hand plucks. Purring top spinnedyspins inside. Black shorthair my coat hides. Ballet shoes prip prip prip, allee, courtyard, footbridge, dizzy brown water, allee stones, wheel barrow, dirty bones, allee narrow, broke wagon, round corner, white pickets, leaky dormer, Dollhouse. Black shorthair cries.

Safely you may always hide. my mouth says.

Gate, little weedy court, rattly ivy leaves. Stocking hat, earphones, Ivy scratches. Darkness. Dusty old shop. Black shorthair meous, dim stairwell cats crouch, eyes pingping.

Upstairs, flickery doorway, dim flat, brown sofa, Freda lies. Eyes, skinny pale arm hides. Freda says, So, youre alive. And in one piece. And you bear our scent. I knew youd do it.

Earphones Hand pulls, earphones fall, mattress. Purple glasses Fingers take. My arms flap flap.

Dont be that way. Swan wanted to know how youd do. I had to.

Black coat Fingers open black shorthair my hand shows.

Miaou. shorthair says, legs stiff, paws wide, whiskers twitch sidetoside.

Freda arm lifts blue eyes blinkblink blue eyes my eyes. My eyes hide. My mouth my hand hides.

Baby. my mouth says.

Freda rises. Floorboards creaks, Freda comes. Shorthair hands take. Crooked Freda nose pink nose rubs. A baby. cawing Freda says. How sweet. Yes, we must save the babies most of all. Who knows what trap youdve fallen into, little one. And what nightmares youdve faced in your short lil fork n knife. Youre so skinny, flea bitten. Ill call you Mittens, cos a your big funny paws. Mittens, lets get you a snack.

Freda turns, walks creakcreak wood floorboards Skinny torn red stockings cats swarm, rub. Stained kitchen counter Black shorthair sits. Dented tuna can lid Freda fingers peel. Eat up, little one. Freda says, hands shoo cats bye bye. Shorthair crouches. Blue eyes, my eyes.

Me you. my mouth says. Little purring mouth eats.

Freda turns, blue eyes my eyes. Fabulous. Freda says. Youre fabulous, Oboy. You whispery mystery.

My hand, coat pocket, Freda comes. My eye Orange supermiracle bubble wand hides.

I have a present for you, too. says Freda. Fingers black crosses. Black collar thumbfingers pinch. Metal tag has black collar. I was going to wait until after your first solo mission, but surviving Swans inspection deserves a prize.

Metal tag clinks. Black collar Freda hands put my neck. My eyes hide. Dont fuss. Freda says. After a while, youll forget its there. My throat, chin, fingers tickle, buckling collar. Freda lips parted. Freda smell my smell. My throat Freda breath warms. Collar cold. Metal tag my fingers hold. Freda hands fall. Counter Freda leans. Botty bounces.

Youre part of us now. Freda says.

Red paint smears mouth. Tooths white. Black paint rounds blue eyes. Eyes damp dark. My eyes hide.

O, you smell so good. says Freda, coming.

My rope belt Black cross fingers tug. Its okay, chickpea. Freda says little. Cotton candy, sweat, wood smoke, mint, Freda. Me.

Cage birds fweepfweepfweep Ceiling shadows flap. Pants button pulls, zipper zzzzt. My pants fall. Legs. Bruises. Knee. Red cut. My mouth says Hum.

Freda says, You smell like Swan. Mmm. Its the greatest scent.

My arms flap. Candlelight shivers. My underpants Freda hands pull Flap flap Darkness curls Cui cui cui cui Little Lulu trots byebye.

My mouth says Hum.

Blue eyes flicker, candlelight. Cage birds hop, twitch ack ack ack, black shadows flutter cracked ceiling. Cat eyes bingbing.

Torn red stockings fall. Black undies fall. Pink tshirt lifts. Pink tshirt falls. Candlelight, pale Freda comes. Nonees sway. Freda eyes shine.

Freda says, Cats of Frankenstein.

My hands Freda hands take, pull, Freda turns, pointy shadows back shows. Skinny waist my arms hug. My peepee Freda botty tickles. Yellow hair, cinnamon, dry flowers. My mouth groans.

Freda says Look, sir. Look, sir. Mister Knox, sir. Lets do tricks with clits and cocks, sir. Lets do tricks with dicks and twats, sir.

Hum. lovebird says. My mouth says Hum. My peepee warm Freda botty rubs. My mouth says Hum.

Hug me. says Freda. Thats it. Quiet. Stay with me, Swan.

My peepee fingers take. Oboy. my mouth says.

So hard. Freda says. My hand Freda hand takes. Soft thighs my fingers tastes. Fur my fingers taste. Fur soft, wet.

Wet and soft. Freda says. My hand Freda hand pushes, wetness my fingers poke. Dont be afraid. says Freda. Thats, like that, ouai. Thats it. Right there. O. Boy.

Oboy. my mouth says.

Your other paw goes here. says Freda. Fondle my breast.

My hand Freda hand takes, puts soft nonee.

Nonee. Freda says. Soft. My hand squeezes. Yellow hair, dust, sweat, flower. My peepee hand rubs. My peepee tingles. Nonee My hand squeezes. Freda groans, turns, my chest hand pushes. Dont spill just yet. Mattress Freda kneels. Mattress hands knees. Candlelight shines dirty heels, curved botty, wings shoulders, flutter. Kitties come, whiskers twitch, Freda nonees Noses sniff. Freda hisses. Scat.

Kitties prip prip prip.

Freda shoulder, cheek, red mouth, puffy lip, blue eyes my eyes. Dont just stand there, Oboy. botty says. Get on your knees.

Striped botty wiggles. Kneel. says Freda. My calfs Rough scratchy heels kick tongue clicks my knees bend Mattress my knees thumpp Freda botty wiggles Hands knees Stripes glimmer candlelight. Dark split botty smells dizzy. Fur shows. Yellow hair falls, pale neck glows. Black collar candlelight. Reaching hand thighs show. My peepee black cross fingers rub. Hold still. Freda says. My peepee Freda fingers rub sidetoside, scratchy fur. Wet. My peepee Freda fur tickles.

My peepee wet pushes, fur hides.

O. Freda says.

Cats of frankenstein. Freda says.

My tummy striped botty slap slap slaps Tags clink, clink, clink, wet fur, peepee, pushes, rubs, birds Ark ark ark thrash cages, feathers drift Fweep fweep fweep Shadows wings blink Wallpapers Cat eyes bingbing Miaou My arm Freda hand takes, pulls Freda says Lie on me Freda lies flat mattress My peepee Freda wet Freda groans back damp.

Burning comes little. Burns. Pushing.

Thats it. says Freda. Move with me. Im almost, Im almost, almost there. God. Damn. Swan.

My head tingles My peepee tingles Freda wet Not yet Not yet My chest, top spins da dah da dah da dah Hot my mouth wants Water My head Sparkles hit, tingles Hollers come My mouth says Hum My peepee pinches, burns, my peepee pinches, pinches. Hollers. Come.

It burns. rocking Freda says, shoulders shrug It bnrus, O, it bunrs, O god, I cnat tkae it, btie my ncek, cmoe on, cmoe on, btie my ncek, fcuk me, god, it bruns, it bunrs, O, I cnat tkae it, I cnat sotp, hrury, sotp, stop, sotp Black collar Neck My tooths bite Freda hollers Mattress shakes Candle falls Birds holler Bang bang cages Cats spit, paws hit, cats yowl hiss My ears hurt Goddamn it Freda head turns fast Collar pulls hurts my tooths Eyes wet candlelight Get off me you fuikcng ioidt Freda arm swings, my cheek Claws scratch Freda mattress floorboards drop. My botty wood floorboards hits. My back, my head. Thonk.

My tummy, peepee, shine wet. Pinching gets little. Freda rises, turns. Floorboards. Wax fur drip drip drips. Shiver. Wax drips glow. Freda comes. Darkness comes, my eyes darkness hides.

Raggedy Andy jumped out of the little doll bed and tip toed to the door. The night was dark, but Raggedy Andy had two very good shoe button eyes and as they were black shoe button eyes, Raggedy Andy could see very well in the dark. And what do you think. Raggedy Andy saw Raggedy Ann standing in the moonlight of one of the doll house windows.

Shoe button eyes shine. Metal tag black collar twinkles. Cotton stuffed head falls, shoe button eyes yarn hair hides. Raggedy Ann spins, toe big black boot spins. Flash flash White cotton thighs, long brown coat hides. Raggedy Ann chin lifts, white cotton throat, darkness moonlit.

Raggedy Ann says, A. E. I.   O, you. White cotton knee lifts, long brown coat. Knee Moonlight shines. Black boot kicks, white leg stiff, trembly moonlight. Brown coatsleeves rise, darkness cotton soft fists punch flip flap Big paper wings open. Floorboards black boot heel stomps Raggedy Ann arms drop, white knees red wing hides, blue wing flutters red wing, sigh.

If I were a dickory dock Id be seven thirty on the dot. Raggedy Ann says.

Black shoe button eyes shine.

My shoe button eyes hide. Snoring birds Draped cages hide.

Raggedy Ann says Look at me, chickpea. Me, your visual semaphoric cue for aleph, alpha, A. A number one, A the scarlet letter, I am wot I am the beginning of time and matter, from the glottal plosive uh o to old Plutarchs lunar vowel.

Raggedy Ann jumps, big black boots klonk klonk floorboards, my ears hurt, red wing, blue wing, flutter moonlight. Raggedy Ann says, A is for acid, for alanine, adenosine, or a red blood cells antigen, or the federal reserve bank of boston, or the mass of an atom per annum carved in the forehead of the golem, the la la la frequency, the ox in metonymy, ox, the first of all necessities, the deevine energy of creation wot animates business and agriculture, society and its delectation, you know the fucky and the sucky, from anarchy to zukofsky.

Big black boots shuffle heel toe heel toe clic clac clic clac clic Raggedy Ann slides, moonlight, darkness, moonlight, Toro, toro, like the matadoro. says Raggedy Ann, From newfoundland to labradoro, aces in my gilt edged corner pocket, A is well fleshed and normal in shape, the grade only the best animal carcasses and eggheads make, though only the carcasses are free of protruding hairs and feathers, A is the hit side of a 45, top notch, first rate, better than okay, on the flip side theres not, nothing, dee void, and who hasnt forgotten that oldie but goodie, the black plague.

Yarn covered head folded Raggedy Ann arms hide, wings wave blue, red, Raggedy Ann turns, she turns, black boots clic clac clic, Poke your tongue against your lower front teeth and say A, ah, aa. A, ah, aa. Diphthong, broad or flat, lets make papa mad as a hatter without his vitamin, be it alcohol, or carotene, so he dont go night blind, see.

Redblue wings swing, rag doll head, darkness. Long brown coat opens, cotton shoulders shrug, coat falls, cotton wrists show, darkness. White neck, collar black, moonlight. Metal tag shines. Black shoe button eyes watch soft cotton nonees sway, moonlight. Raggedy Ann says, Come on, say it.

Bubble wand my hand holds, hides my shoe button eye.

Not even going to try, huh. Raggedy Ann says.

Feeling shy, chickpea. Raggedy Ann says. White cotton body moonlight shines. Cotton arms, cotton legs, darkness.

Raggedy Ann turns, she turns, darkness, arms flap, long brown coat jumps, hides cotton shoulders, paper wings flutter, red moonlight, blue darkness, blue moonlight, red darkness, candy heart spins, cotton soft chest hides.

Okay, heres your visual for E. says Raggedy Ann. Red wing flaps high. White cotton knees blue wing hides. One thirty on the dickory dock, see.

My shoe button eye Bubble wand hides.

Remember this now. fluttery wings say. All anthro intellect is based on E, E as epsilon, epsilon as ei, ei meaning if, if, if the wise men, old and wooden, those semites, greeks, romans, lent me their Es, E for the sound of breath, the sound of prayer, then thou art fully Apollos holy letter, if the fifth, then the number five, five senses five sages, hey, if blind Euler moiled all night over his transcendental number, two point seven one eight two eight, et al, then who et all the monosodium glutamate, if Plutos five tidy solids, then Homers five poesy worlds, if E is a rhythm and power constantly renewed, if the shape of E evolved from a semitic dude to a phoenician kitty, then why cant anthros evolve into a cat. Answer me that.

E is epsilon, is electron, is naked like me, a fetish in this vestibule of delphi snuggled up beside Octavians golden wife Livia, E is for eta, for electric fields and brazen athenians, E is creamy fat soluble antioxidants smeared copiously on the sunburned skin of that age old question, the feminine direction.

Moonlight Raggedy Ann spins, floorboards black boot stamps, E means man in prayer, and this sinners not just praying, hes shouting for joy.

O boy. my mouth my hand hides.

E is the worshipper seeking at first transcendence from some long distance divinity to transcendence from the galoot next door, you know, that so called god in all of us. E is Mercury, is Venus, or flute and violin, the big apples subway line, E is the sun, the wind, the soul, breathe and blow a happy clappy Mi mi mi mi mi mi mi, E is new brunswick and east london, is semisynthetic entactogen, em dee em ay, anthros all of fourteen rolling ecstasy, grasping empathy, euphoria, exhiliration, evenhandedness, heightened self enlightenment, energy, in the end, little more than a sweaty, raving, mysterious mummy, whos got Spanish class mañana.

Raggedy Ann turns, she turns, black boots say clickety clic clac clickety clic clac, long brown coat opens Cotton skin flashes white moonlight. Black collar tag winks. You can say E just by baring your teeth, the tip of your tongue touching the lower gum, E, though of course, there are fifteen other sounds E makes, including none.

Raggedy Ann spins, comes, moonlight, darkness. Floorboards spin byebye, my cotton foots, my cotton hands, flashing moonlight, Raggedy Ann shoe button eyes shine darkness. Come on, chickpea, dont run away.

Birds coo, birds snore. My shoe button eye bubble wand hides.

Dont really fancy the sound of E, huh, my crouching, hyperventilating, chickadee. Raggedy Ann says. Does the sound buzz like bees inside your head, do its wings stir the albumen, scuff the albedo, or perhaps, like E, you realized being silent covers up a lot of shortcomings.

Swinging red wing falls, passes cotton soft waist. Blue wing swings high, covers cotton stuffed head. Seven of the clock. Raggedy Ann says, chin lifts, darkness. The letter I was once a questionable, voiced pharyngeal, fricative, that is. To the phoenicians the word was yod and it came from yad and the meaning was hand, I began life as the pictogram of an arm and hand, which meant force, violence Snap snap paper wings shut, paper wings open Unless the pictogram had an arm with a hand holding bread, Brot, pan. Then it meant offering or gift. I was the same as J was the same as Y, but when you get down to it, I is the majestic majuscule wot forms almost all other letters. Are you still with me, chickpea.

Raggedy Ann arm high, elbow bends. Blue wing turns. Raggedy Ann says Alive, the letter bends and rotates, articulating at the elbow and the wrist Blue wing waves With or sans serif, the miniscule with its tittle distinguishes itself from the hoi polloi of nearby scrawly letters, to the greeks I was iota, the arm reversed, the only difference between homoousios, Jesus the same substance as God the papa, and homoiousios, Jesus of similar substance. What the fucks the difference, why dont we rabbit and pork about I as blinding supergiant stars, I as the planet mars, a trombone, svelte and internecine, as the roman numeral one, or the number nine, isoleucine and iodine, as interest rates, as spit takes over orbital inclination, as electrical currents wot burst like celebratory smash cakes from miletus to corinth to bocotia, as hot cakes poured in imaginary units, as identity matrices or inertia, like postcards of minarets.

Cotton knee raises, knee swings wide. White cotton thighs. Black yarn shows. Wings wave. Say I with your lips open, tongue held at the front of the mouth, behind the lower teeth. I. I. I. Crazy. Wont you at least try. Raggedy Ann says. Black boot stamps floorboards. What Im trying to teach you needs to stick in your crust of bread, chickpea, even at best as pentimento or palimpsest, not simply the rant of some verbigerating termagant.

Raggedy Ann yarn hair hangs damp over black shoe button eyes. I broke up with Y in 50 BC or so. Poor guy, hated to see him cry. That is to say, I is the most personal of vowels, the most personal of pronouns. I meaning me emerged as pastiche of the old English pronoun ic, the German ich, during the 1400s, the great vowel shift, to be polymathic. Raggedy Ann spins, pink cotton skin flashes.

I meaning Freda emerged from a test tube only 20 years ago, 25, 30, whos counting. Raggedy Ann says. Tag red wing touches. Tag trembles. Freda. Say it. Can you say it, fudgling. Say my name. Freda. Raggedy Ann comes. Clic. Clac. Clic. Shadows moonlight moist pink cotton body flutter. Damp cotton tummy big little, big little. Pink cotton nonees sway, darkness.

I realize, unlike me, youre not given to prolixity, but can you at least. Can you at least. Cant you at least tell me Im pretty. says Raggedy Ann. Just this one thing.

Tell me Im worth more than a jot and a tittle, and not just cos, not just, not because I just let you fuck me. Red wing blue shut snap snap. Wings fall chac chac floorboards. Draped darkness, birds whistle, snore. Long brown coat falls whoof darkness. Raggedy Ann stands close, naked hot, hollers bubble. My shoe button eye bubble wand hides.

Fuzzy white bit has red felt lip.

I was just dancing for you, like a fool with those cheapo paper fans. says Raggedy Ann. Its not like I expect you to shower me with roses or silver, but a girl needs a little validation. Especially after she just. I dunno, I just wish. I wish you could talk so you could tell me Im pretty. Im pretty, arent I, even though Im all bruised up and my hairs tangled n greasy and my teeth are yellow. Arent I.

Hell, Oboy. I always forget your mouth is painted on.

Raggedy Ann spins, she spins, cotton botty stripes shine, big black boots clic clac floorboards, Raggedy Ann spins, comes clickety clic clac, clickety clic clac, wet glistens arms, back, spinny candy heart Pink cotton chest hides, shoe button eyes black, felt lips red,

White bit has red felt lip

Raggedy Ann spins close, fuzzy white bit has red felt lip, White bit puffs, spins, my cotton hand catches.

Little bird feather.

Raggedy Ann says I know, its terrible. Its awful, I know. But sometimes I just cant help myself. Candy tooths Red felt lips show. Tooths wet red.

Sometimes the catside wins out. Raggedy Ann said.

Raggedy Andys cotton soft hand closed around the feather. The birds grew quiet in the cages. The candlelight flickered and hissed and went bye bye. In Raggedy Andys shoe button eyes came the darkness. Darkness.

My eye orange supermiracle bubble wand hides.

Little me, black tree, blue sky, magpie.

Rusty updown drainpipe rattles crumbly red bricks. White quoin stones clip clop updown corners crumbly red bricks. White stone mouldings sigh.

Fig parrot whistles. Oriel window open high.

Sitting brown bench, stripe meridien top spinnedy spinspins. My throat collar pinches.

My mouth says hum.

Supermiracle bubble wand coat pocket hides. My eyes purple glasses hide. My ears earphones hide.

My mouth says hum.

Coat pocket my fingers fumble tumbly cream cups.

My mouth says hum.

Little cup White tape fingers pluck. Lid fingernails tear. Cream pours cool sweet. Cup my tongue licks. Lip my tongue licks. Brown bench little cup sits.

Old chaires to mend, old chaires to mend

My mouth says hum.

Rusty drainpipe comes. Collar tag clinks. Rusty drainpipe my hand rattles. Blue sky sighs. White quoin stones rise. My arms reach My knee lifts Stone joints Fingers tootsies grip. My arms tremble shake, taped fingers pull joints, hurt, tootsies push, climb. My breath hot, purple glasses steam.

Court. Little black tree. Little brown bench. Magpie. Little cream cup little black beak pecks.

Climbing. Oriel window open. Grey curtains rustle. Fweet fweet fweet. Windowsill my hand grabs. Stone moulding my foot pushes. Windowsill my hand grabs. Tweet tweet twee.

Windowsill my hands pull. Sill my tummy slides, foots kick, my cheeks earphones grey curtains brush. My hands Stiff blue carpet comes, somersault, backbottyfoots, rise. Cigarette smoke, damp, dust, meat, boiled cole. Spoiled milk. Splintery wood perch red cheek Fig parrot sits. Head twitches.

Who you. fig coos. Blinkblink red eyes.

Raisin my fingers pinch. Green wings fluster, cage bars claws hop hop cluck cluck fweet, cluck cluck fweet. Raisin Darty beak snatches Gimme. Chuckles.

Little red hanging house says Toc tic, toc tic.

Cage, splintery perch, black beak rubs clic, clic. Red bib fluffs. Green wings flap Sweet sweet sweet. fig says. Raisin my fingers pinch. Black beak darts hahaha.

Cage hook hangs. My hand lifts cage. Green fluttering. Door comes. Doorknob my hand pulls. Lock my fingers turn. Snic snac, snic snac. Knob my hand pulls. Shut.

Wrong way. says black beak.

Earphones say Dadum dadum dadum. Lock fingers turn snic snac Doorknob hand pulls.

Door shut.

Wrong way. says chuckly red cheeks.

Dadum dadum dadum. My mouth says hum.

Shivery grey curtains come. Swingy cage my hand hangs, hook. Gate my hand opens.

Grey claw Dirty tape finger pokes. Green wings fan Cage bars claws climb Hop hop hop Green head flickers. Blinkblink red eyes. Fig peels. My finger grey claws pinch. Green wings flitter.

Tell me a secret. black beak says.

Fig my hand lifts. Little green forehead my finger scratches. My mouth says, Happyhalloween.

Little red hanging house says, Toc tic toc tic toc tic. Hall, cracked door, squeak, squeak, squeak.

O, Felix.

O baby.

Fig chuckles, Check it out my finger claws pinch. Hall. Cracked door comes, my foots blue carpet scratches. O, o, o yeah. says cracked door. My hand pushes.

Bed arms legs tootsies pinch Green blanket pushes, pulls. Head hands hold Mouth mouth rubs Back hands pull Green blanket pushes, pulls. Bed shakes, squeaks, rattles, bump bump bump wall Thats it thats it Fig leans sidetoside, blink blink. Oolala.

What the Scwee saw scwee, arms wave, legs kick Who the fcuk are you Waht are you donig wtih taht brid.

Door my hand shuts. Blue carpet spins, scratches, green wings flutter, my foots puh puh puh. Clink clink collar tag.

Toc tic toc tic. says little red hanging house.

Saw screee saw. Thump thump. Get up, Felix.

Green fig wings flap, fweet fwee fwee My finger claws pinch Doorknob My hand twists rattles Dark shine metal locks snic snac, snic snac. Wrong way, ach ach. Shut.

Hall door swings. Light shines. Faw faw faw faw comes swingy nonees. Hey. Gimme that damn bird.

Its that pet burglar, baby. The papers say call the police.

If we wanted the cops we shouldve called yesterday. Baby says. Hey. Black coat Red fingernails grabs Brown eyes hot hurt my eyes Gimme that bird
Hollers come

berfoe I taer yuor eras off

Red fingernails black hat byebye.

Cuckoo. Cuckoo. hollers jumping blue bird, little red hanging house, peekaboo blue bird jumps jumps Cuckoo my arms flap Hey fig jumps, wings blink thathathatha My dusty red hands chase Green tablecloth hip bumps Hes lost it baby watch out Fig parrot flies thapthapthap grey curtains ruffle.

Byebye Fig.

O cishrt. holler nonees. Yuo bsartad uoy let hre go.

My arms Red nail hands slap Grey curtains Hands push My foots Windowsill comes My shoulder Sash hits Windowsill foots pap pap O Little courtyard. Little black tree. Little fig parrot. Come find me.

Grey curtains flap flap My botty Rednail hands push Windowsill spins Drainpipe jumps Bang hits my hands My foots crumbly brick wall hits Drainpipe squeaks black coat Foots patta patta pat crumbly red bricks. Falling.

Hoo wee. oriel window says. Lookit im go.

Rusty drainpipe breaks Aawwiiii falls Courtyard stones jump hits my red dusty foots, my hands. Drainpipe bang. Owie.

Lamppost chattery magpie flutters. Black tree fig parrot clic fweet fweet, clic fweet fweet. My arms legs tremble. My damp skin Cool crosses.

Baby hollers, Goddamn it, Felix, my parents just got that damn bird They get back from holiday theyre going to shit Get down there and get Bertie back.

He broke the drainpipe.

O, and takin stairs just wont do, huh, hero. Here, Bertie. Bertie. Here pretty boy. Come to mama.

Well, I dont think it minds like a dog, baby.

You got all the answers, dont you. Wall, ah caint sleep with Bertie cheepin in the baidroom, he says.

Baby.

Say, whah cant lets kipe im in the livinroom, bah thet big ole winder, he says. N lets keep thet there winder waaaad open, sos he got thangs t see. And burglars can climb up and steal him from me. You nitwit.

Baby, it aint my fault.

Shut up.

Baby.

Window shuts.

Little me, black tree. Twittery fig parrot hops branch branch. Red eyes blink. Red bib ruffles. Brown bench my dusty red foots stand. Mouth whistles. Raisin dirty tape fingers show. Happy happy happyhalloween.

Redgreenyellow head shakes. Fig twitters I m I m I.

High tree, high eaves, pink sky, fig flies.

Bubble wand has my hand. My eye hides.

Allee, shadows. Allee, bunny cries.

Bunny tummy hungry hurts. Bunny cries. Bricks, pink tippy top window, bunny cries. Elbows my crouching knees sits. Hurty ears my hands hide. Boxes, ashcans, torn plastic sacks. Purple sky. Upstairs bunny cries. Glow, shadows, pink window shows.

Chim chiminey, chim chiminey, chim chim cheree.

Bright downstairs window, hot greasy fish fries. Fishy fish waters my eyes. Bright downstairs window hollers Badda badda badda. Beebeebeebee. Bad badda badda. Beebeedybeep.

Allee whining mopeds pass. Allee shoes pass Clop clop clop. Cobbed grit cold, my back. Collar my fingernails scratch. Coat pocket, little cups, cream.

Chim chiminey, chim chiminey, chim chim cheroo. Good luck will rub off when I shakes hands wit you.

Lid my fingernails pinch, pull. Cream cool, my tongue. Torn little cup my fingers sit stones. Allee. Rooftop. Glow, tippy top window, bunny sighs. Door shuts, glow hides. Darkness comes, purple sky.

Cream cool, sweet. My foots. Torn little cup my fingers put torn little cups. Rising black coat Cob scratches. Cob coldrough my palms. My knees hurt. Hurt my legs kick, kick, kick byebye. Purple glasses my fingers push.

Allee, bricks, windows comes. Cobblestones hardcoldwet. Fire escape drips. Shivery me. Ladder Corner bricks make. Ladder my taped fingers pull. Fingers legs arms tootsies hurt. Fire escape balcony comes. Balcony railing my hand takes. Dark sky. Breath goes, railing swings, balcony hits tum tum my foots. My fingers my mouth sucks, byebye hurt.

Bright open window greasy fish fries. Grey sleeve, little hand, hot fish red spatula flips, frying pan. Beebeedy beebeep beebeep. hollers grey sleeve red spatula.

Badda badda badda. hollers waving fork.

Metal stairs cold my climbing foots. Pink window, dark. Black coatsleeve my hand pushes. Skinny jimmy bracelet my fingers ravel wang wang. Windowsash jimmy slips. Jimmy pushes Round catch. My hands hurts. Round catch turns. Chattery hollering bright downstairs window. My wrist Jimmy wraps, black coatsleeve hides. Sash lifts Rattle rattle rattle.

Tape fingers dirty. Black coat my dirty hands rub, rub, rub. Dirty.

Darkness pink curtains show. Ceiling monkeys hang, turn. Fuzzy rug my foots. White cage, little breaths. Wisp. Wisp. Wisp. Curled bunny white cage has. Bunny smells soft. Warm. Fuzzy bunny my hands lift, put bunny black coat sling. Bunny my black coat hides.

Pink curtains my hands push. Dusty sill my foots tastes. Little allee windows shine. Pipes, grey boxes, spinny metal onions, cob roof. Fire escape colds my foots. My tummy Bunny bumps Black coat bunny whines. Soft black hair my taped fingers rub. Big dark eyes. Bunny nose twitches, bunny mouth sighs. Soft fuzzy ears my fingers rub. Big dark eyes shut.

Downstairs window, pale moon black shirt leans. Badda bad baddabadda. pale moon says. Pale moon shines damp, streetlamp. Redtip cigarette Hand waves. Badda badibad. Redtip cigarette Hand puts damp pale mouth. White smoke blows. Smoke rises. My nose, my eyes. Dizzy.

Fire escape. Allee. Cob roof. Allee stones shine little allee. Cob roof. My hair cold flutters. Little white dots torn cream cups allee allee allee. Cob roof.

Bunny black coatsleeve hugs.

Fluttery pink curtains window. Bricks. Yellow curtain window. Bricks, cracked window, noisy glow. Corner ladder bricks make. Little allee glows.

Downstairs window redtip cigarette Damp pale moon smokes.

Pink curtains wave. My foots Windowsill comes. Bunny sways, black coat. Window my palms hold. Fog makes.

Bricks my hand grabs. Rough bricks my foot slides, taps windowsill. My tummy Bunny kicks. My damp hair cold flicks. Breath comes, breath goes, my foot jumps windowsill, kicks my foot, bricks my hands grab, hold.

Fog makes, dark yellow curtain window. Sill, white paint peels, scratches my foots. Red bricks my arm hugs. My foot slides, black coat red bricks scratch, scratches my cheek. Bricks my arms hug. Little allee stones shine. Breath comes, breath goes, foot jumps, windowsill hits, bricks hands grab. Cracked window flutter noisy light. Skinny legs. Socks dirty white.

My arm, black coat, bunny sighs. Wisp. Wisp. Wisp. Brick ladder my fingertips my tootsies grab. Bricks rises slow. Heavy hurts my arms my legs, my shoulders. My hot damp hair, cold. Black coat brick ladder rubs. Bunny sighs.

Badda badda bad. says downstairs moon.

Pale moon Smoke hides. Blink blink. Moon eyes my eyes. My eyes hide. Red bricks rise. My fingers, my arms shake. Bad badda bad. pale moon hollers. Bad badda bad, bad badda bad.

My tummy tickles Brick ladder pulls Bricks my tootsies fingernails scratch Bricks fly byebye, bunny black coatsleeve hugs, allee stones jump, my ankles my knees sparkles burn owwwwieee, My hands stones slap slap, fussy bunny swings Baddabaddabadda. pale moon hollers. Beebeebeebeebee. red spatula hollers, high windows open, hollers, hollers.

Stones run, my hands, my foots, corner, rue, allee, ashcans, streetlamps, corner, bobbing downstairs trees, shrubs, white pickets comes. Dollhouse. Bunny whines. Bunny leg kicks, tickles my side.

My mouth says, Safely you may always hide.

White pickets, peely entrée door, dusty shop, squeaky steps. Hallway cat eyes bingbing. Flickery doorway. Candle fires flutter. Freda turns, candlelight. Shiny tag black collar winks. Purple glasses my hands take. My eyes hurt, watery. Blink blink.

What took you. Freda says. Youre all sweaty.

My mouth my hand hides. A, e, i, o, u. my mouth says. Black coat my hands open. Sling. Bunny. Bunny eyes shut, bunny mouth huffs, fuzzy head my arm rests.

What the hellre you doing with that.

Bunny. my mouth says.

O. Good one. Freda says. Dont bunnies have fur. Dont bunnies have long ears. Dont bunnies have whiskers and carrots and easter eggs. Do bunnies wear diapers and pjs and gaga and googoo you bloody dipsy doodoo.

My ears Buzzing buzzes. Freda comes, breath hums, blue eyes my eyes.

You cockeyed cockleshell. Freda says. You errant errand boy. Havnet you eevr seen an anthro baby before. Are you relaly taht blodoy daft.

Fuzzy bunny head my hand pets. Big grey bunny eyes show. Bunny mouth opens, bunny gums, bunny tongue, bunny lips big, red. Bunny cries.

Freda says, They might sound a lot alike when they bawl but adam n eve me, a baby is no bunny. So, you need to take it back right now. Huh. Wha. You cant. Course not. Fuck. My collar Freda fingers pull. Choking. I go and give you your own collar and this is what you do. And wot hppeaned to the gddoman fig prarot I snet you to rcesue.

Bunny Freda hands grab My chest Freda elbow hits. Hollers come, burn, bunny Stiff Freda arms hold, hollering bunny mouth big, legs kick. Waht in hlel am I sppuosed to do wtih tihs rdonet besdies go to jial, huh, wrehe did you get it, thnik, do you eevn fickung remeebmr you jsut kpdnapied tihs rnut, you mammreing, tieklebraincd luot.

Freda arms fly. Bunny spins, candlelight. Shadows wing wallpaper cracked ceiling. Torn sofa bunny hits, bounces. Cats jump, bunny screams yoooot yooot bunny mouth sofa hides.

Bunny top spins r r r r r r r.

Thats another thing. Freda says. Your rabbit cant hop.

Bunny arms push, bunny mouth lifts, bunny legs kick, big bunny mouth hollers. Water bunny mouth makes, bunny eyes. Bunny eyes my eyes. My ears my hands hide. Freda jumps, perches sofa, cats jump. Bunny Freda hands grab Stiff Freda arms shake. Bunny kicks, waves fists, cries.

Tlel me waht the fcuk we are sppuosed to do wtih tihs gmddaon tnihg, Ooby. Huh.

Closet. Metal hangers. Hangers my fingers push, g rrrring, g rrrring. Freda lifts bunny. Sharp Freda tooths holler Waht the hlel are we ssppoued to do wtih you, you mweling gkleineg gpoher, you punchay homunculus. Huh. Bunny Freda hands shake. Suht up. Suht the fcuk up.

Bunny cries. My eyes buzzing waters. Hangers my hand push, ting t tingting t tingting.

Enoguh wtih the bldooy hanregs. Freda hollers. Hand swats, hangers spin fall ting ping, tingtingping, closet spins byebye, my arms flap, dive, catsup packet, my eye bubble wand hides, bunny Freda shakes, Suht up, shut up, bunny legs flap, twist, bunny head bounces, bunny cries.

Bunny nose, bunny mouth white tape Freda hand hides.

Youve screamed your bloody last. says Freda. Fucking die.

Bunny eyes shine, candlelight. Bunny eyes my eyes. Bunny eyes wet, red.

Freda says, Once youre dead, we can cook you up, make a succulent rabbit stew, yes, or bread you, fry you, broil you Cry, you. Fuck.

Bunny nose, bunny mouth shows Bunny cries, breath comes, yellow chest big, little, big, top spins waow waow waow, bunny Freda arm hugs, bunny botty Freda hand swats, bunny hollers, red fists shake, Freda walks thumpthumpthump Window Freda hand lifts squeee, cold comes rattly ivy leaves. Bunny Freda arms hang.

Freda says, We have to stop this goddamn racket one way or another, vraiment. Can bunnys fly, Oboy, you expert you.

Bunny kicks, top spins, bunny cries.

Freda sighs. Bunny falls mattress, bounces, bunny screams, bunny cries. Window shuts. Cages Pillowcases towels hide. Hidey birds whistle, birds fweet fweet awk awk awk. Freda walks thumpthumpthump darkness, grey cat orange cat prip prip prip Freda stamps, hhihh, cats scatter byebye. Candles flutter, candles sigh. Bunny cries.

Floorboards mattress comes. My lap crying Bunny my hands put. Fuzzy bunny hair hand pets. Bunny kicks, bunny cries, water makes bunny mouth, bunny nose, bunny eyes. Bunny eyes my eyes. Sparkle have bunny eyes. Darkness, white cage, warm blanky, warm skin, warm milk, singing. Mama.

Dusty floorboards, little cream cup. Lid my fingers tear. My finger dips. Bunny mouth my finger touches. Bunny mouth shakes, bunny cries, stiff red tongue, cream white.

Hot fuzzy black hair my hand pets. Chim chimmy, chim chimmy. my mouth says. Chimmy, chimmy, choo. Hot fuzzy hair my hand pets.

Bunny sniffles. White cream drop, my finger. Red bunny lips move, my finger red gums pinch, hurt. Shiver my back. Big dark eyes wet, red. Bunny sniffles, bunny coughs. My pinkie bunny fingers squeeze. Mama.

Chimmy, chim chim chimmy. my mouth says. Cream my finger pokes. My fingertip, wet, white. Black cross Freda fingers. Black thumbnail Freda tooths bite.

What are we going to do, what are we going to do, what are we going to do. Freda says.

Bunny mouth my finger rubs. My finger bunny mouth pinches. Bunny nose sniffles, mouth sucks. Freda whines, pulls hair, stomps boots, scares bunny, scares me.

On wood floorboards Freda foots walk. Floorboards creaks. Freda coughs. Yellow hair drips. Shivers me. Freda stands by window, newspaper Blue eyes watch. Out window, bubbly rain rotted gutters spill. Foots turn, walk, creak, creak, creak.

Forehead white tape hand wipes, pushes yellow hair. Blue eyes shine. Fuck, fuck, fuck, fuck. Freda says, newspaper blue eyes watch. Freda coughs. My ears hurt. Newspaper Freda hands shake. In kitchen doorway Trinity, Whiteblack sit, curled tails. Greenyellow eyes bingbing my eyes. Cream cup lid my fingers tear off. Cream tastes sweet. Cup falls, hits floorboard cups. My collar clinks. Cats blink.

Ceiling wires drip drip drip. Shiver. Holes has ceiling, wood slats show. Ceiling holes drip in pots pans jars cans, green plastic pail, plip plip plip. Shiver. Pail spills, floorboards wet. On brown sofa my botty sits. Collar my fingernails scratch. Brown sofa arm wet, ceiling water drips thap. Thap. Thap. On my lap jumps blue Korat. Blue ear my hand rubs.

Shiver. On floorboards, dresser drawer sits. In dresser drawer Bunny fusses. Newspaper diaper rustles.

Poop.

Fweet fweet.

In doorway, Freda foots turn. On wood floorboards foots walk. White candle stubs tumble, spin. Cage birds whistle. Window ivy trembles. On wood floorboards Big Orange David falls flumph. Curled paw, red tongue licks. Cardboard box, guinea pigs. Fuzzy tummies little, big, little, big. By window Freda stands, holds newspaper, trembly hands. Freda coughs.

Your snafu in species identification has become bleeding page one news. Freda says. Authorities say a six month old infant was kidnapped from a fifth floor flat in the Favelle Sunday evening. A resident saw a man climb down the buildings façade and flee carrying something inside his overcoat. It wasnt until next morning the baby was discovered missing.

Newspaper flutters. A wallcrawling cat burglar, so says this putz who was front row center that night. I can just hear him. Oi was smokin a Wragge waitin fo me chips to froi when oi sees im, cough cough cloimin down the wall loik a spoidah, a floi, sum koinda spaceyman. Note specimen, spaceyman. Wuzzah. Aa, bugger off. Oi onee ad fie points.

Big Orange David rolls, furry white tummy glows, dusty floorboards back rubs. Paw red tongue licks, whiskers white paw rubs. Furry tummy gets little, big, little, big. Green eyes blink blink my eyes.

Big Orange David says, Crème.

Collar tag my finger flicks. Clink clink.

By window Freda stands. Ivy trembles. Freda turns. On floorboards, dresser drawer Bunny foots kick, drawer sides chubby hands grip, Bunny cries. Floorboards creaks. Torn red stockings crouches, crooked nose sniffs. Great. Your little rabbit filled her newspaper with pellets again. Dresser drawer Bunny foots kick. Kicky Bunny foot rolled newspaper swats. Ceiling shadows seasaw. Newspaper drops.

Hand takes musty red towel. Yellow hair red towel hides.

What the ding dong bell am I going to do. red towel says.

Musty red towel Freda hand pulls. Throp throp yellow hair shakes sidetoside. Blue eyes, my eyes. Skinny Siamese rubs skinny red stocking leg. Abyssinian Tape hand pets.

Ears Red towel dries. To brown sofa Red towel flies, birds flap, whistle, cui cui cui. Bunny cries, chubby fingers pull dresser drawer sides. Green Big Orange David eyes squint, red mouth yawns.

Lets see. Freda says. I could take the little rodent to the coppers. Right. Thats as good as saying I stole it. And the mama aint even offering a reward, so whats the point. Newspaper Freda hands spread on floorboards. I could leave it on some church doorstep. Sure, with my luck I pick one with some flesh eating psychopathic priest who would love to have his feverish fervid perverse way with an anthro baby before he dressed it and baked it and served it for easter dinner. Newspaper Freda hands tear. Who needs that kind of karma. If Im going to hell its not alongside any priest. Freda coughs. Newspaper Freda hands tear.

My tooths my ears hurt. Hollers come. Whiteblack ears flat. Big Orange David rolls on tummy. Quit kvetching, Oboy. says Freda. What, was I supposed to save you the football scores. Your horoscope. Or was it your moment in the spotlight you wanted. Starting a scrapbook, are you.

My arms flap, dive, room spins.

Freda says, You couldve stolen some diapers and powder and jumpers and rash ointment when you stole this baby. Then we wouldnt have to cover her arse with the daily tattler.

Hum. lovebird says.

Shut up. says coughing Freda.

Bunny Freda takes from drawer. Bunny kicks on floor. Poopy newspaper Freda hand pulls. Poopy botty shows. Yech. Freda says. What halfnhalf does to you.

Poopy paper Freda hand puts in brown paper sack. Kicky Bunny foots hand holds. Poopy botty newspaper hand wipes.

Ick. Freda says. Gross gross gross. Poopy paper falls in paper sack. Big Orange David rolls, yawns, stretches. Torn newspaper Freda hand takes, wipes poopy botty. Bunny botty black smears.

Swan. Freda says. I could go to Swan. Of course now that its hot news he will probably tell me to drop the little rat in a dumpster or off a bridge or leave it in some pissoir or on that flesh eating priests doorstep after all.

Freda sits. Poopy paper hand holds.

More likely, hed find some way to make bees n honey off your fuckup. Sell her into prostitution, or something. O, god. I cant tell Swan, either, can I.

Poopy paper falls in paper sack. Black smears Bunny legs, botty. Freda blue eyes blink. My collar tag clink clink. Freda coughs.

So what does that leave me. Freda says. Leaves me smearing tattler ink all over this larvas shitty little arse. Newspaper hand tears. My throat hurts. Hollers. Sing it, chickpea. Im sick and wiping dung from tootsy bung and youre complaining. Typical papa.

Big Orange David rolls, rises, prip prip prips to shadows.

Black Freda eyes my eyes. You should be immensely thankful youre not the one cleaning this soupy pooper. Yet. Bunny legs hand lifts puts torn newspaper on floorboards. Bunny legs drop Newspaper Freda hand pulls, tucks paper on Bunny hips. White tape black cross fingers tear. Tape Fingers put on newspaper. White tape Fingers tear. Newspaper tape tapes. Bunny Freda lifts. Bunny legs kick. Freda coughs.

Taped torn newspaper falls off.

Smeary black Bunny botty shows. Legs kick kick.

Paper diaper Freda eyes watch. Foot kicks, rattly paper diaper spins. O yes. Freda says. I only have one choice in the matter. Dont I. Dont we. We are safe as long as we avoid Swans routes, or cross them only when hes elsewhere. The Vivians, though. We have to be very careful. Cough cough.

Freda walks to skinny cabinet door by kitchen. This is where the old ironing board used to be. Freda says. Cabinet door squeaks. In door, dust, darkness. I tore out the board, knocked out the panel behind it. Look. Its narrow, but theres enough space for skinny cats like us between the lave and kitchen walls. If for some reason we cant get Bunny out before Fouroclock or whoever comes for the birds, one of us will have to squeeze in here with her. And somehow keep her quiet until Fouroclock leaves. Understand, chickpea. Hide and seek. Shit, who knows if this would work. Grab your coat. We have to go to the library. We need baby manuals. And we need to clean her up. And, Christ, the things a cat never imagines she would ever say. We need to get some diapers.

P sst. Oboy.

My bent knee on stone windowsill. Window sash my dirty fingers hold. Down my shoulder, in courtyard, little Freda stands. Kick kick Bunny brown coatsleeve hugs. Yellow Freda hair shines in lamplight. Freda eyes bingbing.

Freda finger lifts. Shadow moves on stones. Freda hisses, See that. Hanging from that balcony up there. Up there. Dont stare at my finger. Look, upstairs there, the balcony. See. The savonnerie. The rug. I want it.

Window. Green blinds. Snoring Macaw hides.

No bird tonight, Oboy. Freda voice hisses. No bird. Non. Non. Non. Non. The rug. Get the rug.

Window dirty fingers shut. Collar tag clink clink. Stones Hands grab. From sill knee slides, to stone moulding foot goes. Stone joints fingertips grip. Bent corner, drainpipe, come. Drainpipe my hands pull Stones my foots climb. Shadows on stones. My foot steps, my foot steps to windowsill. Tippy toe balcony. Rug hangs. My arm lifts, fingers flutter. Bracelet jimmy shines on my wrist. Rug fingers scratch. Bunny cries.

In courtyard, in lamplight, yellow Freda hair flaps sidetoside. Bunny arm waves, legs kick, fussy. Sh sh sh sh. Freda says. Bunny Freda hip bounces, Sh sh sh sh. Eyes shine on my eyes, blinkblink. Metal tag winks.

Hurry, Oboy. Bunnys going to wake the natives.

Knees bend, legs jump, to hand balcony grate comes. Balcony squeaks. Little courtyard rocks sidetoside. Fingers hurt, arm swings Rug Hand slaps Rug goes. My shoulder pulls fingers Grate hurts. My hanging legs swing, twist.

Quit monkeying around, Tarzan. Freda hisses.

My legs swing, dirty foots stones hit, push, arm swings, rug hand grabs, Rug says shhhhhtwap From my fingers Rug pulls whoowhoowhoo falls Jesus jumpy Freda hollers, lamplight shadows swing Bunny Brown coatsleeve hugs Stones Rug slaps.

Shoulder elbow fingers hurt. Arm lifts, to fingers grate comes. For downstairs windowsill Tootsies kick. Legs swing, swing, swing, Grate Hands let go Foots stone windowsill hits Knees spakspak window Dripcap stones Fingernails scratch, catch.

Breath comes, breath goes.

To rug little clic clac Freda walks. Freda says, Remind me not to take any magic carpet rides with you, swami.

Black pants kneels. Bunny Freda hands sits on stones. Stones little hands hit hit, fussy Reeeooo. Shadow bounce in lamplight.

Rug Freda hands roll. Roll gets big. Freda rises, hands clap, black boot on roll. Come on, lets go. says Freda. Pale forehead lifts, eyes pingping, mouth opens. O, bloody hell. Freda hollers, Beware the Irish confetti.

Windowsill Onion hits My heel twists Onion skips off stone wall to courtyard, bounces.

Ma savonnerie. balcony says. Thieves.

Fat green sweater sleeve on balcony railing. Vegetables green sleeve holds to big tummy. Grey hair, glasses shine. Gypsy scum, stealing from a poor godfearing old woman. glittery glasses say.

Tomato flies Splat My hair, my forehead my eyes Wet sprays. Drainpipe my hands grab. My shoulder Lettuce head hits leaves burst shadows leaves flutter, fall.

High window hollers, Ils volent la couverture de Madame Chuvot.

Courtyard hollers, Bastardes. Stealing poor old womans prize heirloom. And you bring your baby to your crime, for what, to riun her by yuor werchted wyas you dnemad foilosh gsyipes.

Trembly cucumber Wrinkly balcony hand shows. Rattly drainpipe my falling hands clap clap clap, my dirty foots stones scrape, falling shadows swing sidetoside. Drainpipe Cucumber hits bang cucumber bounces off my coatsleeve, falls to courtyard.

Windows get bright, sashes squeal grumble groan courtyard door opens striped pajamas holler, Arrêtez.

Non, Emile. They always carry knives.

Drainpipe flies Stones leap hit my foots My hands stones slap slap. Dirt, straw, seeds, burnt broke cigarettes, bones. Tomato hits, busts.

Rug Freda boot kicks. Pick it up Oboy allons y. Rug my hands lift. Bunny Freda hands lift, tsokk tsokk tsokk black boots run In brown coatsleeve Bunny bounces twinkles haw haw haw haw Rug my arms hug, my hip rug bounces, rug flops, brushes running stones. Stones carrots hit, tumble.

Basement window hollers, Gspyy trsah, you oghut to be steond to dateh.

Apple, can, parsnip, pan, cabbage, potpie, artichoke fly, bounce clatter spin, stones. Freda caws, boots run tsokk tsokk tsokka tsokk Bunny bounces, in brown coatsleeve twinkles In my arms rug bounces, rubs my hip, rug dips Rug Hands knee swing to shoulder Rug smells smoky skin mold dust Lip curls throats shut Arm hugs rug shoulder Black

⟨181⟩

Freda boots tsokka tsokka tsokk corner, byebye, down crinkle crankle curvy stone walls, torn coloured papers, skinky trees, collar tag tinkles, triptrap bridge shiny dark canal whispers, spills, dizzies me.

White pickets. White pickets comes. Dollhouse. Gate Black boot kicks Clap Freda runs Bunny bounces, Ivy ruffles pink Bunny hat, Bunny eyes on my eyes, brown coat shoulder Darkness hides. Black Freda boots say clacclac up steps in shop, in darkness.

Gate my hip bumps Hand Ivy scratches rug Darkness up steps my foots thup thup thup, Freda bootprints glow in darkness. On steps, cat eyes blinkblink. Manx hisses.

Tippy top stairs, doorway, candlelight flickers. In cages birds brrr birds awk birds cui cui cui cui. On mattress Freda lies, hahahaha. Bunny Freda hands squeeze. Bunny Freda arms shake, Bunny twinkles. Little Bunny FooFoo did you regardes le visage de vieille when she caught your papa stealing her rug. Did you see the look on your papas face. Have you ever seen your papa get hit by a bloody tomato before.

To Freda mouth Bunny falls on round Bunny cheek Ribbet Ribbet Bunny twinkles wheeeee legs kick Bunny Freda hands fly to mattress Freda rolls to floorboards Freda rises. Brown coat shakes skinny shoulders show Coat Black sweater sleeve on floorboards throws. Black sweater sleeves Hands push. Pale arms, candlelight.

Okay, lets unfurl Madame Chuvots priceless objet de famille. Rug Freda hands pull Hollers come Let go, Oboy, off my shoulder rug falls to wood floorboards. Dust paffs in trembly candlelight in cages hollering Greenyellowbluewhite wings flapflapflap. To floorboards Sofa tabby leaps, darty tail. To my botty Mattress comes. Bunny my hands take. Bunny mouth open, grey eyes on my eyes. My collar tag Bunny fingers pull. Papa. Black Bunny hair My fingers scratch.

Bunny twinkles. Cage bars Blue parakeet gnaws.

Plastic cups, cream cups, black Freda boots kick, wrappers, books, newspaper, shoes, soda can, clothing, pizza box. From cold silver radiator purring grey longhair comes.

Creeammm. grey longhair says, green eyes on my eyes, my knee fluffy paw pets.

In coat pocket my hand fumbles cream cup. Cup shows. Cup cooing Bunny fingers grab. Cup my fingers take from Bunny, tear off lid. Cream Furry red tongue laps from cup, grey ears twitch. Bunny fusses, little hands grab. My lap dirty Bunny booties kick.

Rug Black Freda boot kick, kick, kicks. Rug goes flat on wood floorboards. In cage Brer Rabbit twitches pink nose.

Grey longhair sits. Fluffy paw Red tongue licks, whiskers paw rubs, eyes shut, purrs. Torn cream cup Bunny hands take. Cup Bunny mouth tastes. Bunny fusses, cup little hands throw pinkle pinkle.

On books Wood icebox stands. Icebox hides ice block, milk carton, cream cups, sardine tins, yellow cheese, prosciutto, halfnhalf, salami, plastic bottle. Milk. Plastic milk bottle Hand holds to little Bunny lips. My fingers little pink fingers squeeze. Bunny mouth sucks. Bunny heavy in my arm.

Time for night night. says green parrotlet.

Corner of rug Pale Freda fingers grab on wood floorboards rug slides shhht. Grey longhair ears twitch, in silver radiator longhair hides.

This is the spot. says Freda.

Rug Turning black boots stomp, hips pale hands grab, yellow hair hangs, hips shoulders Freda turns, boots stomp. Whiteblack comes prip prip prip to rug.

Hsst. Freda hisses. Whiteblack skips turns to kitchen Darkness in doorway Eyes flash pingpingping. Bottle Bunny mouth sucks.

This rugs perfect. Freda says. It makes our darling Dollhouse top of rome. It really sets off the peeling moldy wallpaper and wet cracks in the ceiling. Seriously, though, if we had some fresh paint, and some decent furniture and window treatments and electricity and running water and heat and social status and love, and, uh, and. Blue eyes on my eyes. Tooths show in candlelight.

Look at me, Oboy. Freda says. Im nesting.

Wood icebox door squeaks. Cage birds cui cui cui. Milk carton Freda hand takes. Need another block of ice. Icebox door shuts. Tails flicker, Tortoiseshell, tabby, mackerel come Miaou, miaou. On ceiling shadows Black fingers cross, fall. On wobbly table Milk carton sits.

On brown sofa my botty sits. Bunny my arm hugs. Dirty pink socks kick. Collar tag Bunny fingers flick. Dirty nose, chubby red cheeks puff.

Holes in black Freda sweater. Black sweater Freda hands lift. Pale white tummy. Tummy grey tshirt hides. Elbows, pointy white. Chin, pointy. Forehead shines. Black sweater pulls, greasy yellow hair falls, blinkblink, blue eyes. Blue eyes my eyes. My eyes hide.

Aquarium mice scurry, tumble, hug, kickkickkick. Lantern fluttery moth bumps, Bdddda bdddda Shadows gutter. My knee purring Black Bart cheek rubs. Bunny fusses. Chim chimney, chim chimney. Cheroom cheroo. Chubby Bunny cheek soft   my fingers pinch   Peach   Bunny eyes, my eyes. Brown eyes has Bunny. Grey eyes. Papa. Warm sweater. Hairy chin. Cold nose honk honk. Papa.

Black sweater falls Poof paper bits cat hair dust feathers spin on wood floorboards. Fweet fweet fweet whistle shadows. Chicken Little cluck clucks, cage bars ruffly white feathers. Grey tshirt Freda hands lift. Hand hand tummy shows nonee nonee elbow elbow bruise arm chin cheek nose eyes peek peek. Greasy yellow hair falls, taps damp forehead.

On dusty wood floorboards Grey tshirt falls.

Enjoying the show, Papa. Freda says. Pale throat. Long cord necklace hangs. Hook has necklace. Freda turns, pale skin flashes, cages elbow bangs Oops wings flaflaflap Cats pripprip flickery lantern light. Nonees, shadows. Bdddda bdddda.

Bunny cries, dirty socks kick, stripe meridien little fists pull. Tears snots hollers drool. My kisses on hot fuzzy Bunny hair Shh shh shh shh.

Bloody hell, Im hurrying, leetle one, kayate kayate.

Plastic bottle Freda hand grabs. Long tubes, bottle cap. Plastic bottle cap Fingers twist. Milk carton hand grabs. Milk pours from bottle Googoogoogoogoog.

Freda says, Only till my milk really starts to come in. It is a little. See. Nonee tip fingers pinch. Shivery white drop. White drop finger rubs fussy red Bunny mouth. Little red mouth bites. Bottle Necklace hook hangs. Bottle hangs, tubes hang, down. Milk lappy white, seesaw, seesaw.

Christ thats cold. says Freda, nonees hands rub.

Miaou. blue Korat cries. Sofa cats snuggle sidebyside. Goffin cockatoo sighs. Chicken Little clucks co co co.

White tape roll. Freda hand takes. White tape black cross fingers tear wshht. Bottle cap tube. Long tube fingers pinch. Tube fingers wind down, up, soft nonee tube wraps. Tube fingers tape to nonee. White tape fingers tear wshht. Tube tip to nonee tip, fingers tape. Wshht. Tape tape crosses. Tube tape crosses. White crosses tape makes. Now the other one. Freda says. Black crosses fingers White tape tears wssht. Bottle cap tube hangs. Fingers tape tube to nonee. Fingers tear white tape. White crosses tape makes.

Cawing Freda says, Youve seen me do bride of Frankenstein five times now, but each times like the first, innit. Or maybe youre just stymied by stiff pink nipples.

Bunny Freda hands take from my hands. Bluegreenyellow wings flap flap cages. Red Bunny mouth hollers, hurts my ears There there, little foo foo. Freda says. Soft fuzzy hair

Freda arm cradles. Dirty pink socks kick. Fweetfweetfweet Nonee Palm lifts Fingerthumb pinches tape tip tube. Little red lips fingerthumb rubs tip. Soft pink tip Little red lips nip.

Here, darling. Freda says. Komm schon.

Red mouth sucks nonee, tube. Red mouth moves. Red mouth opens, red gums show. Bunny cries, red eyelids hide grey Bunny eyes.

Nonees Shadows hanging bottle bumps. Bottle Freda hand squeezes. Forgot to prime the pump. Freda says. Tube milk fills. Bunny mouth opens, fussy. Okay, okay. Christ. Hush lil one, hush. Lets try again.

Nonee Freda palm lifts. Thumb presses. Red mouth nonee tickles. Red mouth opens Red gums red tongue Tip tube rushes little red mouth. Bunny whimpers, hurty tummy.

Little red mouth sucks. Soft fuzzy hair Freda hand pets. Chubby Bunny cheeks red, wet. Milky wet, little Bunny chin.

So. Freda says.

Bdddda bdddda. Moth flutters, lantern. Black Bart paw bats, moth spins, paws catch, paws tump tump floorboards. Broke moth glitters. Black Bart sits. Chicken Little clucks.

Arms rock. Freda says, Can I tell you a little secret, Oboy. You were my first rescue of our kind. It took me a long time to find you, to find the right you. Little did I know youd take to the life so well, so well that youd surprise me with your first independent act. What do you do. You find me a little baby booboo. You didnt understand. But you knew.

If Im to be a mama, I must go all the way. You n me, Oboy, our mama was a test tube, an electrical current, a few genetic bullion cubes. Breastfed. Right. Not us. Just formula. Ding dong bell, we were formula. I despise that word. As the bastard offspring of science, I can say that. The f word, ha. Artificial, soulless, bloody perfect. Anthro or no, I cant feed my baby perfection I cant Its not right Its not bloody honest. Freda says.

Bunny twitches. My ears hurt. Cat ears flip, eyes bingbing.

Awk, whos honest. says Congo grey. Head tilts sidetoside. Blink blink eyes. Wings flapflapflap cage.

You see the way Bunny looks at me. rocking Freda says.

Little red mouth sucks. Grey eyes Freda eyes.

She wants to trust me. Im her food, after all. Shes all about trust. Survival. Leben heißt kämpfen, Bunny. Its a war renewed everyday. How can I know it wouldntve been better to throw you away.

Soft nonee Bunny hand grabs. Red mouth sucks. Bunny eyes wet. Bunny whines. Tummy hurt gets little. Tummy hurt goes byebye.

Freda hand pets. Freda makes noises. Hurt gets big O dear o dear o dear Freda shakes god damn Freda groans Water Freda eyes make Whatm I doing, whatm I doing, whatm I going to do with you. Fuzzy Bunny hair Freda hand pets, hand pets, hand pets Goddamn it. Freda says, hugs Bunny. Bunny coos. Hand pets. Hand pets. Red mouth moves. Freda arm has greenyellow bruise.

Freda coughs. Lantern flickers Torn brown sofa cats push, rub, miaou, miaou, Shadows wings flutter ceiling What Im going to do is turn over a new leaf. says sniffly Freda. Thats what mamas do. Mamas get their shit together. Mamas give the best they have to offer and then some. Whatever it takes to raise the best of all possible beings. Even if she is an anthro. Fuck. Anthro or no, shes my little fudgling.

On my shoulders tortoiseshell sits. Big Orange David flops, head pushes my knee. My lap Korat paws knead, claws scrit scrit.

Bunny Freda arms rock. Nonee little red mouth sucks. Freda hums. Fuzzy black hair Freda lips kiss, rub. What can be better than a little girl. Bunny FooFoo. You mightve come from anthros, but I love you just the same. What makes an anthro is the indoctrination, the brainwashing. Bunnys not anthro. Shes still pure. Like the animals, she can be saved.

Black socks spin, walk, Bunny bruised arms cradle Tic toc Black Bart tabby mackerel jump, follow, bump, prip prip prip Freda spins, shadows spin, lantern shines Freda says, Such big eyes So unblemished, the whites, Mysterious the way the colour goes from grey to blue to brown and back again. How wild this thatch of hair This skin, so soft, si parfait and these chubby cheeks O What is it with babies Why do we want to pinch their cheeks Their chubby little arses Doesnt she smell insanely good Shes darling, int she, chickpea When you look into her kaleidoscope eyes dont you just want to give her your love your blood the whole wide world Dont turn away, look at our Little Bunny Shes yours as much as mine.

Hissy Lantern wick flickers. Lovebird hums. Hallway cat eyes bingbing candlelight. Sniffly Freda says, Raggedy Ann and Raggedy Andy were so filled with happiness. It seemed as if their cotton stuffed insides were filled with golden sunshine instead of nice, clean white cotton, and their cotton stuffed heads were full of lovely sunny thoughts.

Dear me. Freda says. Raggedy Andy and I are just filled with happiness. Arent we, Andy. If we were any happier all the stitches would rip out of our cotton stuffed heads.

Bunny Freda rocks. Little pink socks curl, rub. My baby Bunny. You fit just right on the swell of my hip. Your face is so open, so ready for delight, watching, studying me, listening to my voice, so. Eager. The way your little hands touch my face. The way your eyes stare into my eyes. O, stop, before you break my heart. We are both trying to understand arent we. I understand the way you snuggle against me, your breath warm. The way you nurse, your fingers tugging my other nipple, making sure its there, all yours. Its staggering to think of everything wot needs to be done for you. Its hectic n borderline hysterical, where to begin, how to get it all done. You need so many things, baby. I figli sono cure sicure e consolazioni incerte.

Freda turns, rocks slow, arms show. Look. Oboy. Shes drifting off.

Bopbopbopbopbop. says Chicken Little.

Shut up, you bleedin picnic entree.

Fuzzy hair Freda arm holds. Nonee little Bunny hand pinches. I was waiting for you all my fork n knife you know. My love precedes you, dormant, suspended upsidedown like a bat for you, mon petit raisin juteux. My love for you was there before I was manufactured, even. I never played with dollies, but once imagined what fun it could be. It is fun. The tinkle of your laugh. Your smallness. How you. How you.

Water red Freda eyes make. Freda says, Christ Bunny Foo Foo. I see in you who I want to be You seem invincible to me And I hate myself for the sad pathetic twit I was made to be How could anyone not fall in love with you instantly, at first sight What a shit I was, that first night Im so sorry you were frightened. It was criminal. I thought there was nothing more than nothingness. Now I love you so much it kills me. I feel young. I feel new. I feel like you, with your clear eyes and your good smell even amongst this filth, your skin, your hair, your breath. I wish Swan could love you too. But Im afraid what he would do.

Freda sniffles. Dodo, dinette, Dodo, dino. Ma petite poulette, Va faire dodo Uho. Poops. Nipple Freda finger pops from Bunny mouth. Bunny eyes open. In my hands Freda hands put hollering Bunny. Its your turn to change her, Papa. Freda says. Use the zinc. Her bottoms getting chapped.

C eiling lights shine. Wood library table shimmers. Paper crinkles. On paper pen scratches. Sniffle. Pantlegs walk brushbrushbrush. Mouths bzzt bzz bzzt. Cough cough. Watery eyes. My eyes purple glasses hide. Metal collar tag my thumbfinger plucks.

Rozlyn.

Black hoody black pants. Black trunk. Tied purple cloth strips has trunk handle. White hairs poke from trunk. White hairs flutter. On table, scissors, big paper cup, plastic sacks, pens. Black sunglasses. Big white mane.

Freda comes. Bunny brown coatsleeve hugs. From fur shoulder, black haversack hangs. Yellow hair, black hair, wet. Okay, got us all cleaned up. says Freda. You know you can lock the door to the kiddies loo. We could take our time, get Bunnys little bottom squeaky clean. Mamas too oo la la. Bunnys clean from head to toe, without too much fussing, even though shes not her usual self lately. Now we just need to get you to clean up, tarzan.

Zzt. Yellow raincoat falls. Scruffy chin, fingers scratch. Nose finger picks.

Freda says, Here, take her.

Bunny my hands take. Bouncy bouncy.

While we were in the loo I got to thinking about Dolittle. Freda says. Sure, he sells pets. But its a front. Hes not there to run a pet shop. Hes there to collect freaks like you, collect government bees n honey to collect freaks like you. Dont you think he replaced you, wrote you off, on his taxes, that is, soon as you were gone. He pretends hes all sugar n spice cologne. But hes draining us to the marrow in our bones.

Book pages black cross fingers ruffle. In my arm Bunny fusses Wet rubber kitty Bunny mouth chews. Hurt in Bunny ear. Cough. Sniffle. Door shuts. Page finger turns.

Freda says, Maybe shes teething. Hm. Still so little though, int she. Maybe colic, whatever that is. This howto manuals no help. I wonder whats wrong with her. Something, dont you think. Getting sick.

My eye orange supermiracle bubble wand hides. Scissors. Wrinkly spotted hand takes. Big paper cup. Shwit, shwit, shwit Scissors cut. Pen Hand takes. Hole pen pokes in cut cup. Hole pen pokes in cut cup. Black ribbon Hand takes. Cut cup pen holes black ribbon laces. Sniffle. Black hood Hand pulls. Grey frizzy hair shows. White lion mane wrinkly hands take. Mane shakeshake, turns, turns. Grey frizzy hair white lion mane hides. Mane hangs, hides eyes. Hands pull, pull, pull. Wrinkly hand goes pat pat. Arms fall thump thump table. Big little, big little, lumpy tummy goes.

Killer tea cozies. Let me take a look. No, I havent read it myself. No copies in today. Would you like me to reserve one.

Bubblegum pops. Crooked tooths show. Eyebrows updown updown go. Green cap. White cap. Ho ho ho.

Dolittle pretends hes cake and ice cream while he stores you like canned tomatoes in the root cellar. Hes of the old school. Probably just cashes the checks and tucks the bees n honey under his old pallet, telling himself he doesnt do it for the payoff, poor gmo knuckleheads like Oboy would be so lost without me, Im giving him a good life, not just a roof over his head clean undies clean sheets, but a purpose, a, a sense of self worth. Long as the checks read pay to the order of Doctor Dolittle, tout le monde est heureux.

Bang wood table leg wood chair hits.

Whitegreen rainboots walk twit, twit, twit.

Wrinkly hands flat on shimmery table. Cough cough. Arms rise, big white mane hands pull sidetoside. Bangs fingers push up. Wrinkly forehead shows. To forehead Cut cup laced ribbon Hand holds. Cut cup white bangs hide. Black ribbon Fingers pull tight, to head fingers tie. Mane crookedy fingers pluck, pluck, pluck. Cup Mane hides, black ribbon Mane hides. White mane puffs. Arms fall on table, thump thump. Lumpy tummy goes big little, big little.

We should tender for our consideration the appropriation of Dolittles freak show funds. We should collect the collectors collections. Comprendes.

Plastic sack wrinkly hands open. Pins fingers pinch. Pin fingers poke in white mane. Pin fingers poke in white mane.

I know. We dont take money. We have a bloody mission. But plans change. We have to get out of here, dont we, for Bunnys sake. We have to get out before Swan finds her. Swan finds out about everything. Its never pretty. But without money or a place to hole up, we are stuck.

Curly goblin shoe curly goblin shoe rubs.

We cant stay with Rozlyn. says Freda. We make a move, we have to get out completely. The country, the continent, even. We need money for that. With a baby.

Book falls bang. Freda jumps. Little round mirror Wrinkly hand holds up. Eyes shine Blinkblink mirror. Gold tube Hand takes. Wrinkly lips gold tube paints red. Lip mumbles lip. Fingertips Gold tube paints red. Wrinkly cheeks fingers rub red. Black tube paints black wing on wrinkly cheek. Black tube paints black wing on wrinkly cheek. Mane hangs, trembly.

Once we do it to Dolittle, we move to south florida. Freda says. For the exotic wildlife. Because of the weather there, the tropical weather. Key west. Gulf stream. Port of miami. Pet birds live outside. Can you adam n eve it. With all the sanctuaries, aviaries, breeders, avian vets, enthusiasts, shops. Its the pick of the litter. Cream of the crop. We hit a breeding facility, pinch fortyorfifty birds at once, I bet. Thats eightythousandamericandollars retail, all in one swooping swoop. No more climbing crumbling façades like bloody chimps, dangling from ledges, tiptoeing round snoring chumps. No more drip drop thefts, one rescuee at a time.

Green paint crooked fingers smears on eyelids. Plastic sack rustles. Gold tube black tube green case Plastic sack hides. Black trunk silver zipper zzzzzzt. Plastic sack fingers spin shut. Plastic sack Black trunk hides. Cut paper cup Trunk hides. Zzzzt.

I saw her last The whole time Thats okay I love ringsides happy hour We didnt know Steak bites Quest que tu es faisant ce soir.

Ceiling lights shine. My eyes hurt. Palm holds hairy chinny chin chin. Lumpy tummy updown, updown.

And the absolute richest part is the suckers keep the whole thing going. Most of the market for stolen birds, most of the marks, are breeders and shops. We could steal the same bird, sell it to a different sap

Door shuts bang

       Those fortyorfifty birds stolen twice become onehundredfiftysixgrandamerican. With that kind of nest egg, we could buy food, clothes, a flat. Resume our mission from a place of comfort. Imagine that.

Brown stocking cap. Long white coat. Forehead fingers tap. Sall she wrote. Rustle, paper sack. Ceiling lights. Orange bubble wand hides my eye. Collar tag clinks.

Once in miami, we would have to ape the anthros in a different way. Dior or chloe bikini. Clarins self tanner. Chanel bronzer. Huge dior sunglasses. Chanel or dog flip flops. Anna sui sundresses. Dvf beach mat. Prada messenger. Smaller chloe handbag. Gucci belt bag, why not. Pucci headscarves. Burberry headband. La roche posay sunscreen for Bunny. And for you, a pair of swim trunks. With those wallcrawling muscles, you dont need much else. South florida. Perpetual summer. Itll be fab to be always warm, wont it chickpea.

Window, rain, grey branches wave. My beard supermiracle bubble wand scratches. On windowsill Sparrows hop. Beaks peck peck. Cheek Wand scratches. Chin. Throat.

Oboy. Are you even listening to me. Freda says.

Baby cries. Tranquilles, Hazel. Bunny cheek turns. Little ear little hand touches.

You see that. says Freda. She keeps touching her ear. Is that the problem. An earache. An infection. Oboy.

White mane Hands pluck, poke, push.

O, for christs sake, enough of this hocus focus. Freda says. Freda rises. Ole Rozlyns a spider drunk from the caustic juices of a hundred glittering flies Shhh Shes some withered purse of a witch counteracting a ladybugs vicious curse Meanwhile Ive got work to do. No big fraidy cat eyes, you. Ill be right back. Here, have one of these.

Red candy, sweet. In haversack, baby book Freda hands put. Zzzt. Haversack swings Black boots tic toc carpet pink roses, byebye.

Scarf hand pulls. Pale throat. Ahem. Snots has Bunny nose. Bunny twinkles on my bouncy knee. Ear hand hides, bzz bzzt. Hurt pushes ear.

Dadaaaaa. Bunny whines.

Bunny my arm hugs. Freda my foots follow.

Upstairs. Downstairs. Eenie meenie minie mo.

On bench my botty sits. Bunny my knee bounces. Shoes come, go. Zzzt. Tap tap tap. Bzzt bzzt. Books dirty green coatsleeve hugs. Door shuts. Squeak. Squeak. Cough cough cough.

Oiya kittycat. big white lion mane says. Made you jump.

Goblin shoes squeak. Brown tooths show. Trunk hand pulls, tiny wheels roll. Dint know ye patronoize the loibrary. Ah, ye got a wee one whered ye foind her. Shes a doll. Lil fussy. Got a earache, but a doll. Dont be frightened, dearie. Tis me. The woilds greatest luvah. Of cats, that is.

Red paint lips. Black paint eyes. My eyes Bubble wand hides. Big white lion mane. Curly goblin shoes. Cat hairs has dark blue coat. Cat hairs has my black coat.

I wont turn ye in, dearie. Nevah. You are magic. You are blessed. Nothin loike us, the rest. Look, I got a tin a sadines fo ye. Two. Tis the best I can do. I got some string cheese, but I dint want to insult ye. Uh o.

Tic toc tic toc running brownshirtsblackpants up steps, shoulders crackle. Watery eyes go tic toc tic toc. Lumpty tummy gurgles. Tin Wrinkly hand holds, trembles. Red mouth coughs. My eye Bubble wand hides.

Crooked eyelash chapped lips says, Theyre thugs. Outlaws. Lot a cozzahs out there wit mental problems. They shouldnt be given a gun, they should be given a labotomy. One cozzah wit 70 incidents of assault. Some a that creeps victims were innocent. E got the wrong guy. Or woman. Or choild. But so wot. Wot is that. Those cozzahs kilt me son. Seventeen. No record, no violent bones anywhere in his body. E relieves himself in the bushes n ends up kilt. Fo wot. Twenty six bones broken. There were three cozzahs on top of im. They couldnt get the handcuffs on, they said. Are you kiddin me. Three big well trained lunatics against one skinny undernourished baby. They couldnt restrain him so they beat im to death. And all e did was tinkle in the bushes. Executioners. Lots a calls go in to the prefecture, offring cozzahs money to off somebody. And a lot of em take the deal. Moonlightin as paid killahs, thats wot theyre doing. Is that the only way to make a buck, I ask ye. Wot you think. I think the cozzahs paid those oods to thrash me las noight. I got to be careful on the streets now. I got to watch out fo the oods and the cozzahs. Wot koind a loife is that. This new prefects a damn nazi. And shes a woman no less. Shes come out n said shes not gonna prosecute any cozzah for anythin done while wearin a badge. Damn nazi. Wotta ye gonna do. The people the prefects supposed to protect n soive are no bettah. Ooligans who run n yell. Curs. Im 72 years old, n Im afraid to go ome. Afraid those thugsnooligansre waitin fo me. The cozzahs dont loike that I wroite lettahs to the Pope, Mothah Teresa, to Monsieur Le President. They detest that I get lettahs in retoin. Three from the Pope. They dont loike it one bit. And they wont stop till they get m Wot in heavens.

Upstairs hollering.

Fuck you.

Bunny twitches, ear hand hides. Ear hurt pushes. Bunny my arm hugs.

Miss. Weve spoken to you before about rearranging the collection. We cant have it. Wait miss. We need to talk to you.

Sprechen zie Deutch, Schwienhund.

We told you, do it again, youll be excluded for one year.

Ich bin eine Bibliothekariner.

Wait miss. Please. We need to see your eye dee.

Railing Freda jumps Stairs Boots hit Boots run tsokk tsokka tsokka. Byebye. Brownshirtsbigtummybaldhead run One year, miss dum ditty dum ditty dum ditty dum.

White lion mane says, Toime to go, dearie. Take these sadines. Two tins. Dented but you could usem. The lil one.

Bunny cries. Little ear little hand hides.

Little umbrellas redgreenblueblack twirl in crinkle crankle allee. Little arms swing little foots kick run in rain. On ledge my botty sits. Ledge cold wet. My pants wet. My foots. Wet brick my heels kick kick. Collar tag clink clink.

Yours not is baby. Mother needs baby.

Freda mama, Bunny.

So thinks she.

Freda save Bunny, save birds, save me.

Herself or others save she does.

Rain falls. Earplugs my fingers tap. Green moss have stone Gargoil robes. Robes dripdripdripdrip. Shiver. From stone eyes Water comes. Cracked stone tootsies wet cold to my fingers.

Tickles, that. gargoil says.

Bunny head on my shoulder. My beard Fuzzy black Bunny hat itches. Bunny botty my arm hugs. Wind whistles in my eyes. Little Bunny mouth whistles, little sighs. Bricks my heels kick. Puffy dirty Bunny coat my hand rubs. Bunny nose snuffles. Come little rabbit come inside. Safely you may always hide. Dark room comes. Soft eyes comes. Soft eyes in dark. Soft eyes in light. Cage white.

Mother dreaming is baby. gargoils say.

Soft nonee Bunny lips pinches. Cinnamon, soap, flowers, Ma cantaloupe, tooths shine, soft brown eyes. Milk.

Bunny hiccups, Bunny whines, Bunny cries.

Fuzzy Bunny hat rises. Wet grey Bunny eyes open blinkblink. Moon in Bunny eye. Redface Bunny cries. Ear hurts. Wet Bunny cheek my fingers wipes. From gargoil eyes Water drips. Shivery me.

Little Bunny hand my hand takes, cold metal fingers my lips pinch. Bunny hiccups, fussy, ear fingers tap. Bottle my hand takes from coat pocket. Bunny lips Bottle rubs. Bottle Bunny mouth sucks. My fingers little Bunny hands squeeze.

Redhead pigeon lands flapflapflap on stone hair.

Bricks my heels kick. My mouth says, Bunny Freda hugs.

Windy rain sighs.

Love true not, love know not, does she. gargoils say. *Mother or her, love baby does. Of dream baby does whom.*

From Bunny mouth bottle falls. Bunny fusses. Little ear little hand hides. Puffy dirty Bunny coat my hand pats. Milk Bunny mouth spits on my black coat. Bunny coat my hand pats. Bunny hiccups, my coat shoulder mouth rubs. Milk bottle my hand puts in pocket. Bunny my hands lift

Careful. gargoils say

Bunny goes in pink pack on my chest.

Bunny arms waves, ledge dirty pajama footies kick, fussy. My foots stand on ledge. Cold stone robe my hand grabs, my legs rise. My pants, foots, wet. From my shoulders Pink pack Bunny hangs.

Twinkla twinkla leadl star. my mouth says on Bunny hat.

Wrong and right is there. gargoils say. *You are one. Which.*

Gargoils watch sky. Rain rain goes away.

Stone robe my hands, foots climb. Pigeons warble. On pigeon poo shoulders, on pigeon poo hair, my foots stand, rock. Parapet my hands grab, bricks my tootsies push, climb. Bunny twinkles eeeee, bricks chubby hands pat, foots kick my tummy. Parapet hits my foots, twinkly Bunny bounces. Pigeons roost on parapet, tucked wings, beaks in chests, eyes shut. Snoring.

From coat pocket, millet my hand takes. On parapet my foots walk. Millet my hand sprinkles on parapet. Millet falls, spills, drifts to allee. Bicicletta rides down allee down allee down little crooked allee. Millet my hand takes from pocket, wet parapet millet sprinkles. Ivy corner comes. My foots turn. My knees crouch. Bunny hiccups Parapet pajama foots kick. To my hand Millet sticks. My knee my hand rubs.

Pigeon eyes open, heads twitch, pigeons warble hop, march on rooftop, wings flap, on parapet pigeons land, coo, strut, bob, peck millet.

Happy halloween. my mouth says.

My legs stand. Bunny my arm hugs in pink pack. Parapet runs my foots twinkle twinkle little eeeeee, clinky collar tag, pigeons squawk, pigeons jump wings flap, blinkblinkblink in rainlight, feathers purple green shine in rainlight, millet hard to my foots, slippy, Bunny twinkles, eeeee parapet corner comes, my foot swings, little heads little shoulders in crinkle crankle allee, my arms spin, foot swings, parapet spins, my legs crouch.

Little Bunny arms wave. In grey sky drifting coloured papers wheel, fall, flutter, perch on parapet, pigeon heads twitch, legs march, peck millet, perchy pigeons say Qui pigeons say Quoi pigeons say Coo.

Parapet runs my foots bumpbumpbump my hair flutters, my arms wide, wave, little Bunny arms wave, pigeons whistle, shriek, spin off railing, my coat my hair wings slap, Bunny twinkles wheeeeee.

Rooftop jumps to my foots. From my fist, millet falls to parapet, spills, rolls byebye. Pigeons come. Pigeons strut cluckcoo peck millet.

My fingers snap, my tongue cluckcoo. Redhead pigeon comes, wings flaflaflap. Redhead pigeon claws grab my finger. Cooing. Head twitches sidetoside. Little black eyes blink.

Sweet, sweet. redhead pigeon says.

From coat pocket Cookie crumb my fingers take. Cookie crumb Redhead pigeon pecks from fingerthumb, bobs throat, swells ruff.

Bunny twinkles, redhead tilts Little Bunny hand pulls grey feathers. Redhead pigeon tail fans, wings flares, oohrr, ohhrr. My tongue clucks, hard pigeon beak my fingers pinch. Cooing pigeon lowers wings.

Sweet sweet. my mouth says.

Beak my fingers give cookie crumb. Pigeon my hands take. Feathers wings thin bones little top spins My hands un, deux, trois Throw pigeon to sky, wings thapthapthap redhead pigeon gets little. Byebye. Bunny bounces in pink pack little arms waves Bunny twinkles eee eee eee. Bunny is warm. My chin Fuzzy Bunny hat bumps. My finger Bunny hand grabs. My palm turns up takes cold little Bunny hand.

Dada. says Bunny. My hand Bunny mouth kisses.

O boy. my mouth says.

Down bricks, down moulding, down juliet balconies I run. Allee stones jump, hit my foots. Bunny twinkles.

Any work for the cooper

In allee. Little black lab puppy trots. Oua oua. lab pup barks. Oua oua.

Doggy dee. says twinkly Bunny.

My hands show. Fun pup. my mouth says.

Doggy dee. says Bunny, clappy hands.

Down allee my foots walk. Puppy follows. Non, non. my mouth says. Non, non.

Down allee my foots run, Bunny bounces, ee, ee, ee, ee. Puppy chases, barks, Oua, oua oua.

In pocket my hand goes. Cookie crumbles my hand takes.

Yum yum. my mouth says. Cookie crumbles my hand puts on stones.

Little black lab puppy comes. Wet black nose sniffs cookie crumbles. Crumbles puppy tongue licks byebye.

My foots run. Bunny hollers Non. Doggy dee. My foots stand. Black lab puppy comes, pant pant pant.

Four pair for five francs, Holland socks

Colly molly puffe

My knees crouch, puppy my hands take. Round corner, up gravel allee, down stone steps. Upstairs tree branches wave. Downstairs white pickets sway. Gate my hand pushes. Puppy ear Bunny fingers pull. Bunny cheek little pink tongue licks. Bunny twinkles. Up steps, entrée doorlatch hand takes, in doorway my foots walk. Staircase creaks. Upstairs light flickers.

That you my dears.

Doorway comes. Bunny twinkles. Little Lulu hisses, cats run, prip prip prip.

Was wondering where you went after the library. Can you adam n eve they kicked me out. Freda rises, turns. What the ding dong bell are you doing with that.

Puppy. my mouth says.

I know what it is, I just cannot fathom why its here. We dont rescue mutts, how many bloody times have I told you. Your brain truly is of infinite density and zero size.

Bunny twinkles, pulls floppy black ear.

I dont give a shit if Bunny likes it, it needs to go.

My knees crouch. On savonnerie Puppy my hand sits.

Whatre you doing, Oboy. I said get it out of here, now. Freda hisses, stalks sidetoside. Black lab pup barks Oua oua oua oua. Hissing cats scatter, jump, crouch.

Bunny my hands take from pack. On wood floorboards Bunny my hands sits. Black lab pup Bunny hand grabs.

Black lab puppy crouches. On savonnerie, black lab pup pees.

God damn it. hollers Freda. I cant fucking I said get this thing out of here Little black tail Freda fingerthumb lifts, puppy yelps, to window Freda goes Window hand opens This is all your fault you idiot Out window little yelping lab pup Freda hand swings.

Window slams Bang.

Freda turns. Yeah, fucking holler all you want I told you we dont have anything to do with dogs. Never ever again, comprends moi. I call the shots here, you mold, you mump, you measle.

Closet door my hand opens. Metal hangers my fingers push, g rrrring, g rrrring.

Dont start that rot. Me Freda hands push. Hangers Freda hands catch sheeee. Window opens screee. Hangers go Pin pin tin pin pin Window slams Bang.

Bunny cries. Bunny hands grab table leg Bunny rises, Bunny wobbles. Ear hurts.

O my god, shes standing. says Freda. I cant believe it int that incredible look at her.

Standing redfaced Bunny cries.

L ittle window little door. Raingutter drips plip plip plip. Shiver. Car splashes, passes. Latch Freda hand takes. Red Freda lips says, Let me do the talking. Haha.

Door opens. Din don. In Freda walks tic toc Bunny brown coatsleeve hugs. Bright lights. White counter. Come on, Oboy. Brown wood walls. Chairs. In chairs hands folded. Legs crossed.

Sandrine, jai dit non.

Maman, mais Henri

Assieds.

Bunny Freda sits on counter. Hello. white counter says. Pointy glasses bingbing. Help you.

Freda shoulders shake, water drops on floor. Bon soir our infant has an ear infection and is in need of antibiotics Amoxicillin I believe.

Pointy glasses says, The little one does look out of sorts. Though very adorable. Whats your name, pretty girl.

Bunny. says Freda.

Bunny. Thats a cute nickname. The np can certainly take a look at the poor dear, then make her diagnosis. First, we just need you to complete our new patient information form, and also sign our acknowledgement and consen

Forms. This babys in need of immediate attention.

Bunnys obviously experiencing some discomfort,

For days now

and I apologize for the delay, but we do need her information before we can provide care. And of course there are other patients ahead of you. Im sorry, like most, its a busy day.

Lines, lines, thats all you anthros know.

Pardon.

Its a fine line that makes lines fine. Paper pen Freda fingers takes. Pen thumb clic clic clics. Lets see. Patients full name. Date of birth. Sex, okay, there we go, female. Race. Haha. Telephone. Address. Look, no telephone number no address. Why do we have to put all this info when its a free clinic.

Pointy glasses pointy nose. Nose sniffs. Im sorry for any misunderstanding, but treatment isnt free, per se. We bill your insurance, of course, and depending on your

No insurance.

Freda thumb clic clic clic clic.

Ahem. If youre uninsured, the fee is four hundred eighty francs.

Four eighty are you bloody daft.

That is our minimum charge for walkin service, madame. Its very reasonable in todays economy, but we can put you on a payment plan if you cant pay today. We will need eye dee.

Little white cards dirty Bunny hand takes. Nein, Bunny, leave those. says Freda. Bunny falls on counter, fusses. To floor fuzzy Bunny hat falls. Freda hisses. Bunny, hat, Freda arm takes, gives to my hands. Freda says, So with your little payment plan we can get the medication.

The np can give you a voucher, which you have filled at the chemists.

Papers pen Freda hand throws on counter. Freda says Rules and procedures and plans and vouchers. Thats the hoops of the anthro world, innit. Christ, I just want to get my baby fixed and leave paperwork to the bean counters.

Truly, madame, I understand. And my apologies for upsetting you. I know youre only concerned for Bunny. Moi, aussi. Why dont you tell me what I need to know and I fill out the form.

Freda hisses. My nose twinkly Bunny pulls.

Sandrine

Maman

Pen thumb clics. What is Bunnys full name.

Just Bunny.

Bunny is her given name. Daccord. Surname.

Okay if you insist. Bunny Petite then.

And when was Bunny Petite born.

When.

Her date of birth. Oui.

Hm. Fingers Freda thumb touches. She was six months. That was two or three months ago, so 8 or 9 months, no 10, That would be this year early sometime. January, February. Yes. Put, o, the fifteenth. That sounds right.

Im sorry, I dont understand. January or February.

Ouai. Maybe March.

Paper pen taps. Chair creaks. Ahem. You seem uncertain about your daughters name. You dont know when she was born. Perhaps your husband. Monsieur.

Pointy glasses bing bing my eyes. My eyes hide. Black Bunny hair my hand pets.

Sandrine, o la la

Do you know your daughters date of birth.

Sandrine oo la la. my mouth says.

Ha ha. says Freda. The ole pot and pan doesnt know anything. He doesnt have a thought in that pretty loaf of bread of his, do you.

Do you. my mouth says in Black Bunny hair.

Pen Hand lays on paper. Fingers cross. Madam, Im very sorry, but I must ask. Is this your child.

Wot. Why would you make such an affront. I never.

You dont seem to know much about her.

Freda arms wave. Of course I dont, shes still so new yes We are still getting to know each other. A lifelong endeavor.

Chair creaks. On desk, flat hands. Thats not what I mean.

Names, dates, hardly relevant when shes tugging on her ear and crying all the time.

A childs wellbeing is always the first concern.

Fah. Its the money, innit. Cos we are homeless, yes. You think we cant pay. Despicable gypsies, we must be. That it.

Not at all. Something doesnt feel right here. You dont know your, the babys information. You have no contact information, no insurance.

Youre a free clinic we are your demographic.

Your, your partner is obviously disabled. And most likely incapable of caring for himself, let alone a baby. You yourself seem barely capable. Your hygiene. You both look in need of attention as well as, your, as the baby. If youre under 21, we can help you too. But, I need you to be straight with me.

Awp. That tough love piffle Ive read so much about.

Okay, Ill be straight with you. We are mandatory reporters at this clinic.

Wots that. Byline at gunpoint. News at six or else.

Meaning, if I suspect somethings amiss regarding the welfare of a patient, I must report my suspicion to the authorities. Now, I ask you again. Are you this childs legal parent or guardian.

Bunny Freda hands take from my hands. Freda says, Perhaps in our world its always two thirty, but I can get you the sausage and mash. Pas de problème. I can get more money than youve ever seen. Just like that. And I will. When I do, we will be back, and we will expect respect. Right. And we will take the damn voucher.

My coat Freda hand pulls. Lets go, sorry and sad.

Wait, Miss, please, I think you should

We will get your fucking money. Freda hollers. Door opens, darkness, rain. Freda runs, fussy, Bunny bounces in brown coatsleeves, ee ee ee ee.

To my eyes, black eyes go. White plastic bottle caps on cardboard box sit. Box edge my finger rubs. Bottle cap my fingers lift. Red pea shows.

My wrist oily hot brown hand grabs. Hurt. Bottle cap brown fingers take.

Dont be handlin nothin shithead. squeezing brown hand says. Red tip cigarette, crooked white tooths. My wrist burns, up my wrist burn burns, up my arm, up my shoulder, burns, from my mouth hollers come. Burning.

Brown wrist Freda fingers black crosses grab My wrist Hot brown oily hand squeezes. Hollers. Freda says, Oboy doesnt like to be touched any more than you, dearie.

Dumbshit sucka better get a clue. Fur coatsleeve flaps. Just cos he got that shiny new collar dont mean nothin.

Brown hands clap clap clap. Pardon d commotion, messieursdames. Blondie here aint got no sense but she been lucky enough to win. Luck be all it take. Now, who next to play. Come on. Quelquun. Somebody.

Black bowler hat say, Ill give it a

Freda shoulder bumps Ow says, Oboy wants a turn.

Idiot wit less sense than you. Come on.

Freda caws. You flat joiner, hes smarter than you think. If you do. He doesnt get caught in crossfire. He can beat your game. Just like a dumb blonde.

Crooked white tooths shine. Black chapped lips. Brown throat twists. My mouth burns. Black eyes my eyes. My eyes hide. Black marks on cardboard box sides. Black dirt have allee stones. Butts. Bones.

Your boy want to play huh. redtip cigarette says.

Cest vrai.

He got somethin to bet wit.

Rainbow paper Freda puts on cardboard box.

Freda says, Hes got what I just won off you.

What. Hm. Well, awful big a you, throwin in yo. Money. Like dat. An after you worked. So hard. Fo it.

Let him try. blue coat says.

Ouai. Ouai. pushing arms coats hats say.

Long fur coat says, Now I startin to worry yall got nothing better to do today than specklate You too broke or too cheap or too scairt to step up. Alors, so you gonna let einstein lose it all. Thass on you blondie.

Rainbow paper Long brown finger scratch scratch scratch mumbles, Six, sept, huit.

Long brown fingers throw rainbow paper on rainbow paper on cardboard box. Dirty tape has cardboard box.

Eighty francs, yose to win o lose.

Orange supermiracle bubble wand my hand lifts. My eye wand hides.

What, that thing give you the xray vision, einstein.

No, it makes him invisible.

Psh.

Fur coat lapels Brown hands grab. Coat flaps. Down long fur coat Brown hands slide. Red tip cigarette chapped black lips. Red pea brown oily fingers pinch, show. She be what you after, chucklehead. She yours, alls you got to do is keep yo xray eye on her.

Red pea brown fingers put on cardboard box. Red pea White plastic bottle cap hides. Bottle caps fingers switch.

Sh, sh, sh, sh. say dancing plastic bottle caps.

T tp t tp t tp. hidey red pea says to my eyes.

Long fur coat rises. On cardboard box white caps sit. Brown hands clap clap clap, my ears hurt Ooo playa dont like dat Shhh quiet now, quiet he concentra

Arm hugs head. Cap my hand lifts. On cardboard box red pea rolls. Rolling red pea brown hand catches.

Rainbow paper brown fingers flick. There yo go, lucky star. Eighty francs, jus like that. Okay, now who next.

Me, me. says pushy rooster hair.

Tais toi, Mignonette. says bumping Freda. Rooster hair stumbles. Oboys going again. Double or nothing.

Non non, give somebodys eltz a turn to win. You sire.

Let im go again.

Encore, encore.

Wha the fuck you doin. scratchy black lips says.

Freda says, Its a gas, baby, youll love it.

Little cigarette Fingers pinch. Chapped black lips suck. Cigarette brown fingers flip away. Cigarette bounces Red sparks on stones. Okay, one mo shot, lil bro. Double on un six o. Rainbow paper hand throws. But then I want one a yall to step up.

Red pea dark thumbfinger pinches. Lines in hand sparkle. Torn skin has thumbnail. My back shivers.

Keep yo eye on it. scratchy black lips says. Pea cap hides shows hides See dat shows hides Caps fingers switch on cardboard box. Sh, sh, sh, sh. Hidey pea makes little t tp t tp. Pea brown fingers hide cap to cap to cap, say, Lil bride flees wit dirt on her knees d champagne and brie and into d breeze and into d trees Beau hollerin please to d seven seas n the fotty theez say Lil bride free eeze.

On cardboard box White plastic bottle caps.

Quelque parfum veux tu. High rolla.

Cap my fingers lift. Red pea shines. Cawing get big. My ears hurts. My coat hands tug, slap my back. Hollers come. My arm hand squeezes. Freda caws. Hum, Oboy. Hum.

Damn. long fur coat says. Rainbow paper Freda hands take Whoa whoa whoa Hold up now, hold up. chapped black lips says. Folks, this chap take d bread out my mouf, me, a Woman who got to make a livin, aint she, she caint jus be the life a the party. So, turnip seed, you take my hunnert sitty francs. Rainbow papers long brown fingers put on cardboard box. And that be another un, deux, trois and twenty.

Gee, I dunno. says Freda. Lips twitch.

Double down on three hundred twenty. hisses coats hats shoes. Wet allee stones Wet shoes shuffle. O la la.

We really must be going. says Freda.

Psh. Yo boy got to gimme a chance to catch even. fur coat says. Three hunnert, fo hunnert, five, it dont make no nevermind Caps fingers push Pea rolls Red pea little curled finger hides cuz turnip seed I is through foolin which you. I is clawin back every centime I done charitized yo arse and what you think bout that. Here go.

Sh, sh, sh. caps say.

Long fur coatsleeves cross. Okay. Where the bride be.

Its the one on the left.

Non, centre, centre.

Non.

What who playin, you playin, back up, pipples Dont crowd the man Give him room to think He need

Brown wrist my hand grabs
what the fu

Wrist hot damp. Thp thp thp. says brown wrist. My hand pulls. Yo man. hot brown wrist says. Whatchoo doin. Get yo muthafuckin hand off me fo I break it off. Brown hand pulls, Brown oily hand my hand turns.

Open your hand, Dainty. Freda says.

What the hell you sayin, bitch.

Ouvrez la main. checked cap black beard says. Grumbly coats arms legs come.

Dark hand opens. Red pea.

Fuckin cheatin, shes cheatin, look.

From balconies pale moons holler, We told you.

Rainbow paper Freda grabs from cardboard box. Arms legs bodies come close, brush my coat, push, hollers come. Cardboard box shoes kick, stomp.

Mignonette Pussy Willow Down allee Arms legs boots run patpatpatpat get back here. Damn. Fur coat Hands grab. Street gonna hear about this, Freda. says fur coat.

I want my money back, you bitch.

Puta.

I going to cut out your heart.

Hands Brown oily hands push Fur coat hands grab Va te faire foutre Long fur coat spins away, arms flap flap Fuck all yall Down allee Boots run tamptamptamp Hollering arms legs chase, Up bricks Fur coat boots run Fire escape brown hands grab Ha Ladder arms legs climb tong tong tong. Fists shake, bottles hands grab, garbage from ashcans, throw. Long fur coat caws, climbs ladder. Mangez ma boîte, suckas.

My coat Freda hand pulls. Pavement, corner, allee. Now we have the bees n honey, we can get the antibiotics for Bunny. Speaking of, we better get back to the Dollhouse. That cough syrup we gave her has probably worn off.

Dirty black haversack falls bam wood floorboards. We slipped that collar by a whisker. Freda says. Clic clac boots. Hand pulls off red stocking hat. Yellow hair hides blue Freda eyes. Yellow hair shakes sidetoside. Across black Freda pantleg Angora back rubs.

Red hat falls onto chair. Angora cat black pantleg pushes away. Fiona, stop. How could animal control have known we were going back to the kids clinic. That pompous bitch at the front desk with her mandatory reportage. But for all she knew, we were never coming back. So how.

My eyes, Freda eyes. On torn brown sofa my botty sits. My foots. Little Bunny hat my hand takes. Fuzzy black hair my fingers pet. Lantern fires flicker.

Theres only one answer to that question. Freda says. Of all Doctor Frankensteins postulations and perpetrations, this is the permutation Ive feared the most.

Over dirty black haversack Freda crouches. Cats come, tilting tails. Zipper black cross fingers pull zzzt. Yellow papers Freda hands take from black haversack. Papers Freda thumb ruffles. Physical control of the mind toward a psychocivilized society. Freda says. Jose delgado. Its all right here. Another important tome for the library of us. Let me show you something else.

Into black haversack Freda hands dig. Bunny nose snuffles. Bunny tummy my arm hugs. Fuzzy hair my hand pets. Nose sniffs. Bunny fusses.

I know, Bunny foofoo, I know. A few drops of onion juice are all we have for that poor little ear of yours.

In taped hand. Candy.

Not candy, chickpea. Freda says. An ultra submicrominiaturized radio equipped electrode array. A Stimoceiver. Eye of Frankenstein. Brought to you by the CACI. Culled from the hamburgered head of one of our fallen sisters, Dandelion. You never met her. Five stories. A button pushed, a signal hammered down, arms and legs bound right off into space, against all sense or grace. Candy fingerthumb tilts in candlelight. I found this, herr doktors derring do, right there in the marketplace, a gem spinning in a puddle of red goo.

Red goo, red goo. says blue eyed cockatoo.

Candy Fingerthumb holds toward ceiling. Bunny fusses. Little carrot pudding jar my hand takes. Little spoon for Bunny. Yum yum. Across my foots scratch eared cat curls.

Birds say, Fweet fweet fweet.

Freda says Yes, the chronicle of evil only gets more pernicious, more pervasive, the guvmint in its thou shalt not question our slackwittedness rubber stamped Doctor Frankensteins laudable humanitarian effort to screw electrical probes directly into our brains. If he couldnt fabricate our minds and emotions genetically, Daddy Franky would do it mechanically. With these neural implants he could hack into the wetware between our ears, not only to track us, but to manipulate our every move, to know and to control what we are feeling and thinking, directing all parameters of excitation to turn us into big cuddly dolls not even remotely in control of ourselves. Freda arms swing updown blue eyes get big Legs kick toward doorway. Kitties scatter. On heel Freda spins, arms swing, Fee fi fo fum, yo ho ho and a bottle of rum, dum dada dum dada dumdumdum.

Candy Freda hand drops into black haversack. Yellow papers Hand puts into haversack. Freda rises, turns, clic clac. Carrot pudding drips down Bunny chin. Jar spoon rattles. Freda spins.

The bastard, our god. Meting out our feelings. Stimulating the limbic system to induce fear, rage, lust, garrulousness, hilarity, heeheehee, varying the intensity, filling our heads with phantom odors, flashes of light, hunger, fatigue, sleepiness, tickling our whiskers via microchips, stimulating the motor cortex to make us scratch our ear, twitch our phantom tails, jump or salute, sieg heil, stimulating the caudate nucleus to control our voluntary movements, try as we might they would not allow us to scratch an itch, to lick our paws tic tic tic We have no rights, we are mutated corn, kosher pickles to be experimented on. But in the meantime, hes got us on the dial.

Ceiling shadows flutter. On book stack Freda botty sits.

Papa Frankenstein would cure the foibles of anthro existence. Paralysis, parkinsons, lost nerve function, schizophrenia, epilepsy, panic attacks, ocd, alzheimers, paralysis, homosexuality, which is just so fucking funny, to reduce anthros innate aggression and hostility, which is just so fucking funnier, as aids in neurosurgery, alleviating chronic pain, other ills of injury, defect or disease.

Cui cui cui. birds say.

As the god of perfection, correction, erection, Papa Franks wanted to create a less cruel, healthier, happier, better woman and man. How bloody noble. How positively grand. What greater edification than building a master species impervious to illness or disease, that can regulate its emotions and feelings, reduce anxiety, interpersonal conflict, neuroses. It would be paradise on earth. Paradise in every body.

Carrot pudding byebye. Jar fall to floorboards, roll into books. Jar Dirty Boutin sniffs. Dirty Boutin sits, eyes blinkblink. Bah. Bunny my knees hold. Scratch eared cat twinkling Bunny pats. Tail flicks. Little cream cup lid my fingers tear. Red tongue laps. Bunny fingers scratch.

Hode e. says Bunny.

Cat eyes shine.

Dont you see, its really just global scale slavery. Through us, through our blood and fear and vivisection, he can control society. Like you sitting crosseyed cuddling pets in Dolittles shop, cleaning your paws, awaiting your reward of comfort, security, meat. Its a matter of anesthetizing everyone. When youre complacent, whats there to live for. What needs to be done.

Bunny twinkles. Cream cup Bunny fingers hold. Red tongue flicks. On brown sofa Dirty Boutin hops, nose sniffs. Grey paw swats. Cream cup spills. Bunny fusses. In pocket my hand goes. Cream cup my hand shows.

Hode e. says Bunny.

Red goo. hollers blue eyed cockatoo.

And even when we do do something, how do we know someone tucked cozy hidden in our minds didnt tell us what to do. What makes you think you chose to go down this allee or that avenue, to climb this purlieu or that tenement. How do we know anything we have done up to now has been our own doing. Our responses to things naturally integrate themselves into the flow of our so called daily lives so as to appear less automatic and more social, ie, normal, haha, yeah, right, thus we cannot know in terms of being where we leave off and the stimoceiver begins.

Broke window Ivy scratches. Birds burble in cages. Hungry cats come, miaou, miaou. Dirty Boutin hisses, cream cup falls. Cream spills on brown sofa. Cat heads dart, ears twitch, tongues rasp. Bunny twinkles, pats backs.

Freda scratches Chester cat chin. Comment nous savons nous sommes nous. Ill tell you how. Cos we free the pets. Int that right, Chester. Why would they instruct us to do something against their best interests. Its proof we have control over ourselves. Proof short of opening our own heads.

But not controlling our every flicker doesnt make him any less a menace to us. Hes still a dirty voyeur, observing us, crooked metal prick spurting black spikes of ink across graph paper congealing onto shiny stainproof linoleum. Again, how else could animal control know we were at the clinic. The library. The cinema. The market.

Freda crouches. Skinny green box taped hand takes from black haversack. Skinny green lid Freda hands open.

In lanternlight, silver shiny roll flickers.

Freda says, Ironically, the best way to blind Frankensteins eye is as simple as his methods are complex.

Shiny roll Freda fingerthumb pinch. Shiny paper turns from skinny green box, crackles cross wood floorboards. Scratch eared cat rises, stretches, jumps from sofa.

Kiki. Bunny says. Kiki. On wood floorboards Bunny my hand puts. Tag clinks. Bunny crawls, chases cat, little hands thump thump thump. Fweet fwee fwee. birds say.

Silver shiny paper Freda hand holds on floorboards. Box fist pulls Shiny paper tears shhhht My ears my hands hide. Birds whistle, flap. Blue eyed cockatoo feathers ruffle. Red goo. Wicker cage bars black beak gnaws.

Torn shiny paper Freda hands fold over. Across fold Black thumbnail scrapes. Folded shiny paper Hands fold. Black thumbnail scrapes.

Its not paper its foil and the conclusive square must be shiny front n back. Freda says. In laternlight taped hands turn shiny foil hat. My eyes blink.

Its the shiny wot repels the signals. Freda says.

Cui cui cui. birds say. My fingertips Dirty Boutin licks.

Black Freda boots clickety clic clac clickety clic clac to broke mirror. In mirror, Freda eyes glow. Shiny hat Freda hands put on yellow hair.

Here comes the bride. Freda mouth says. Of jolly Frankenstein.

Shiny paper Hands crinkle round yellow hair. Toward mirror Freda leans, cheeks turn. Crinkly hat flashes in lanternlight.

Red goo, red goo. Hahaha.

Bunny stands, cage bars little fingers grab. Parakeet head ducks, blink blink. Bunny my hands take. Bunny fusses, kick kick. Birds fweet fwee fwee.

Tape roll has Freda hand. Black cross fingers pinch, tear tape. Tape ring fingers make. Tape ring sticks onto shiny crinkly hat. Tape fingers tear, make ring, put tape ring on shiny crinkly hat. In mirror Freda cheeks turns sidetoside.

Freda knee Big Orange David head bumps, stiff leg, tiptoe, scritchscratch, ron ron. Tape Freda fingers tear, make ring. Stick to shiny hat. Red stocking hat Freda hands takes, pulls over crinkly shiny hat. Red hat taped hands pat. Yellow hair Black cross fingers push from blue eyes. Freda turns, blue eyes bingbing my eyes.

More fetching, dont you think. Freda says.

Red goo. cockatoo cries.

Kiki. says Bunny. Toward Chester cat Bunny crawls.

Red hat Freda hand pats. Green skinny box Freda hands take. Silver shiny foil Fingers pull. Taped hand pulls, tears shiny sshhhht.

Freda says, Together we will be atlantis fighting phoenicia, or europe against the catholic church. Torn shiny foil Freda hand folds. Across fold Black thumbnail scratches. Shiny foil Hands folds over. Black thumbnail scratches.

Clic clac clic Freda boots comes. Over me Freda stands, shiny hat, fingerthumb.

Time to bake your potato, chickpea. Freda says.

My blue stocking hat flies byebye. In my eyes Hair falls. Foil hat hands push on my hair. Swatting hollers come.

Freda says. I know, Oboy, I know, its scary and its outer space but animal control might use what little mind you have to trace us here. Bust the Dollhouse and our mission to toothpicks. Shut up. You dont want to end up like Dandelion, do you, Dandy Walker.

My throat chokes My eyes water Freda hands my hands swat, take blue stocking hat. Hat my hands pull over foil hat, window, door, ceiling, spin, my back hits, my head hurts, my legs clop clop across dirty woodfloorboardsFredaspinbyebye. Darkness.

O Christ, hes here Swans here Dainty Some of the others. Bunny Freda hands push into my hands You have to get Bunny out Come on.

Baby gate bang. Down hallway to redbluegreen window Freda foots prip prip prip prip. Tinfoil hat shimmers. Dust spins. My foots follow, Bunny my arm hugs. Window frame Freda hands hit. Damn it. Pussywillows got the allee. Here, down the back stairs.

Doorknob Freda hand twists. Dusty yawny steps door shows. Shadows, rustling ivy, rattly stairwell door below.

Miaou. miaou. Tee hee. Shh. Surprisem good, Maidenhair.

Door Freda hand shuts slow. Click. My sleeve Freda hand grabs, pulls. Quiet. Back inside. Into flat Freda runs, tippytoe.

Yellow tail flips sidetoside. Foil hat red stocking hat hides.

Freda says, Vite, vite, Ironing board cabinet.

Skinny door Freda hand pulls. Inside, skinny broke tunnel. Dust, darkness.

Downstairs, entrée door squeaks. Stairwell flashes, shadows.

Get in. Hide n seek, just like we practiced, dac. They have to find you, remember. Past cabinet doorway my shoulders squeeze. Inside, my foots, shoulders turn. Bunny fusses.

Stay put. Keep quiet. Keep Bunny quiet. Luisa, Simone, Mittens, Trinity, everyone, sing.

Red mouths yowl, sharp tooths gleam.

Raggedy Ann Hand throws. Clac clac.

Here, books, pictures. Hide n seek. Keep quiet.

Cabinet door shuts. Crack has door. Crack shows book stack Freda pushes across floor. Door books bump. To crack Freda mouth says, Stay put. Keep quiet. Keep Bunny quiet.

Downstairs sings, Little Polly Flinders, her home among the cinders, warming her pretty little toes.

Crack shows Freda run sidetoside. Into closet diapers, blanky, dresser drawer Freda throws. Closet door shuts. Under sofa, dolls Freda boot kicks. Bunny coos.

Shhhh. my mouth says. Hide n seek.

Crack shows cats, torn brown sofa. Front doorway. In doorway comes long fur coat, rooster hair, spotted coat, white coat black fedora Damn, you got every cat in town up in here Shaddap Black pantleg kicks. Squawking Tivoli, Bart run.

By sofa Freda stands. Freda says, Swan.

Baby gate Bent white coatsleeve swings sidetoside. In cabinet door crack, gold tooths shine. Ha. A gate. For wayward infants, is it.

Past crack red coat walks tic, toc, tic, toc. Floor creaks.

Sometimes we let the guinea pigs and rabbits hop about. says Freda.

Gimme a sack, Ivy.

The, the gate keeps them in. White coatsleeve Freda hands touch. Lover, you dont usually come for the birds

Bo peep. You know why we have come.

Fuckin right. Brown hand shows, finger jabs. Thanks to you and yo retard I caint even show my face round dat arrondissement no mo.

Bang bang bang. Birds squawk Nein Stop Please Too dark in sack

Freda shoulders shrug. Freda says, I dont like how Dainty disrepects Oboy. I wanted to show her hes not as stupid as she thinks. Besides, Oboy didnt cheat at her game, Dainty did. She just didnt do it right.

Brown finger shakes. Got me a garrote I can do right.

Now, now, Dainty.

Hm. Furry coat comes. Bunny lips my finger touches Tell me I aint doin it right, putain Over my shoulder, broke boards, skinny tunnel, splintery Lets see her fuckin run the game Little wood stool. Dirty pillow. Shiny dust curls from ceiling holes, walls holes, holes near floor. Into hole wiggles calico. Miaou.

On book stack long fur coat sits, cabinet door shuts. Crack byebye.

When her days work is done, her business more properly begins.

Swan.

He aks what you did
        Papa
              wit the money.

Cats yowl. My mouth says, Voilà. Cream cup my hand shows. Bunny bounces in darkness, little hand takes. Cup lid dirty little fingernails scratch.

Freda says, Well, it wasnt all about Dainty. The birds are getting sick. Stress. See how Ivys stuffing that parrot into the sack. Odds are its either going to die or lose all its tail feathers. So, I had to buy medicine. Vitamins, too. Got to keep them healthy, right, so they hold their value. My operation brings in more than Daintys

Bullshit. Cabinet door bangs

I just have no bees and honey to keep things going.

Ironically, its true, Dainty, my dear. Alors, what you are saying is your nondurables were perishing before you could get them to market, yes. To remedy your lack of immediate cash flow, you saw a less capital intensive yet income generating activity as the answer to your operational quandry.

Investing Daintys gains into my operation increases the value of the money I borrowed.

You dint borrow it, bitch. hollers cabinet door. Door bumps. Crack opens. Long fur coat to Freda goes thonk thonk thonk. **Keep mouthin off, you little conasse an Im gonna**

Point is, nothing was lost, Swan. What I borrowed will come back to you at greater value.

Cept I gotta give up dat cornah. Dats a loss, Street.

Birds holler **Non, stop, Bang bang Ow,** damn bird bit me Just a canary peck quit yer crying Ivy Cats yowl, trot past cabinet door.

Freda says If shes as good as she thinks she is, Dainty can run her game anywhere in town. Time she moved on, anyway. The natives were wise to her.

Little cream cup little chubby fingers scratch. Bunny fusses. Bunny my arm hugs. Lid my hands pull, give cream cup to Bunny hands. Cream spills. Crack shows white coat black fedora rise, walk toc, toc.

What a beautiful savonnerie you have, bo peep. Where did you find it.

Freda stands. Arms cross. Well. Making our rounds.

Ah yes, look at the backing. Its hand knotted. Wool. A century old. How well its color holds. Dense bouquets, beautiful medallions, the leafy rinceaux ces bons. What are your thoughts, Dainty.

Swan, no. Please

Now dat you mention it, Street, dis rug be tres belle. Get a good price from Kurdish.

Brown sofa pushes across floorboards. In crack black hair darts. Books tossed on sofa. Jus get this baby roed up. Oo. Heavy. Quality, ouai. Prix très bon. Hep get this up on my shoulder, Ive. Ouf. Hop là.

Out door walks bouncing savonnerie, says, Sang, sang, what shall I sang, cat run away wit the puddin strang, haw haw haw. Rooster tail spotted coat follow, carry fluttery sacks. Baby gate boot kicks bang. Byebye. Birds in sacks cry.

Swan, how could you let that bitch take my

Whats this peeking from under the sofa.

On brown sofa arm, white coat bends. Rises. A doll. says black fedora. Is this the Raggedy Ann.

Its Oboys.

Plays with dolls, does he.

He, hes simple, you know. As we all were.

Where is the mooncalf.

Hes out hunting, Swan.

Hunting. What else is under here. Childrens blocks.

Well those are Oboys. As well, I mean. Trying to teach him the alphabet.

White coat says, We noticed not only that lovely rug, but youve added some other touches as well. Curtains. A splash of paint. Lanterns. Air freshener, for the cat urine, eh. The icebox. Glad to see you and mooncalf are playing so nicely together. What good little humans youve become.

Its not like that, Swan. I mean, I just got tired of

Toys, rugs, baby gates. We almost think you are, whats the word. Expecting.

Funny, lover. Just got tired of living in squalor.

Bunny fusses. Cream cup my hand shows. Cup Bunny hand slaps. Shh shh shh shh. Raggedy Ann my hands show Bunny. Book Bunny hands slap, Bunny cries. Poop.

Whats that.

What.

It sounds like.

Like a baby crying. says Freda.

Incredible timing, bo peep. Is it a baby. Crying.

Bunny mouth my hand hides. Bunny kicks, arms swing. Under tinfoil hat, my head itches. Collar chokes clink clink.

Cats meou, yowl, hiss, run sidetoside.

Its one of the Siamese. says Freda. Elvira. Shes got an absess and whines just like an anthro baby. Shes been hiding in the wall and wont come out.

Perhaps you should rob Live Forevers pickpocketing operation, get some meds for the feline. Baby. Ha ha.

O, Swan, you always like to tease.

White coat collar Freda arms hug. Freda white coatsleeves hug. Rocking sidetoside. I miss you so, Swan. Why dont we take a trip sometime, just you and me. Roma.

Tell us what else you have around here.

Freda eyes blinkblink my eyes.

If we looked in the closet, that armoire, that dresser, cabinets. Would we find anything to intrigue us.

Swan, theres nothing, just me.

Freda White coatsleeves push away. Freda shoulders hands squeeze.

What is it. says Freda.

Your blouse has sprung a leak.

Red stocking hat turns down.

Lactating. Are you.

Freda lips tongue licks. Freda swallows. Round white coat Freda arms hug. Blue eyes my eyes. Well, Swan. It just happens sometimes. When I feel. You know. Aroused. Like now, baby. Some anthro thing, I guess.

Yellow tail long fingers grab, pull. Red stocking hat falls off.

Ow, Swan, that hurts

Heres Sulky Sue, what shall we do. Turn her face to the wall till she comes to.

Yellow tail hand pulls. Ah, Swan, baby. Please. Why are you doing this. Youre hurting me.

To ceiling Freda chin points. Freda throat long nose sniffs. Sniff. Sniff. Freda ear lips kiss.

Keeping secrets We can tell. Secret keeper neer do well.

I wouldnt keep anything from you, Swan. Freda cries.

Gold tooths say, We are catching. The most subtle flicker. Of something. But what. We sense forward motion. We sense. Wanderlust. Are you planning a vacation.

Course not. Just concerned about Haussmann. Hes getting closer, you know. Been thinking about moving. Not leaving town or anything, silly. Just, out of his path.

Yellow tail Hand lets go. Good. Cos we wouldnt advise it. The others will make sure youre no. Stray.

Swan.

Lets refresh your scent, my dear. White coatsleeve moves. Long fingers twist. Freda throat long fingers dab. Scent is all. black fedora says. Turn.

Freda turns. Long fingers lift sweater. Freda back Fingers dab. Dont forget who owns you, bo peep. Dont forget who you owe. Turn.

Freda throat mouth kisses. Much as we have valued our relationship, we hope our trust in you is not misplaced. We would feel very badly about that. Is there nothing else you would share with us before we go.

Non. I mean, theres nothing. No secrets, Swan.

White coat rises, spins, coatsleeves stretch up, spin. Doorway flashes white. Downstairs thump thump thump thump. Entrée door squeaks. Shuts bang.

Freda falls. Bunny cries. Cabinet door my hand pushes. Book stack falls bam. Yellow hair flies up. Idiot. hisses Freda. Freda jumps up. Hook stick Freda hands take. I tell you you could come out yet, goddamn you.

Cabinet door hook stick jabs shut. Beside me, in darkness, Bunny cries.

On redbluegreen window Freda hands my hands Bunny hands. Across allee, past little rooftop, Razor wire has chainlink fence. Past chainlink fence, oiled red hoses, bricks, metal gas cans. Big white drill big red drill Metal barrels have drills. Slots, tooths have barrels, drill dirt.

Big pit. Dirt steps has pit. Updown, updown yellow hats go. Hi ho, hi ho.

Laws of the ant heap. Freda says. Bunny Freda hip bounces. Tinfoil hat Stocking hat hides. My fingers scratch.

Dirt Yellow lobster tail claws. Yellow lobster spins, black smoke huffs, Lobster tail swings. In growling lorry Dirt Lobster pours.

On dirt sits long metal bars. Corkscrew drillbits. Rubber wheels, chains, long greygreen metal tubes.

Gas. Freda says.

Sidetoside yellow hats stand. Yellow hats make fire, sparks.

The yellow hats make that wall of planks, to keep the pit from collapsing. Freda says. Otherwise, six oclock news.

Yellow tape hangs from orangewhite stripe plastic posts. Yellow tape tail flutters. Wood scraps concrete chunks has Big orange dumpster. Wood pallets. White metal shed. Long metal bars planted. Orange plastic buckets. Blue plastic pipes. Long metal bars have wood planks. On planks yellow hats stand.

Scaffolding. says Freda.

Ladder. Lobsters sleep, folded, metal tails curled Great metal claws. In lobsters, chairs wheels. Levers. On dirt Big plastic pipe lies. Metal coiled wires have metal bars. Wood sheets. Drink cups paper plates. Plastic bags. Lumpy burlap sacks. Lobster tracks. Bent metal poles. Wood sawhorse falls. Broke streetlamp lies, wires show. Fallen trees, limbs stiff trembly. Across pit yellow hats run.

Tinfoil hat my finger scritch scratch.

Near corner big cement rocks. Rope orange crane beak holds. Big metal pipe rope holds. Pipe sways rockabye baby. Pipe Crane beak lowers, into pit, into yellow hat hands.

Like schoolboys playing in a box of sand. Freda says. Playing with trucks and blocks. Pretending to be world builders. Big men o so happy to tear down what came before, the old, the quaint, the in the way. Make way for the new the shiny the big, the money grubbing pigs. Clear the decks. What could be more beautiful than these crooked little allees, these tinpan rooftops. The signs above the shops. The cobblestone streets like the skin of snakes ferrying carts and cars and mopeds on their backs. The pedlars shouting their wares. All the old playbills lacquered one over the other, papering the boulevard level façades. The soot and grime baked into the stones and bricks of the higher up places. The old windows and shutters, the wrought iron balconies and flower boxes and gargoyles. Going going. Gone pecan. Why, goddamn it.

Freda turns, red sunglasses flash, Bunny bounces. Now its all these slick buildings, big dark soulless windows wot dont open. Even the façades are smooth and slick, no fire escapes. Theyre internal, now. How are we supposed to get in. How are we supposed to carry on with our, with our mission. Our habitat is being wiped out and no one cares and theres nothing we can do about it. Gasoline and sugar, a sock in a bottle. Then what. Christ. Doesnt matter, anyway, cos Swans got us trapped here.

Pale fingers pet fuzzy Bunny hair, fingertips stroke foil hat. We dont have much time left. Only one block between us and Haussmann. Less than that between us and Swan.

Dirt Yellow lobster tail claws. Hollering tail swings up, around. Dirt drops into growling lorry. Lorry rumbles away. Hose yellow hat holds, cobbles water sprays.

Like washing the blood into our grave. Freda says.

Oua oua. barks doberman above. Broke moon shines. Oua oua. Scrit scrit scratch.

Fire escape. Water drips. Steam drifts. High window. Glass Steam puffpuffpuffs. Doberman claws scritch scratch glass. Oua oua.

What the hells Rolo barkin at up there.

Probably his reflection, as usual.

I wish hed quiet down.

He will. Its just what he does.

I wish Martins would muzzle him before he goes out at night.

Now Clara. Its just a dog.

Macaw window. Macaw window has drawn blind, has bright light, shadows. Macaw goes Ha ha ha.

Pretty bird. Pretty bird. Say it.

Awk, pretty this.

Ha ha ha.

Idiot.

Give him some more panaché.

Give that Doberman one, too. Hes making a real racket.

In allee, legs crouch, my mouth drinks cream from cup. Cup falls to cups between my foots. My legs stand, legs kick kick. Collar tag my fingers pluck. Drainpipe comes. Creaking drainpipe my hands climb. Bricks tootsies push. Oua oua oua above. Cobblestones swing below. Macaw window shines bright, comes. Shadows move on blind. Fire escape comes, swings sidetoside. Hands grab, foots climb, jump railing tong tong. Window dark, raindrops. Puff puff window. Wet nose bangs doberman barks Oua oua snarling steam puffs white tooths snap Oua oua oua oua. My ears hurt.

My head drops. My hands open. Oua oua oua. My fingers flutter, run, jump. My finger pokes my palm. My finger pokes my chest. Mister. Warm little shop. Oua oua. Rock you in my lap, long leg pup. Sore tummy my hand rubs. My fingers make rainrain go away. Doberman cocks head. Nose glistens black in darkness. Wet spots glass. Hanging tongue bounces, pant pant pant. Under shop lights. Puppy lies curled in my lap, tummy hurts. My hand pets.

Brown eyes blink blink my eyes. Whimpers. Window steam, drool, smear. Steam pants. You. Top spins inside doberman, hurts. You. doberman whines. You. You.

My hands flicker shut, open, show. My hands rub, wsh wsh. Lovey boy. my mouth says.

Nose glistens, darkness. Black lips hang, show pink tongue. Eyes shine. Window puff puff puffs steam.

My hand ravels bracelet jimmy from my wrist. Jimmy slides inside window sash. Doberman whines, paws clic clic clic window, steam gasps Puff puff puff Lock squeaks Bracelet jimmy my hand wraps round my wrist. Window Hands push up. Doberman jumps Oof My shoulders rough paws hug pushes me Oop falling Tongue licks Bang fire escape Ha ha Black lips, black rimmed eyes, black wet nose snuffles my pushing hands Pink tongue licks Brown eyes my eyes rolling sidetoside. My throat my cheek pink tongue licks Non non non Ha ha ha Doberman pants Huh huh huh huh licks, stiff tail whipwhipwhip. Withers my fingers scratch. Into throat my fingers dig, stroke, tags clink clink clink.

Floppy ears my fingers rub. My wet eyes peek in ears. Peek at tooths. Tummy my hand pats. Warm. Tight. Full.

Byebye go hurt. my mouth says. Here dog big. There, Mister shop skinny long leg pup. Byebye go hurt, ouai. Hurt go byebye.

Petting. My arms hug pup. Collar you collar me. I say. Tags clink clink.

Doberman pants, brown eyes my eyes. He calls Rolo. Throws ball. Walks. Feeds dry food. Wet. Meat. Bed sleep no. Plants dig no. No Rolo no.

O boy. my mouth says against hard warm panting jaw. Happy Rolo. Happy me. Curtains flutter. Broke moon shines.

Little comes he. Glasses bingbing. Yellowgreen jacket sleeves flap flap, black stripe shoes scrip scrap cobblestones. Fuzzy dust Red balloon tied to wrist float over shiny metal helmet.

Green ivy leaves flutter round broke hole high over rue. Magpies bawl. Crouched in broke hole, my finger scratches under tinfoil hat. Hair damp. Under clink clink collar Finger scratches throat. Cinnamon raisins my mouth eats. Torn little cream cup my mouth drinks. Torn little cup falls to torn little cups between my foots.

In rue below he hollers, Sey sey sey sey. My earplugs my fingers poke. He comes, red balloon floats. Floppy orange hat walks beside. Brown dress Grocery sacks bump bump. Puddles shine. Allee gutter glitters.

Karl, laisse cette eau tranquille. Its filthy.

Scrip scrap past dusty wood planks. Bricks. Posts. Broke cement wall.

Brass pott or iron pott to mend Any old iron take money for

Past sleepy yellow lobster. Grocery sack Hands grab. Red balloon bounces sidetoside.

Floppy hat says, Now, Karl. The cotton candy was a special treat. No more sweets before supper. No licorice, Karl.

Iuo iuo iuo. he hollers. Hands pull sack. White dirty shoes stumble Karl arrête Black stripe shoes stomp stomp stomp under flowery tree. Twittering sparrows Flowery tree hides. Red balloon bobs.

O, Karl. Dont make life hard on your mama.

He hollers, yellowgreen sleeves flap flap flap, red balloon bobs. Metal helmet shakes, glasses bingbing. Past white car.

Under brown pigeon poo awning, windows bars hands grab Grrrr yellowgreen sleeves pull pull pull grrr.

Karl.

Outside postern, bicicletta stands. Bicicletta has bell Ringringringring Karl, you know to Ringringring Molestes pas Monsieur Richards Ringring bicycle. He asked Ringringringring you not play with the bell, truly.

Ringring.

Into postern hollering yellowgreen jacket stomps byebye.

Long thread laces, long and strong

My foots stand in broke hole over allee, knees bent. Tinfoil hat Ivy leaves scritch scratch. Magpies rant. My arms go forwardback, forward, foots push, lamppost jumps, hits my coat Ugh collar chokes my arms hug, legs spin round post, fall, my foots cobblestones hit.

In postern Shadow hops, voice big Hawp hawp hawp. Bicicletta comes. My hands twist shiny bicicletta bell from handlebar. Bell coat pocket hides. Awning pigeons coo burrr.

Youve surely got a big strong voice, Karl. Allons y.

Rattling window bars my hands foots grab, climb uh uh uh Fingers tootsies grab dripcap over window, grab voussoir joints over dripcap, pull, tootsies in voussoir, gargoyle wings hands grab, hang, hands foots climb broke balcony railing over gargoyle, over postern. Foots stand on moulding beside railing, slide across moulding to dented stovepipe. Arms shoulders hurt. Dented stovepipe Hands pull Foots push, rooftop comes.

Tile rooftop Hands foots cross, past chimney stacks, dormers. Parapet. My botty sits. Breath goes huh huh huh. Under collar fingers scratch. Below, little he stomps away from postern Yellowgreen jacket sleeves flap flap flap, red balloon jumps, Goy guy gye gay goo. he hollers. Pigeons flapflapflap, scatter, hop run skip.

Thats right. Goodbye, pigeons, goodbye.

Hands foots walk parapet. Corner comes, grey rooftiles below jump, hit my foots, my hands. Pigeons cry, flapflapflap chimney pots, byebye.

Black stripe shoes scrip scrap stones, follow floppy orange hat. White shoes pwump pwump pwump past old stable, past hay bales. In hands grocery sacks twist.

Sun shines. Shadows cross cobblestones in allee, under my foots shadow darts Run past chimneys, past spinning metal onions metal hats, magpies wheel in blue sky, metal tag clinks Running under clotheslines My cheeks purple glasses Clothes scratches, rustle Gap comes Wood siding jumps runs ch ch ch under my hands my foots Splinter stings, hands grab broke eves, lead roof comes warm.

He stops, metal helmet tilts. Glasses bingbing my eyes Haw haw haw haw. My eyes Sweat stings. Breath goes hun hun hun. He lifts arm. Finger sun.

Karl. says floppy orange hat. No staring at the sun, remember. Viens.

Across rue, little black slate roof has white pigeon poo. Green siding, white windows. In pink tree Bluejay whistles. Red thistles. Purple glasses my fingers lift. My eyes Red thistles pull. My eyes Purple glasses hide. Down pavement he comes, helmet shines.

Our little green maison. says floppy orange hat below. Whew. Quite a walk for us. And quite a day. You must be tired. Well, Karl, Im very proud of how well youve behaved.

Little metal gate Grocery sack pushes Squeak. Black stripe shoes scripscrap past gate, stomp stomp steps, bobbing red balloon. Grocery sack pushes metal gate shut.

Goo gye guy gay go.

Goodbye, goodbye. floppy orange hat says. Sack Hand sets Jingly keys Red door Hand opens. Sack Hand takes. Inside doorway Metal helmet Floppy hat go.

Now lets put you in the garden while I make the soup. Such a glorious day, you certainly thrive on Red door shuts Click the sun as much as anyone.

My botty Lead roof welts poke. Tinfoil hat is warm. Collar chokes. Little black slate roof below. Brick chimney stack. Tall brick flats sidetoside. Tall black tower little in bright blue sky. Little green siding. Little white window. Shutter broke black. White window. Red planter box. White drainpipe. White window. Black slate roof.

Okay, Karl, keep your pretty balloon company while I make the soup.

Rain gutter my hand grabs Botty slides off lead roof, Botty falls Wrist gutter pinches, my tootsies cornice hits corner drainpipe hand grabs, drainpipe slides, Window below jumps Shutter foot kicks shut What was that Drainpipe rises between hands foots Moulding hop Windowsill hop Lintel hop Cobblestones Ankles pop. Crouching. Foot hurts. Splinter. Shoulders hurt. Hands. Little green maison. Green grass. Red thistle. Corner flats tall beside. Fuzzy dust spins, floats. Brown shoes come clomp clomp. Terrier comes, pant pant.

Window above says, Evie, you wont believe this, I just saw this guy climb down that office building in nothing flat like aint the circus in town. Hey you. Hey. What you doing.

Brown shoes terrier come oua oua. Corner flats come. Pavement round corner.

Who did. What you talkin about.

This guy wearing like a tinfoil hat. Hes gone now.

Was it that pet thief.

Crinkle crankle allee. Ashcans. White cat blue eyes comes tail up, mouth opens, wheee. Trellis arch. Green vines. Baby gate. White patio stones. Whiteorangeyellow daffodils.

On chipped blue rocking horse he sits. He hollers, rocking horse ears hands grab, horse goes forwardback, forwardback, ta dup, ta dup. Metal helmet, eyes roll behind glasses. Baby gate. White flowers garden tree has. Smell is sweet to my eyes. In tree sun shines. In tree red balloon hides.

Green wood. Open white window. Red screen door.

O, Karl, you lost your balloon. window says. I warned you about taking it off your wrist. Well, I need to finish preparing the sole just now. Your balloon will have to wait.

Non non non non. he hollers. Black stripe shoes stomp, metal helmet shakes sidetoside. Rocking horse ears Hands grab, horse rocks forwardback forwardback. Iuoiuoiuoi.

Hes not going anywhere, dear. Dont break Toute de Suite.

Me, trellis hides. Mlllllk. white cat says, blue eyes wide, on hindlegs, head butts my knee. Baby gate latch My fingers pinch. Squeak. Baby gate White cat passes prip prip prip.

Blue horse rocks, tadup tadup tadup. Glasses bingbing sunlight Metal helmet turns away. Rocking horse sits.

Happy halloween. my mouth says.

Haw haw haw haw. Crooked tooths show.

In a minute, Karl. Be calm. says white window.

White cat my hand lifts. Soft. my mouth says.

〈243〉

Metal helmet. Eyes roll behind glasses. Freckly hands Yellowgreen sleeves have. Purry white cat Freckly hand hits thump thump. Cat ears flatten. White coat My hand pets. Soft. My mouth says. Soft. Trellis leaves rustle. Sun shines. Sparrows cheecheechee.

In my pocket Freckly hand goes. Haw haw haw haw. he says. Cinnamon raisins Freckly hand squeezes. Raisins Hand hides in chewing mouth. Hm hm hm.

Dring dring inside white window. O la la, le telephone. Un moment, Karl.

White cat jumps to patio, rolls on back. Jump, flowery tree branch my hands catch. Bark rough to my climbing foots. Branch Knee hooks. Elbow hooks. Arm leg hang, rock toandfro, collar tag flutters. My tinfoil hat falls to patio stones. He claps, chews. Sey sey sey.

Salut, Ava. red screen door says. Im putting supper together. Oui, just Karl and myself. O, fish soup. With Rouille and garlic croutons and Gruyere. Ha ha. My mothers, oui. I just put the sole on to boil. Hm. Karls in the garden, enjoying whats left of the sun.

Red balloon string My hand pulls from flowery tree branch. Sparrows twitter. He rises, wobble comes, blue horse rocks ta dup, ta duh, ta. Red balloon string my hand gives to freckly hand below.

Haw haw haw. he says. String Freckly hand pulls, red balloon goes updown updown. Tree branch my arm, leg, let go. Dirt jumps, hits my hands, foots. Me, flowery tree hides.

We went to the circus. screen door says. O, yes, we had a wonderful time. So many happy children. Non, never seen an elephant before. He had to cover his eyes but he handled it quite well, for all its size. A clown gave Karl a balloon which he just lost in the dogwood. I will need the ladder, oui.

Bicicletta bell my hand takes from pocket. Ring ring. bell says little, hides behind flowery tree. Ring ring.

Glasses turn sidetoside Bingbing. Fingers pinch, Sey sey sey sey. Red balloon, metal helmet shine. Fuzzy dust twirls. My hair my finger taps. Tinfoil hat byebye.

Me you. my mouth says.

Red screen door says, Im worried as well. Sais pas. I dont know what we will do. Our only option seems to be, move in with Karls grandparents in Villard. O, non. Non. I wont be paid what the house is worth. Its awful, truly. That Haussmann.

Ring ring ring ring.

Our little house is so perfect, so, so wonderfully perfect. The gardens one of the few aspects of his waking moments that give Karl peace. Pauvre petit garçon. And Haussmann is just going to raze the whole thing. Rebuild the city. To improve things. On est dans un beau petrin. Bien sûr, bien sûr.

Under trellis, out baby gate, cobblestones scritch scratch my foots. White cat follows, blue eyes blink. Ring ring. Ring ring. says bicicletta bell. He comes, hoots, white cat black stripe shoes follow Clip clop under trellis, past baby gate, allee. Freckly hand pulls, red balloon wobbles, shiny bobble. In allee gutter Water shines, glitters between my foots. Ring ring. Ring. In my hand Bell shines, ring ring, backward my foots walk up allee. Moss between stones damp soft to my foots.

Iron falcon calls. *Careful. Him miss, will mother.*

He hollers Sey sey sey sey, fingers pinch. Helmet flashes. Puddle splashes.

Down Allee goes, past dark shops, past café. Overhead pigeons coo, snore. Round corner. In my hand bicicletta bell says Ring ring ring. Black stripe shoes come. Round corner, down rue. Gaslamp shines blue New sprats new Ring ring. Clotheslines crisscross overhead, clothes flutter. Metal helmet tilts up, Ringaring, he comes, shadows scatter. Ring ring. Under postern, dim. Pee smell. Ringring. Pigeons march, bob. He runs, hollers eeeeeoooo yellowgreen sleeves flap, pigeons flapflap Ringringring he comes, Psh psh stone Black stripe shoe kicks, he comes, hand reaches for bell Red balloon floats, rocks, string twirls over rooftops, byebye.

Kaarl. voice hollers little. Kaaaarl.

He hollers, Sey sey sey freckly hands come. Fluttery leaves. Picket fence. Dollhouse. Windows above, dry brown vines green vines hide. My pantleg Big Orange David rubs.

Miaou. Miaou. say Luisa Gare Trinity, tails up, arching backs, stretch tiptoe.

Bell my hand shows. Freckly hand takes.

Safely you may always hide. my mouth says.

Ring ring ring ring ring ring ring ring ring.

Behind white picket fence cat eyes bing bing. Cats meou, Me, No me, No me. Ring ring, ring ring, ring. bicicletta bell says in crouching freckly hand.

Purple glasses My finger pushes. White picket gate my hand pushes Scree Dollhouse birds Fweet fweet fweet.

Round my foots blackbluegrey cats prip prip prip. Up stepping stones. Cats meou, tails up, paw entrée door, rub my pantlegs.

Ringring. says bell.

〈246〉

Inside entrée door window Freda says, We could hear that damn bell a kilometre away what the bloody hell are you doing where is your foil hat. Bunny peeks beside. And whos that.

Ring ring ring ring ring ring.

Latch my hand takes, shakes. Entrée door Freda holds.

Get the fuck out a here with that thing, you mewling, onion eyed measel. Get out, now. Take that bloody sack of guts n drool with you, take it back where you got it. Now. Before someone sees. Youll ruin the whole bloody operation.

Durdy dee. Bunny says, waves arms, mouth open, little bunny tooths shows. Fuzzy black hair waves.

Yellowgreen sleeve my hand pulls. He hollers, my hand bell hits. Down stepping stones. Out white picket fence. Allee. Hollering. Cats meou.

Dollhouse. Sun. Turning. Sparrows twitter in green leaves. Inside Dollhouse Birds fweet fweet fweet. Turning, turning. Yellowgreen jacket Hands pull. My hand freckly hand hits. Hollering. My eyes sun hurts. Shadows jump. Turning.

Karl.

Turning. Door window dark. Freda, Bunny, byebye.

Kaarrel. hollers red mouth. Puffy red eyes go to my eyes. My eyes hide.

You. red eyes says. Frying pan comes. Inside brown dress top spins dadut dadut dadut. Forehead shines.

Villain. Where do you thnik yruoe tinkag my bbay.

My arm Frying pan hits. Hollers come, my arm burns. Frying pan swings. Black iron. Pocks. Rust. Scratches. Dented rim. Pale hand, fingertips pink, squeeze black handle. My head spins away Fahh frying pan breathes on my cheek To stones pan clatters Black handle spins bow bow bow bounces. Brown dress tumbles Oof stones hands slapslap.

Yellowgreen jacket my hands pull. He hollers, waves arms, stumbles, helmet goes bang bang bang on crinkle crankle Karl Non non non Bicicletta bell flies bounces ping ping Inside jacket Top spins Tico tico tico tico Safely you may safely you may safely you may always hide My arms lift He is heavy to my shoulder He hollers, Non non non non hits, kicks, glasses fall clac clac, spin Allee stones pap pap pap under my foots stumbling Cinnamon raisins my hand takes from pocket My hand freckly hand hits, raisins fly.

Brown dress rises, hops on foot. Water Red eyes make. Gypsy bastard. Dont you take my boy. Dont. Brown dress hop comes. Stop him. Someone. Please. I. I.

Up allee my foots run. Over me, Window opens Squeak.

Madame Kettl, quest ce qui ce passe.

Hes stealing my baby, the gypsy. Help me, Inge.

Him. He runs with that lot of thieves. The Favelle.

Hes stealing my baby.

Voilà Madame. Down the allee behind you. Police, police. voice hollers, arms wave in window. Help help.

Black cap black boots come clonk clonk clonk clonk clonk clonk clonk. Windows open What the Who is Look the cozzers Whys he carrying that boy Brown dress Blue sweater arm hugs. Bent knee, white ankle, hop. Madame. Vas ist los.

Officer, that, that man. Hes taking my Karl. Hes stealing my boy.

Drainpipe my hand grabs. Wood siding my foot pushes.

Halt. black cap says. What are you doing, there. Halt.

B lack shoes run come. In red beard, shiny whistle whistles Fweeeet.

Ho, ho. Raggedy Andy cried. Its the Policeman again with false red whiskers.

Squealing drainpipe my hand pulls from wood. Rust flakes fall. Yellowgreen he from my shoulder falls, hollers Wahwahwahwahwahwah. Windows holler above. Tomatoes, cabbage, onions hit bricks, hit stones. Hit my back. My mouth hollers. My foots run. Clucking chickens scat sidetoside. Corner comes.

My legs crouch. My eye orange supermiracle bubble wand hides.

In windows hand hand fingers thumb holler, Stop him The Gypsy Hes getting away. Cobblestones Metal helmet bang bang bangs. He hollers, yellowgreen sleeves slap slap, black stripe shoes kick, helmet bang bang bang.

Black cap blue sweater stands over yellowgreen jacket, hands out, shiny whistle in red beard mouth.

My son My son. says red hair brown dress, pushes blue sweater, kneels beside hollering he. Yellowgreen jacket Brown dress hugs, Brown dress Red hair Freckly hands hit, hit metal helmet Poor mouse, my poor dear joli souris, you must have been so frightened.

My eye orange supermiracle bubble wand hides.

The kind hearted Policeman took a little blue book from his pocket. The book told how to be a detective and the Policeman read it carefully. After a minute or two, he followed the footprints which led up the cobblestones. On and on went the Nice Policeman following the well marked footprints below the crookedy walls of the village.

My eye supermiracle bubble wand hides.

Ha, ha. the Policeman laughed in a loud voice, You are just silly if you think you can fool me with your disguises.

My eye Bubble wand hides. Black cap red beard blue sweater come. To my eyes Eyes go. My hands foots run, hopping chickens holler, co co co.

Fweet. whistle mouth says. My ears Earplugs hide. Black cap black shoes clonk clonk clonk. I seen you before. Your picture. Youre missing. Arrête. Alto. Warten.

Windowsill. Drainpipe. Lamppost. Blue sky.

Whos your caretaker. says red beard. Hands show. Black shoes shuffle. Scratch. Scratch. Come.

The Nice Policeman whispered, Are you all alone.

Raggedy Andy made no reply for he knew it would do no good.

On pavement behind, black cap blue sweater comes. Blue sweater hides big tummy. Baton hand holds. Comes.

Whats this now, Ludovic. A kidnapper.

Put that buzzer away, Jérôme. red beard says. I seen him. The bulletins. Hes one wots gone missing. Cest bien, young man. We are friends. Amis. Freunden. Understand. No worries. We only want to help you get back to the right place.

Raggedy Andy looked right at the Nice Policeman and said with a smile, So you came to arrest me, did you.

Eyes get dark. Hand hand fingers thumb. Big arms black cap red beard come. Dirty yellow nails. Red cut on thumb. Blue sweater cuff blue thread hangs from. Lamppost jumps, hitting my bum, bitty bum bitty bum, bum bum bum. On tiptoe spin, my knee comes up Arms go up My coat Blue sweater bumps, spins me dum ditty dum ditty big tummy comes Allee spins Red beard runs Dum ditty Ugh Lamppost Blue sleeves hug My foot climbs hip We like to hop Blue sweater Black cap We like to hop on top of pop Red beard hollers Stop you must not hop on top of pop.

Lamppost my hands foots climb.

Wha the bloody ell was that. says little black cap little black baton big tummy below.

Red beard tips, lamppost sits between black pantlegs. Black cap Hand pushes, eyes show. As he sat thinking very hard, the Nice Fat Policeman pulled the little blue book from his pocket. He looked carefully to find a way to catch Raggedy Andy and arrest him.

Down below, big tummy bends Help you up sarge baton slips under blue sweater arm. Blue sweater red beard Blue sleeves lift Opah Ludovic black shoes clap clap stones. Black caps blue sweaters stand little, below. Lets get you dusted off. Hand slaps big black botty.

Merci, Jérôme. Okay, thats good. I said thats good. Hand slaps hand. Ça suffit, Jérôme.

Its cos Im holding my baton in one hand and touching your arse with the other, sint it. big tummy says. You should be more secure in your masculinity.

Red beard, hands on hips says, O. Perhaps youd show me the way. You could answer the phones while Eugenia walks the beat.

Palm baton slaps. Right, then. Okay this has gone on long enough get down here you numbskull youll break your bloody neck.

Black cap jumps, lamppost Baton hits bong bong bong bouncy tummy.

Jérôme you look like a fool.

O. Who just tackled this lamppost like his brothers drunk wife at Christmastime.

Halt die Schnauze, Jérôme.

Toro, toro, eh sarge.

Jérôme.

My hands knees pull. In my purple glasses Lamplights glow bright. Blinking. Tipped black caps stand below, hands on hips.

We got to get him down from there.

He dont look like he wants to get got.

Well. I spose we had better just go home then.

Vraiment. Shandys and football classics on the telly.

Pour lamour de Dieu, we are sworn officers, Jérôme.

Okay. hand says, turns cap backwards. Alors, gimme a boost, Ludovic. Ill just pluck him by the toe like a daisy.

Black shoe lifts Black shoe Hands grab Hands lift tremble Lamppost Hands climb Uh err ooo Cripes the crêpes love you too much Jérôme Hand picks an apple Hand picks a plum Brown eyes blink, mouth shows tongue fingers wiggle dum ditty dum.

No good. Hes too far up. Lemme down. Stones Black shoes clapclap.

Red beard groans, hands flapflap.

We need us a bit more lift, boss.

Ashcan Blue sweater arms spin wahgit wahgit across stones. Here, stand on this.

We should ring for a ladder.

Nonsense. This cans high gauge steel. Bang bang. None too rusty. Dont go way, lad. We will be right there. Okay, Ludovic. Sur tu va.

Black shoes step, stand on creaking ashcan. Red beard tips up, down. Arms fly, wave. Mein gott. Lamppost blue sweater sleeve hugs.

Alors, here I come, boss.

Black shoes step Whoa stand before black shoes. Lamppost Blue sleeve hugs. Blue sweater Blue sleeve hugs. Blue sweater tummies rub. Teeter.

Ive never felt so close to you.

Lunacy. I smell it on your breath.

Okay, now, boss. Gimme the heave ho.

If only.

Botty out, black shoe hands hold, lift. Ashcan rattles. Hand on shoulders, push.

Ye gods. You. Bloody. Tonne.

Lamppost Blue sweater arms hug, pull. Blue sweater arm reaches, my heel fingers scratch. My mouth hollers, my arms hug lamppost, knees foots push up post, metal bar my hands grab under lamplights. My pantleg hand grabs.

Gotcha now, kidnapper.

Attends Jérôme the can

Crunk black shoes trip black pantlegs kick Oof red beard hits stones, ashcan bounces rolls down allee Dum ditty dum ditty dum dum dum. Post blue sweater arms hug. Hand hand fingers thumb. Turned black cap blue sweater grunts Uhh pulls lamppost Uhh pulls

Get. Down. Here. You. Bastard

Brown eyes get big Blue sweater arms spin, falls. Blue sweater on stones big botty hits. Oof. Black pantlegs tip arsy versy Tinkling coins spin roll down allee.

I am glad, Mister Policeman, you are in no hurry to arrest me. Raggedy Andy said with a chuckle and the Nice Policeman was sure he saw him wink his eye.

Metal bar hard to my foots. My hands on lamplights.

Down allee, black cap blue sweater comes. Curly black hair Black cap shows. No worries, lads. I saw the whole thing. I even got the plate number of that lamppost.

Maurice. The art and science of better late than never. So good of you to join us.

Jérôme, you whale, get off me. says red beard. Hands, blue sweater elbows push. Black pants somersault, pants rip, show white.

Magnifique, sarge. You made me tear another pair of trousers. Central takes that out of my pay, you know.

That your boy in the crows nest. says curly black hair. How in hades he get up there.

Ludovic gave him a boost.

Red beard groans, rises. Black cap hand wiggles. Jérôme, your pay was getting docked no matter what you did to your trousers.

Wot.

Chut, chut.

Surely we three can get one nutter down from a streetlamp. Especially considering theres only one way down.

Youd think so, wouldnt you, Maurice.

I say we wait him out. Ring Eugenia for sandwiches and beer and the playing cards.

My foots jump from metal bar Hhhh Pigeons tha tha tha Window sill comes Hits my foots Glass bangs my knees My hands Window frame hits My fingernails dig into soft wood.

Awning below. Water has awning. Awning my toe taps. Water shivers. Hands on black caps, black pants black shoes clump clump clump under awning.

You seen that jump he made.

Incroyable.

Now what.

My foot steps. Awning snaps. Water spills Putain splashes sputtering hollering mouths. On pavement wet cap lies. My foots slide along wood moulding. Down below, hand on hip, fist shakes, dripdripdrip. Shivery me.

Hep. Look whos here now.

Arm in arm more monkeys come. Many more fingers. Many more thumbs. Many more monkeys. Many more drums.

Mario, Jacques.

Boss. Why you boys all wet.

Wet black cap Hand takes from pavement.

Eh, Jérôme tore his trousers again.

How many pairs this week, buster.

Renzo, Franck. From the smell Id say you lads have happy hour firmly buttoned up.

Whistle Red beard blows Fweet. Enough. Redirect your attencion above Baileys old launderette.

Black caps Eyes eyes eyes turn to my eyes.

That your kidnapper. Howd he get up there.

Lamppost. After Sarge gave him a boost with his arse.

The Nice Policeman shook the water from his clothes as best he could and then walked around and around the pavement. We must follow and capture him. the Nice Fat Policeman cried, Come on.

Heel to heel, my foots slide over moulding. Wood splintery to my hands, my cheek. Corner comes. Broke wood slats my fingers tootsies climb. Magpies bawl, hoot.

Hes heading for the roof. To the fire escape.

Blue sweaters, black caps run dum ditty dum ditty dum dum dum.

Up that ladder, Mario.

Why me.

So you can lead your four little brothers to glory.

Ha ha. And you and Jérôme.

Youve not had the years of brie and moules frites and duck confit they have, petit frère.

En haut, maintenant. Hes getting away.

Tong tong tongtongtong goes ladder under black shoes, climbing hands.

Rooftop comes. Allee below. Dry wood snaps under my foots,

slats pinch my tootsies. Pigeons flutter, bob. Dum ditty dum ditty black caps come We got im now boys Black shoes over rooftop stumble dum ditty waving batons.

Across allee, slate rooftop below. Over my shoulder, black caps run. Black caps come. Wood rooftop my foot pushes.

Over allee, hum. Tummy tickles. Byebye.

My foots Slate rooftop hits forearms Rooftop tumbles under my back Huh huh huh.

On wood rooftop Black pants trip, fall on botties, black shoes stutter dudda dudda da Mother Mary You see that Almost four metres Not even a running start Even with it whod try that jump It aint human.

Foot hurts. Splinter fingers pull from toe. Red dot shows.

In allee below little black caps, little blue sweaters.

That daft little cuss is pushing his luck.

Ludovic, he aint daft and he aint lucky. Hes the bloody pet thief.

No. Him. No. Hes, hes feeble. You saw.

And what are we. Seven of us dwarves and we aint caught him yet.

Feeble or not, hes finally made a mistake. Theres no way off this building. To the roof, Jérôme.

Little black caps run, door blue sweater shoulder hits, byebye. Roof rough to my foots. Corner comes. Tall tree below.

On wood rooftop above sit huddled black caps. Monkeys drum and monkeys hum. Hum drum hum drum hum drum hum.

Que est quil fait.

Ask him.

My breath goes in, out. Green leaves shiver.

What the hell you think youre gonna do.

Tree jumps. Hollering.

My chest branch hits. My cheeks, nose, leaves slap purple glasses byebye Branches my hands grab, break, fall My foot trunk catches, hurts Bark fingernails scratch pavement sky spin My back tree trunk hits, cough cough, my ankle twists pavement jumps toward my hands My hands grab trunk behind my head Bark burns my wrists pavementskyspin. My foots botty back Pavement hits Wham.

Owie. my mouth says. Over tree, blue sky moon.

High above, rooftop eyes stare.

Incroyable.

Hes dead.

His eyes are open.

Hes dead. He spun about like a bloody ragdoll. No one could take that.

Hes on his feet.

Hes dead Im tellin you.

Hes running away down the allee.

Above, red beard hollers, Whered he go.

The morgue, if You go by doctor Marios diagnosis, boss.

Cawing echoes updown allee. Running. Ankle hurts. Hands burn. Windows doors dark. Dust. Down stone steps. Canal. Up allee. Croa croa crows holler above. Round corner.

Courtyard. Big wood doorway comes. Red drops drip from my fingers, my wrists. Doorstep curls under my hip. Dust puffs under my mouth. Darkness.

The Raggedys gave a happy shout, for there, not over twenty feet from where they sat, was a mud puddle of chocolate ice cream. Of course, an ice cream mud puddle is nothing like an ordinary mud puddle, except that it looks a good deal like one.

The difference, though, is that an ice cream mud puddle is just as good to eat as one of Mothers nicest puddings, and the grass all around it is covered with white frost, just like the frost you see in the garden in the fall. If you ever see an ice cream mud puddle, you will know it immediately.

The Raggedys were pleased to see one, for they knew just how nice and sweet Despierta a chocolate ice cream mud puddle Despierta   Sun waters my eyes. Sun hollers, blinks, bright. Hand hides my eyes. Hip hurts. Mouth dry. Pigeons coo, strut, fly.

Despierta. No puedes dormer aqui. Es prohibido. Entiendes. You can not to sleep here. Ah.

Shaky broom wrinkly spotted hands hold. Torn hole in my pants broom bristles. My knee prickles.

Levantate. You go somewheres else. Thees a church. Iglesia. Entiendes, mishito.

My hands push. Botty sits. Collar tag clink clink. Doorstep cold hard to my botty. Red scabs wrists ankles have. My eyes hands hide, sun hurts, head hurts.

Levantate. Vamos. Broom scratches my tootsies.

My mouth hisses, legs jump, stalk sidetoside.

Ay ay ay. says wrinkled hands big watery eyes wiry hair. Broom shakes. S s sacate de aqui barrabas. O llamo a la policia.

Down allee my hands run. Over footbridge. Narrowboat ropes creak in canal below Twelve centimes, oysters Past broke cart, wood wheel tipped on stones. Dogs bark. Magpies hop. Hand has bow, saws violin. Toe taps cup of tin. Eye winks, tooths show. Cui daaaa do. Cui daaaaaa dohh. Down broke stone steps. Eyes bingbing, shadows. Cats stand, stretch, meou.

Cest tu.

Etais tu.

Sh. my mouth says. My pantlegs Cats rub, my hair hanging leaves scratch, cheeks, coatsleeves. Down broke steps, cats pripppripprip to little square. Cats meou. Spinning sunlight. Picket fence. Dollhouse.

In little square Black caps stand. Hands on hips, they turn sidetoside. Me, crouching leaves hide.

Viens viens. meous mangy Boutin.

The Nice Policeman stood there and listened and listened until his ears turned red as his false whiskers but not a sound could he hear coming from inside any of the houses.

He says, The Frau alleged the kidnapper was trying to take her boy into one of these condemned buildings.

Make a tasty croque monsieur out of him probably.

Jérôme.

Well, the pet thief might be daft, but he aint stupid. He will not back to here again. Go way, cat.

Red beard hand scratches. All these abandoned monuments, these hovels and huts, these rockpiles. He probably watches us.

Why dont we just search everything, sarge.

Red beard says, Warrants, Franck. No judge is gonna give em, not when Haussmanns involved. We find something, the premises become evidence. You think Haussmanns gonna be held up by an attempted kidnapping by a missing party who dont want to be found. The baron would blow the courthouse down. The stationhouse. Our houses.

Although he felt it was a rude thing to do, the Nice Fat Policeman went around peeping in at all the windows, but he could see nothing for all the curtains had been pulled down.

Id hoped to find a clue. he says. A scent. The suspect. Something sure, that dont need a judges sayso.

Mais si cest vrai, boss. What Jérôme says. If that was the pet thief.

It wasnt. red beard says. He was stealing a person, not pets. Who bloody knows the why.

But the frau heard a womans voice just before she caught up with the kidnapper. I bet it was the blonde.

Even if he was the. Pet thief. It would make no difference. Except the papers would paint us even bigger fools than we already are.

Vraiment. Ssst. Scat, cat.

Black shoe kicks, hissing Ginger tabby jumps runs.

Red beard says, My gut says hes here, despite Jérômes panaché and escargot laced opinion to the otherwise. The lad doesnt know where to go. What to do. Hes afraid, he ran. But he also wanted help. I could see it in his eyes.

How we get him out, boss. If we cant get a warrant.

Big blue sweater belly says, Why we cant get a warrant is why we dont need a warrant, boys. Haussmanns tearing this all down as we speak. The pet thief either gets crushed, flushed or becomes another districts cuss. So why, uh, fuss.

Hmmm. the Nice Fat Policeman mused as he went to the old fountain and sat down to think.

Crouching, red cards Hands throw on red cards.

You ever seen so many cats, Maurice.

Sure. In roma. Or was it hell.

Ha ha.

Hand throws red card.

Sabot.

Emmerdeur.

Back up broke steps. Chirping cats my legs push. Into bushes, past trees, ivy leaves my arms push. Crumbly bricks fingers tootsies climb.

Où vas tu. whines Little Lulu.

My nose Green ivy scratches, my cheeks, coat, collar, foots. Broke window Ivy hides. Glass bits coatsleeve sweeps byebye. My botty soft wood sill holds. My knees my arms hug. Me ivy hides. Darkness comes to my breath. Darkness hides my eyes. Miaou.

The two Raggedys caught hold of hands and ran over to the large stone and when they reached it they saw little steps leading to the top. Up the steps they climbed until they could look over the top of the great stone.

My nose Ivy tickles. Wind blows. My eyes Hands rub. Up ivy, up bricks, my arms legs climb. Wood parapet. Purple sky. Across broke rooftop, rusty pipes growl Wood parapet hand holds Down bricks foots slide, drop to blue tarp rooftop below. Rolling, tree branch hand catches Branch knee hooks below Tree spins downup allee stones hit my foots.

Dust. Stones. Dung. Bones.

Behind Dollhouse, Big Orange David groans. David crouches over purple feathers, tongue licks, green eyes squint, my eyes.

Yvette.

Hands clap. Purple Yvette Big Orange David mouth bites, David runs prippripprip under fence byebye.

Old splinter barrel behind Dollhouse. Red blue green yellow orange feathers has Barrel. Beaks open. Eyes shut. Red Lovebird. Yellow Honey. Green Tintin. White Curie. Blue feathers, Hyacinth macaw. Eye blinks, yellow black, yellow black. Pokey yellow stripe tongue Black beak shows.

Water. hyacinth squawks, blinks yellow black.

Hurt. keens hyacinth.

Hyacinth my hands take from barrel. Hyacinth my arm cradles. Hand pets. Cats come. Miaou. Miaou.

Maaaaaama. he hollers, trembly yellow cheeks.

O boy. I say.

Flies bzzbzz. In splinter barrel orangeyellowred feathers riffle. Over my tootsies, up cobblestones, green feather spins. In allee, in yellow weeds between bomes, crouching cats meou, blink blink.

Grey board on stones. My hand takes. Over splinter barrel grey board lies, birds hide. Flies spin, bzzbzz.

Dirty Boutin grumbles Faim, faim, faim.

Gone pecan they, scat you you. I say.

Chattery groan. Smoky plume. Behind white bricks hollers big Boum Boum.

From yellow weeds cats run. Jinx Tivoli Saraband wriggle byebye under Dollhouse ivy. Ivy rattles. Broke lattice. Redbluegreen window above, blue eyes hide. Ivy my hand pulls. Broke window. Hyacinth macaw my arm hugs. I crawl inside.

Dust. Damp. Pee smell. Poo.

Darkness says, You lost your hat. So the coppers followed you. You yeasty boil brained ultramaroon.

On stairs, in darkness, Bunny Freda arm hugs. Tinfoil hat shimmers. In stairwell above candlelight flickers.

Durdy dee. Bunny says, arms flaflaflap.

Why dost thou cradle that dead bird. Freda says. Down stairs clic. Clac. Clic. Slow black boots. Blue eyes bingbing my eyes, tinfoil hat flashes. You saw I had to rid us of the lot of them, those bloody lollipops snooping right outside. All this hooting n screeching, like they thought they were going to be freed. Well, I ate what I could. And since Bunnys taking solid food now. Still, what a waste.

Outside, big Boum Boum. Floorboards shakes. Tooths tickle. Ceiling dust.

Freda boots come clic clac clic. Tinfoil hat shines. From my hand, hyacinth macaw Freda hand takes. Bunny comes dirty pajamas to my hands, twinkles Papa Papa Pa. Ivy Freda hand pushes Out broke window Macaw arm swings spins out window. Plaff. On stones, shiny blue wings spread over dry horse dung. Inside beak, yellow stripe tongue.

Toward macaw Boutin creeps, yellow eyes my eyes.

Freda rises, allee ivy hides. Behind ivy, Dirty Boutin says, Miam, miam, miam.

Bunny my arm hugs. Fuzzy black hair my hand pats. Little pajamas damp. Pee.

Hands on hips Freda says, I know, you piedpipered that bloody cretin all the way back here cos you saw it was kin. Lets entice this cuddly pinhead to the Dollhouse, recruit it to our club. You could even be its mentor. Codswallop. Cant you tell them n us apart by now. That lot in particular. Bloody helmet. Think he can climb anything higher than his rocking horse.

My nose Bunny fingers pinch. Durdy deedee. twinkles Bunny, mouth drooly, nose runny.

My collar Freda hand grabs. My throat Freda claws scratch. Burning hollers come. Collar Freda fingers take. Into shadows flies collar clink clink. Bunny I hug.

Freda hollers, Youre daft as a brush Why the ding dong bell did you have to lure that rotting vegetable here Youve ruined everything inagimable I tried to show you how to be You think Sawn wlil uadrnstned Ha I cannot stomach the sight of you Your sorry looks the pzzueld glance the poised stance Not knoiwng whether to run or cower Jseus Cirhst How did you eevr mkae it tihs far in lfie, The way you bungalow bill

Boum boum Dollhouse shakes

makes me want to

Black boot kicks my botty

Owie. I say, into dusty shelf I tic toc bump

Christ You gleeking beef witted lout Quit that bloody bleating Now look Youve upset Bunny

from my hands Freda hands pluck hollering Bunny

Shh Shhhh I said Shut up you mewling flea bitten rodent do you want to end up in the barrel too.

Freda turns, on dusty wood shelf hollering Bunny drops Stay put Bunny falls back, kicks My eyes Freda eyes burn And if the sight of you int revolting enough What is that ungodly smell Its fish oil Its fear Glands Gdadmon I ought to kick your disshevelled butt again you smelly geek you fishified scut I ohgut to torhw you in the seetrt What the hello did I think bringing you here I must be dumb as you are Dnot gimme tsohe big bworn doe eeys You fool born, half faced foot licker You booby prize You popped blister Why the hlel ddint Dolttile do me n the taepayxr a fvaor Stuff you in a sack a rocks Throw you in the bloody lock Quit looking at me like that you wretched fraidy pussy cat

My cheek Freda hand scratches Owie Hollers come, my cheek hurts, my mouth burns Freda boots flash My legbottyarmhead Freda boots kickkickkick Bunny cries Under my clothes crouching hollers burn, from my mouth hot hisses Dont sass me Freda hand swats my jaw Room spins Edges of my eyes burn darkness. Darkness.

Dont you pass out on me now, you snot bubbling chimp Under my arms hands grab, pull Youre going to give me the satisfaciton of yuor compelte attention

Freda hands push me Shelf hits my back Rocks tic toc

Whilst Im kicikng the shit out of you

On wood shelf Bunny cries.

Freda hand hums. Black cross knuckles. Red scratches thumb Dum ditty dum ditty dumdumdum Arms up I spin Hand comes Boot comes Hand comes Boot I spin duck cartwheel jump hands foots huh huh huh huh. Shelves crash bang.

In flat above, birds fweet fweet. Freda eyes tinfoil hat hides. Freda mouth huff puff, huff puff. Tinfoil hat hand pushes up. Blue eyes, my eyes.

Sirens pin pon pin pon outside. Hear that. Freda says. You lost your hat. So animal control will be here anon. And if not, then Swan, with a different hat for me n you.

In flat above birds fweet fweet. From shelf kneeling Bunny cries, Papa. Black hair stands. Freda chest big little. Blue eyes big, dark. Freda says, Youre divine, you botched experiment. You heart without a head. Je taime, Scarecrow, all the way down to the flaky russets of skin round your broken toenails.

My cheek my fingers touch. My fingertips red wet.

But you dont love me, chickpea. Freda says. Tinfoil hat shines. From shelf, Bunny. Freda hugs, bounces. Bunny back Freda hand rubs. Shshshsh.

Bunny cries, Non non non, little fists red, stiff legs kick toandfro.

Outside big **Boum Boum**. Windows rattle. Up steps, on hip Bunny, Freda boots clomp clomp clomp.

Be upstairs ready my angel. Freda sighs. Not bloody likely. Am I just doomed to give my soul and blood and womb to blokes with tiny hearts who only yawn at my perfume. Freda says. Upstairs Freda goes, steps creak creak. My hands foots follow.

Bunny on landing Freda stands. Bunny comes thap thap thap, arms up, eyes nose mouth wet. Uppy, uppy, **Papapa**.

Wood landing creaks. In flat birds fweet fweet. Bunny my hands grab Arms hug Chubby cheek smoochy I say, Chim chimney, chim chimney, chim chim cherroo.

Freda boot stamps. I jump. Freda says. Why dont you kiss me, too, damn you. Im pretty enough, arent I.

My jaw Freda hands grab I step away, hug Bunny On my mouth Freda mouth Freda breath in my mouth I holler, hot Freda lips chew my lips My chest Hot Freda nonees rubs calmate calmate Freda nonies my hand pushes Kiss me back, you idiot My cheeks my lips Non Hisses spray Love me, just this once love me goddamn you My hand pushes Shy away. I say.

Freda turns. From yellow hair hand pulls tinfoil hat. Hands squeeze hat. Tinfoil ball tumbles ish tish down dusty wood steps. Freda says, I just want to mean something to someone. If only a whit, a scintilla, a crumb. I want someone to think Im beautiful and special. I want someone to love me before Im done. My lives arent numbered, but my days are. Yours too. CACI or Swan or Haussmann, we are through.

Outside, big Boum Boum. Dust twirls. Cough cough.

Blue eyes shimmer.

In flat birds fweet fweet fweet.

Why youve been gone for days, Oboy. says Freda. I thought the CACI or those coppers got you. Freda arm waves. I thought I had to get out, why wait. So I hit the shops where I knew I could score fast and I didnt have to scale tall buildings with Bunny on my sore old hip. That included Dolittles. You know, I searched high and low for his bankroll, even under his pallet while he was passed out on grappa. But I couldnt find the money. So, I took more birds. Cant be empty handed for Swan.

Cheeks wet, Freda spins, walks clic clac into flat. In door follow cats. O boy. parrot says.

Lantern light shivers. In flat, in cages, cockatiel, parakeets, parrots. In cage on books. Pretty Boyd dances foot to foot. Orange Pretty Boyd eye goes to my eye. Blink blink. Green wings flap. Green feather head ducks sidetoside.

Freda says, An old freund.

O boy. says Pretty Boyd, blink blink.

O boy. I say.

On dirty mattress, under torn rumpled duvet. Snores. On lumpy pillow Greasy yellow hair lies.

Psst.

Pretty Boyd rainbow mask tilts sidetoside. Orange eyes my eyes. Blink blink. Candlelight shadows flicker. On floorboards Bunny I sit. Bunny nose drips. Snots.

No Papa. Uppy.

To cages I crawl.

Uppy uppy Papa.

Chk chk chk chk. On my back Bunny I put. On my ear Wet mouth twinkles, Hortsey. Chk chk chk. Past snoring Freda, past duvet feathers, to cages I crawl. Gate latch my fingers pinch, gate opens Squeak My hand Pretty Boyd claws grab My arm Pretty Boyd climbs, greenredblue wings thapthapthap my cheek. Bunny twinkles. Down my neck wet trickles. Claws pinch my shoulder. My ear beak tickles.

Pretty Boyd whispers, Ach. Hallway, Mac. Go.

Us too. says cockatiel. White wings thapthapthap.

Take with you. says yellow mask parrotlet.

Ach, bird brains. Clam up.

Arm hugs Bunny. Over baby gate I step. Tails flicker, Anabel Tomas run. Down hall I crouching tiptoe. Bunny tumbles Thump. Whee. Out redbluegreen cracked window, past white bricks, past tile rooftop. Yellow lobster in pit. Black dirt into lorry lobster tail swings. Lorry shakes. Pit. In boulevard beside white bricks, wrecking ball sits. In dim sunlight black ball sways rockabye baby.

Ach, ole charcuterie all wots left. Big boum boum for you next. Pretty Boyd says. Yellow hats come. Set up bad. Mon ami, grimalkin sleeps. Gotta amscraaaayy Pretty Boyd spins on my shoulder, green wings flap flap flap my cheek Pretty Boyd squawks, Scat, fleabit furball spies

Past Bunny, Cecil Tony Simone run, hiss blackwhitebrown byebyes.

Bunny twinkles, thump thump thump comes. Candybiddy. Bunny says.

Bunny. says Pretty Boyd. Us grimalkin kidnaps all.

Green tail feathers Little fat fingers grab. Down green head goes, rubs chubby Bunny fingers, Bunny nose.

Bunny twinkles. Pretty Boyd beak Bunny fingers pinch. Honk honk. Pretty Boyd says. Greenredblue wings stretch. Bunny eyes big, wet. Bunny mouth wet. Twinkles. In wet mouth little piece of white. Little piece of white My finger pokes.

Milk tooth. says Pretty Boyd. Chipmunk crack nuts soon.

In flat, cockatiel hollers, Gemme outta here.

Shaddap. says Pretty Boyd, wings flapflapflap. Cockatiel always me me me me me me meez. Lucky no salt tail.

Rainbow feathers fat fingers pull. Hey, no piñata.

Chubby hand Greenredblue wings flapflapflap.

Bunny twinkles. Candybiddy, Papa.

Tweedledeedledee. says Pretty Boyd. Babies call you Papa. Woild upside down.

Out redbluegreen window, past tile rooftop, yellow lobster hollers, tail lifts. Smoke puffs. In lorry, dirt pours. Lorry hoots, shakes, rolls away. Tinktinktinktink huffing Lobster goes.

Look, Mac. My eye.

Mister stands outside shop. White hair sticks up. Mister looks sidetoside in allee. Mister turns eyebrows shoulders hands raise updown. Wrinkled fingers smell smoke brown. How can he make it out there alone. Mister says little.

Remember him. Pretty Boyd says. Old lush wants home, you. You, Mister papers town. Talk to cozzers, lips turn blue. Bet real papa want Bunny, too.

Ahem.

In doorway behind. Elbows on doorframe Freda. Simone Cecil Tony sit, lick lips, forepaws. Blink blink.

Meeting adjourned. says Freda.

Ach. Pretty Boyd says. Down hall rainbow wings flapflapflap, red door goes, byebye. Candlelight flickers.

Look who back.

Enjoy vacation.

O, choke on millet.

Cages bangbang, flapflapflap. In allee, round wrecking ball, Yellow hats stand.

Come on, chickpea. says Freda. Watching the mayhem wont make it go away. It wont even slow it down. Worse comes to worst we slink away to another hideout. Saying goodbyes simple as pie. We just have to watch out for Swan.

Yellow hair byebye. Down hall Bunny I walk, my fingers in chubby fists, cats run prippripprip. In flat, in cage, Pretty Boyd preens, orange eye winkwink. On mattress Freda lies. Time for lunch. Freda says. Hands reach, fingers wiggle. To Freda hands Bunny goes. Against Freda tummy Bunny curls, snuffly nose. Tshirt Freda hand pulls up. Pale nonees. Nonee

⟨273⟩

Bunny fingers clutch. In Bunny mouth pink nipple moves.

Oboy, lie down with me. Im freezing. Lie down and keep me warm while I tell you a story from the raggedys.

Round mattress Cats curl, eyes bingbing.

On mattress Freda foots black pants pale nonees. Bunny lies, sucks. Bunny legs kick. Eyes shut. Tweet tweet.

Lie down I said.

Mattress is cold lumpy to my elbows knees. Sweat. Pee. Ceiling cracks drip. Shiver. Candlelight flicks. Prip prip prip.

Closer. Freda says. You arent doing me any favors laying way over there. My sleeve Freda hand grabs My arm hollers Hollers stab fingertips shoulder.

Bunny cries. Ear finger pokes.

You dizzy eyed mongrel. Freda says. Cant you do one thing my way for a change. A little body heat is that too much to ask All this nsruing drians me of calicum and wtaer and all tsehe ohter thigns ctas need Im freizeng and Bunnys cold too and Swans out there waiting for me and you so

To my feet I rise. Red Freda glasses I take. Out doorway. Down stairs, cats meou.

Mac. hollers Pretty Boyd.

Get back here. Where are you going. hollers Freda.

Dollhouse door creaks. Cold comes Fweet fweet fweet To my foots doorstep roughcold. In my hand red candy. Sweet. In my nose plant smells sniffle. On white picket fence green buds tremble. Black Bart Mittens slink slink between white pickets. Tails kink. Yellow eyes blink blink. Pointy white tooths.

Miaou. says Bart.

Miaou. says Mittens.

Poisson. says they.

Hsst. I say.

Prip prip prip into crackly weeds.

On doorstep, white paint flakes. My dirty toe pokes. Red Freda glasses my finger pushes. In fog above, lamp glows. Blink blink. Around white pickets Fog curls.

Miaou.   Miaou.

My hand pulls Dollhouse doorlatch shhhtah. Under my foots cracked pavement moves. Broke gate passes. Cold wet cobblestones have green mosses. Prip, prip, prip

Miaou.

Up broke stone steps I run. In courtyard above, Movsha plays *Caw see own. Caww seee ownnnn.* Branches Bushes have smelly blossoms, yellow blinky eyes. Mittens. Red mouth says Enfuis, enfuis.

Pigeons warble above. Scritch scratch haha down below. In fog shadows move. Up broke steps I go.

Down steps fog rolls. Shadows flicker. I leap into bushes into trees Mittens springs My arms push rattling ivy leaves, broke bricks hurt My foots climb Hee hee flees Fingers tootsies Green ivy scratches my nose, cheeks, clothes Hiding windowsill My hands find, climb Rusty metal blind Cooing eaves Wood parapet.

Miaou, miaou. Where goest thou.

Across broke rooftop I run Pigeons strut hop thathathap oorrh oorrh Over holes I jump Roof splinters under my foots Off wood parapet my hip slides Down powdery bricks Heels run ch ch ch fall Rusty drainpipe my hands catch Squeeeek Broke window Blue tarp roof soar above me Over wood parapet shadows peek Tee hee My foots hurt Oof.

Cobblestones. Allee. To Dollhouse I run.

Fog puffs, curls, shadow sings, On the border of the wood, All alone the Ghost Flower stood. Like a moonbeam dressed in white, such a very pretty sight.

Behind me Fog hands grab push pull off red sunglasses Hi Oboy Hey You Comment va tu The cops the pigs they come n go but always come on back you know ha ha ha

Green eyes glitter, gold tooths shine. Black fedora tips.

O, mooncalf. You piedpipered the cozzers right to your doorstep. Attempted kidnapping, wot.

Twas a retard, Street.

We cant have you thinking for yourself, its true. We told Freda to keep a leash on you. Clearly now we must intrude.

Arms pull my arms. Hurt. For your own good, O, Yeah boy we want you veddy veddy success On my foots boots step, hurt Just got to make sure you dont fuck up again I holler Hand slaps Mouth hurts Owie owie owie.

We will palaver with Freda soon enough. For now, your peers

Lemme learnm, Street.

Fog hides. Shadow clomp clomp clomps cobblestones.

White jacket Pointy elbows Hands on hips. Gold tooths shine. Dainty, dear girl. You wish to play tax collector.

Fog tumbles Brown boots come, ch ch. Cigarette mouth spits. I aint forgot that shit he pulled wit my trick. An I sure as hell aint forgive the prick. Black sunglasses come. Dusty brown Fists get big. White tooths shine. Now this dumb sucka got the cops snoopin, on top o stealin from me. Hell yeah, I got to be taxman, Street.

You have a contract, then.

Je sais, je sais. I takes the tax, or I pays the tax.

Être et durer, Street.

Hands let go my arms, push me, pinch my botty Oo oo, sad but true, you Daintys bitch now, silly fool.

Hot breath black lips say Think you can keep yalls xray eyes on my hands this time, muthafucka Fist jumps Stars my mouth hurts bzzzzt Gotcha Hollers come My chin Gold rings fist Pow Dats got to hurt I spin away Get back here, bitch For my coat Hand grabs I duck, spin, across wood fence my foots run bam bam bam Crac Hole boot kicks Muthafucka Big hands come, boots shuffle, arms out to sides What You think you fass, boy You think you fass, you nuttin but a hollerin billy goat Arms jump, hug I duck, somersault, jump up Back of long furry coat has tear Fog pushes me Dont go away teddy bear Furry coat spins Arm swings I fall away Lamp shines in fog My hands catch cobblestones my legs swing above Cobbles hit my foots Ta dah.

What the fuck. crooked white tooths say. Bitch, I get true which you you gonna wish dem handsprings was bedsprings.

Under boots Bricks tunk tunk tunk, come. Toward my tummy Boot swings.

Scrapes. Scratches. Boot. Drops dried. Red on boot. Comes.

Kicking boot My hand slaps I spin away O lookatim go Under my foots stones scrape sideways Fog pushes me, caws, Get bcak in trehe, litlte mosue

Brown fists come God dman it cockkucsa you daed now I was jset gnona baet yo asre Now I mo cut yo haert out n eat it rgiht in fornt a yo eeys.

Raggedy Andy knew it wouldnt hurt him even if the Howloon did eat him, for he was made of cloth stuffed with nice soft, white cotton. So even though all the guards and men of the court who liked to see fights yelled with the king, Andy just smiled his painted smile and didnt say a thing.

Into furry coat Brown hand goes. Brown hand shows.

Knife shines.

Knife comes.

Scratchy blade.

Chipped blade.

Dusty brown cha cha cha blade Knuckle drips red Owie I spin Past my cheek Knife flashes Knife whistles, cuts my coat Thass right You dead sucka Cmon Toward my throat Knife hums Raggedy Andy and the Hungry Howloon rushed round and round the candy apple tree. The Howloon tried to grab Andys cotton soft arm, but Raggedy Andy spun and the Howloon slipped on an ice cream mud puddle and fell.

Thats the time I fooled you, Raggedy Andy laughed.

Ill get you for that. screamed the Hungry Howloon, hooves pounding as fast as they could. Raggedy Andys feet went ratatatata up the candy apple tree and before she could stop herself, the Howloon crashed right into the trunk. Candy apples tumbled boop boop boop all over the ground.

Long furry coat rolls over, sits. To knife Big hands knees crawl huh huh huh.

On knife Brown boot steps.

Street. Cest quoi ce bordel. I aint true wit him yet.

From cobbles Knife Long pale fingers take. Flashing gold tooths says, Dainty, my dear, you crawl about on your hands and knees. Your defeat causes us no small embarrassment.

Pink palms show. In hands brown lines. Fingers wiggle. Gimme my blade, Street.

You used to be so fast. black fedora says. We reveled in your speed, your power. But mooncalf punked you at your game. Now hes gone and done it again. What makes the victor. Honour thy contract, dear.

Hep, Street, cmon, baby.

Tut, tut. Mignonette. Maidenhair.

Furry coatsleeves Hand hand hand grab Green pantlegs kick Black boots clonk clonk cobblestones. Street, baby.

Sleep, Dainty, sleep. Our cottage vale is deep. The little lamb is on the green, With woolly fleece so soft and clean, Sleep, Dainty, sleep.

My mouth says Hum.

Furry sleeves Fog arms pull Get the fcuk off me Arms legs kick Setret you owe me dnot do it I lvoe you

Dainty shall have a new bonnet. And Dainty shall go to the fair. And Dainty shall have a blue ribbon To tie up her bonny black hair.

Furry coat collar Gold ringed fingers rub.

Street nooooo

And why may not I love Dainty. And why may not Dainty love me. And why may not I love Dainty

White coatsleeve Hummmmmm

Cos Daintys a lifeless body.

The Hungry Howloon stood still with a queer expression upon her face as if she felt very sad and greatly surprised at the same time.

Then everyone heard a tiny whistling sound and the Hungry Howloons legs began to sag beneath her. No one said a word while the Hungry Howloon shrank and wrinkled until she fell to the floor a shrinkled heap.

My mouth says Hum BumBumBumBum hurts my head Cobblestones jump My cheek darkness hits. Papa Papa Pa.

Over me white coat spins. Arms wide. Knife sprays darkness sidetoside. Whatve we here, what have we here, Bo Peeps lil secret We fear We fear We fear

Mouth dry. Grey sky. In grey sky Lamp glows. Starling flies. Magpies weyweyweywey. Hurting, my eyes, my head. My fingertips red. Pigeons coo, strut, bow, peck peck peck. Scattered millet on cobblestones. Millet red fingers touch. My pants pockets out. Silver paint on my coat. Catsup packet flat beside me, red spout. Orange supermiracle bubble wand broke.

What this. Rattle rattle. Pills. Abbondanze.

On tummy I roll. Pigeons hop, flutter, oorrrhh, ooorrhh. Bubble wand ring my fingers pinch. My eye Ring hides.

Across allee little silver hands pull out green pants pockets, coins spill ping ping ping. Hep, Culai, that kass is alive from the dead. curly black hair says.

Broke. Bubble wand loop my fingers drop.

So what. puffy yellow coat says. All his pockets have is fucking bird seed.

Red cap says, Ya, you not esposed to feed pigeons, ha ha.

Hey you. big black sunglasses say. You not worry about we. Your dyke whore, she dead, she not care we take this.

Silver hands dig in long furry coat pockets. Francs. Silver fingers wave rainbow paper Abbondanze Gimme gimme Silver hands pull Let go asshole Its mine hand hand slap, legs kick Fuck you Some francs, some pills. says puffy yellow coat.

Little silver hand pulls red knife from red tummy. Puffy yellow coat says, And this blade. Old but good.

On furry coat shoulder Red knife wipes red. Pigeon tails fan beside. Millet beaks peck peck, coo. Brown boots little silver hands pull. Brown foots, curled tootsies. Long furry coatsleeves little silver hands pull.

Perché lei prendere queste cose. puffy yellow coat says.

Red cap says, These boots good, no holes, that is cos why.

But dumbshit they too fucking big Red cap Hand slaps I sell them so Fuck your mothers ancestors Boot throws tonk tonk Hand hand slaps Fuck you they got blood You so supastar you think can you sell bloody clothes, huh Hand slap sneaker kicks Caca Mama.

Beside cracked bome, Metal bottle hand tips. Into plastic sack Silver paint spills Pour me Get away Cmon Dont hold me Plastic hands put to nosesmouths, puff inout, inout.

I hate thees Dainty all the time. curly black hair silver nose says. Beetch kick me always.

Nose plastic sack hides. Dirty foot kicks furry coat botty.

Now who keeck the arse, Dainty. Huh. Sniff sniff.

Little botty Sneaker kicks Black sunglasses holler Ha I keeck your arse, beetch Hep, fucker pock pock pock sneakers run Hahaha Vamanos Rainbow paper silver hand waves Pigeons fly Down allee Little dirty shoes chase into fog, doom daka doom alaka die doom alala flapping silver bags byebye, hollers Fuck you, Fuck you.

I crawl. Dusty brown foots, curled tootsies. Down cobblestones red puddle goes. Green pants, red, wet. Pockets out. Shirt, red, wet. Grey lips sigh. Red puddle grey eyes spy.

Rough dusty foot my hand takes. Dusty foot my hand pets. I say, Why not I love Dainty. Why not Dainty love I.

Under foot hides little red pea. Little red pea my fingers pinch. I stand. Pockets out.

Pockets my hands push inside coat, inside pants. In coat pocket, little red pea hides.

Allee door broke. Inside, kitties meou. Pigeons peck peck peck. Up creak creak stairs I go, head hurts. Tootsies dirty. Open door. Down hall. Into flat. Freda, Bunny, byebye. Bird cages byebye. Aquariums broke. Glass glitters on wood floorboards.

O boy. I say. On brown sofa I sit.

O boy. On broke chair Pretty Boyd perches. Wings flap flap. Ach. One n only me, Mac. says Pretty Boyd. Slipped cage, hid. Long Tall, babes, stormed joint.

I say, Pretty Boyd byebye. Bunny Freda do byebye, ouai.

Pretty Boyd wings flaflaflaflap, come. Cross wood floorboards scurry mice. Pretty Boyd claws pinch brown sofa arm, wings flare.

On floorboards, little pink pack. Little pink pack I take.

Ach. Bunny in pickle, Mac. How find her.

Find her. I say. Out door I run. Down stairs, running.

O boy. Pretty Boyd says, flaps behind me.

On my shoulder Pretty Boyd sits. Yellow beak makes clic clic clic. Drainpipe whistles up sooty red bricks. Big metal blacksmith key. Juliet balconies creak. Rottled planter boxes leak. Dripdripdrip little eves. Shiver, I. Little stone dresses sigh. Grey sky.

Ach. Wot here, Mac. says Pretty Boyd. Black tongue red mask orange eyes watch sky, blinkblinkblink. Only fleabit pigeons.

Courtyard broke carts wood slats chairs. Cool brushes my hands neck hair. Fingers tootsies I grrr climb bricks. My shoulder Pretty Boyd claws pinch, green wing flaps my ear, my hair. Lintel, bricks, lamp, flapflap, bricks, moulding flapflapflap Ach, no offense, slowboat, Pretty Boyd springs, thathathatha green wings, tail sails, up, up, Catch you on the flipside Rainbow feathers black under grey sky, Windowsill, shutter, balcony I climb. Grey stone dresses gargoils come. In my throat goes dum ditty dum. Pretty Boyd swoops above, flaflaflap, Peekaboo ach ach ach Dark pigeons scuttle ooorhhh, oooorhh Wings flare, hop hop hop round stone gargoil foots Say, Who this messabout.

Beside gargoils on cracked cornice Pretty Boyd lands, Pigeons hop hop, Rainbow wings flap flap. Behold good breedin model, rats. says Pretty Boyd.

Pigeon throats swell, O, fancy birdy rooroo Circus in town roorooroo Payaso rooroo Clown rooroo Pagliaccio roorooroo How big schnozz rooroorooooooorrhhhh Pigeons scatter thathatha byebye Ats wot I thought hollers Pretty Boyd.

Huh, huh, arms tremble, balcony rail my hand takes. Rail shakes. To balcony Planter box falls Crack dirt spills Pfff on railing I stand. Streaked stone foot comes to my hand.

Look. Returned has friend, only

Foot our tickles he.

Ledge my hand takes, Huh, huh, huh. Down my back trickle tickles. My hands pull, rail shakes, bricks tootsies push, I jump, spin, sit between cracked stone foots.

Feathers ruffle, head shakes sidetoside, Pretty Boyd says, Friends in high places, Mac.

Pretty Boyd. I say.

Pretty, certainly. Boyd Pretty, acquaintance your make to pleased are we.

Ach, aint sure wot said, but hoid pretty twice. Broads classy for grotesques.

Oboy, troubled are you. Wrong is what.

Bunny Freda byebye. Scary hurt. I spy.

Danger in is life, baby. Happened what.

Baby kidnapped. says Pretty Boyd. Find Bunny before kaputski.

Find Bunny Freda. I say.

Gargoils stare.

Awooogah canal boat. Bee bee bee whiteredgreen cars. Pigeons grumble, Ooorrhh Oorhh That flying piñatas nuts.

Gargoils stare.

Cool ruffles my hair. My hurting foots. Bricks, my heels kick pap, pap, pap. Across allee, turret. Window. Windowsill pigeons roost, coo, fuss. Oua oua Down below Pekinese paws paddle dirty window.

Gargoils stare.

Cross little court, arms legs swing forwardback, forwardback. Crouching terrier poops. Terrier chases arms legs clic clic clic clic. Little streetlamps flic flic flicker.

South. Roof mansard, metal red. Dormers three.

Ach, south, south, red roof, see them. hollers Pretty Boyd, flapflapflap.

Little yellow Freda hair. Little black fedora. Little white coatsleeve hugs little pink spot. Red coat blue coat grey coat black, stalking rooftop forwardback.

Go. Baby save you.

Balcony below. Spilled dirt, planter box. Off ledge my botty slides Fingernails scratch stone tootsies Ow Rail jumps tong hurts my foots, from wall balcony pulls Screeee tips I fall Tummy jumps, Legs kick, tootsies stiff I fall Hummmm Balcony rail below comes tong hurts foots Owie I fall Rail arms grab, Legs hang I fall Big metal blacksmith key jumps Hands foots catch Wuurrrrrt falls Hum Windowsill comes dum ditty dum ditty dum dum dum Wood shutter snaps falls spinning Broke streetlamp comes Hum foots kick bricks, hands let go lamp Bricks slide up shhht scrape palmsfoots, cobblestones jump thupthupt.

Owie. I say.

Ankles hurt. Fingers bleed. Cobblestones coldhard. Pretty Boyd blue tip wings flapflapflap grey claws land beside me. Taker easy, Mac. Why kill self. Give cats chance ach ach ach.

Bricks windows rooftops lean. My eyes black shadows cross. Darkness comes. My mouth says Hummmm.

Hurry. little black dresses gargoils say.

Down allee I run knees elbows foots tsa tsa tsa tsa.

Rainbow wings flap beside. Aaaaach wotta we do, Mac. Pretty Boyd hollers, flaflaflap behind, ahead, beside.

My mouth says Hum. Up pavement I run.

Once inside the Magicians castle, Raggedy Andy went upstairs to the room where the Magician usually sat upon his throne. But everything was topsy turvy. The chairs were turned over and the Magicians throne was upside down.

Dear me. Raggedy Andy exclaimed as he ran his rag hand up through his red yarn hair. I wonder what could have happened. So Raggedy Andy scampered up the winding steps of the castle in search of Raggedy Ann.

As he climbed, a strange rapping noise echoed from above. A little voice in his cotton stuffed head told Andy, Wait, Mac, wait. If see you, hurt Bunny. So, Raggedy Andy tiptoed quietly to the tippy top.

Give Street bebe.

Fuck off Fouroclock.

Give Street bebe.

Again Raggedy Andy heard the Magicians cane rap three times upon the floor. In a shadowy garret atop the castle, Raggedy Andy espied the Magician.

Intery mintery cuttery corn, Thumbkin is sold upon the morn. Bo peep. Dont turn your crowning achievement into an embarassment for our family.

Raggedy Ann stood silently and proudly before the tall man. Again he rapped three times upon the floor with his cane. Will you speak. he cried in an angry voice.

The black shoe button eyes of Raggedy Ann seemed to glow with a light of hatred, but her voice was soft and flutelike. I have nothing to say. she answered.

Will you not consent. the man screamed. Even though I promise to lift the enchantment and restore all of the old time loveliness, just as you see it now.

Swan. Raggedy Ann replied, Your power is great and you have brought terrible misfortune upon us, but I shall never consent. You may work your evil enchantment and destroy the beauties of our castle, but your magic is not strong enough to overcome the love in my heart. Nor is it strong enough to overcome the love of those who are near and dear to me. Work your evil sorcery forever, if you will, but I will never agree. You will always remain just as far from attaining your evil desires.

Fool, fool that you are. the magician shouted. I shall give you one more opportunity. Refuse me, and I shall never again lift the enchantment from you and your people. This castle shall crumble to dust and I shall forget you.

You shall never forget. Raggedy Ann said. Deep within your selfish heart a small voice will always remind you that you have destroyed all this loveliness. And that small voice will never let you know peace or happiness. Your heart will always be filled with remorse for the evils you have brought upon us. In true justice, as you know, you receive in exact measure as you give.

Come now, Bo Peep. Did you really believe youd be able to raise little thumbkin. Did you think it wasnt a commodity to be exploited. Do you really believe in happily ever after.

You cant sell her, Swan. Ill die.

Kits, cats, sacks, and wives. How many were going to St. Ives.

I wont give her up. said Raggedy Ann.

Ill show you. the Magician howled. You do not know what a good blower I am. And he puffed so hard his eyes stuck out and it made him dizzy, but still he huffed and puffed.

Raggedy Ann drew herself up proudly and folded her cotton soft arms across her breast, but remained silent.

Once more, and only once, I give you the opportunity to save yourself and your people. the magician roared.

Raggedy Ann remained silent.

He waited a moment, as though considering everything in his mind, then said in a terrible voice, I have given you your last chance. He raised his cane as if to strike Raggedy Ann.

Fog drifts. Little headsarmslegs move toandfro in allee below.

On my shoulder Pretty Boyd head turns sidetoside. Orange eyes blink blink. Pssst. Over there. Pretty Boyd says. Greenblue wings thapthapthap. Pretty Boyd lands on ledge below. Grey claws turn, Pretty Boyd rocks sidetoside. Red mask tilts, orange eyes blink blink. Ach, up here, under dormers. Use for cover.

Down metal ladder I go, to fire escape balcony below. Under my foots balcony creaks. Over railing, to ledge, windows. On my shoulder Pretty Boyd hops. Hear. says Pretty Boyd. Window. Others.

Dormer window dirt my sleeve rubs. Inside, cage birds whistle, holler, flutter, Look. Look. Help. Save us.

Bunny first, Mac. Pretty Boyd says.

Rust stained pilaster My fingers tug. I climb. Rattly metal cornice Hand grabs. Rattly metal cornice Hand grabs. Pilaster Tootsies push green wings flutter beside Ach Hop lá I jump Fishtail bang shhh On rattly metal cornice my botty sits. Dormer hides me. Bunny cries.

Round corner of dormer, on roof above. Bunny White coatsleeve holds over slanted metal roof. Freda cries. Bunny cries, eyes red, wet, Bunny kicks, hangs from pink hood.

Metal roof Cane tap tap taps. Sad little Bo Peep. says Swan. Or is she Mary lost her little lamb. She was a fierce soldier once. A fabulous earner. For her, we were king of the cats. The love in her eyes when we played along with this crackhatchery was at turns amusing, and mystifying, but bottom line, lucrative. The dealers and other coparties cant get enough bloody parrots or parakeets, cant pay enough, the francs rolling in from her eccentric focus on bird thievery.

And so we nurtured her process, encouraged her to think she was saving petkind from some degrading dna grinding bureaucratic death colossus. Cest fou.

Swan.

But now, her ripe fantasy grows tedious.

Swan.

Shes naught but a junkie hiding from her next fix.

Swan. says Freda. I dont. I stopped. Why are you saying these things. Of course youre king of the cats.

We have always been intrigued by how detailed delusions can be. Yours, love, take the prix dexellence. You have journeyed to the limits of imagination, a stupendous effort designed to blame everyone but yourself.

Stop.

You live in a condemned tenement where you shit into holes in the floor. You frolic about with a simpleton. All because of, wots it. Gene splicing. Interspecific hybridization. Social conspiracy theory. Cest incroyable.

Swan, how can you deny what we are.

Black coat says, We be cat people, miaou. Miaou.

Red coat, Miaou.

Grey coat, Miaou. Haha.

Silver glasses says, Miaou. Who the hell ist thou.

Striped coat says, One crazy bitch. Wah wah. Ba ding.

Eat shit, Maidenhair Torn red stocking kicks Cawing Striped coat leans away.

Gold tooths show. Conspiracy. Tell us why, dear. Why would

scientists or politicians care one wit about you.

Swan, dont. says Freda. Blue eyes wet. Please.

Fuzzy little Bunny head Lips kiss. All anyone cares about is onehundredthousandAmerican.

Swan. Freda says. Freda eyes red swollen wet. Dont.

What makes a loser a loser, baby, is the search for those circumstances in which you cannot fail. Leave nothing to chance, nothing to luck, nothing to skill or to pluck.

White coatsleeve holds up Bunny, nose to pointy nose. Bunny cries. This thumbkin, however. A whole new ball of wax, verdad. We realize losers give themselves not one, but two choices. The pursuit of that at which she cannot fail. Or the pursuit of that at which she cannot win, conclusion foregone, yet the loser can say, I was this close.

Little fuzzy head lips kiss. Bunny cries. Gold tooths say, In the real world, David gets pulverized.

Freda arms Red coat black coat hold. Let us go, you bastard. Freda hollers. Please. Just let us go.

Bunny Pink sweater hood White coatsleeve long fingers hold. Gold tooths show Green eyes shine Bunny hollers, kicks. Bunny legs Freda hands grab. Freda arms Red coat Striped coat Yellow coat grab.

Oboy. says Pretty Boyd on my shoulder.

O boy. I say.

Oboy. Pretty Boyd says.

O boy. I say.

My ear yellow beak pinches, hurt. Listen me, Mac. Pretty Boyd says. Save Bunny.

Along metal gutter My hands foots stalk tiptoe, dormer to dormer. Loose rusty metal rattles little under my hands, foots. Green eyes, blue Freda eyes, hollers, red faced Bunny white coatsleeve hugs. White coatsleeve brown coatsleeves pull. Arm arm arm arm arm arm grab Freda. Gold tooths shine in light, sing, A seasonable song, Piping hot, smoking hot, What Ive got You have not Bunny falls bang Hot grey pease, hot, hot, hot Bunny pink tumbling tumbles down metal roof hollering Hot grey pease, hot Freda hollers, Noooooo

Red coat black coat stripe coat Caw.

No God Big Bunny eyes, my eyes Save baby Mac catch her now Bunny slides ssssssssssss

                                    down

                                          down

                                             metal roof.

Crying pink Bunny tumbles Peekaboo into my arms.

What in hell. hollers above. Mooncalf. Bunny cries Waaahhhhh. Seagulls cry Wah hahaha Grey sky White coatsleeve flaps BangBangBang hollers canecanecane White pantlegs brown boots come dum ditty dum ditty Oboy Run White pantlegs Skinny Freda arms hug Gold ring fingers Hand holds cane You cannot be seriOboy get Bnuny out fo hree Skinny red Freda stockings Brown Freda coat Striped coat Sleeves pull Rrrrr Bunny I hug, pat, little pink back shshshsh My shoulder Pretty Boyd claws pinch Hoid the lady Lets go Lets go From my chest hangs Dirty pink pack. My thumb pulls open Shshshsh Fussy pink Bunny my hand puts into pack Sokay

Screee

Dormer window rattles up Black eyes sharp tooths red coat comes Red boots bangbang metal roottop I scoot back Coming red coat says,

Where you gonna go, boy o.

Fire escape. Red coat comes. Uh uh. Black tree trunks wiggle downdowndown to pavement. White scrap flutters across humming wet stones. Long drop for a lil baby. says red coat. Seagulls wah haha wah ha. Red boots bang. bang. bang come. I kiss fuzzy sniffly Bunny hair.

Thwap Rooftop hollersAhhhCane White coatsleeve swingsAhhhYellow Freda hair flips Red coat caws Bitch finally gettin what she desoive Brown boot kicks Freda tumbles bang bang Why do you think we hold services on the roof Freda Stripe coat Spotted coat hit kick Fuckin bitch White pants white coat spin Cane jabs

Knockm off, Maidenhair

My chin Red boot kicks Owieeeee Greenblue wings
flapflapflap On my back I fall Bang Bunny cries Hugging
Bunny Off metal gutter I slide Metal gutter Weeeee My
fingers catch Oof legs swing, hang, My arm hugs Bunny
swings up Metal gutter Fingers grab come red boot stomps
bang Owie my fingers shake shake Wahhhh Stomp Bunny
cries My legs twist sway Elbow hurts

hanging
Cobblestones yawn
below

Ach, dirty pool Pretty Boyd Dark wings flapflap under
Grey sky Bunny gurgles Cnady bdriy Bang bang bang
Window across allee shows Red coatsleeve swing Red boot
kick Wings flap Fuckin bird Corbel my hurty hand takes
Ledge comes to my foot Bricks my shoulder bumps Foots
sidebyside In Bunny hair I sing, Safely you may always hide
Metal roof Bang Black pantlegs tumble slide fall O Fuck
Red coatsleeves hang beside me, holler,

Shi. Wai. Im caught.

Red boots kick, kick, kick Metal gutter squeak, squeak,
squeak Red coatsleeve pulls, stuck. Window shows metal
gutter Pretty Boyd perches beak peckpecks fingers Make it
black eyes my eyes stop Red boots kick window glass breaks
Help me

On ledge I stand, hug Bunny.

Help me, goddamn you.

Bang Bang above. Window shows white pantleg kick cane
flashes Get away Damn bird

Ach Pretty Boyd flies Grey sky Red coatsleeve tears, red
sleeves, flap flap fall No, no, noooooooo.

Above hollers, Maidenhair.

Little red sleeves little black pantlegs crumpled below.

Wee wee hahaha wee wee wee.

Flap flap, greenblue wings Pretty Boyd perches on ledge. Pretty Boyd says, Window, Mac. Elbow hit.

My elbow swings glass cracks greenblue wings flap flap flap Otra vez Elbow swings pshh glass scatters window frame my coatsleeve sweeps, tinkly glass. Bunny my arm hugs shshsh sokay under sash I crawl My foots step into flat. Dim. Dust. Cage birds shake shriek fweetfweetfweet Look Look Save me No me No me

Shaddup Listen What I say do. hollers Pretty Boyd round room, round room O my O my howd him make boss On high cage Pretty Boyd perches, wings flutter Shaddap wanna get saved or ate Birds cower eyes blink Ergo Cages open, Mac Bunny cries Shshshsh My hands open gate open gate open gate open Shshsh Cecil Perry Buñuel Mimi Rico Kojak Muenster Raquelredpurplegreywhite birds fly, ceiling shadows spin. Squawk, cry.

How.

Where.

Why.

Hollers Pretty Boyd, What I do do flaflaflaps byebye. Out doorway follow greenyelloworangeblue.

Outside broke window says, Whered he go Down below The birds

Across dusty wood floorboards I run. Bunny my hands hug. Hallway. Flapping wings fly round darkness cracked ceiling Trapped trapped broke lightbulbs dripdripdrip. I shiver. Door. I pull handle. Stairwell.

Thump thump thump above Hep les oiseaux, ils volent nos oiseux

Up stairs comes bobbing black homburg Red bandana, Chk chk chk chk Hep, its Ob Down stairs troops Pretty Boyd hollers behind thathathatha hit My hair, shoulders Raww raww cheepcheepcheep Comin through I duck hug Bunny, feathers spin, wings tails cut sidetoside, curl fweet fweet fweet fweet down stairwell.

Black homburg hollers Sacre merde Shrieking wings rain flaflaflap Red bandana hands grab Beaks nip hands Black homburg trips bumpbumpbump somersaults down stairs

On stairs above clump clump clump hollers, Sounded like Pussy Willow Pussy whither art thou Below says She fell, the birds they bit off my finger Above eyes eyes eyes bingbing my eyes Regardez Oboy We going to wring your neck, little mouse Up stairwell comes Pretty Boyd Green wings thathathat My shoulder Grey claws pinch Vite vite, Mac that door In stairwell below, tweeting, In my eyes tweeting, round my ears, tweeting Doorlatch My hand pulls.

Dark hallway. Stripes glow bing bing bing below doors Pretty Boyd I chase Door swings shut behind.

End of hall fluttering Pretty Boyd says, Open.

I pull knob. Rattlerattlerattle.

Pretty Boyd says, Kick. Tres vite, pommes frites.

Door I kick. Tootsies hurt, hop Owie owie owie

Pretty Boyd says, Again kick, foot bottom silly, not foot toe

I kick

Break door, Mac. Arm hugs Bunny I hhrrah Crack Wood flies Door shivers Bright light bang.

Dusts spin. Pee smell. Ceiling rust. Window. Window. Close door, Mac. Pretty Boyd fflaflaflap perches sill. Cmere. Pretty Boyd says, Ach, baby cries. Scary. Happy her, Mac.

Thump thump thump outside Binkie my hand sees in coat pocket. Happy Halloween. Bunny cries. Binkie my hand holds Oooooo Inketty Binkie Bink Hold it. says Bunny. Bunny fingers take Binkie Bunny mouth sucks Shhshhshh Bunny cries little, sniffles, sucks. I kisskiss fuzzy head, bouncy bounce oo oo oo, sokay, sokay, sokay. To floorboards my coat falls. Bunny, pack, on my back put, bounces oo oo oo. Strap I pull. Snug Bunny coosucks. My ear Bunny fingers pull

Hows Pussy Willow Her necks bloody broke Bastard threw Maidenhair off the roof Where the hell that sunnuvabitch go

Hep Down this hallway Allez allez

Crack.   Crack.   Crack.

Pretty Boyd says, Door to door salesmen, Mac. Open window. Rattling window my hands lift Shhh Dust Big light Out window greenblue Pretty Boyd flies Out window I climb, ledge under my botty Bang hollers door I stand Into flat arms legs run Get im Out window swings arm arm arm Fingernails scratch ledge Fog comes. Seagulls wahwah hahaha. Corner comes, my foots shuffle, Pigeons fuss, fly thathathatha. Drainpipe. Round drainpipe on ledge Fog curls. Black fedora green eyes gold tooths shine, We had a little moppet. We put it in our pocket. We fed it corn and hay,

Long red hair whips, comes

There came a proud beggar, And swore he should have her. He stole our little moppet away.

I jump. Grey sky hums. Across allee, Juliet balcony comes. My armpitelbowknee railing hits bang My back Bunny head bumps Bunny hollers Waaahh Bunny fingers grab my hair pull Balustrade my fingers scrit scrit scrit. Cobblestones below. Rooftop above.

Risktaker. says behind. Nous aimons cela.

Over my shoulder gold tooths shine, mouth spits palms rub. Fog comes. Pretty Boyd flaps, Up, up, get a move on, Mac To roof I climb, pigeons flaflaflap oorrh oorrh oorrh

Make way, rats Pretty Boyd chases, Crazy clown bird. pigeons holler. I say, Bunny Funny Bunny Funny Fun fun fun, Across metal rooftop Under black wires I run dum ditty dum Metal vent pipes hiss Metal cowls spin Fog gutters Puddles plouf Over allee I jump Greenblue wings flash flutter, brush my hair, Pretty Boyd swings sidetoside, Rusty metal rooftop comes bang bang

Fouroclock Mignonette

Boots sneakers Tonk tonk metal rooftop behind me Fogs run come chakka chakka chakka, caw Run run as fast as you can Bang Bang I run across sloping metal panes my foots slip sideways skip seams Torn brown glove hand reaches Now I gotcha barefoot fucka

I fall botty hits valley bang Bunny fingers pull my hair I slide shhhhwwt down valley Fucker legs leap over me Stripe coatsleeves pinwheel run along metal ridge above My foots p pang gutter Up dormer I run Dormer dormer dormer I hop skip jump Stripe coat caws above Yellow cap caws behind Metal seams hurt my foots run Hand grabs chimney cap I swing to rooftop dormer below I jump hands grab party wall I climb, leap between red chimney pots Up rooftop I run on hands foots Arms legs swoop sidetoside Torn glove punches my shoulder Tag yer it Eyes Tooths shine Boot kicks my botty Bullseye Torn glove pulls Bunny arm Give us the

worm Pretty Boyd swoops nips Fuckin bird arms swing
Pretty Boyd wheels, wings thathathatha Over ridge I jump
to metal roof
foots scrat scrat scrat run
down
down
between dormers
allee below
Seagulls wah wah hahaha Open window sings My eyes
smile senseless and I got some golden diesel

Highs

Raingutter comes. Across allee wood shingle roof, ridge.

Thats a big jump mon petit frère. caws spotted coat.

Cawing yellow cap hides green hair.

Over allee I jump Tummy tickles

Whistle in my ears Eeoooeeooo Geronimo

Sidetoside me spotted coat yellow cap

In allee below

Handswashhair Biciclettawobbles Greycatlickspaw

Rooftop ridge comes, hits my foots, hurts Sidetoside me
kaPow kaPow, On ridge I run, jump allee to tile roof, turn.
Huh, huh, huh. Holes in wood roof behind. Dust drifts.
Pretty Boyd lands on my shoulder. Whered everybody go
Ach Ach Ach. says Pretty Boyd.

BleedingHeart PoisonIvy BlackeyedSusan

On wood roof fog spins Pak pak pak along ridge silver
sneakers run past broke holes Dingalingling sneakers flash,
come

I turn, run, skip skip jump to slate rooftop Metal roof comes Across metal rooftop Stripe Coat runs chok chok chok chok I jump over party wall Across metal rooftop runs Rooster hair tsh tsh tsh toward Stripe Coat

Pretty Boyd hollers Cuttin you off, Mac

Chain Rooster hair blue sleeve swings Metal pipe has Stripe coat Behind me comes silver shoes In tooths shiny knife

Come to mama

Behind black coatsleeve swings I lean Knife flashes I spin duck spin Owie My wrist hurts Thats right You bleeding now I kick Ooof Motherfucker I spin run Bunny bounces hoo hoo hoo on my back, running.

Cracked chimney comes Up sooty bricks I run jump Grey sky Knife hits Crunch sooty bricks below, I fall Black coat shoulders my heels hit Ahh black coat falls back Black hair rooftop hits Ughh head bounces Silver shoes kick Knife flies knife skitters down roof My foots stomp stomp tummy Ooo Round chimney I run Red wrist flashes in my eyes

Rooster Hair blue sleeve swings My forearm chain wraps stings Gotcha Pipe Stripe coatsleeve swings I duck Chimney pots break

Stripe coat has torn elbow

Rooster Hair red scratch behind red earring Red scratches has hand holds chain Metal pipe swings I pull my arm Rooster Hair stumbles Pipe hits Crac Rooster Hair Hoooof Ahhh Stripe coat tumbles down rooftop bangbang Noooo boots slide byebye I run jump Bunny twinkles rooftop comes You dnot konw the hevaens yet I spin push chimney Pap pap pap my hands on rooftop, Bunny on my back I run chachacha

Rooster Hair catches my shoulder Ill kill you chain swings rowrr rowrr White sneaker kick kick kicks I jump, spin, hands catch sneaker Puddles plouf White sneaker kicks I trip fly My tummy Rooftop hits Ooof Bunny bounces on my back Binkie tumbles Waaaaa Rooftop rasps across my stripe meridien, sliding tummy hurts Waters plouf Ha ha Gotcha little mouse My legs swing up Handstand On my hands I run dum ditty dum ditty dum dum dum Parapet comes Circus freak My tummy white sneaker kicks Owie I fall

Allee below

Pantleg my hand grabs I hang, spin My shoulder hurts bump stones Wot the Bam Bam botty falls knees elbows white sneakers slide shhht Falling My hands grab gutter Hands grab my hands I kick Falling white sneakers pedal Nooooooo

> Rooster hair
> arms legs pedal
> catch snapping clotheslines

My hands patty cake bricks Drainpipe comes ping chachacha Drainpipe flies up between my hands fweeeee burn Fire escape railing Hands grab I bounce knees bang Owwww I hang Bunny cries

> Rooster Hair
> Ashcans
> Bang
> Dust flies.

Over fire escape railing I climb. Chest hurts, throat. Blue sky. Bunny cries, Hurty, Papa. Want Mama.

Shsh shsh. I say. Sokay, Bunny. Sokay.

PrettyBoyd parakeets finches canaries lovebirds flflflaflaflaflap twitter, perch. Look who I found. says Pretty Boyd. Red drips off my hand.

Oua oua. Barking. Oua. Oua.

I go crungcrungcrung shaky legs down metal stairs. Bang goes landing. Crungcrungcrung bang crungcrungcrung bang crungcrungcrung

Dusty window comes. Big pink tongue Huh huh huh huh.

Rolo, Bunny. Happy Halloween.

Bunny hands clap. Doggy dee heehee. On railing, fluttery yellowredbluegreen wings. Cui cui cui cui. My fingers push at window Rolo whines, paws window scra scra scra scra

Behind me Shadow moves Rolo barks Oua Oua Oua I spin, Gold tooths white coat black fedora says, Young Sweet William, sad to tell, Rang the Canterburys Bell. Just for that, his father said, William, Im gonna bash in your head.

Cane swings Scattering parakeets lovebirds sing, I spin Bunny hides My spinning shoulder cane hits Owwiiee Cane swings my hands slap Cane hits bricks Brown boot kicks, hurts

    Cane
        Swings
                Swings
            Stabs

I twist Glass goes Pash Rolo jumps Oua Oua Oua Oua glass flies White coat hollers White coat railing hits Bongg Black fedora tumbles Flittering black butterfly downdowndown Long red hair spins Rolo tooths bite white coatsleeve rr rr rr rr Ay chingada Red comes to dirty white coatsleeve Up fire escape I run crungcrungcrung follow Pretty Boyd

What the hell is going on Broke window hollers below, Ingrid, Quick, ring the police Rolos got the pet thief

Long white pantlegs brown boots tip up, white coat pants

Rolo fall over railing Christ Rolo No Hand grabs Screee
Railing pulls away White pantlegs swing, spin, green eyes
my eyes, white coat white pants

f

a

l

l

Rolo hit cobblestones below.

Hands push Rolo away

Rolo, my baby, my poor baby, no

Dont look Ingrid, dont look

Bloody christ. red tooths say. Just a dog. Now this. This.

Brush pokes purple shirt. Trembly fingers poke brush. Red
tooths caw. We had never. Considered it. Our own. The
closest we could get to. Ha ha. To be killed by a hairbrush.
Ha ha. How bloody ridiculous. Hoisted on my own pi, pi, pi.
Pi.

Sirens pin pon pin pon pin pon pin pon.

My eyes wet, hurt. Fluttering birds come.

Pretty Boyd says, Sorry Rolo, Mac.

I run crungcrungcrung up metal steps. Red on my hand
drips. Shivering, I move pack straps, Bunny says Candy
birdie ee ee ee. Red mask Pretty Boyd flaps Greenblue wings
wings wings wings fly up up up byebye.

Arms legs run come down allee. Holy shit. Street.

Red white coat lies. Blackbluebrowngrey pants kneel. Hand
hand hand take. Dum ditty dum more monkeys come. Striped
coat. Red bandana. Baby o my baby He love me most Fuck

you I was his one and only Yeah, he one n only ho Hand pulls out drippy brush. Street. Christ. No. Swan. Who gonna take care a us now. Up metal steps my foots go. Rooftop comes.

Sirens pin pon pin pon pin pon pin pon.

Fuck it. Lovers gone pecan. Lets go.

Down allee arms legs run.

Pretty Boyd perches on my shoulder, flap flap. No worries, Mac. Pretty Boyd says. Lets go home.

A ch, found it, Mac.

Grey door. Bars on grey door. Shiny doorlatch. On windowsill, Pretty Boyd perches. Bars has window. Between bars Shadows flicker.

Door new. says Pretty Boyd, blink blink. Grimalkin broke two. One fo me. One fo you.

Down allee, rooftops hide big boum boum.

On my shoulders, on my hair. Parakeets canaries finches twitter whistle chirp. On fuzzy Bunny hair lovebird perches. Red beak darts pic pic pic.

Bunny twinkles, Tee hee hee Ticky biddy.

On stones round my foots hoot, sneeze, squawk, preen, march, parrots, macaws, cockatoos.

Casement window squeaks above. Out window long nose says, Whats the fuss down there, Magda.

Freckly balcony arms say, Cest clair, non. The swallows have returned from Capistrano.

O. I thought the lot took a wrong turn on the way to Bombay.

Hahaha, Gertie.

Allee. Boiled cabbage. Steam. Inside tipped box yellow kitty sits, licks paw, green eyes squint. Boum Boum. In gutter silver water shivers. Stones cold to my foots. Grey door. Black bars. Shiny doorlatch. Bunny my arm hugs.

Open sesame, Mac. says Pretty Boyd.

Doorlatch my dirty red hand takes. Red smears shiny.

Jingleelee. says bell. Into shop yellowgreenblue flock twitter Flapflapflap round ceiling, swoop updown aisle cui cui cui lamps wink What in heavens Glasses bingbing Brown sweater sleeves wave Coat shoulders hunch Coatsleeves hide eyes Orangeyellowgreen spinning rings, thathatha chattering wings From whence came these birds Birds perch on cages, sills, curtain rods, fishtanks, banister, flutter twitch blinkblink Safe Thought we was gonahs See that cat Hey they eat Zupreem Feed me Feed me Feed

Brown sweater green pants brown shoes come. Singing white hair Crinkly grey eyes blinkblink my eyes, holler, Young man, what on earth is the meaning of this.

My ears hurt. Jingleelee. In my nose shop makes bright smell. Wood shavings, feathers, fur, feed. Hoots cage birds. Whistles Dollhouse birds. Bloop bloop fish tanks. Yip yip puppies. Twinkly Bunny.

Young man, why have you, you. Glasses bingbing. Scratchy white chinny chin bobbles. O my. O my.

O my. I say. O Boy. O Bunny. O Dollhouse. O Freda. O Mister. O Pretty Boyd. O bubbles.

To my dirty foots Brown shoes shuffle. Watery grey eyes blinkblink my eyes. Tobacco. Garlic. Mothballs. Mister hands lift. Hands tremble, float. Yellow fingernails. My shoulders twitch. Mister hand folds round Mister hand.

My prayers have been answered. says Mister. My poor lost boy is found.

Pretty Boyd jumps, flap flap greenblue wings, on cozy brown sweater shoulder perches.

Surprise. says Pretty Boyd. Beak tickles ear.

O my. says cawing Mister. Pretty Boyd, you rascal. I missed you fiercely, as well. And look. Charlie. Mathilde. Beatrix. And so many I dont recognize. Didnt recognize you at first, my boy. That long hair. That marvelous beard. And heavens, a baby in tow. My, haha, such a racket in here. Behind glasses, watery grey eyes glow pink. Wrinkled fingers hush singing white hair. My boy. Mister says. I thought Id never see you again.

My arms flap. I say, There is nothing wot brings such happiness, is loving friendship.

Watery eyes blinkblink. Mister caws. Zounds. You can speak. How is it that, did you. Why, I can hardly hear myself think, with so many birds

Ach, Hear ye, shaddap, pigeons. hollers Pretty Boyd.

O ere we go Rainbow tyrant Little power goes right to big beak

Fweeeyoooooeeeet Quiet.

Birds burble, cough, snicker. African grey sneezes.

Mister caws. Finger tickles red Pretty Boyd cheek. Thank you Pretty Boyd. Im awestruck by all the many surprises at once. My goodness. I cannot fathom it all. My goodness.

Bunny hair Wrinkled hand pets. Whos this little one, then.

Bunny. Pretty Boyd says.

Bunny. I say.

Bunny. says Mister.

Funny. says Bunny. Lumpy nose Bunny fingers squeeze.

Yellow tooths say, Shes adorable. In need of a hot bath, though, like you. But adorable. O, a booboo on her lip. Now, where did Bunny. Is she. Are you her. Is it possiNo. No. The timings wrong, isnt it. Where did you come from, little

Kidnapped, kidnapped. says Pretty Boyd. Ach, us all.

Grey eyes go to my eyes. Kidnapped. says Mister. Eyes blinkblink behind glasses. Wrinkly fingers rub wrinkly forehead. Mister says, Kidnapped. But who. How.

Ahem. coughs white coat behind Mister.

O my. says Mister. Brown sweater turns. Green pantlegs walk shuh, shuh. On brown sweater shoulder Pretty Boyd flutters. White hair sings. Wrinkled hands say,

Folks, Im so very sorry Hm I must, we, we must close early today O Family emergency Im afraid O dear Please, please, come again tomorrow, Hope everythings alright Yes, yes, fine, we will reopen tomorrow with, as you can see, a haha larger selection of fine feathered friends Yes, haha, Adieu Adieu

Jingleelee. says bell. Wrinkled fingers turn clic clac door lock. My hand turns window board Shut. Brown sweater turns, sleeves cross. Big breath. My arms flap.

Mister says, Now. Uh. Why, I dont know where to begin. When I take another look at you all. Little Bunny is filthy, scalp filled with dandruff. Shadows under her eyes. You, my boy, are also in dreadful shape. So very thin. Is that a rope holding up your pants. Youre bleeding. So many bruises. Your feet. You, Pretty Boyd, some of the others birds too, your new feathers show stress bars. All of you, youre all the worse for wear. Who among you can say, well. I can only wonder what happened to you. And where you have been.

Ach, tell him, Mac. says Pretty Boyd, Ring ring, ring ring. Recuerdas.

Bunny I put on floorboards. To yipping puppies twinkly Bunny stomps, arms out.

Pretty Boyd says, Ring ring, ring ring. Go on.

Arms up, I spin. I sing, Ring ring ring ring. Brokey telephone bells tonight. Freda hands go wings. Byebye Mister. Dollhouse hello. Miaou miaou was machst thou Herr Doktor. Raggedy Andy Raggedy Ann. Hi to meet you Big Orange David Dirty Boutin. I am once upon a time.

Fingers untie rope, pull down pants, hands hold cheeks to Mister. I say, Señor Lion Gezundheit.

Mister says, O my.

My hands pull up pants, tie rope. I jump, crouch, say, Bird thieves terrorize flats in Bercy. Crooks turn pet store arsy versy. CACeeooeeoo runaway Oboy run. Hen hen hen hen Tippy toe updown Every rooftop in town. Supermiracle bubble wand broke. Cream yummy too. A e i o you.

I say, Chin chimney chin chimney chin chin cheroom. Freda Oboy Bunny makes poo. Chut chut. Freda hollers no. Oboy no. Cockeyed cockle shell. Diapers.

My arms flap flap flap, I scamper toandfro, puppies bark, nattering cockatiels flutter. I say, Swan has a purple berry you is very naughty very. No no no. Scary. But do. How could not we love you. Foo foo. Fraidy cat where you lost I tinfoil hat. Hand hand fingers thumb. Cozzers come Swan comes strumming on a drum. Fogs say Peekaboo. Kiss kiss cest que ça Bo Peep. Bunny cries. Freda cries. Chut chut.

In my pocket My hand hides. My fingers show For you see Little red pea Little red pea come back to me.

Boum boum.

O mother dear me sadly feared le grand boum boum. Come little Bunny come inside. Safely you may always hide. In florida.

I clap my hands, I run run run. Ringa ringa roses Pocketful of posies Hush rush hairbrush they all tumbled down. Poor puppy Rolo Mister. Où etait Raggedy Ann.

Wrinkled Mister hand my hands take. Shake shake. Here me speak to you Hi how I do Shakeshakeshake My eyes look to your watery old eyes to show we am like you. Heart with love always shines and kindly ask we do.

Grey eyes wet. Mouth gawps. Into fist Mister coughs. O, my boy. Im afraid I. Im not used to the garrulous new you. I am enthralled and mystified nonetheless. Are you saying you. No. I dont understand. Who are Freda and Swan and Oboy.

Boum boum.

I. I. I. I am I.

On floorboards I sit.

Egads, whats wrong.

Hurt, Mister. says Pretty Boyd. Mira. Cut hand. Knife. Bumps bruises. Rooftops, chains n canes. Ach, arse kicked.

On floorboards I curl. Floorboards colds my cheek. Round my eyes swims darkness. Pink Bunny foots come stomp stomp stomp Papa, no. Soft green pants kneel beside. Tobacco. Mothballs. Garlic. My hurty shoulder Wrinkly hand holds. My hurty elbow hand holds. Warm Mister hands hurt me. Bunny cries. Bunny hand in my hand. Hurting.

O my boy, what happened to you.

Pretty Boyd wings flapflapflap my hip claws pinch. Pretty Boyd says, Pay attention, Mister. Killers. Big bad danger. Chase. Escape. Bangbangbang.

Darkness spins round my eyes, spills, fills my eyes in darkness. Darkness.

R aggedy Andy did not like the idea of Raggedy Ann not being in her place next to him. What if that big dog next door should be chasing cats during the night and wander into the playhouse, he thought. He played so roughly and might easily harm Raggedy Ann.

Raggedy Andy wasnt a bit sleepy. He just lay there thinking for a long, long time. The house had grown very quiet. All the real for sure people had gone to bed and the moon was shining brightly through the nursery window.

Raggedy Andy had an idea he could think better over by the window. He got up quietly, climbed up on the chair by the window and stood with his elbows resting on the window sill. He enjoyed the fragrant night air and the lovely moonlight and there in the orchard was the playhouse with Raggedy Ann probably sound asleep.

Just outside the window was the back porch roof. Without really thinking, Raggedy Andy pulled himself up on the window sill and dropped quietly to the roof. He walked over to the corner where the rainspout went down, slid down it so easily he hardly realized he was there on the ground. He hurried to the playhouse. Raggedy Ann was gone.

He looked everywhere, inside and out. Raggedy Ann. Raggedy Ann. he called softly. What could have happened to her. Where was Raggedy Ann.

He ran straight for the hole in the orchard fence where a tiny path led to the deep, deep woods filled with fairies n everything.

Raggedy Andy had not gone far along the path when he met Eddie Elf. Hello, Eddie Elf. Raggedy Andy called, Have you seen Raggedy Ann.

Good evening, Raggedy Andy. the cheery little elf greeted.

Yes. Raggedy Ann passed by a long time ago. She seemed to be in a hurry. Said she was following a beautiful golden butterfly and she was sure it was a good fairy. You will find her if you go right down the path.

Raggedy Andy thanked Eddie Elf and hurried on his way.

H es waking up. Thats a boy. Youre safe. Youre home.

Pretty Boyd says, Rise n shine, sleepy head. Mister make his yummy bread.

Cake.

Lets eat fo petes sake.

Now Pretty Boyd.

Closet curtain sways. To tippytoe window in closet, rain comes pic pic pic. Cracks in yellow ceiling. Under me, cot. On squeaky cot I sit.

Easy, my boy. says Mister. Grappa. Wrinkly hands on knees. Yellow fingernails. Tobacco. White hair sings.

Blue sweater, me. Black corduroy. Dry wool socks. Foots hot. White hides my wrist.

Mister says, Gauze bandage, to help heal your wound. I rang Giles, he made a house call. Helped bathe you, then tended to your wounds. He put a couple stitches into your wrist. Had you on a sugar iv, to hydrate you. Thats the bandage on your left arm. A bit persnickety, old Giles, but a good doctor nonetheless. Someone attacked you with a knife, Pretty Boyd told me. Giles confirmed. It grieves me, the thought you were all alone out there, and a victim of such violence. What if youd been killed, God forbid. Idve never seen you again.

You said it, Buster. says Pretty Boyd.

Youve got bruises head to toe. Giles noted how old some were. Whoever beat you has been doing it awhile. I wish I knew what happened, where youve been all these months.

Behind curtain, chittering birds, bloop bloop fishtanks. Oua oua. barks bichon pup. Foots hot. Wool socks. My hands pull.

Floorboards cools my slippery foots. Lotion. Cheek chin smooth to my hand.

I took the liberty of shaving you. Trimmed your hair, too. Hope thats alright. Had to be certain you were you, haha.

Bunny. I say.

Yes. The baby. Shes home safe, thanks to you. You did a wonderful thing, rescuing her, and at no small personal cost. By any measure youre a hero. After I got you into your cot, with Sergios help of course, I rang the prefecture. Child Welfare came and fetched her. Shes gone home.

I jump. Cot squeaks. Bunny. I say, arms flap flap.

Little Elsie thats her name Elsies mama rang, wanting to thank you

Greenblue wings flaflap Damn straight she better thanks

Pretty Boyd, hush. But youve been sleeping all this time, almost three days. Besides the, the   Watery eyes blink

the prefect

ordered no contact beyond family members for now.

Bunny. I say. I hop, flap flap flap. Fart.

Now, my boy

BunnyBunnyBunnyBunny

Okay, I understand you are

No, Bunny. I say. My head my fist hits. Non non non no

Mister hands yellow fingernails come. Wrists my hands grab. Non non non. I say. Dry wrists creak in my fists. Grey eyes blink blink up to my eyes. Mister says, Youre hurting me.

Ach, wots problem, Mac. Greenblue wings flap flap My shoulder Pretty Boyd perches My ear beak pinches.

Please, my boy. Two men from the prefecture are here. Theyve come everyday, to wait. I tried to tell them you wouldnt be able to help any more than little Elsie, even though you, you can say things now. But the prefects men are persistent. Please. Let go.

Wrists Mister pulls from my hands. Closet curtain pulls back shhhhhk. Pretty Boyd thathatha into shop, takes perch. Cockatoo cage black jacket pokes. To angelfish tank brown trench bows. Black jacket brown trench rise Black eyes blue eyes. Black hair shines. Grey entrée door shut behind.

Ah ha, Sleeping Beauty awakes. says black jacket black moustache. Il était temps.

Good afternoon. says brown trench. Blue eyes my eyes. I am Inspector Duran. This is Inspector Morel.

Mister says, Hes still fairly shaken, discombobulated, gentlemen. As I said, I would be very surprised if he could help your investigation.

Bien sûr, grandpa. As you said. says black moustache. And as we said, he was a missing person who had a missing person and tens of thousands of francs worth of stolen exotic birds in his possession when he was discovered. Ouai.

Not discovered. Returned. He escaped the kidnappers.

Ach, damn right. says Pretty Boyd on perch.

Escape, eh. Your rendering remains to be seen. The pet thieves are still at large. You read the papers, oui. This lot matches the description of the male dodger.

So do fifty percent of the young men in this city. Is my boy on trial here, in my shop, Detective.

Brown trench comes Hand on black jacket shoulder. Forgive Inspector Morel, sir. says crooked grey tooths. His commitment to justice at times appears abrupt.

Black jacket shrugs. From black jacket shoulder, hand falls. Madame le Prefect wants answers, Henri. says black moustache. That is what we are here to obtain, non.

What Jacques wants to say is, its nothing personal. says crooked tooths. There are simply too many unanswered questions. If your son can resolve one, just one, we may better ensure no more defenseless children will be endangered.

Coming black moustache says, The baby was kidnapped nine months ago. How did you come across her. When.

Sausage. Onions. Dijon. Red eyes hurt my eyes.

Bunny. I say.

What of the murder victim found not far from here, in Gobelins. A Favelle gang leader you were observed fleeing, then engaging with in mortal combat. Viens, parles plus fort.

That gang person was the pet thief, the papers said. says Mister.

Bunny. I say.

Papers were wrong. says crooked grey tooths. The murder victim did not match the description.

Black moustache says, I said, speak up. Hand grabs my blue sweater, burns. Hollers come.

Jacques, hes afraid. Let him go.

Damn it, Henri, I dont buy the idiot routine. This ones been missing longer than the baby, and somehow he survived. Could a true idiot survive on his own. I think pops and the pet shop here werent big enough for him. I think he fell in with that Favelle scum. Then he got scared and wanted out. You are too fond of the dance, Henri. He knows

I told you, detective, hes not like you and me. says Mister. If you persist in upsetting him I will ask you to leave.

My sweater Black jacket hand grabs. Bien, we leave. But we take this lot with us, to the prefecture.

Jacques.

Hes a suspect. Henri.

Non, non, non, non, Bunny mine

Wot

BunnyBunnyBunnymineBunnymineBunnymine

Alors, he confesses at high volume, Henri

Wait now What do you What does he mean

Leave him be, hes terrified, he doesnt know what hes

BunnymineBunnymineBunnyBunnyFredacries

I spin, black jacket sleeves fly Hep Brown trench sleeves come

Stained cuff Snagged thread Hairy wrist

I duck

Blue pants knee comes to my foot pap pap Brown trench Black jacket shoulders under my foots Beard scratches my ankle To door I jump Fish tank falls Pawshh O no, the angelfish Get him Jingleelee says bell Bang says door Into allee I run, puddles plouf Rain rain go away My sweater Fingers grab, I run up stones, somersault Oof Black jacket Stones hit Black jacket falls Plouf Buzzing baton Brown trench waves Arrêtez I dont want to hurt you Ashcan lid

I throw Pangggggg Buzzing baton tumbles Pok pok pok My boy come back My hands foots run.

Pinponpinponpin. Grey sky. Bobbing white clotheslines. Allee I run run. Aroooooo howls balcony bouceron. Running I jump huhhhhands grab blue lamppost Legs swing over wood gate Down stone hall I run pitta patta pitta pat Bobbing archway comes   Shadows   Stone hall wet rough Hands foots push, climb, Hn hn hn hn Rooftop comes I roll, run, pigeons thathathatha Off parapet I fall, catch Rusty drainpipe, my knees gung gung gung. Ooof. Big red bus gasps, steam sighs, Big red bus I chase behind Black platform comes, Metal railing I grab Arms flutter Lordy he came outta nowhere Pinponpinpon Redblue lights byebye. Bus turns, hisses steam Stones jump Pap Pap hands, foots Round corner Green bottle my foot kicks cling cling bottle skips Puddles plouf plouf. Court. Cimetière. Trees. Broke columns. Léglise. Shutter bangs. Cloche rings, Din Dan Don. Din Dan Don.

Rain comes. I run. Arms legs toandfro, raincoats, big hats. Shop window, grey cat. Lhôtel. Fountain rain boils. Jardin. Rain drifts under yellow lamp. Oboy. hollers red spark. Yo man. You snuff Swan. Up bricks my foots ch ch ch Lamp hands grab. Lookit im go. He king o the rooftops you know. I hear he clear Boulevard Arago. Windowsill. Drainpipe. Cornice below. Cross rooftop I run, jump, down rooftops, down, down, under black sky, over shivering treetops I run.

Wood parapet comes. Darkness below. Across broke rooftop, rusty pipes growl. Off wood parapet, down wet ivy, crumbly bricks I slide. Ivy rattles. Windowsill crumbles, I fall, tear ivy. Ooof. Owie. My breath hurts, chest throat hurt, babum babum babum. My eyes raindrops peck. Ivy wets my hands, my neck. Tree branches rattle above.

Miaou. says Dirty Boutin. Eyes bingbing. On my sweater wet Boutin curls. My fingers scratch purring chin. I sing,

Front, petit front, Yeux, petits yeux, Nez de croquant, Bouche dargent, Menton fleuri, Quiriquiqui. My finger Boutin bites.

Miaou. says blue Korat, says Little Lulu.

Me, you. I say. Cats come pripprippprip out darkness, slink slink ivy, cry Faim, faim. Fuzzy wet heads butt my hands, wrists, arms, purr Ron ron ron, cheeks, stiff whiskers rub my fingers, Faim, faim.

From my eyes rain cries plouf plouf plouf. Rain rain go away. I roll, hands knees. Foots. Trees, bushes. Arms push.

Crumbly steps. Down I skip. Above me, meouing kitty cats prip prip prip.

Below, Dollhouse pickets scattered white on stones.

Wire fence. Wire fence traps Tumbled rocks wood bricks plaster metal stones. Yellow lobster sleeps beside big metal can. Big metal can hums. Window bright.

Dollhouse byebye. Wire fence I stalk sidetoside. Links my fingers grab. Links I shake shakka shakka, water drops fly. Rattling fence I climb, links hurt fingers, tootsies. Miaou. Tssst. Over fence I jump, ground hits foots. Concrete hunks. Splintered wood. Twisted nails. Broke glass. Plywood scrap. Black strap.

My hands pull up muddy black haversack.

Metal can door squeaks. Light shines. Roosters, lobsters, in mud behind. Yellow hat comes. Flashlight. Koennen Sie nicht lessen. Eintritt verboten. Die Polizei. Verschwinde.

Black haversack I put over my shoulder. Clonk clonk wood steps yellow hat comes. I turn, jump, climb rattling fence, Hep Yellow hat runs, jingling, My legs spin over fence, black haversack falls Bang fence rattles behind. Cats crouch.

I see you here again.

I hiss. Haversack I take, I run. Cat eyes bingbing, blackwhiteorangegrey legs run beside.

Allee. Courtyard. Bench. Streetlamp, running. Arms legs tables chairs under striped awnings. Smoke. Clink, clink. Boulevard. Dingdingding goes steamy streetcar. Léglise. Lhôtel.

Courtyard broke carts chairs. Black sky. Little stone dresses sigh. My pantlegs cats rub. Mew. Miaou. Faim. Lintel, bricks, windowsill I climb.

Non, non. say cats, red mouths wide.

Black haversack bumps my back, climbing. Juliet balconies up up up, fallen planter box dripdripdrip. I shiver. Ledge hands take. Pigeons flutter, hop, coo. Moped zoum zoum. Past rooftops, canal. Little white little red car lights little horns beebeebee cross pont, cross quai. Rain shines. Tour is bright. Whitegreenred stars below. Darkness below. Dollhouse.

Tonight, beautiful is city. Dies it, however. Again beautiful, be will, city.

On ledge between stone legs I sit. Pigeons march, strut, ooorrhh, ooorrhh.

Hello. Gargoils say.

Black haversack falls paff beside me. Rain hisses. I hunch, pull sweater sleeves, hide my hands.

Frightened are you. Matter is what.

Cat eyes in doorways bingbing. Stars shine below. Across black sky, little red light blinks. *Safe is cache. Cold are you. Come.* Stone legs behind I go. Alcove dry.

Pin pon pin pon pin pon. In darkness, wool blanket my hand finds. Coat. Hat. Cream cups.

Baby is how.

Bunny byebye safe. I say. Chim chimney.

Again mother has she. Best is it.

Arms I put in coatsleeves. Hat I put on head. Blanket I put round shoulders. I sneeze, shiver. Hide foots.

Sleep. say gargoils.

Freda. I say. I drink cream cup.

Ask you, she is where. Here up from is, there all see we. All see we. See not do we she. Now sleep, do.

Cream cold to my tongue. Blanket hides me. Alcove curl I. Rain sighs. Sleep baby, sleep. Miaou. Miaou. Where goest thou, Oboy.

Freda. say I. Darkness.

T*here.* gargoils say.

Across allee, over rooftops, brick chimneys. Smoke curls, blows. Sun shines on boulevard below. Beebeebee. Under streetlamps, under windows. Past bobbing hats coats shadows. Yellow hair flashes.

Black haversack I put over my shoulder. Stone ankles I grab, I slide Pigeons thathatha Hanging I fall Bangngng Rusty juliet balcony squeals, tilts. *Caution.* stone dresses say. *Fall to going, is balcony.*

Planter box dirt spills from shivery railings. Over balcony railing I go, I hang, strap pinches, balcony shakes, squeals, bends. Allee. Ashcans. Courtyard below. Bicicletta ringring. Shutter I take, shutter breaks, windowsill, down bricks, cross ledge I tilt, black haversack bump bump, my coat bricks scrape. I jump. Whistling drainpipe my hands catch Down I slide shhhhh. Cobblestones Foots pitta pat.

Round corner down gravel allee I run scrat scrat scrat. Miaou. miaou. says blue korat. On my hip Black haversack bumps. Boulevard. Cars, motocicletta zoumzoum. Past legs Arms Swinging bags Bobbing balloons Ice cream I run. Good sasages Aqua vitae Buy gazette here Torn red stockings Black boots tsokk tsokk tsokk down stone steps. Yellow hair flaps. Grey coat Black haversack bumps Hep watch where yeer go Red glasses flashflash below. Fuck. Freda runs.

Down steps I skip, black haversack bounces. In allee Waterpump black boot jumps Up cob boots run Rattling wisteria Freda hands grab, boots climb sh sh sh sh. Up blue car I run bang bang jump Streetlamp comes Wisteria Big wood sign Hands foots take creeeak *Faites vous questceque* hollers gargoil above Stone skirt my hands grab Hips Cold stone nonees *Pas moi molestez* Stone crown fingers grab Stone shoulders foots push *Bastard* Windowsill Hum

⟨325⟩

Crumbly cornice Hum Parapet Hum Rooftop. I run.

Black Freda boots tsokk tsokk tsokk rooftop Freda I chase Brown coat jumps Yellow hair waves byebye. Cross rooftop, parapet. Below, Freda runs, elbows tic toc tic toc. Sun shines. Clotheslines. Clothes Spin I jump, run Get the fuck away from me Seagulls cry Wah wah hee hee Wings flaflaflaflap On my shoulder Black Freda haversack bumps, torn red stockings jumps Black boots my foot catches kick kick Boots slip, skip, Freda falls Fuck Rooftop Yellow hair red stockings tumble wop wop wop wop. Freda lies, shiny. Rooftop Elbows pale fists hit. Bootheels kick. Hot blue eyes, my eyes.

Freda says, You have been, and always will be, conduct disordered.

Raggedy Andy remained real quiet, though he was very anxious.

He sat down beside Raggedy Ann.

My bag. Raggedy Ann said.

Black haversack my hands open. Out haversack my hands take Apple Dried cherries Chocolate Cheese Baguette if you please. I say.

Black haversack Freda hand takes from my hand. In haversack crooked Freda nose peeks. So youve taken up shopping. A picnic, no less. No wine. Ah but my very important journal papers, all safe and sound. Thats bloody fab. Haversack drops. Red stockings knees Brown coatsleeves hug. Freda rocks slow.

I thought it all boiled down to identity, you know. Freda says. Its not who you are, its who you think you are. Rarely those are the same. No one is that consistent. No one is that sane.

Identity. A persistent entity. A sense of self. An equation wots always most of all never completely true. How can it be, when consciousness is a yammering narrative, memorys a falsehood, and language, a killing tool.

I. say I.

But there is no point to I. says Freda. Blue eyes wet. My eyes byebye. Blue sky.

Brown coat pocket. Freda hand hides in pocket, rustles. Folded paper. Torn newspaper Freda fingers shake.

Freda says, Pet Thieves Hideout Uncovered. 12 April. Demolition crews stumbled upon a grotesque bestiary of starving animals in a heatless storefront flat above Rue Bosquette. District authorities notified the Center for Animal Care and Industry, or CACI, which arrived in hazardous materials suits, gas masks and gloves to find 28 malnourished cats, 47 equally mistreated snakes, guinea pigs, rabbits and other rodents, one 25 year old turtle, and more than 100 feline and other animal cadavers. Augmenting the horror, in a barrel behind the storefront, the dessicated, partially eaten corpses of 33 Well those birds were as good as dead no matter what I did. says Freda. Besides it was your fault Oboy You brought the heat What was my alternative.

Dried cherries I eat. Sun hurts my eyes.

Necropsies of the dead pets, performed at the School of Veterinary Medicine in Reuilly, revealed advanced symptoms of malnutrition and neglect. The more startling discovery, however, was that virtually all the animals matched descriptions of pets stolen by the socalled pet thieves, who have terrorized city districts over the past two years.

This is a major find said Antonini Finocchio, Gobelins District Commander. I believe we will soon crack this case.

With Tuesdays chilling storefront discovery, the belief the pet thieves were trafficking in stolen pets has given way to the possibility they suffer from a largely ignored psychiatric disorder, animal hoarding.

Heres the best part of the article. says Freda. Hey, dont eat all the Comté. The CACI defines a hoarder not by the number of animals collected, but by the condition in which they are kept. According to Laurent Trichet, director of Public Policy for the CACI, a hoarder fails to provide minimal nutrition, veterinary care, or sanitation, fails to act on the deteriorating condition of the animals or the environment, and fails to act on or even recognize the negative impact on his or her own wellbeing. Rather, animal hoarders usually ardently believe they are rescuing the animals they incarcerate, often calling themselves saviors and describing their charnel houses as shelters for the victims.

Trichet has published several papers arguing that hoarding results from a combination of disorders, in particular obsessive compulsive disorder, or OCD, perhaps explaining the emotional bond between hoarder and animals, and the hoarders alienation from fellow humans Ha Fellow humans Freda caws.

On my back, watery eyes blink blink blue sky. Hurting.

Unlike most hoarders, who typically gather animals from humane societies, classified ads, or well meaning neighbours, the pet thieves stole all their victims.

This distinction is not lost on the CACI, which announced plans to seek criminal charges on 187 counts of animal cruelty and neglect. These charges would be in addition to 224 counts of burglary and breaking and entering, and two counts of assault.

Presently, however, there are no leads on the pet thieves whereabouts. Complicating matters, an unfortunate miscommunication caused the storefront, one of numerous Favelle structures expropriated for destruction under the Haussmann Plan, to be demolished before any clues or further evidence could be gathered.

It is a painful setback, admits Finocchio.

For now, the healthiest and least feral of the troubled cats have been moved to shelter care to await adoption. The majority, however, are in the CACIs Clichy isolation ward, where, Trichet says, Our job is to make them as healthy as possible. They need to be rehabilitated, and the court has to figure whats going to happen. In this ongoing saga, Trichet explains, These cats arent merely victims or potential pets. They are evidence in a law enforcement case.

There you have it. says Freda. All the months, the bruises and bumps, the runs in my tights, the pounding hearts and highwire frights, trying to do whats right and defend those lacking might, and they end up in Doctor Frankensteins clutches anyhow. That bites. And the media cements my image as a piéce de merde collector. Me. This world is so meanspirited in its irony.

Torn newspaper flutters byebye.

On red stockings knees Freda forehead sits. Knees arms hug. Yellow hair flits. Crumpled drink cup. Cigarette butt. Ice lolly stick.

Bunny binky.

What I told you is true, Oboy. Freda voice hides between skinny red stockings. The first time I saw you, I thought I was seeing an alien materialized on this planet by a miracle, or a mistake. Prospero wanted to bring forth the real you,

Caliban. Hellenisthenai ten glossan. But you were already you, no airs n graces, no deception, self or otherwise. So really, I only served to corrupt you. What do you need with language. For myself, Im headed in the opposite direction. Identity mistaken. Raisondêtre misunderstood. Unidentifiable. Anonymous. For good.

I crawl. Binky comes. Binky dirty in my hand.

You should go back to Dolittle, Oboy. You cant survive out here on your own. You cant look after yourself alone. Especially cos Im not feeding you those little red antianxiety meds any longer.

Me, you. I say. Me, you.

Thats miaou, I keep telling you. Freda says.

Binky I put between black boots. Freda coughs. Skinny hand takes. Mustve fallen out of my pocket.

Freda forehead lifts. Blue eyes blink. Water comes. Across blue eyes coatsleeve rubs. Fingers show binky. When shes older, will she remember scaling tall buildings, sliding down steep rooftops, running pell mell along parapets. Do you think Bunny will remember me, chickpea.

Bunny will remember me, chickpea. I say. My cheek Fingernails scrit scrit.

Binky Freda hand hides in coat pocket. I was a good mama to Little Bunny Foofoo, wasnt I. Freda says.

Freda hand my hand takes. My hand burns. My hand Freda hand slaps. Freda mouth my mouth. Lew see nay ma. I say. Love stories are the best for learning.

Freda pushes me. I want you to get away from me now, O. Get away from me, cos I need to get away.

Cats of Frankenstein You are amputee like me. I say, arms flap flap.

Just get the hell away from me Black boots jump Boot kicks my knee Owie Boot kicks my arm shoulder Owie Owie I curl on rooftop, roll, Boot kicks Get away from me, you pribbling half faced hedge pig Hurts on my knee, arm, shoulder, hollering mouth Goddamn it You screwed up when you kidnapped Bunny and you screwed up when you gave her back You fucked everything up, god damn you My hand Black boot stomps Its not us against them Boot kicks Freda spins, stalks, turns. Its me against you.

Brown coat huh huh huh huh. Eyes yellow hair hides.

I say, Tell me Im pretty Im pretty arent I, Oboy. Yes.

We are all alone and on our own. Freda says. And then we are gone pecan. Dead and dumb. All done.

Freda bows, arm swings, black haversack strap hand takes. Brown coatsleeve throws. On my chest clink clink. Black Freda collar. This is for you. And now, without further ado. Wet blue eyes, my eyes. Breath loud. Chest swells. Freda cries. Freda turns, runs, Geronimo, torn red stockings jumps.

Bang

Bang

Bang

Bam. To parapet I run.

Raggedy Ann lay just as Marcella had dropped her, all sprawled out with her rag arms and legs twisted in ungraceful attitudes.

Her yarn hair was twisted and lay partly over her face, hiding one of her shoe button eyes.

Freda.

Raggedy Ann gave no sign that she had heard, but lay there smiling below the fire escape.

Round my neck black collar I tie. Down ladder I slide. Cobblestones. Papers, books. Apples. Cheese. Baguette.

One of Raggedy Anns legs was twisted up over the other, but it wasnt the least bit uncomfortable, for Raggedy Anns legs were stuffed with nice white, soft cotton and they could be twisted in every position and it did not trouble Raggedy Ann. No indeed. Her little candy heart with the words I love you printed upon it went pitty pat against her nice cotton stuffed body.

Red drips from pale ear. Dripping red My finger pokes. Gasping mouth red, wet. Yellow hair my hand pets. Water bottle on pavement. Water bottle my hand takes. Hand lifts Freda head. Hand puts bottle to mouth. Water Red tongue licks. Off chin red water drips.

Brown shoes blue pantlegs green sneakers run come chka chka chka chk. Omigod. What the hell happened. Hey.

She falls. I watch of my kitchen window.

Omigod.

I ring ambulance. I hear coming now.

Howd it happen. Hey. Hey you. What, is he deaf.

Roma. I say. Piazzo vittorio.

Wet red hair my hand pets. Raindrops from my eyes plouf, plouf, plouf. Siren hollers pinponpinponpin. I sniff Freda lips, Freda eye, behind Freda ear. My hand pets red Freda hair.

Wasnt it just like a fairy tale. Raggedy Andy asked Raggedy Ann as they put on their nighties and hopped into bed.

Indeed it was. said Raggedy Ann. Raggedy Andy laughed. And I spect, just like all nice Fairy Tales, everyone will live happily together here in the wonderful Magic Castle forever.

And the two Raggedys, their shiny shoe button eyes looking happily up at the top of the playhouse, felt in their little cotton stuffed bodies that indeed, this would prove true, for unhappiness can never creep in when hearts are filled with the sunshine of unselfish love.

I say, And all you have to do, is just give your heart a sunshine bath by saying, I love everyone.

A BIBLIOGRAPHY

BOOKS AND STORIES

All God's Children: Inside the Dark and Violent World of Street Families. Denfeld, Rene.

Animals in Translation: Using the Mysteries of Autism to Decode Animal Behavior. Grandin, Temple.

The Body Language and Emotion of Cats. Milani, Myrna M.

Caspar Hauser: The Enigma of a Century. Wassermann, Jakob.

Catwatching. Morris, Desmond.

English Prepositions Explained. Lindstromberg, Seth.

Eugène Atget (55). Badger, Gerry.

Flower Children: The Little Cousins of the Field and Garden. Gordon, Elizabeth.

Frankenstein. Shelley, Mary Wollstonecraft.

Hand, Hand, Fingers, Thumb. Perkins, Al.

Language Visible: Unraveling the Mystery of the Alphabet from A to Z. Sacks, David.

Letter to a Child Never Born. Fallaci, Oriana.

Mysteries of the Alphabet: The Origins of Writing. Ouaknin, Marc-Alain.

The Night Climbers of Cambridge. Whipplesnaith.

Nobody Nowhere: The Remarkable Autobiography of an Autistic Girl. Williams, Donna.

Old London Street Cries and the Cries of To-day: With Heaps of Quaint Cuts Including Hand-Coloured Frontispiece. Tuer, Andrew W.

Paris from Above. Arthus-Bertrand, Yann.

Raggedy Ann in Cookie Land. Raggedy Ann and the Nice Fat Policeman. Raggedy Ann and Andy and the Camel with Wrinkly Knees. And many others by Gruelle, Johnny.

The Real Mother Goose.

Shadow Cats: Tales from New York City's Animal Underground. Jensen, Janet.

The Sound and the Fury. Faulkner, William.

The Subterraneans. Kerouac, Jack.

Thinking in Pictures: And Other Reports from My Life with Autism. Grandin, Temple.

Under the Overpass: A Journey of Faith on the Streets of America. Yankoski, Mike.

Walks Through Lost Paris: A Journey into the Heart of Historic Paris. Pitt, Leonard.

PAPERS AND ARTICLES

"Advance in Stem-Cell Work Avoids Destroying Embryos." *The Wall Street Journal*, November 21, 2007. Naik, Gautam.

"The Argot of the Three-Shell Game." *American Speech*, October 1947. Maurer, David W.

"Construction of Biologically Functional Bacterial Plasmids *In Vitro.*" Proceedings of the National Academy of Sciences of The United States of America. November 1973. Cohen, S.; Chang, A.; Boyer, H.; Helling, R.

"First Embryonic Stem-Cell Trial Gets Approval From the FDA." *The Wall Street Journal,* January 23, 2009. Winslow, Ron, and Mundy, Alice.

"The Forgotten Era of Brain Chips." *Scientific American,* September 26, 2005. Horgan, John.

"Inside the Autistic Mind." *Time,* May 7, 2006. Wallis, Claudia.

"Inside the EK." *Portland Tribune,* November 2, 2006. Denfeld, Rene.

"'Matador' with a Radio Stops Wired Bull." *New York Times,* May 17, 1965. Osmundsen, John A.

"On Spectrum: My Daughter, Her Autism, Our Life." *Harper's Magazine,* April 2010. Tisdale, Sallie.

"Onoma—Onomato—Onomatwaddle." *The Kenyon Review,* Fall 1990. Barzun, Jacques.

FILM

Autism Is a World

Blade Runner

The Bourne Ultimatum

Cat People

Children Underground

District B13

In the Realms of the Unreal

Mozart and the Whale

The Matrix

Under the Roofs of Paris

A SOUNDTRACK

Autour de Lucie. "Vide."

Balún. "La Bicicleta de Cristal."

Broadcast. "We've Got Time"; "Phantom."

The Hylozoists. "Hearts and Harps."

Jorane. "Eléphant blanc."

Laura Barrett. "A Certain Major Vinylsky"; "Wood Between Worlds"; "Space Seed: The Musical."

The Long Lost. "Siren Song"; "Woebegone."

Nadine Mooney. The backwards half of her album, *Big Bang Backwards*.

Nine Inch Nails. "3 Ghosts I"; "6 Ghosts I."

Rachel Taylor Brown. "Vireo"; "Hemocult/I Care about You."

Radiohead. "Karma Police."

Rasputina. "Hunter's Kiss"; "Remnants of Percy Bass."

Regina Spektor. "Aprés Moi"; "The Flowers."

The Tiny. "Closer"; "In My Back."

Tracy + The Plastics. "Oh Birds."

IN GRATITUDE

To author Monica Drake, for letting me—some unemployed yahoo she'd never met before—think I wooed her with my account of this new novel I was working on about "cat people." It was cocktail chatter, trying to impress a beautiful woman, slouching against the counter in future Oregon Poet Laureate Paulann Petersen's Sellwood kitchen.

To Paulann, who provided the milieu for me to woo my future wife.

And to Mavis, Funny One, Mousie, Imp, for being born and adding depth and breadth to my life, and consequently, to this novel. She makes me laugh.

And to the workshop writers who caught a glimpse of my first attempt at this story: Monica, Stevan Allred, Joanna Rose, Suzy Vitello, Walter Keutel, Chuck Palahniuk, Cori-Ann Woodard, Kevin Burke, and the late Candy Mulligan.

To Rhonda Hughes of Hawthorne Books, for publishing my first novel, which gave me the desire to resume work on this book six years after I gave up.

To Jeff Baker, book editor for *The Oregonian* newspaper, who gives me work and keeps my name out there.

I want to thank Kristin Thiel, erstwhile fiction editor for the Writers' Dojo, who solicited material from me—she had to ask more than once, bless her!—and published an excerpt from this novel on the Dojo's online magazine.

And to Jeffrey and Rachel Selin, founders of the Writers' Dojo and publishers of the Dojo's online magazine, for providing such valuable resources in service to the writers' community.

To the annual Wordstock Festival and its former executive director Greg Netzer, for supplying the venue for me to read from this novel.

To Moira McAuliffe and RV Branham, founders, editors and publishers of *Gobshite Quarterly*, for inviting me to read with them from this novel for Oregon Literary Review's reading series.

To David Elsey, who invited me to read from this novel and other work for his own reading series.

And my gratitude to the one and only Tom Spanbauer, for trying to hook me up.

To Matt Love, Oregonian extraordinaire, for his boundless enthusiasm, and for including my essay in his anthology, *Citadel of the Spirit*.

To my friend and brother Daren Dougan, who was there when I began writing this novel, who was there for me on countless other occasions, but sadly, is no longer. I miss him.

And to my friend and brother Shawn Rodgers, for his invaluable feedback on this novel, and many other topics as well.

I want to thank Multnomah County Library, for making available its abundance of research tools—including good old-fashioned books.

Thanks to Vanesa Kelmendi, for her Bosnian; to Markrid Izquierdo, for her Spanish; and Jan Chciuk-Celt for his German and Polish.

To Shantina of the Children's Community Clinic on NE Killingsworth in Portland, who was thoroughly professional in regard to my unexpected appearance, and patient and helpful with my odd questions when she had more important work to do.

To Temple Grandin and Johnny Gruelle, for using animals and dolls to teach me about humanity.

And finally, I want to thank Lidia Yuknavitch, writer, publisher, rock star, a knight in shining armor, my savior, my champion and sponsor with Fiction Collective 2. Lidia's efforts substantiated my vision. She redeemed me from a canyon of self-doubt; a mountain of hope she gave me.